# Walls of Jericho

*Best Wishes,*

## JONATHAN HOPKINS

*Jonathan Hopkins*

*For Elsa*

*'The battle that never ends is the battle of belief against unbelief.'*

- Thomas Carlyle (1795-1881)

# Prologue

# The
# Golden Calf

# 1805

# Elchingen, Austria

Louis-Henri Loison could not die.

Putrid grey smoke exploded from a hundred Austrian muskets. Bullets hammered past the French general as he raced forward, hurdling the stream in his path. But none touched him.

Loison's lungs rasped from his efforts, the enemy so close the stench of their burnt powder stung his nostrils. His legs were tired, long boots blistering raw heels, but he must run on: *must*. Behind him his blue-coated infantrymen struggled desperately to keep up, anchored by heavy backpacks. He shouted, swore; encouraged the men onwards. Into the musket smoke: into hell.

In front, the Austrians reloaded. Strain scored soot-stained faces as they thrust ramrods down hot barrels. Men desperately fumbled unfitted bayonets; but they would be too late, Loison saw. He laughed at their indiscipline, and in his joy the sound became a scream; a visceral cry to loosen bowels. Now he would kill them.

More bullets tore the air about his face. He threw himself at the Austrian front line, slashing at the nearest man with his sabre. The infantryman fell, clutching a face bloodied to the bone. Another Austrian thrust forward with his musket. Loison saw the weapon coming and ducked underneath, cannoning sideways into his opponent who reeled back from the blow. He brought his sword across, a vicious sideswipe that cut into the man's midriff. Then a French bayonet punched through the Austrian's lungs as he tried to twist away. Loison's men had caught up.

As their attackers forced the Austrian infantry to give ground, something tugged at the shoulder of the general's coat. He was shoved roughly in the back and almost fell, but a hand grabbed his collar. One of his sergeants hauled him upright while plunging his short sabre into the belly of the Austrian whose bayonet thrust had narrowly missed piercing Loison's neck. The grenadier offered his commander a muttered apology, yanking and twisting at his sword as he struggled to free it from the Austrian's sucking flesh.

More of the enemy pushed forward to join the fight. Loison's gold-braided coat seemed a magnet for steel and lead, yet nothing found a mark. He cut at another man. The Austrian jinked away, only to be smashed in the head by a French musket butt. A pistol exploded directly ahead and the general tensed, knowing he must be hit, but inexplicably the ball went wide. Loison lunged at the perpetrator, his razor-honed blade sliding easily through the man's coarse clothing to split his ribcage. Fear and realisation flashed in the Austrian's eyes before he fell away, writhing and screaming.

Bluecoats on each side of Loison stabbed with bayonets, driving the Austrians back, but now the enemy were too many. In such a tight crush of bodies the general's pace slowed to a crawl. He found no room to swing his sword. The Austrian infantry began to drive the French back by sheer weight of numbers; Loison's brave attack balanced on a knife-edge of failure.

Except for one thing; a fact no enemy could have foreseen. A miracle, so inexplicable, so fantastic, the French general had only just come to believe in it himself. In all the battles he had fought, against every man he had killed, no blade had spilt his blood; no bullet even caressed his skin. Whilst all around him others bled and died, he survived, impervious to harm. He was immortal - a god.

Summoning his strength, Loison screamed at the sky. Again and again he jammed his sword-point into the crush of bodies ahead; he hacked and thrust, stabbed and slashed; a warrior without fear of death. Until, abruptly, the Austrians faltered. Loison saw their panic begin. The packed ranks surrounding him thinned.

His infantrymen piled into the weak spot he had created. Jabbing forward, their long bayonets scattered the enemy; encouraging their flight. More and more Frenchmen poured into the gap, shrieking like demons, until the whole Austrian front line seemed to explode outwards. They ran.

And the general lowered his sword, laughing out loud in triumph and relief. For here he was god, and no-one could stand against him.

Splashing back through the stream he had jumped across only minutes before, Loison drew his sabre again just as a water-rat dropped from a hole in one bank with an audible plop.

"Hah!" The Frenchman slashed his gore-crusted blade through the shallows, scaring the tiny animal so it arrowed away upstream. He would be another *Tudieres* - he knew that now - the ancient Hammer of the Franks, voracious slayer of Moors and forever victorious in battle. The general raised his arm to let his sword drip, frowning that the running water had not scoured it of blood. His servant must see to that later. As he slid the sabre back into its snakeskin-covered scabbard, his stomach grumbled, reminding him he had not eaten since he woke. His servant could solve that problem, too.


Marshal Ney galloped towards him. French engineers must have repaired the bridge over the Danube. When the Austrians collapsed its roadway into the slowly swirling water, only the two main arches remained intact, crossing the river. Loison had led his men along one narrow ribbon at daybreak, boots sliding, musket shots whistling about his ears, only inches from falling. Now thick timbers spanned the arches, allowing cavalry to stream across without any risk of soaking their fancy uniforms. They were too late, though. He had won the battle without them.

Ney pulled to a stop. "You are injured?"

Mounted, the marshal towered above him. Damned cavalrymen always looked down on the infantry, Loison thought. He stared at Ney with disgust before realising what his commander meant. With one hand he scrubbed at his face, and his glove came away rust-flaked with drying blood. "It is not mine."

Ney grunted. "Brigadier Villatte?" he asked.

Loison had charged his subordinate with concluding the attack; re-forming battalions which would be scattered and disorganised from pursuing the enemy. He should be able to do that without having his hand held. "I left orders for him to consolidate, once he has taken the abbey."

Ney grunted again. "The Emperor will reward you for this day's work, Louis-Henri." He gave the general a curt nod before galloping on.

Loison watched him go and spat on the ground. Bonaparte would never reward him; the bastard Corsican was too busy handing honours to his usual cronies, including Ney. But Loison did not care. He had fought and won. Again. He *was* immortal.

Even the damned Emperor could not say that.

# Part I

# Crossing Jordan

# Gloucestershire, England

# Chapter 1

Joshua Lock stabbed a grubby forefinger at the book's yellowed pages. His mouth worked, fish-like, over the text, which bled badly from one gauzy page to the next. Crossly, he pushed unruly brown hair up from his forehead. He was fourteen, now. He could manage the other words, so why not this one? Moving the table nearer the window did not help, either. Lifting the heavy oak was easy; hammering iron had muscled his arms and chest; but there was no moon that night to add to the feeble halo of light cast by his sputtering oil-lamp. He tried again

"Supp…" he began, his lips making an involuntary popping sound at the end. "Supp-or…"

*BANG!*

Lock's crashing fist made the old table leap a good inch off the stone floor. Motes of dust rose up from between its thick planks, and the oil lamp teetered precariously. Instinctively he grabbed at it, scorching his fingers on the glass.

*"One…"*

He fumbled with the lamp, at last righting it on its base. Between stifled oaths he blew furiously on smarting fingers.

*"Two…"*

His anger was subsiding. His grandfather had taught him the trick soon after his parents died; how to count up to ten before the emotion consumed him and he lost control. Then, he had been angry all the time. Now, he rarely got past

*"Three!"*

Lock sighed. He felt stupid, for what had angered him was merely a word. He looked at it again, squinting in the lamplight, and ran his finger under it on the page. Supp – *something*.

The lamp flickered as the door behind him opened and a draught caught the flame. He knew it was his grandfather; Lock could hear the old man's rasping breath and the slow shuffle of boots over the flags. He straightened on his stool.

"What is it, boy?"

Lock pointed at the damned word. "I can't read that, Abraham."

His grandfather picked up the old book with reverence. Its end boards and title page had been lost long ago. Abraham raised it so that it was just a couple of inches from his face, his eyebrows working comically as he strained to read the words in the meagre lamplight.

"Suppurate," he enunciated the word, a subtle note of pedantry in his tone.

"What's that mean?" Lock had never heard it before.

Abraham paused, as if in thought. "When a wound fills with pus: means it needs a poultice." He placed the book down carefully and put his finger under the word. "Look; *sup-you-rate*," he said, jabbing each syllable for emphasis. "It's not difficult."

Lock snorted. "That's easy for you to say."

"You shouldn't be reading in this light, anyway," his grandfather scolded. "Do you want to end up with eyes like mine? God made the daylight for reading and the dark for the devil's work."

Lock shrugged. He could not see himself ever being as old as his grandfather. But he obediently picked up the book and crossed to the shelf where it was stored, alongside the only other book in the smithy. That was a heavy, leather-bound Bible with faded gold lettering across its wide spine. *The word of God.* Once, Lock enjoyed its stories, but he never read them now. God had taken his parents, he had been told, so why should God's word matter to him? He could go to hell, he thought, feeling no guilt at the blasphemy. There was a piece of oilcloth on the shelf. He carefully wrapped it around the book he had been reading and placed it alongside the Bible. He still had chores to finish.

It was quiet and still outside the cottage. Ice had begun to form on the surface of the water barrel. Lock stuck a dirty finger into it, tracing a pattern and breaking the thin skin. His breath steamed in the cold air. He walked away from the smithy and down a short track to the meadow where a horse grazed. Earlier, he had left an armful of hay under the hedge. Now he pulled it out, shaking the new frost from it. The horse looked up as he walked towards her, calling, and eventually she ambled over, whickering in recognition. Lock dumped the hay in a pile on the ground in front of her and watched as she took a mouthful and chewed contentedly.

She was old, and her coat grew thick at this time of year to keep the cold at bay. As a small child, Lock had been thrown up on her broad back and led around, up and down green pathways, holding tightly to her long mane. When he was older, he had ridden bareback through the woods and meadows, fancying himself an armour-clad knight of old. In his reverie he would charge into battle, standard fluttering from his lance, beating down enemies with a razor-sharp sword to save the lives of kings and princesses. Lock patted the mare's sway-back affectionately and traced his steps back to the cottage.

Even though he closed the door behind him, cold air still trickled in where its frame warped. He hooked up a piece of thin leather that served as a curtain across the window. The fire was almost out, he saw; if it died now the cottage would be freezing in the morning, which was bad for his grandfather's chest. But bringing the coals back to life would mean fetching more from the forge inside the smithy next-door, and he decided that tonight he could not be bothered. He looked into the iron pot by the fire containing leftovers of vegetable stew they had eaten earlier in the day. It was cold and congealed. Lock prodded at it with a spoon, but could not bring himself to eat it. There was bread and some cheese in the larder, but if he ate that there would be no breakfast, so he left it. But there would be meat tomorrow, for, with any luck, he planned to go hunting coneys in the afternoon. Rabbit stew for supper! He could almost taste it, and the thought made his stomach growl. He was used to that feeling.

Lock sighed. He would go to bed hungry. Stepping into the back room, he lay down on the cot that served as his bed, but left his boots on when he pulled the blanket up over his head. At least his feet would be warm in the morning.


The Honourable John William Killen stood on the landing that served all of the rooms on the first storey, right at the summit of the staircase. It was a massive structure, with two wide wings which curved downwards into the hallway of Halcombe House. He laid his head on top of the right-hand banister rail and sighted along it.

The polished wood was cool against his cheek. This time, he decided, he would go all the way down.

Killen had practiced for weeks when no one was looking. He started low down, near to where the end of the rail curled to meet its final support, and had gradually moved upwards, one stair at a time, until he reached the half-way point. But today was a special day. It was his father's birthday, and in honour of the event, dinner was to be served in the main dining room. He would sit at the head of the table, below the huge portrait of his father his grandfather had commissioned. Killen felt unworthy of this honour, and had decided that, to deserve it, he must do something bold and reckless; a dare that would surely have made his father proud.

Killen hitched his right leg up so his calf lay across the rail, and shifted his body so that he was half sitting on it. Years of polishing made the banister slippery as ice; that would be a boon once he was moving. He inched his way slowly along to the point where the rail started to fall. Now he could see the whole staircase curving downwards. It looked an awfully long way! Perhaps he should start lower down? No! He had decided he must brave the entire length. Steeling himself, he flicked away the lock of hair that habitually fell across his forehead. He took a deep breath: it was now or never. He wriggled a bit further, and suddenly he was off! Killen wobbled slightly as he accelerated. Then he was whooshing madly down the rail towards the tiled floor below, exhilaration flowing through his frail body. In his excitement, the short journey seemed to last an eternity. He slid past portraits of relatives and ancestors whose stern faces seemed to glare disapprovingly as he flew by. Then suddenly he was at the end. The banister dropped him towards the floor and he landed feet-first, staggering for a couple of steps until he regained his balance. He smiled broadly, for though his heart was hammering he had done it. *He had done it!*

"I wish you wouldn't, Johnny." His grandfather emerged from the corridor on his left and scolded him gently. "It is all too easy to break one's leg. Dinner will be served shortly, if you are ready?"

Killen looked at him sheepishly. "Sorry, grandfather," he said, but without much conviction, for he did not feel contrite. *He had done it!*

Roberts, Lord Halcombe's manservant, had lit both large silver candelabra on the dining table. There were two places set, and Killen walked slowly to his seat at the far end. He touched the back of each chair he passed; there were ten of them, for the table had been extended to its full length. Before he sat down he walked the few extra steps to the end of the room.

On the open lid of the harpsichord which stood there he noticed his grandfather had stood a small portrait of his grandmother, but it was dwarfed by the picture above. Killen stared up at the huge painting on the wall behind his dining-place. It celebrated a young man in the uniform of a cavalry officer; bright gold braid on a dark jacket, a crested helmet on his head and in his hands a great, curved sword. Killen had gazed at the portrait a hundred times, but its magnificence always twisted his stomach into knots. His father was standing, moustached and smiling with his sabre in front of him, tip propped on the stump of a tree and with his gloved hands resting on its pommel. The portrait's background was dark, brooding almost, but around his father's feet spring flowers bloomed in a coloured carpet that slowly faded into the shadows behind. A willow tree sprouted at one side to frame the shining figure with sad, drooping branches.

Lord Halcombe seated himself heavily and rang a small silver bell. As he replaced it on the white linen tablecloth, his manservant appeared.

"We'll eat now, thank-you, Roberts."

The servant gave a small bow. "Very good, my lord," he said quietly, and disappeared again.


Killen put down his glass. He was not allowed the best wine very often, but this evening the cellar had been searched for an exceptional bottle of claret to mark the occasion.

"A toast," his grandfather said, "a toast to William Grenville Killen. My son: your father." They both turned to the portrait, raising their glasses. It was odd, Killen thought, to be celebrating a man he had never known, although he often had to toast the King, who he did not know either, and that was deemed acceptable. His grandfather seemed to have a watery look in his eyes as he took a draught from his glass, but Killen could not be sure, so said nothing.

In the awkward silence afterwards, Killen wondered if now was the right time to broach a subject dear to his heart. His grandfather picked up a napkin, dabbing his mouth. It was white linen, matching the tablecloth, and Killen noticed that when he put it down his lips had left a red stain. "Grandfather," he began, "I'm old enough now." He paused, not quite sure how best to continue, but Halcombe stayed silent so he plunged on, "And you did say you would write when the time came." He gave his grandfather a pleading look.


George Arthur Killen, Lord Halcombe, looked back at his grandson and smiled sadly. He knew what the boy was after, and while it was true that his fifteenth birthday was two weeks past, he was not yet ready. Neither was Halcombe ready to lose his grandson to a service that had already killed the boy's father. He mulled over different excuses for weeks, knowing that the boy would soon ask him to write a letter requesting a recommendation to join a cavalry regiment. "Have you decided yet," he asked slowly, "which regiment you wish to join?"

"The Seventh." No hesitation, "Lord Paget's."

Halcombe nodded gravely, "A good choice."

"You know him, don't you?" Killen asked.

Halcombe was non-committal. "Only slightly," he said carefully. "I have dined with him once or twice, but he may not remember me."

Killen smiled at him. "Of course he will! When will you be able to write?"

His grandfather looked serious. "I believe the Seventh will only take officer recruits who are over sixteen," he said. "Perhaps it would be better if you were to wait a year."

"I'm sure they would take me," Killen refused to be dissuaded. "William Meacher joined the 33rd last year, and he was only fifteen."

Halcombe sighed. "The infantry are less particular, so I am told," he said with distaste. "And in any event, there is plenty for you to do on the estate. I need you here, to oversee my affairs if I must travel away. My bones grow older," he smiled, teasing. "Who would take over if anything should happen to me?"

Killen scoffed at the thought. "You're not that old, grandfather! And you have the staff to help you. And in any event," he added as persuasion, "you promised you would! Please.... will you write?"

Halcombe decided to drop the matter for now. "We'll see," he said vaguely. "Have you anything planned for tomorrow?"

Killen seemed not to notice the smooth change of subject. "I thought I'd take The Tempest out again," he said. "He's getting much easier now, and I must keep working him."

His grandfather nodded agreement, "He should make a fine hunter for next season," although privately he thought the thoroughbred horse he had purchased as a birthday present might be proving too difficult for the boy. "Now, off to bed with you. Goodnight, Johnny."

He watched his grandson trot gaily down the length of the dining room and out through the door. He was young for his age, Halcombe thought. Johnny's slight build and poor constitution did not help matters. In that he was unlike his father, who had always been of robust good health. Halcombe felt protective. Johnny would not find the rigours of a military career easy to bear, even cushioned by an officer's more privileged lifestyle. And if he were ordered into battle? Halcombe did not wish to consider the possibility, but Napoleon's seemingly unstoppable progress across Europe made that likely at some point if the boy insisted on a military career.

Halcombe rose from the table and stood in front of his son's portrait. He looked up at the gaudily dressed cavalry officer, seeing Johnny's fair hair and smiling blue eyes "Damn you," he cursed the painting quietly, under his breath. "Damn you."

Retrieving the oval frame he had placed on the harpsichord before dinner, he stared at the face of the picture it held; a woman, young, fair haired and smiling. Halcombe had ordered the painter to capture her happiness as that was what had first drawn him to her. Always a smile, he remembered. Always laughing; filled with joy. His late wife's eyes looked back at him, and he put his right hand on the picture, trailing his fingertips gently over the contours of her face. "I shall keep him close, my dear," he promised the likeness. And clutching the portrait to his heart, he turned away from his dead son.

# Chapter 2

Smoke poured out of the open workshop doorway and, blown by a gentle breeze, turned wispy as it rose upwards. It shredded through the winter-bare branches of an old horse-chestnut tree that in better seasons would throw shade onto the tiled smithy roof. A few small birds, perched on the ridge, scattered at the hammering noise from inside. It was not the ring of steel on steel but a flat sound, like driving a metal spike into timber.

Lock pushed the horse's left hind foot off his knee and straightened up from where he had been crouched beneath its belly. He brushed filings from the hoof trimming off the leather apron that protected his legs and looked down critically at the animal's foot. The bright metal clenches, where the shoe-nails had been turned over, were filed smooth. At the outside edge, where the wall of the foot met the shoe, the horn was neatly rasped. And the line of nails showed a third of the way up the foot. A good job, he thought, satisfied.

The big bodied cob stepped sideways, putting its weight on the hind leg as if testing the fit of the shoe Lock had just applied. Then, seemingly happy that all was well, the horse rested its opposite foot. The animal's owner, the parish priest, a stout young man recently arrived in the village, stood to one side leaning against the rough stone wall. He put a hand inside the black woollen cloak he wore over his cassock. His purse was hidden there, and he drew out a palm-full of copper coins.

Knowing his grandson would not take money from the fat clergyman, Abraham Lock stepped forward, chest wheezing, and accepted the payment graciously. Still holding the coins, he put his hand into the pocket of his apron. The garment was more patch than original, and the old gnarled leather scraped at his calluses like sandpaper. He remembered his son making it, years ago; before the fever took him, together with his wife, leaving Abraham to bring up a small child alone. Years later, Joshua patched it, once Abraham had shown him how to stitch. He smiled, remembering the boy's curses when the sharp awl slipped and he stabbed a finger. It was not long afterwards that he began teaching Joshua to read. He shook his head sadly, half to himself. Joshua was a good boy. It was a worry that he would no longer go to church, but Abraham prayed for him. The Lord would forgive a child.

Money was tight but the coins warming in Abraham's palm would feed them both for a while. War with France had stopped virtually all trade with Europe, and the hardships felt by wealthy merchants gradually filtered downwards. When they spent less money, fewer people were employed. Food prices fell. There was no money to pay farm-workers. They went hungry, and when they went hungry their work-horses went unshod. Abraham believed that Bonaparte, for all his fine words about freedom, was an agent of the devil. But God would deliver them all from the tyrant.

The clergyman retrieved his broad-brimmed black hat. He had left it alongside the forge, presumably hoping its heat would drive out the February dampness while he waited. He untied the cob. The horse followed him sullenly outside where the priest stood and waited under a grey afternoon sky that matched his expression, for there was no mounting-block in the yard. Farm-workers mostly vaulted aboard by themselves, but the clergyman obviously expected a further service. Lock was forced to leg him up into the saddle, grunting a little at the man's weight. The priest failed to notice Lock wipe his hands on his apron straight afterwards, and did not bother to thank him either, seeming to believe the courtesy was merely his due. He clapped heels into the horse's sides and the cob, reluctantly, trotted off. Lock stared after them. Bugger you, he thought crossly, though he dared not say it out loud.

Back inside the smithy, Lock raked through the coals in the forge, dragging unburned fuel to one side, for there would likely be no more business that afternoon, and no need to keep the fire hot. His grandfather shuffled over and stood beside him.

"I'll be away shortly," the boy said, without looking up.

Abraham nodded. "Where are you going this time?"

Lock sighed with frustration. His grandfather had forgotten already! "I told you last night; over to the combe. We need meat for the pot, and there's a warren I haven't tried yet."

Abraham was warning. "You take care. His Lordship's gamekeepers have been busy of late. I hear they caught someone from the next village over at Mile End, and he's for the magistrate."

Lock smiled. "I'm always careful," he said on his way out.

"That was what Our Lord said to Pilate," his grandfather said seriously. "And the weir will be flooded," he reminded loudly, but Lock was gone out the door.


At the back of the stone cottage, the boy kept a hob polecat in a timber hutch with barred front. He opened the door and peered in. The animal uncurled from its bed of dried grass and chirruped in anticipation. Lock picked it out gingerly because it had not been fed that day, and a stray finger was as good a meal as any. He tied a string lead around the polecat's neck and stuffed it carefully inside his heavy wool coat, before collecting a canvas knapsack from inside one of the outhouses. Then he strode away, down the muddy track that led to the village.


Killen ran down the grand staircase into the wide expanse of tiled hallway at its foot. He took the steps two at a time, flushed with enthusiasm. Lessons were finished for that day which meant time for the more important things in life; for riding, or hunting. His dusty ancestors still seemed to stare down on him with disapproval, but now he stuck his tongue out at them irreverently. Skating across the floor at the foot of the staircase, Killen turned sharp left, arms flailing, into the first corridor. The maids would have to scrub at the marks his boots left on the tiles, but, well, that was their job.

The panelled oak door with ornate brass handle that led into Lord Halcombe's study was ajar, and muted voices came from within, but Killen's momentum sent him skittering through as he tried to slow down. All three men around the huge desk looked up, slightly startled, as he went in. A clock ticked on the mantel; the only sound.

"I'm sorry, grandfather," he started, contrite.

Halcombe smiled. "Come in boy, come in," he beckoned. Killen knew the two men who stood opposite his grandfather; one short and stout, the other tall and thin. The Head Gamekeeper and the Estate Manager. The keeper, Trollope, offered Killen something between a bow and a nod, though the boy noticed he held his cap nervously in front of him as if expecting a dressing down for some error. But the Estate Manager, who seemed to Killen to have a touch of arrogance about his manner, ignored the boy completely and turned back to his employer. "As I was saying my lord," he continued, "we seem to be suffering more and more from the depredations of poachers. If you will only allow me…"

Lord Halcombe interrupted. "Yes, yes, Perkins," he said tiredly, "you've told me all this before." He looked the Estate Manager in the eye. "And I have told you, I will not entertain those damned man-traps anywhere on my property. I've heard tell of them catching children, severing a limb even, and I will not be made party to that event. You must do your best without." He picked up a sheet of paper that had escaped to one side of the desk stuffing it unceremoniously beneath a large grey pebble balanced on an untidy pile of more loose papers. "And if that is all, gentlemen, I bid you good day."

The two men nodded at his lordship and left, the Estate Manager stalking imperiously from the room while Trollope hovered behind him, an anxious satellite, politely closing the door.

Halcombe turned to his grandson who was studying the carpet intently. "Well, m'boy," he said, smiling slightly, "what did you say you were planning for the afternoon?"

"I'll be taking The Tempest out," Killen said in a serious voice, as if to prove to his grandfather that this was to be no frivolous undertaking.

Halcombe pursed his lips in thought: The Tempest. The horse was proving to be a handful, even for a rider of the boy's undoubted talent. It was entire, a stallion, and it was in his mind that castration might make the animal more tractable, more amenable to discipline. Unfortunately, his grandson had immediately seen mastering the horse's temperament and manners as a challenge, and would no doubt object to having it gelded.

Halcombe smiled. "So you've not given up on it yet?"

Killen shook his head determinedly. "He just needs more time, grandfather, and more work. I waste too many hours on boring lessons instead of being out there." He waved his hand in the general direction of the stable-yard. "And what use are Mathematics and French for schooling the best hunter in the shire."

Halcombe sighed. When it came to his grandson, he found it difficult to be objective. And there was no doubt that the boy was a fine horseman; the Hanoverian riding master he had employed said as much. He nodded, "Very well." Killen smiled and turned away, but Halcombe called him back. "Will you be going far?"

The boy grinned. "Oh, just down to the combe, through the fields, probably." The wooded valley was a half-league away, reached over galloping pastureland.

Halcombe watched his grandson leave and felt a great surge of love. Ever since his son's death he had treated the child as his own, hoping Johnny might grow up in the father's image. True, he was a quiet boy, but friends assured Halcombe that was not unusual in one who had lost both parents at so young an age.

With no wife to help him, Halcome had done his best. The child was sickly at first. The nurses he employed cosseted the boy unduly, and Halcombe was convinced that was the reason for his poor constitution. Even so, as Johnny grew he ensured his grandson was tutored in the usual subjects; the arts, the sciences and languages. But he knew that it was horsemanship that the boy both excelled at and loved best. He shot and fenced well, and Halcombe was glad of it. Though he realised that these, the arts of war, might take Johnny far from home in troubled times, he had prepared him as best he could. And in any case, now he had made a promise to his late wife. He would not let the boy go.

He stood and stepped back to where a tall bookcase leaned against the wall, pulling at a tasselled cord which hung beside it. Less than a minute later, his manservant entered the room and bowed.

"Tea, I think, Roberts," Lord Halcombe said, "and I shall take it in the drawing room, if you'd be so kind."

Killen could smell the harness room before he reached it. He walked across the stable-yard with a spring in his step and a whistle on his lips. The clean-leather smell of soap and oils, the sharp tang of polished brass and steel caught in his nostrils and made him think immediately that he was home. This was where he really belonged.

Edward Gaunt, Halcombe's Stud Groom, was stooped in the far corner scrubbing at a horse blanket. A cloud of dust and stray horsehair rose into the air. Daylight shone only weakly through a heavily barred window, forcing him to squint at the blanket as he brushed.

"Hullo, Edward." Killen dumped a hunting rifle and leather cartridge bag on the table. There might be the chance of some game in the combe.

The Stud Groom turned and inclined his head. "Master Johnny?"

"I thought I would take The Tempest out for a hack."

Gaunt nodded again. "The work won't hurt him," he agreed. He hesitated before asking, "Will you be going far, Master Johnny?"

Killen shook his head. Edward Gaunt always wanted to know where he was going. And it was not just because he was nosy. Killen's grandfather would want a full report. And it did make sense, he supposed, in case of an accident

"Just thought I'd take him down to the combe," the boy said easily, "and see if he'll leap a windfall." He noticed Gaunt was looking at the rifle, and hefted it almost apologetically. "I might come across some game," he added offhandedly.

Gaunt grunted. "I can't say as he's been schooled to a gun, mind," the Stud Groom warned, but Killen was dismissive.

"Oh, he'll be fine," he said, blithely. "Would you mind awfully dragging my saddle out, Edward?"


Lock met two of his friends in the village. Well, they had been friends, once. Now they just annoyed him, still stuck in childish ways. Lock had stopped stealing birds' eggs and scrumping for apples years ago.

"Where're you going, Josh-wah?" Terrence Tranter danced around and kept getting in Lock's way. Showing off; being stupid. The other boy hung back.

"Why don't you get lost, Terry?"

"Huh!" Tranter muttered. "What's got into you then? What's got into him, then?" he repeated to the other boy.

"I'm busy." The polecat stirred inside Lock's coat and started to wriggle.

"I've got something," Tranter tried a different tack, "want to see?" He reached inside his jacket. Lock only kept half an eye on what Terrence was doing, but was glad of it, because the boy produced a knife. It had a six-inch blade, pointed and sharp, and he shifted it from one hand to the other, back and forth.

"See. Scared of me now, aren't you, Josh-wah."

Lock stared at him. "No."

"Yes you are, you liar. Want to fight?"

"Bugger off, Terry," Lock said heatedly, and stalked away towards the river.


Abraham had been right. The weir was in flood; the tops of its flat stones submerged under rushing water. Lock studied the barrier carefully. It was crossable, just. But he would have to take his boots off or suffer cold, wet feet for the rest of the day.

He tied the laces round his neck so that the boots hung down on his chest, and pulled the string tighter round his waist. It would be a pity for the polecat to fall into the river to drown. Carefully, Lock inched his way across the top of the weir. The water was incredibly cold and the current tugged at his calves, but its force had scoured the stones of slippery green weed so his bare feet gripped the rough surface easily. He made it to the other side without so much as a slip.

After half a mile, a track turned off the lane, and Lock took it. The path led into a wide meadow, where grass tufts were browned and dead from winter frosts. A few teasels remained, seed heads standing proudly, attracting a small flock of goldfinches which fluttered around them. Lock watched the birds for a while. Their bright red faces and flashing gold wing-feathers were jewels under a glowering winter sky. A charm; that's what a flock was called, he remembered. It was an apt name, and made him smile.

Lock's breaths condensed in the cold air, and the breeze that was making the tree-twigs dance and tap scattered the vapour over his shoulder. It seemed to be getting colder. He pulled his coat tighter to his body, re-tying the string belt, and felt a wriggle inside it as the polecat snuggled into a more comfortable position, warm from the wind.

The track dropped downhill. Even though an easterly wind blew into Lock's face, he could still hear the river scurrying through the valley. It meandered quietly in summer, but now it was enraged, biting at its banks, swollen by melt-water from January snows that filled it close to overflowing.

At the tops of the first stand of trees Lock passed was a rookery, occupied even in February. The big black crows were beginning to build nests. Each pair squabbled with its neighbours over the ownership of twigs or perches, and their angry cawing disturbed the landscape's peace. Lock's feet were cold. The long, wet grass had soaked his scarred leather boots and one of them was untied. He knelt to re-knot the lace, and thought he might as well have left them on to cross the weir.

Above the woods, the river sound was muted. If he kept a sharp ear out he would hear if a gamekeeper approached on horseback. And if it was a 'keeper on foot he would run. They would not be able to catch him. Amongst the trees it was more dangerous; easier for one of them to creep close and surprise him. But Lock had no need to go deep into the woods. The rabbit warren he was searching for lay just outside, where the meadow shelved steeply down to the tree line.

The first burrow Lock found was dug beneath the trunk of an ash tree that stood tall and alone, separated from its neighbours by a well-worn track running jagged and stony along the hillside. Tree roots curled around the rabbit hole, their heartwood stained orange-brown from sap where the animals' chisel teeth had stripped the bark. Lock hunted for scrapings in the earth and scattered droppings at the entrance, proof the warren was occupied. Satisfied, he dug in his knapsack and drew out a small, bell shaped net, fixing it over the burrow with four wooden pegs. Further along, he found four more holes and fitted nets over them in the same way. There were probably more entrances, he reasoned, but he had no nets left, so they would have to remain undiscovered and unblocked. Then, going back to the first hole, he drew the polecat from inside his coat and tucked it carefully underneath the net. The animal needed no further encouragement. It gave several deep sniffs and immediately scuttled off underground, leaving Lock to lean against the ash tree. Now all he had to do was to wait.

Killen had been smiling to himself the last mile. The black horse beneath him strode out with enthusiasm, ears pricked so far forward they almost touched. It must be glad, he imagined, to be free of its confining stable. The Tempest's black mane was rippled by the cold breeze and its thick winter pelt gleamed with health, and from hours of strapping by the grooms. Killen checked his stirrups were level and saw again how the brown leather straps and panels of the saddle and bridle had been soaped and oiled, and buffed to a rich sheen. The steel of the bit in the horse's mouth and the stirrups at his feet had been burnished by hand so they caught the light and sparkled as the horse tossed its head or it skittered to the side when an unexpected movement caught its eye.

They crossed the five-acre field that in summer would yield a crop of oats, keeping to a grassy headland to avoid muddying the horse's feet in plough already prepared for spring sowing. The horse jogged a little, for Killen's hunting rifle, hanging muzzle-downwards behind his right leg encased in its leather holster, tapped its flank. It was not used to the feel. He steadied the horse lightly with the bit, holding the reins in one hand and stroking its neck with the other until the animal settled.

At the far end of the field was a gap in the hedge, which was otherwise ragged and overgrown. Killen knew that there was a rail across it, wedged a few feet above the ground. He shortened his reins in anticipation and urged the horse forward, but kept to a trot to allow The Tempest to see the obstacle clearly. The horse pricked its ears and, gathering itself momentarily, took off and leapt easily over the rail. Its jump carried it way out into the open ground beyond and Killen let the horse canter on across the grassland as a reward. He could see the trees of Combe Wood in the distance, and after a while slowed to a trot, then a walk. The horse was blowing after its short gallop, clouds of steamy breath floating backwards across Killen's face. He loosened the reins, letting the horse stretch out its neck to relax.

The track that led down into the valley was strewn with dead leaves and twigs that cracked dully under The Tempest's feet. The animal was startled at first, but soon accepted the strange feel and noise as normal events that warranted no response. Its ears swivelled this way and that, picking up woodland sounds; the rustle of mice and voles that the thaw had awakened early; the hollow hammer of a woodpecker chiselling grubs. Green shoots of early snowdrops poked through the carpet of dead leaf-carpet. And here and there lay the last icy remnants of snow; white patches that might remain for weeks in shaded corners that feeble early sunshine failed to warm.

Killen could hear the faint sound of the river rushing through the valley below. The wind seemed to have swung to the north, blowing the sound away from him. That was a shame, because it would carry his scent into the woods, spoiling any hunt. He pulled the horse to a halt, considering. He might as well load the rifle, because one never knew if the wind would change, and he might just be lucky.

Killen dropped the reins onto the horse's neck, and the animal stared about, not bothering to move off, while he pulled the gun from its holster. It was awkward, loading on horseback. The Tempest fidgeted, stepping forwards, and Killen was forced to take up the reins to halt it again. The animal flicked its ears at the tapping sound when he rammed the ball down the barrel, but then seemed to settle. He managed to prime the pan without spilling too much from his powder horn and drew the hammer back to half-cock. The frizzen clicked smoothly into place, sealing in the powder, and Killen pushed forward the safety-lock lever to prevent the gun discharging accidentally.

When he dropped the rifle back into its holster, the small thump as it hit the leather stop made the horse jump, but Killen did not correct it. He was ready now, so simply picked up the reins and sought out a track that led downwards through the trees.

The net over a burrow five paces away from Lock shook and a brown furry body tumbled out, thrashing as the cords snagged it. He strode over and grabbed the rabbit before it managed to free itself, snapping its neck with a practised flick of the wrist. While he tied its long back legs together, the polecat stuck its nose out into the fresh air, and, finding its quarry had disappeared, turned again into the burrow and waddled purposefully back underground.

Lock grinned. Tonight's supper caught, and perhaps a couple more that could be sold in the village tavern or used for barter. He walked along the line of nets, listening intently.

On the north side of the valley, a roebuck made its way down through the trees to drink.

Over centuries the river had carved its way through the valley, its path changing the land. Now, the water was deep and fast flowing, swollen by melting snow and with foaming eddies where it ran over large rocks near the surface. But here and there, where its course curved, it widened, and the water slowed to drop its cargo of small stones and silt. At these places, the river bed shelved upwards and the midstream squall quietened.

The roebuck, in the way of its kind, was wary. It stopped frequently, looking about with huge liquid eyes. Big ears, flicking constantly from side to side, caught the tiniest sound that might indicate danger. It stepped daintily, small cloven feet avoiding fallen twigs, and ducked its head so its two miniature pointed antlers would not catch on drooping branches. The buck stopped right on the riverbank and looked around again before dropping its head to the shallow water.

The Tempest noticed the deer first. Turning its head and pricking its ears, the horse alerted Killen to the slight movement through the trees almost a hundred paces away. The boy's hand went to the rifle's stock, and, very slowly, he drew the weapon out. The trigger guard made a small scraping sound as it cleared the leather holster, but the wind had changed again. It blew into Killen's face now, and the deer remained undisturbed. He made his movements very slow and deliberate, raising the rifle to his shoulder and leaving the reins on the horse's neck. The deer was down to his right, which made the shot more difficult; he had to twist his seat around in the saddle. He dare not move the horse in case the deer saw it.

Then the roebuck lifted its head, as if sensing something, and Killen went very still. It must have looked straight at him, but then seemed to relax and lowered its head to drink once again. Killen slowly let out his breath. Now was the critical moment. He must cock the rifle, and the click as the hammer locked into place might be heard. But the mechanism was well greased. He pulled back the safety lever with his thumb and hardly heard the pawl seat, trapping the cock in its firing position. He sighted down the barrel, breathing in deeply, willing his heart rate to steady, because its thump threatened to spoil his aim. Just behind the shoulder. That was the place; where the heavy lead ball would pierce the animal's lungs and heart and drop it, dead, in an instant. He let his breath out slowly. The hammering in his chest eased a little, and then the roebuck raised its head again and he pulled the trigger. Too quickly! Everything happened too quickly, after that.

He should have squeezed, not pulled. The hammer snapped forward onto the frizzen and flicked it forward. A shower of sparks from the flint-strike dropped into the pan to ignite the powder, which flashed to the main charge in the barrel. Flame and smoke spat from its muzzle as the rifle hurled the spinning lead ball away. The butt hammered back into his shoulder. And in the same instant that he realised he had rushed the shot and missed, the horse, frightened to the point of blind panic by such an unexpected explosion, took off through the trees.

Killen grabbed desperately at the reins, but they had fallen down the horse's shoulder and he missed them. He ducked down over the horse's neck to avoid a low branch which scraped his hat off, and the rifle barrel caught on a tree and was snatched out of his hand. Caught in the trigger guard, his index finger broke. He cried out in pain as he felt the bone snap. Killen's right hand was useless. He tried reaching for the reins with his left, but it was hopeless. The horse galloped down a dip in the ground and up the other side, smashing his right leg against another tree. The impact almost knocked him out of the saddle, and he twisted his good hand into the horse's mane in an effort to keep his seat.

Then the river turned towards them. At the top of the rise, the ground fell towards the rushing water, an almost sheer drop, and the horse, panic receding, instinctively shied away to its right.

Killen's right leg was numbed. He had so little grip that the horse's sharp turn threw him out to the side. His head crashed against another tree and he fell, a limp body tumbling down the drop and into the river. Where the rushing water picked it up and carried it, ever quicker, downstream.

# Chapter 3

Lock heard the gunshot. Its distinctive crack was not particularly loud but the sound, echoing, seemed to go on for a long time. He stood up.

He had been kneeling in front of one of his nets, but his eyes were drawn to the opposite side of the valley. A few birds started up from the treetops; rooks circled cautiously, cawing indignation, and a quartet of woodpigeons clapped their way across the canopy before wheeling and side-slipping down to a new resting place. Perhaps one of the 'keepers had fired. It was early in the year for crow-shooting, but if gamekeepers were about then he ought to make himself scarce. Coneys were only food for foxes, or target practice for the landlords, but poaching them for the pot was still a crime. Transportation was the sentence; even hanging, in those counties with a harsh magistrate. Most 'keepers turned a blind eye, though; trout and partridge were more their concern. But it made sense to be careful.

The woods went back to sleep. Lock bent to re-peg the net, but a distant movement caught the corner of his eye. On the other side of the valley, a horse had come out of the trees. A black horse, moving fast: reins trailing and stirrups flapping to fuel its panic. With no rider to guide or steady it, the horse careered out of the woods along a dirt path. Lock watched its wild gallop until the animal disappeared out of sight over a low rise without slackening speed.

Someone was in trouble. It was none of Lock's business, but curiosity made him walk down to the tree line. He stared downhill towards the river but could see little through the densely packed trunks, and he cursed, because fading afternoon light made the woodland floor darker still. Shrugging to himself, he made to turn back, but his conscience stabbed at him. *Someone was in trouble.* He hesitated, and the polecat chose that moment to poke its nose above ground.

Lock sighed and climbed back up the hill. Lifting the polecat from beneath the catch-net, he reversed its body so that once again it faced into the burrow. The animal happily scuttled back underground and Lock stuffed his bundle of dead rabbits in the hole to block it. He would come back for all of them later.

An animal trail led down towards the river; a well used track that, though narrow, was clearly visible through the undergrowth. Lock followed it. The trail twisted and turned through the trees, sometimes running along the side of the hill, sometimes dropping straight down. Leaf-mould slid away under his boots. Fallen branches crossed the track and he was forced to clamber over larger boughs, clumsily scraping off layers of damp moss and rotting bark. The river-sound grew louder; the light dimmer as the clogged canopy above his head filtered out more of the weak afternoon sun. He moved faster, accelerating down the slope without realising, his breath turning cloudy. Deep in the valley the air was colder.

Then he was at the river, and almost fell in. A section of bank had collapsed, scoured out by melt-water, the trap masked by a mat of twigs and dead leaves. The boy only just kept his feet, arms wind-milling wildly, twisting his body backwards so he sat down heavily.

Lock let his breathing slow to normal while he carefully scanned around him. He often walked in the woods so his eyes adjusted quickly to the poor light, but there was nothing unusual to see. The noise of the river swirling over rocks and slapping against its banks drowned out all other sounds. He thought to call out. "*Hello!*" It sounded loud to him, but rushing water seemed to whisk the word away. "*Hey!*" he called again, but there was no answer.

Lock got to his feet and began to walk downstream. Keeping away from the bank where he could, wary of the edge, he crouched every so often to check beneath overhanging branches. Nothing moved except the river.

He kept searching. Lock shivered, even though wrapped in his warm wool coat. The temperature must still be falling. He called out again, and this time his voice echoed across the water, for the river had widened. Its banks rose higher on each side, and its rushing slowed. In the quiet after the echo he froze, hoping for an answer. Nothing; it was hopeless. Whoever the horse belonged to was gone. Lock sighed in frustration, cursing his nosiness. Now he must climb back up the hillside, and the time he had wasted would most likely mean having to re-cross the flooded weir in twilight. He took one last look across the water.

And then, as he was about to turn back, he noticed something. Just a shadow; a dark shape bobbed by the swell, downstream and against the far bank. He hurried towards it, and as he drew closer there was a pale spot; a face. He could see a face, and the shape was clothing. A body, caught in branches that trailed in the water; snagged there but moving as wavelets lapped it. Lock was opposite the body now and shouted, but got no response. Perhaps it was dead and just floating. Bodies did that, he knew, buoyed by gas as they slowly putrefied. He should check, though; he could not just leave it there.

It would be impossible to wade to the far bank; the midstream swirl betrayed how strong the current was, and there was no telling the river's depth. Lock needed a way across, so he pushed on downstream as fast as he dared, slipping and stumbling over tree roots.

At last, he found what he had hoped for. Torn out by autumn gales, a huge larch straddled the river. Its tip did not quite reach the far bank and dangled into the water, but it would do very well. Enough of the big tree's roots had remained in the ground to anchor its trunk and stop the whole massive structure from being washed downstream. Lock jumped down into the crater where the tree was once anchored and began to climb upwards, using broken roots as hand and footholds. Once he reached the trunk itself, the rough bark offered some grip for his boots, but its branches, sticking vertically upwards, slowed his progress across the makeshift bridge. He struggled to find gaps for his feet and was wary about using the boughs as hand-holds in case one should break to send him crashing into the water below. The last few yards were the most difficult because the top of the tree was spindly and weak. It bent alarmingly under his weight, dipping below the water's surface. In the end he was forced to jump, landing on his knees on the far bank.

Lock rushed back upstream. The body was not a man, more a boy. A pale face; white, almost. He must be dead, Lock thought. He had seen a corpse once, frozen to death in the fields. Lock shivered, pulling his coat closer because the boy's face reminded him of the corpse. His horse had thrown him, he had landed in the water and drowned. His coat must have tangled in fallen branches, stopping the body from drifting further.

Lock felt his feet sinking into the ground. The riverbank moved. He got to his hands and knees, worried the earth might fall into the river. Freezing water soaked into his breeches: now he had cold legs as well as feet. He reached out towards the body but he was not near enough. The river was deafening. Getting down onto his belly, he inched forward until his hand was in the water. Stretching his arm out as far as he could, he touched cloth. Lock grabbed the boy's collar and heaved with all his strength, but realised too late he had made a mistake. Without warning the bank collapsed and he was tipped into the river.

The current whirled both of them away. Lock's face went under, then broke the surface again. He flailed wildly with his right arm to keep his head up while his left hand still clung grimly to the boy's coat. The water tore at him, flinging him this way and that, bumping over underwater rocks that caught at his jacket and bruised his back. Waterlogged clothing dragged him deeper as he struggled to keep his face above the torrent. The weight of the boy's body began to make his arm ache, but he would not let go. And then they were approaching the tree-bridge across the river, the one he had climbed across. Lock knew it was his chance. If he could just grab one of the shattered branches, he would be saved. He spluttered, spitting out water as the river dragged him under again. Then the larch was above him and he reached desperately upwards.

He had one! Desperately hanging on, buffeted by the torrent, the boy's body threatened to break from his grasp. At least now he could keep his face out of the water, but his sodden clothes were so heavy. He could not kick out to reduce the strain on his arm because the boy was in his way. His grip on the branch grew weaker: the force of the water was just too strong. At last it wrenched him away from the tree and threw them both downstream.

Another branch saved them. Lock's coat snagged it, and the current pulled him down below the surface. He held his breath, searching desperately with numbed fingers until he touched

44

something solid, then pushed with all his strength. It was enough to force his face out of the water. He gasped for air, and as he did his jacket came free. Once again the current tore the two boys downriver.

Lock's legs smashed against an underwater branch. He managed to grab it, but the rotten wood snapped off in his hand and the water swept him onwards. When he next jerked to a stop, the right sleeve of his jacket was caught. It felt like the river was trying to tear his arm off.

Lock fought to free himself and immediately wished he had not. A sharp spike drove through his clothes, digging into his upper arm. He cried out, but the river filled his mouth and forced him further onto the spear. The boy struggled, thrashing water to get away from the agony, but the current held him while the river fought to drown him. In desperation Lock grabbed for something - anything - to help lift his weight from the jagged thing tearing his flesh. The wound made his arm feeble: the water's intense cold sapped his strength. The spike dug deeper still and Lock's pain grew so unbearable he thought he must let his burden go, to save himself.

Afterwards, Lock believed he imagined it. A voice spoke to him; a memory from years past. His father and mother lay stone cold and pale on their cots. *"It is God's will,"* the voice said. The old priest's lips moved, mouthing the words, but it was not his voice. And as he watched the sheets drawn up to cover both dead faces, he cried out in anger, *"You'll not have them, you bastard!"*

Then the wild currents below the river's surface moved the branch from where it had lodged. Lock was free. But his right arm was near-useless, and the river washed him and the boy further on, until all at once it changed its course in a wide sweep, and the flow pushed him towards the bank. Lock felt the riverbed shelve upwards. His boots scrabbled amongst the stones until he found some purchase. Soon he could sit on the rocky bottom with his head clear of the water; nearer the bank the current was not strong enough to move him on.

Lock coughed up water that had found its way into his mouth and lungs between taking great gulps of air. He still had hold of the boy's collar, and with a struggle managed to drag the body up a gently sloping bank until it was half out of the river.

Breathing great clouds of steam into the cold air, Lock sat for a while. Experimentally he tried flexing the fingers of his right hand. They moved, which was something, but the arm was so weak: it hurt abominably and he could not make a fist. He fingered the hole in his dripping coat very gingerly, but could not see inside. Gritting teeth to ignore whatever damage the thick cloth hid; that was the only way.

The boy still lived. Lock reached across to feel his chest, finding a thump of heartbeat beneath the soaked clothing, faint but regular. His face was death-pale, fair hair plastered across his forehead. Lock saw he had a deep, jagged wound in his scalp but ice-cold river water had staunched the bleeding and washed it clean. Lock did not recognise him. He knew most boys from the village and this one looked about his own age, though his clothes seemed new.

Lock felt through the garments but found nothing to indicate who the boy was; only a sovereign in one coat pocket. He turned the gold piece over in his fingers, feeling its weight. Not much of a reward for saving a life, he thought, and put it back. He started to shiver. The light had almost gone, and though deep in the valley, Lock could feel the wind had changed direction. It picked up speed, rattling bare twigs in its path. He must move very soon, for this time of year a north wind might bring snow. The air would freeze, and he was soaked through to the skin.


Lord Halcombe sat writing in his study when Edward Gaunt burst in without knocking first. Halcombe stood up, startled. The ornate French mantel clock had just chimed six.

"My lord," the Stud Groom spoke into the silence.

"What is it?"

Gaunt hesitated. He hated to bear bad news. "Master Johnny's horse has come back without him, my lord." He looked at Halcombe, whose face had paled, and forced the rest out. "There's worse, my lord. There's blood on the saddlecloth." The Stud

Groom thought that if it were possible, his lordship's face grew even paler.

Halcombe slumped heavily back into his chair, staring at Gaunt as if he could not believe his ears. "The horse's?" he asked.

It sounded feeble, even to Gaunt who shook his head sadly. "I checked him over myself, my lord," he said, matter of fact. "Couple of scratches to his legs, like he'd run through brambles, that's all."

Halcombe got up and steadied himself by leaning on the desk. He looked worn out. "Be so kind as to fetch a carriage, Edward. And we'll need torches."

"Very good, my lord," the Stud Groom bowed before leaving quickly. There would be a search. Though how they would manage to find the boy in failing light, with no real idea of where he might be, was anybody's guess.

There was only one way he might get both of them home. Lock sat the unconscious boy up against a tree trunk. He found it difficult to drag the body now his right arm had stiffened. The limb hurt if he moved it at all, and on land the boy was much heavier than he had been in the water. Lock crouched down, managing to drape one flaccid arm over his shoulder. Now, if he could just find the strength to lift the boy up.

Then he saw deep scars in the bark. The base of the trunk must have been used by badgers as a scratching post. Strong animals, they were. Men said that if you were bitten by a badger, you had to break its jaw to make it let go. Lock had found a skull once, he remembered, from an old boar with worn teeth. He marvelled that its lower jaw was still firmly attached, and saw why the stories might be true. Now he stared hard at the claw marks, imagining the striped animals' talons tearing at the tree. And as he concentrated he straightened his legs and with a great effort forced himself upright. Bloody hell, it hurt! But all that remained was to hook his left arm under the boy's thigh, and that only seemed a small struggle after what had gone before.

Even so, the effort left him breathless. He had to stand for a while, bent over, leaning against the tree, the body balanced across his shoulders. But the numb fingers of his right hand could feel again - something sticky and wet. His torn arm was bleeding.

The river ran past the village. Lock decided the boy had to be a local. The horse had galloped off in that direction, so he must go there too. He knew that somewhere on the hillside above them was a road. Reaching it would make his trek easier than forcing his way through undergrowth, but the slope was too steep for him to carry the boy straight upwards. He must angle uphill, skirting trees where they blocked his path or stumbling over fallen branches in the dark. Once he slipped on wet leaf-mould and fell into a hole he had not seen, wrenching an ankle. Cursing, he was forced to stop until the joint recovered enough to take both their weights.

As Lock struggled higher, the trees thinned. Deep in the woods, their broad trunks shielded him from the wind, but now its bitterness forced him to clamp his jaws shut to stop his teeth chattering. Doggedly, Lock kept climbing. He took one deliberate step after the other, eyes down, checking where he planted each foot. The boy seemed to grow heavier. That was impossible, Lock knew. His neck ached. He stopped and tried to reposition the body, shrugging his shoulders to get some relief from the discomfort. But he dare not put the boy down; it would be too easy not to pick him up again.

Nearer the road, Lock's pace faltered. He must be almost there, he convinced himself. Daylight had gone. Desperately tired, his soaking clothes impeded every step. His right arm throbbed; it nagged at him each time he moved, and because he felt so feeble, so near to exhaustion, Lock grew increasingly annoyed. How could he have been so stupid? And the boy; what was he doing in the damned woods at this time of year? Lock nurtured the feelings; let them blossom. Soon he was angry with the woods, angry with the mud that sucked at his feet, angry with the branches that whipped his face and with the north wind that frosted his wet hair and chilled his bones. The anger drove him. He would not let the bastards beat him; *he would damned well not*!

Abruptly he lost his balance, pitching forward. Stones dug into his knees and shins. In the dark, he had left the trees, stepping into the road without realising. Exhausted, he fell forward onto his face. He lay underneath his burden and sobbed, for he could go no further.

Then the north wind breathed a snowflake onto Combe Wood.


Edward Gaunt took the lead. Keeping hold of the nearside coach horse's bridle with his right hand, he raised a lantern in his left and stared out into the fields on that side of the road. Truth be told, it was growing too dark. Snow flurries made visibility worse, and the party were forced to abandon their bare torches early on when the wind repeatedly blew them out.

Five men trudged through the dark, for as well as Lord Halcombe and his coachman, Gaunt had pressed two grooms to join the search party. On horseback, they ranged on either side of the road and should be able to see further than if they had been on foot. Each rode one-handed, carrying a lantern in the other, but the horses hated snow in their faces. They tucked their noses into their chests and tried to swing their hindquarters to the wind.

Every hundred paces or so, everyone halted to call Johnny's name. All strained their ears for an answering shout, but each time the wind blew their voices back at them. The only sounds were the jingle of harness as a draught horses chewed at its bit, or the scrunch of hooves grinding gravel. To make their search more difficult, the snow began to thicken. Broad flakes drifted down, speckling any bare ground; settling wetly on clothing and carriage; melting against hot lantern-glasses.

The Stud Groom began to fear the worst. An injured man lying outside in this weather would probably not last the night, and Master Johnny had never been robust. The next time they halted he walked back to the carriage and put his head through the open window. Halcombe looked even more distressed, if that were possible. Seeing his face, Gaunt hesitated, but the words had to be said. "How much further do you want us to go, my lord?" he asked gently for they were approaching the edge of Combe Wood, and if the boy was lying amongst the trees, an army of men searching in broad daylight might miss him. It was obvious that Halcombe really did not want to make the decision to call a halt, but by now all of them were cold and wet. Searching in the dark through a thickening snowstorm was doing no good.

The Stud Groom looked at his master sympathetically. "We'll go to the edge of the wood, if that's all right with you, my lord," he said, and even to him his voice sounded flat, without much hope. Halcombe simply nodded dumb agreement, as if not wanting to accept the likelihood their search would be unsuccessful. Edward Gaunt went back to the coach horses and led them forward, into the wind and snow.


Lock's anger had not completely burned itself out. An ember still smouldered, and as the north wind tugged at his wet clothes, it burst into flame. If he lay where he was, he would probably die. He must go on. *Must!* Wind and snow would not beat him. He cursed them both out loud, somehow struggling to his feet, the boy still on his back. The anger seethed and bubbled inside as he trudged along the road; it forced him onwards, giving him succour, screaming at him. *Don't stop.*

Putting one foot in front of the other, step after step, he did not know how far he walked, or even where he was. Just that he had to keep going, one foot in front of the other; step after step. Snow fell more heavily. Breathing burned his chest. Waterlogged boots rasped his feet raw and his shoulders drooped under the boy's weight.

His arm still bled; a slow, innocuous seep. But it hardly registered now cold had numbed the limb completely, leaving his right hand flapping and useless. So he leaned into the wind and walked ever slower, on and on, until even the force of his anger was not enough to sustain him. At the end, Lock fell to his knees, collapsing in the snow. They had beaten him. He cried out one last time, cursing the wind, cursing the snow, cursing the boy on his back, cursing the whole damned world.

And the north wind took his cries and, mocking him, swirled them uselessly away.

Driving snow muffled the sound of the river, but the Stud Groom could just make out the roar of rushing water over the hiss of the wind in his ears. The search party reached a place where solitary trees marked the beginning of the woods, and came to a halt. Both grooms walked their horses forward with care, wary of holes hidden beneath the snow, but saw nothing.

In desperation Halcombe climbed from the coach and started downhill, towards the river. Gaunt caught up with him in a few strides. It was dangerous to stray too far from the road. Once more, every man called Johnny's name, but only the wind answered. Halcombe trudged back to the carriage and beckoned Gaunt to him, his face furrowed deep in the lantern-light.

"We must give it best, I think," he admitted tiredly. The Stud Groom nodded reluctant agreement and went to fetch the two grooms back.

Halcombe had one foot inside the carriage when a groom called out. Gaunt sprinted towards him. "What is it?" he shouted, cupping hands around his mouth. The groom pointed ahead, "I thought I heard something, Mr. Gaunt." He kicked his horse forward, and with a flush of hope the Stud Groom stumbled along behind.


There was something ahead, Lock thought; a pinprick of light. A cottage maybe, with a lamp-lit window. Face down in the road, he squinted at the glow through one eye. Falling snow made it difficult to focus, but there was definitely a light. He could reach it if he wanted to. Get to the cottage and he would be safely out of the blizzard. Then it moved, he thought; the light moved! With an effort he shoved the boy off his back and rolled onto his side. He tried to call out, to tell the light where he was but his voice squeaked, and the light would not come any nearer.

Lock screwed both eyes tight shut, willing the light to find him. When he opened them again it flickered closer. He was sure. And there was something about the ground; he felt it move! Someone was coming, and he lay down again, waiting an age until he could almost feel the horses' breaths on his skin. Steel-shod hooves stopped inches from his head. Boots scraped through slushy gravel; carriage-wheels creaked. And voices; all speaking at once.

Then Lock closed his eyes and gave a great sigh, for he knew he had won. He had beaten the north wind, and saved the boy from God.

# Chapter 4

For a moment, the Stud Groom was afraid that Killen was dead, and that his master's fears were well founded. He touched the boy's face. It was like ice, but his cheek twitched and Gaunt felt a flood of relief. Halcombe leapt from his still-moving carriage and rushed across.

"What is it?" He stopped, aghast when he saw the two bodies, but the Stud Groom straightened up to reassure him.

"He's alive, my Lord," he shouted to make himself heard above the wind.

Halcombe took over. "Blankets," he commanded the coachman, "quickly man!" He turned to the grooms. "You two; help get him inside!"

They lifted Killen gently and carried him to the carriage, propping him carefully on its upholstery. Halcombe clambered in to sit alongside, wrapping his arms around the boy's body to warm him. With a tremor in his voice he shouted through the open door at one of the grooms, "Ride to the village and fetch Doctor Wyles; with all speed!" The young man was up on his horse quickly, but before he could put his legs to its sides the Stud Groom strode over and reached up to grab his elbow.

"In this weather, you take it steady," he hissed a warning. The groom nodded before setting off into the darkness at a brisk trot. Snow muffled the clip of the horse's feet.

Halcombe rapped on the ceiling of the carriage. "Come on man," he railed at the coachman, "let's be on our way, for pity's sake."

"Just a moment, my lord," the Stud Groom looked closely at Lock who had managed to drag himself to his feet, shivering violently. From the way he carried it, the boy's arm was injured. Gaunt held up a lantern. He saw the tear in Lock's sleeve and beckoned to the coachman, "Give me your apron." The man was reluctant to yield up the thick wool that protected his legs, but Gaunt snatched it down. He draped it over Lock's shoulders, noticing the way the boy winced when the heavy material fell across his right arm. The Stud Groom pointed to the open coach door, "Get in, lad."

Lock needed help to climb up. His shoulder caught on the narrow doorframe as hands pushed him inside. The wound hurt like hell, but now he was out of the wind and snow. He collapsed onto a soft bench seat, not caring that the man opposite stared at him with suspicion. Lock thought he looked familiar, but he was too tired to be sure, or care. The coachman must have flicked his whip at the horses for the coach began to move, and soon the gentle rocking of its leather-slung body sent him to sleep.

He woke with a start. The coach had stopped, and its right hand door hung open. Feet scrunched on gravel and he could hear raised voices. Lock peered out. They had pulled up outside a grand house. The remaining groom, and another man he had not seen before, carried the boy up the steps of a porticoed entrance, through a doorway blazing with yellow lamplight. Sombrely dressed servants fussed around them. Like jackdaws fighting over a dead vole, Lock thought uncharitably. His right arm throbbed. But when he reached across with his other hand to explore the damage, the wound seemed numb.

The man who had wrapped Lock in a blanket climbed back down the steps to the carriage and gave him a friendly look. "We'd best get you out of there lad," he said softly, "or we'll never get the seats dry." Lock offered an outstretched left arm, finding he again needed help. He staggered as he stepped outside and the wind caught him, stripping away the vestige of warmth his body had produced in the closed carriage. He shivered violently, and the man must have thought he would fall. He grabbed Lock around the waist, pulling the boy's left arm up over his shoulders. He was quite short, Lock decided, because he was not forced to stoop. Together they half-walked, half-stumbled across the gravel, and the short man dragged him up the stone steps into an entrance hall. Lock's helper had to tug hard on his arm to keep the boy upright, and his wrist began to ache.

Once in the hallway, they stopped. Lock heard distant voices and assumed the other boy had been carried up one of the staircases which swept majestically skywards on each side. He swayed, and the short man propped him against one wall.

"Can you stand?" Lock turned his head and nodded dumbly. "Wait here then," the man instructed. He started to walk away, deeper into the hallway, then thought better of it and came back. He stared Lock in the face, his eyes flicked up and down as if looking for something. "I won't be long," he insisted.

Lock nodded without answering. He felt so tired; if only he could go to sleep. On the floor lay a rug, an oblong of patterned wool, but that apart the hall was bare of furniture. Perhaps he could lie on it. He glanced downwards, at brown and white quarry tiles crosscut by fine cement lines. The water seeping from Lock's soaked clothes ran into the grout, staining the lines black as blood in the lamplight. He looked away.

On his right, a door stood ajar. Of panelled wood, with a brass knob handle to fill a large man's hand, the room it opened into appeared only dimly lit, as if its last occupant had left a candle burning. It attracted Lock like a moth. Staggering weakly way from the wet stain he had made on the wall he pushed awkwardly at the door so it swung open.

A single lamp burned on a dark wooden table standing at the room's centre, and in its poor light Lock could see that the walls were lined with books. Shelves and shelves of leather and board covered volumes. Starting near the floor, the library rose so high that a ladder must be used to reach the topmost. Barely believing what he had found, Lock stepped across the threshold and shuffled slowly towards the nearest shelf. He had never seen so many books. Reaching out with his left hand, he touched one with his index finger, running the tip slowly across the gold-blocked title. Something he could not read; Latin, perhaps, or French. There were some Latin words in the farriery book at the smithy. He went on to the next, feeling the small ridges in its leather binding, and his still damp skin lifted away a thin layer of dust; a smudge on his hand.

The door creaked suddenly, and he turned, guilty at being caught. Pain shot up his arm as he twisted round.

"There you are," it was the short man again. "It's Joshua, isn't it?" Lock nodded. The man looked satisfied, "I thought I'd remembered." He paused, and gestured back towards the hallway. "I'm Edward Gaunt, Lord Halcombe's Stud Groom," he said, by way of introduction. "You'd better come this way, so we can take a look at your arm."

A huge black cast-iron range kept the scullery warm. One of its fires was being fed by a kitchen maid, unseasoned logs making the flames roar and spit. Gaunt motioned for Lock to sit on a long wooden bench at one side of the room while he fetched a lantern. Holding it close to the boy's injured arm, so he could inspect it more closely, he fingered the tear in Lock's coat. He had to spread the rent apart, making the boy wince.

"That'll have to come off," he said gruffly, indicating the coat. Lock stood so Gaunt could pull the wet sleeve off his left arm, but when the Stud Groom tugged at the other the pain was so great that Lock felt sick. He slumped back down onto the bench.

Gaunt grunted, "I'll have to cut it." He found a sharp butchers' knife that he first used to extend the rip in the sleeve until its cuff fell easily over Lock's wrist. The rest of the coat slipped off. The boy's shirt was stained dark with blood the river had not managed to wash out. The Stud Groom carefully peeled the linen from his skin to examine the wound, frowning as he did. The tear stretched from just below the boy's shoulder to above his elbow. Gaunt grimaced. "That doesn't look too good", he said, shaking his head. It must hurt like the very devil. He caught Lock's eye, "It'll need stitching."


"Well?"

Doctor Wyles straightened up from Killen's bedside. "Well, my lord, I believe he will survive," he said carefully.

"Are you certain? Is there anything else you need do?"

The doctor gave a small smile. "You must keep him warm until he wakes," he instructed. "Change the bed warmer every hour, and his contusion must be bathed in cold water." He moved towards the boy's head, beckoning Halcombe forward. "You will see that there is a wound here, above the hairline," the doctor went on. He parted the hair at the side of Killen's head with his fingers to point out a jagged cut with raised edges that surmounted a large lump. "He has hit his head on something, or perhaps has been hit by someone?"

Halcombe registered shock. "Are you suggesting he was attacked?"

"I merely advance the possibility," the doctor said. He paused. "But I have palpated his skull and can feel no sign of a fracture." He stood up straight. "We must hope and pray he has suffered no damage to the brain," he said gravely.

"Is that possible?"

"There is always a risk, my lord, but I think it unlikely in one so young." He gave a small smile. "Children bounce more readily."

Halcombe frowned toward his grandson, still concerned. "Very well," he said at last.

"And his broken finger has been splinted," the doctor added, "but whether it will set perfectly straight...," he shrugged, "one can never tell." He stooped to pick up the leather case that held his instruments and dressings.

The Stud Groom appeared in the doorway, and Halcombe motioned him to come inside.

"Edward?"

"The boy, my lord." Halcombe raised his eyebrows in query. "His wound is quite bad, my lord. I think it should be stitched."

Halcombe nodded. "Could you avail us of one additional service this evening, doctor?" he asked.

"Of course, my lord," Wyles agreed.


Halcombe kept Edward Gaunt back as they started down the staircase. "Has the boy said anything yet?" he whispered.

Gaunt shook his head. "I think he's still in some shock."

"Try to find out what happened. The doctor thinks Johnny might have been struck deliberately."

Gaunt showed surprise. "I can't believe the boy would have done that, my lord." Halcombe looked unconvinced, so the Stud Groom went on, "Why would he carry him back? Why not leave him there? We would never have known. And, my lord, there's no reason for him to attack Master Johnny."

"The rifle," Halcombe said with a sudden thought. "It was not with the horse when that returned, was it?" Gaunt shook his head.

"Then that must be the reason."

"But why?"

Halcombe had an answer. From his position in the carriage opposite the boy, he had seen Lock's poor clothes. "It is a fine weapon; worth a great deal of money to the right person. The boy probably hid it in the woods and had a twinge of conscience when he realised what he had done."

Gaunt shook his head again, more vehemently this time. "Whatever you think, my lord, I don't believe the boy is guilty of anything more than trying to bring Master Johnny home. I know of his family, such as it is. They're honest people. There must be another explanation."

"Then find it, Edward," Halcombe commanded, "find it."


Wyles examined Lock's wounded right arm, tut-tutting with disapproval. "It is certainly deep," he observed. "How did this happen?" Lock looked into the doctor's eyes, but did not reply.

"They were both soaked," Gaunt said. "We think they'd been in the river."

The doctor pursed his lips, still staring into the tear. "The edges are ragged," he opined, "so it's not been done with a sharp implement. This was not done with a knife, was it?" he interrogated. The boy shook his head, still dumb.

Wyles sighed. He really ought not be treating this…this *peasant*. Being disturbed on such a foul evening to attend an emergency had not been welcome, even for the Lord of the Manor, and now this. But since he had made the journey, and Lord Halcombe would pay, he might as well collect an extra fee. "Lost your tongue, I see. I don't believe he knows what caused it," he said to Gaunt. Moving his head from side to side, still looking at Lock's arm, he beckoned the Stud Groom. "Bring a light closer, if you please; there seems to be a …a foreign body lodged here."

Gaunt found a lantern while the doctor pulled a pair of slim forceps from his case. He poised them above the wound. "This may hurt a little," he said, without sounding at all sympathetic.

Gaunt watched Lock's face as Wyles pushed the tip of the steel forceps into his arm. He saw the pain; muscles ridged under the boy's jaw, but he made no protest.

"I have it," the doctor boasted, drawing out his prize with a dramatic gesture. Clamped in the forceps' narrow jaws was an inch-long black object. Wyles brandished it close to the lantern, twisting it around in the light. "It looks like..," he paused, unsure, and held the object towards Gaunt, "...a sliver of wood?"

The Stud Groom looked quizzically at Lock, who shrugged one-shouldered as if he had no idea what the thing might be. The wound was bleeding again; watery pink fluid running down the boy's elbow. Wyles scrutinised the damage. "I cannot see anything else in there," he said, pulling a grubby rag from his pocket with which he wiped the forceps before returning them to his case.

Gaunt had stitched injured horses and cattle before, but never a man. He watched with morbid fascination as the doctor pulled a length of silk from its reel and ran it through his mouth to wet the thread. The curved needle he produced seemed enormous, and this time Wyles neglected to warn the boy of any possible discomfort. He simply jabbed the needle through Lock's skin on one side of the wound, skilfully piercing its opposite lip before pulling the two edges together with a secure knot. He looked at the first stitch critically, seemed satisfied, and drew a small scissor from his case to snip the thread. Then, impatiently handing the scissor to Gaunt, he dug in the needle once more.

When the doctor had finished there were ten stitches in Lock's arm. Near the shoulder, swollen flesh made the wound edges gape untidily between each knot. And lower down the wound, it seemed the doctor had exhausted his enthusiasm for the job. The stitches here were worse; the final one looked loose. Gaunt thought he might have done a little better himself.

Wyles wound a bandage around his handiwork. "Ensure you keep the dressing wet," he advised. Then backing away from Lock he motioned Gaunt to follow him before speaking in a whisper. "That's the best that can be done, but I cannot promise it will heal. If the wound festers, the arm may have to be removed."

But he said the words too loudly; the boy overheard him. And Lock spoke for the first time that evening.

*"No!"* he said vehemently.

# Chapter 5

"So what happened?"

The doctor had gone, ushered into Halcombe's study for a fortifying drink before he set off home through the blizzard. The kitchen maids were in bed. Gaunt gave Lock a small smile. "I only ask," he said, "because Lord Halcombe thinks someone may have clouted Master Johnny over the head."

"I don't know what happened," Lock admitted tiredly, "I just found him in the river." He shifted position on the bench. Gaunt leant casually against the scullery wall, waiting for Lock to be still before he gently probed again. "Tell me then."

So Lock sighed and told him. He told about the horse galloping from the wood; about grabbing the body in the water; about carrying the boy along the road. The story came haltingly at first; just the bare facts. But eventually it all spilt out in a rush.

"…And I was glad you came," Lock finished.

Gaunt listened without interrupting, growing more incredulous as the tale went on. It must be a half-mile from the river to the road; more like a mile if the boy had angled along the hill rather than struggled straight up it. Then another two to where the searchers had found them. Gaunt gave a small shake of the head, but Lock saw it.

"It's the truth," he insisted.

Gaunt smiled again. "I believe you lad," he said gently. "You say you heard a shot before the horse bolted away?" Lock nodded. "Right," Gaunt pushed himself away from the wall. "Just wait here, will you? I'll be straight back."


The Stud Groom found his lordship in the study. Doctor Wyles was still there, clutching an empty brandy glass. Vainly hoping for a refill, Gaunt thought with a certain relish.

"I think I may have solved the mystery, my lord." The Stud Groom told Halcombe Lock's story. "I believe the gunshot is significant. I said before, we've no idea if that horse has been broke to fire. And if Master Johnny shot at something..?"

Halcombe raised his hand in interruption. "Could his head wound be from a gunshot?" he asked the doctor, but must have seen the look on Gaunt's face. "I merely wonder whether the rifle might have discharged accidentally," he added mildly.

Wyles considered. "It is possible," he said slowly.

"Well is it or isn't it, damn it."

The doctor conceded, "I think it unlikely, my lord."

Halcombe still seemed unsatisfied. "Well, thank you doctor," he said in dismissal. "Roberts will show you out."

Wyles disappointedly put down his empty glass. "I shall return at noon tomorrow," he announced, "to check young Master Johnny's dressings, and bleed the patient."


Once the doctor had gone, Halcombe turned to his Stud Groom again. "Are you certain this boy's story can be trusted?" he asked. "It seems far fetched in the extreme."

"It was the sound of a shot that convinced me," Gaunt said. "Think about it, my lord; if that horse isn't broke to fire, and it's probably not, in my opinion. If Master Johnny shot at something, that would account for it bolting out of the woods. He could easily have hit his head on a tree if he had no control."

Halcombe thought. "See what you mean, Edward," he said after a while. The damned horse would have to go. He sighed. "So it is likely we have the boy to thank, rather than condemn?"

Gaunt was convinced. "I believe Master Johnny might be dead by now if Joshua Lock hadn't happened along."


Lock began to feel cold again, except that his right arm was on fire thanks to the doctor's efforts. To begin with, the discomfort made him sweat, but that soon stopped, and he found if he concentrated his thoughts on something else the pain eased a little. Now it was just about bearable.

He retrieved the woollen apron Gaunt had wrapped around him, but his wet clothes had soaked it. Even though he turned it inside-out it felt damp. The range was cleared of pans; the fire in its belly slowly dying. Lock could still feel the iron's heat, though. He struggled to his feet to stand beside it. When Edward Gaunt returned, steam had begun to rise from the boy's wet breeches.

The Stud Groom picked up the apron but quickly felt why Lock discarded it. "I'd better find you some clothes. Put this around you," he ordered, "we have to go outside. You can sleep in the stables tonight." He looked at Lock out of the corner of his eye. "Will your grandfather expect you back?" When Lock shook his head, Gaunt nodded, motioning the boy to follow him through to the far corner of the scullery where a small porch bulged outwards. "I'll send one of the grooms to the smithy in the morning, to let him know where you are," the Stud Groom offered, unbolting a door at the back which let in a great blast of wind-driven snowflakes. "Be pointless going now, in this weather."

They scuttled across the yard to another door, this one set in the end of a building that seemed to run at right angles to a stone stable block. Gaunt let them both in, slamming the door closed against the weather. Inside, lamps threw shadows from empty harness hooks lining one wall, but it was the smell of horse and leather that assailed Lock first. Mixed with the peculiar tang of dung and urine, it was a stink he was used to; felt at home with. He sneezed. Crossing the yard had stripped away what little warmth he managed to draw from the scullery range, and his teeth began to chatter. Gaunt opened a deep wooden chest in the corner of the room and pulled out a thick bolt of cloth.

"Horse blanket," he said. "Wrap it around you while I find some clothes. And stand by the fire."


When Gaunt returned, Lock was sitting on the chest and had managed to unlace his boots with his good hand. The leather was sodden. He levered one off, pushing the heel down with the toe of the other, but the second proved stubborn. The Stud Groom bent down to help him with it.

"Thanks, Mr. Gaunt."

Gaunt smiled. "You'd better call me Edward." He dumped dry clothes on top of the chest alongside Lock. "Can you manage to change into those? They're not ideal but the best I can do for now."

He frowned, "Then I think it best we take another look at your arm."

The shirt was too big, and the breeches the Stud Groom had brought were tight across Lock's thighs and too short. He hung his right arm out of the shirt so that the material ran awkwardly across his chest, but Gaunt had also found a dark blue cloak that fastened at the throat with a metal hook and chain. Lock gratefully slung it around his neck so that it fell over his shoulders, covering everything up. The Stud Groom reappeared carrying a tray which he set on the floor alongside the blanket-chest. Lock did not much like the look of what it held.

The door opened, gusting snow, and two grooms staggered in dragging armfuls of wet leather straps that made slug-trails on the floor.

"For God's sake, get that door shut!" Gaunt thundered at them. It slammed again, cutting the wind short, and the two men heaved their loads out of sight. There must be more harness racks around the corner, Lock thought.

Gaunt brought a pail of steaming water, poured from a kettle by the fire. He stooped alongside Lock and began to unwind the bandage from his arm. The boy winced as the Stud Groom unwrapped the final few turns. Blood had stuck the folds to his skin. The wound was still seeping.

Gaunt pulled a face. "Want to look?"

Lock gingerly raised his arm, which had turned a purplish-red colour. Between stitches the wound gaped even more. It looked dreadful, and he lowered it again. "My apron's stitched better than that."

Gaunt gave a small guffaw. "You're probably right. Not much we can do about it now, unless you want me to take them out and start over?"

"No thanks."

"I didn't think so." The Stud Groom considered. "A poultice, I think, would be best."

Lock gritted his teeth. The bloody wound had started to hurt like the devil now it was exposed to the air. "Bran," he said.

Gaunt looked up. "What else would you use?"

"Cabbage leaves, maybe? Only if the wound wasn't open"

"Yes," Gaunt grinned at him. "Done this sort of thing before, have you?"

"Lots of times," Lock muttered. "Not to myself, though."

Gaunt mixed bran into the pail with a wooden spoon until it made a stiff paste. He wound a few turns of bandage around Lock's arm so the wound was covered with a thin layer of cloth, then spooned out a lump of hot poultice. "Ready?" Lock knew this would be worse than the stitching.

The Stud Groom lifted the boy's arm and began spreading the steaming mixture over it. He scooped up another spoonful, then another, building them until a thick layer of paste lay above the wound. When at last he was satisfied, he began wrapping the rest of the bandage over the poultice.

This is where it gets worse, Lock thought. Heat from the mixture had already penetrated the fabric against his skin, but now pressure was being applied on top it just got hotter and hotter. Lock's head flopped back and he closed his eyes.

"Not too bad, is it?"

Lock said nothing.

Gaunt must have seen the pain, though. "Perhaps you should have laudanum. I could ask his lordship for some?"

"There's no need," Lock said faintly. "Be fine."

He slept on a cot propped in the eaves of the stables' attic. The youngest groom had been reluctantly persuaded to give up his bed, grumbling constantly about the unfairness until Gaunt threatened him with a horse whip if he did not shut up. Afterwards the boy threw accusing looks at Lock, who, too tired to argue, ignored him completely. There was no pillow, but Lock was used to that. He fell asleep almost as soon as he lay down.

Chapter 6

Lock lay on his back staring at patterns the daylight sketched as it filtered through tiny gaps between the roof tiles. The bright designs seemed ordered; regular. He had never noticed that at home, more often studying the shapes of dusty cobwebs which spiders hung in dark corners, where one huge roof beam met its neighbour.

He rolled off the cot and sat on the floorboards. In the stables below him people moved about. Horses stamped or chewed hay; men's voices softly cursed or cajoled; the sounds of a stable-yard in the morning. Testing his right arm he found muscles had stiffened during the night. He wriggled his fingers, grimacing. They worked fine, but the rest of his arm was pretty sore. He would not be able to work today.

Edward Gaunt's blue cloak had worked its way round his back during the night. Lock struggled to rearrange its folds, tugging the heavy material across so it covered the bandage on his right arm but left the other bare. Stretching pulled at bruised back muscles he never realised he had. He stood with exaggerated care, stooping below the roof-slope. He should go down.

The open staircase Lock found a steep climb the night before was easier to descend. Down below, the harness room was deserted, but a fire burned in the grate and there was bread on the table; Lock could smell it from the foot of the stairs. His stomach protested its hunger for he had eaten nothing since the previous morning.

The loaf was still warm, and Lock tore a chunk off. It was difficult using only one hand, especially as there was a butter-pat with a knife. Not wanting to miss out on a rare treat, Lock managed to roughly slap some golden-yellow fat on the bread. He had just put the piece to his mouth when Edward Gaunt strode in.

The Stud Groom stood in front of the fire, blowing on his hands before briskly rubbing the chill out. Lock stopped chewing, but Gaunt seemed not to see any wrongdoing. He turned his back to the fire, flapping damp coat-tails towards the flames. "Tea's down there," he said, indicating the hearth, where a battered pot stood steaming gently. "Cups are in the cupboard." He drew one hand from behind his back and pointed. "How's your arm?"

Lock pulled a face. "Stiff."

"Only to be expected." Gaunt came to the table and sat on the remaining chair. "Weather's still bad." He pulled off his cloth cap to shake it, scattering water droplets over the floor.

Lock fetched a pair of tin mugs from the cupboard before crossing to the hearth for the teapot. Someone had bound its handle with thick twine to stop it burning fingers.

"You're left handed." The Stud Groom must have been watching him closely. Lock nodded, pouring tea into the mugs which gently steamed while he returned the pot to the hearth.

Gaunt pushed one mug towards him. "We can ride over to the smithy later. Weather ought to ease by this afternoon." He lifted the other mug to his mouth and blew across it. "You look better than half-alive this morning. Think you can work?"

"That depends," Lock had been wondering the same thing.

Gaunt took a sip and put the mug down. "We've plenty of horses to groom. The lot that came in last night are filthy; they've not been touched yet. The lads can take care of the heavy work; mucking out and such. But if you could give a hand brushing them down?"

The Stud Groom walked Lock through to the stables. "Four grooms work here," Gaunt told him. "There's plenty to do this time of year; the hunters haven't been roughed off yet." One of his men hurried past, pushing a barrow-load of dung and dirty straw. As they both watched, the groom left a trail of dirty stalks across the floor which dribbled from his overloaded barrow. The Stud Groom gave an exasperated sigh, "There's an extra job for someone."

Lock looked interestedly at the stables, set in two inward facing rows. Each horse had one box to itself, a compartment around fifteen feet square with a half-door fixed mid-way along its front. Their dividing walls and fronts were topped with grilles made of thin iron bars, several inches apart, which allowed every horse to see its neighbour but not interfere with it.

But one stable was different. The corner box had a full height solid wall between it and the next. Lock wondered why. He wandered over and found it occupied by a black horse. A decent looking animal, Lock decided. Although in need of a good brushing, the horse had an air about it; something he could not pin down straight away. What was it his grandfather said? It had *the look*.

"What do you think?"

Lock jumped slightly when the Stud Groom walked up behind him unheard. He ran a critical eye over the horse, but could find no real fault. "A bit light in the limbs," he suggested eventually.

It seemed Gaunt agreed. "It's called The Tempest. A thoroughbred, of course," he grimaced. "His lordship bought it off the racetrack. That's the horse that dumped Master Johnny and came home without him."

"Can't he ride then?"

"Huh." Gaunt squinted at Lock out of the corner of one eye. "He can ride alright, but the horse is difficult. Only half a job done when they broke it, I reckon." He looked back at The Tempest. "It's well bred; his lordship wouldn't have bought it, otherwise. But Master Johnny won't take any help with it. His lordship pays this Hanoverian riding master to teach him, but all he does is make Master Johnny trot in circles and says '*Gut*'." Gaunt raised his arms with a flourish to mimic Killen's instructor, then leant forward and spat disgustedly on the floor. "I could do better myself."

"I'll groom this one," Lock said.

"He's entire, mind," Gaunt warned, "you'd better tie him up tight."

Lock had been bitten and kicked by plenty of horses. "I've handled stallions before. Have you got brushes?"

Gaunt brought a short-bristled body brush. Just both longer and wider than Lock's hand laid flat, it had a leather strap fixed across the back. The boy could just about slip his hand underneath.

"You won't be able to use a curry," Gaunt said, handing one over anyway. Lock studied it. The curry comb was a flat metal plate, with rows of fine pointed teeth that stood at right angles. He turned it over. It also had a leather hand-strap fitted, attached to the plate by iron rings.

"If you've got some twine," Lock said, "I'll be able to use it." It was simple really, he thought. He took two pieces of the twine, looping them through the metal rings, and, one-handed, tied the curry to his left thigh just above the knee. Then he drew the brush across the teeth of the comb to clean out loose horsehair and dust.

The Stud Groom grunted when he saw the result. "Shame, really."

"What?"

"The horse," Gaunt pointed at the black thoroughbred. "His lordship will probably get rid of it after all this trouble."


The Tempest already wore a leather halter, and Lock found a rope, neatly wound up outside its stable. He retrieved it and unhooked the door bolts, talking to the horse as he went inside. It did not matter what he said, Lock knew, just that he was quiet and confident. Without any trouble he tied the horse to an iron ring set in one wall.

Lock stood on the horse's left side. As he raised his hand to begin the first brush stroke, The Tempest threw its head up and moved away from him. Lock stepped towards it again and gently laid hand and brush against the horse's neck. "Someone's been rough with you, have they, boy?" he said quietly, almost as if talking to himself. He drew the brush in a long, curving downstroke through the horse's coat before lifting it again. The animal rolled one eye at him, showing the white, but this time did not lift its head. And because Lock stood closer it could only move a short distance sideways before its rump came into contact with the stable wall. Lock spoke to The Tempest again before he brought down the brush in a second stroke. Then he drew the brush across the curry comb to clean it before once again laying it against the horse's neck. The stallion did not move. Lock swept the brush down once more then ducked under the horse's neck to its off-side.

This was more difficult, but not because the horse decided to play up. Lock would normally have switched the brush to his right hand, but because that was impossible he had to use it backhand. The awkward motion swung his right arm, which began to protest. The discomfort made him angry, his brush strokes becoming heavier the more annoyed he got. He moved along the horse's body, keeping the brush going. Three strokes: curry. Three strokes: curry.

Lock started to sweat. He went back to the horse's left side again; swung the brush; hissed through his teeth, blowing dusty air away from his face. His arm was hurting, but he leaned on the brush, pushing his whole weight through each stroke. And to his surprise he found the horse leaning back at him as if testing his strength with its own bodyweight. He went back to the right side. Three strokes: curry. The horse leaned harder. Three strokes: curry. His wounded arm was on fire. Sweat ran down his face. He ducked back to the nearside, speeding up his swing. Three strokes: curry. Three strokes: curry; forcing the brush through again and again. Then, just before the next stroke landed, Lock pulled his hand away away, brushing air. The horse, anticipating pressure that never came, slightly lost its balance, moving sideways towards him. Lock stepped back, away from The Tempest, and smiled to himself. He had made the horse come to him. His anger was gone, and he had not had to count.

Edward Gaunt looked over the stable door, frowning. "Are you alright?" Lock nodded. "Well, you look awful," Gaunt said. He went into the stable himself and shooed the boy out. "Go and sit down before you fall down." Gaunt unclipped the halter rope to let the horse loose, and it turned back to its hay, pulling mouthfuls from between the bars of a rack in the corner. Gaunt stared at it as it walked away. "How on earth did you manage to shine it as quickly as that?" he asked with surprise. "You can give a couple of these lazy buggers some lessons."


"He has not woken yet, doctor," Lord Halcombe said with concern. One of the chambermaids had been stationed at Killen's bedside all night, so he knew this was true.

Wyles removed his fingers from the boy's wrist and stared at the white face of his pocket watch. Five minutes after midday. The sweep hand counted Killen's heart rate. His pulse was regular, if a little slow, the doctor thought. "His heartbeat is strong, my lord," he said. "It is sometimes the case that a blow on the head may cause a state of unconsciousness be extended for longer than we might expect." He frowned. "The reasons have not yet been clearly established."

Halcombe grunted. "So he could wake up today, or tomorrow?"

"Or the next, my lord; there is no way of knowing." Wyles reached into his bag and pulled out a small leather case. "I shall bleed him, to ensure no excess fluid behind the swelling on his skull will pressure the brain."

There was a knock at the bedroom door. Halcombe turned. "Ah, Edward; come in, come in." The Stud Groom entered, with Lock shuffling in tow. In the harness room they had stripped the bandage from Lock's arm only to find his wound hot and swollen. Grooming the horse appeared to have made it worse, and several stitches were pulled over-tight by the swelling. Gaunt pursed his lips when he saw it and insisted the doctor needed to take a further look, overruling Lock's protests.

"It just needs time," the boy said, but Gaunt had re-wrapped the arm and all but dragged Lock, still grumbling, into the house.

"How is he, my lord?"

"Doctor Wyles insists Johnny will be fine," Lord Halcombe said, in a voice which betrayed some scepticism, "and we must trust to his ministrations." He looked up at Lock, who had not raised his eyes, and beckoned. "Come here." Lock obeyed. He is just a village urchin, Halcombe thought. But the boy stood tall and straight-backed, and....there was something else there. He could not be certain, but though Lock's head was bowed he did not seem overawed, like many of Halcombe's tenants might have been. "I am persuaded," Halcome said slowly, "that we have you to thank for Johnny's return yesterday." Lock said nothing, but lifted his eyes and looked into Halcombe's face. Lord Halcombe saw he had been correct; the boy had confidence. He turned his eyes away, towards the slight figure of his grandson. "I am most grateful to you, Joshua Lock," he said. "You will be made welcome in my house, at any time."

Lock breathed out heavily. He was not sure what he had expected, but was surprised at the thanks, and unsure how to respond. At last, he gave a small bow. "Thank you sir...I mean, my lord."

"If it's possible, my lord," Gaunt broke in, "can the doctor examine Joshua's arm again? I don't like the look of it."

Wyles received a nod of confirmation. The doctor put his leather case on the edge of the bed and stared suspiciously at the boy's bandaged arm. "Have you been keeping this wet, as I instructed?" he accused.

"We changed the dressing this morning, doctor," the Stud Groom said hurriedly. "Matter from the wound had dirtied it." Wyles seemed reluctant to accept Gaunt's explanation and unwound the bandage, making Lock wince when its weave tugged at knotted stitches. He prodded the swelling with a fingertip and a dribble of watery pus seeped from above Lock's elbow.

The doctor wrinkled his nose. "I see no reason for concern as yet," he said brusquely. "Re-apply the dressing and ensure that you keep it wet *at all times*." He emphasised the words to Gaunt as if speaking to a child.

"Of course, sir," the Stud Groom inclined his head and, as the doctor turned his attention back to Killen, gave Lock a surreptitious wink. But Lock was watching Wyles. The doctor retrieved a leather case from Killen's bedside and unbuckled the top flap, sliding out what appeared at first to be a pocket knife. When he unfolded its three leaves Lock saw it was a fleam. Each blade had a sharp triangular spike protruding from it, and Wyles selected the middle-sized one, folding the others carefully back into the handle. He placed the fleam back on the edge of the bed and then produced a length of thin, rubber tube from his bag.

"Roll up his sleeve, if you please," Wyles commanded the chambermaid, before tying the tube tightly around Killen's upper arm, above the elbow. His bag then yielded a polished metal dish, which the doctor placed on the coverlet in readiness, and a small wooden gavel. With his fingertips Wyles located a suitable vein in the boy's forearm and placed the fleam blade alongside it. Then he picked up the gavel. But before he could strike a blow, Lock interrupted.

"Don't!" he said loudly.

# Chapter 7

The doctor stopped with his hand in mid air. "I beg your pardon?" Lock stared at his feet, embarrassed at his outburst, but then Lord Halcombe spoke.

"Just what did you mean by that?"

Lock did not know what to say. He knew what he meant, but how to explain? There was a small silence; he looked at his boots. "I don't know," he said quietly.

Gaunt tugged at Lock's shirt. "We should go."

But Halcombe was persistent. "You must have had some reason."

Lock did have a reason, but Lord Halcombe would think it wrong and the doctor would disregard it. Still, he had dragged the boy out of the river.

"Sir," he said, "...I mean, my lord; I don't believe it does any good." Halcombe looked away, towards his grandson, and Lock saw he must find a different way. He thought quickly. "My lord, if your horse is injured and bleeding, the first thing you do is try to staunch it. Because if you do not the horse will become ill. Why should a man be any different? If it is important that blood stays in the body, then why wound it deliberately?"

Wyles interjected. "My lord, I really must protest. It is well known," he said in an irritated voice, "that an excess of blood in the circulation can have a debilitating effect upon the body." He stood up, looking down his nose at Lock, who remained unmoved. "Even the College of Veterinary Surgeons approve of the practice," he said triumphantly.

Halcombe was still staring at Lock. "What have you to say to that?" he asked calmly.

Lock shook his head. "I don't know sir," he said. "It just doesn't seem right to me, that's all."

Wyles snorted. "My lord, I think I should be the best judge of that."

Halcombe waved his hand. "Yes, yes, doctor, I understand you have the best interests of your patient at heart," he looked back at Lock, "while you, young man, seem also to want him well, and I thank you for it. But you will see that I must follow the good doctor's advice." Lock shot Wyles an angry glance, but the doctor just smirked and turned back to Killen.

Blood ran dark red down the boy's forearm into the dish the doctor held carefully underneath to catch it. Occasionally, he twisted the fleam to adjust the flow, and at one point stopped and gave the dish to the maid to be emptied. "A gill this time; a half-pint in total will be sufficient," Wyles murmured..

Lock turned towards Edward Gaunt, and the Stud Groom took the hint, "If you will excuse us, my lord?" Halcombe waved them away.

Half-way down the staircase, Gaunt stopped and in hushed tones asked Lock why he had spoken. "You can't go against what the doctor advises."

"I will," Lock said defiantly, "if I think I'm right."


Gaunt paused again in the middle of the hallway. "I'll have to go back," he said quickly, "Needed to ask his lordship something." Turning on his heel, the Stud Groom trotted back upstairs.

Lock saw the door to the library was open again, and he could not help himself; he had to go in. Heavy curtains, which covered the single window the previous night, were drawn back, but the room still seemed like a refuge; dimly lit, with cosy corners and thickly upholstered chairs. A brightly patterned floor rug cushioned his footfall.

On the table, a book had been left open with a stone paperweight resting across one corner to keep the page. Lock stepped closer to look down at the words, but they were written in an unfamiliar language. After a while Gaunt came back and peeked over the boy's shoulder.

"That's French," he said. "Look," he pointed at a word in the text, "*Cheval*. It means 'horse'."

"Can you read it, then?"

Gaunt shook his head. "Not French. A few words, that's all." He sounded pleased with his knowledge though, Lock thought.

"Master Johnny could read it," Gaunt went on. "Speaks a few languages, he does." He grinned, "That's what comes of book-learning. Not like you and me, eh? Now you'd better come to the stables. I'll make a fresh poultice."

Gaunt and Lock re-crossed the yard. The wind had dropped, and though some flakes of snow still fell, they were tiny specks.

"It's getting colder again," Gaunt remarked as they walked. Lock pulled the cloak tighter around his throat. Outside each stable he noticed a pile of forage had been tipped. As he watched, a groom went into one of the boxes and tossed the hay into a rack, high up on the wall

"They aren't fed corn mid-day when they're not working," Gaunt explained. He called for one of the grooms to saddle two hunters before going into the harness room. Lock followed. Under the cupboard that had held their tea mugs was a set of drawers. The Stud Groom pulled open the topmost before rummaging inside. A pistol was tucked into one corner, Lock saw; its short barrel poking out of the oily rag wrapped around it.

Gaunt gave him a sideways look. "You never know when you'll need one in a stable yard." With a triumphant flourish he produced a fresh bandage. "I take it you'll be able to ride?" he asked, and Lock nodded.

Ten minutes later he regretted his confidence. Gaunt changed the dressing on his arm, wrinkling his nose at the smell of the boy's wound. He had not said anything, mind, so perhaps it was not as bad as Lock supposed. The new poultice set it on fire again, or at least that was what it felt like.

A groom brought two horses out into the yard and respectfully legged Gaunt up into the saddle.

"You can have the quiet one," the Stud Groom said, "but I'm only being kind because of that," he indicated Lock's arm. "Can you mount?" Lock grabbed hold of both reins and the front of the saddle with his left hand, vaulting straight up without bothering to put a foot in the stirrup. But pain seared through his right arm from the jolt. He grimaced.

"Are you sure you are alright to ride?"

"It's just sore," Lock said through his teeth. "It won't kill me." At least, he thought, I hope it won't.

Gaunt led him along a narrow path at the far end of the stable block. The track curved around the west end of Halcombe House and although covered with a layer of snow it was flat and relatively easy going for the horses. Bare branches of trees on either side of the driveway were dusted white and their trunks striped from roots to crown. Blown by the wind, in the open the snow had settled to only a few inches deep, and the concave undersides of their horses' feet were coated with thick grease to help stop ice packing hard inside.

Once they reached the main road, Gaunt turned away from the village, heading back towards Combe Wood.

"D'you mind showing me where you were?" he asked. Lock stared at him with some alarm. "I know we won't be able to cross the river; the fords are too deep. And I don't want to go all the way to the bridge. Just show me from this side." Lock knew the hump-backed stone packhorse bridge was three or four miles further upstream and was glad to avoid riding the extra distance. Although the horses were only walking, the movement seemed to jar his whole body and was making him feel sick.


Coombe Wood was black in the afternoon light. Lock stopped his horse to point across the river. "There."

Gaunt saw. "What were you doing?" he asked, and when Lock failed to answer, carried on, "It's no matter, whatever it was," he said. "No-one will find out from me."

`"Why do you want to know?"

Gaunt sighed. "There's a gun out there somewhere, an expensive one, and his lordship won't be best pleased to lose it," he explained. "If we can discover where Master Johnny fell in, perhaps we'll find it."

Lock grunted. That made sense, he thought, and so far Edward Gaunt had acted like a friend. So he told the Stud Groom. "And the polecat's still up there," he finished. "I'll have to come back for it."

Gaunt grinned. "At least it won't starve."

Fresh snow coated the smithy roof, but around the chimney a semicircle of tiles showed where heat from the forge melted the flakes as they settled. Lock slipped his feet out of the stirrups and lowered himself carefully from the saddle. He passed up the horse's reins to Gaunt.

"Thank you," he said simply.

The Stud Groom smiled. "I rather think it's you we have to thank. His lordship said you'll be welcomed at any time."

"I have to work."

"You won't be able to work iron for a while," Gaunt said, "so come when you can. Put your weight behind a brush for me."

Lock thanked him again and watched as the Stud Groom walked both horses back down the lane. His arm hurt like hell, but Abraham would fix it. He could hear his grandfather's coughing as he opened their cottage door, a rasping, hacking sound. Cold weather always seemed to make his chest worse. Lock knew Abraham tried to hide the condition from him, to pretend he was not ill; but blood would stain the old man's pillow every morning until spring. And if that was God's will, then he needed a lesson in compassion.

# Chapter 8

At least Killen was still breathing. Lord Halcombe sat on a chair alongside his grandson's oak bedstead and watched the almost imperceptible rise and fall of the bed linen over the boy's chest. It was the only indication he lived. The boy's face was waxy and pale, lips almost the same colour as his cheeks, and his eyes were sunken like a corpse.

Halcombe rubbed his eyes, gritty from lack of sleep. Although the boy was watched through each night by shifts of maids and footmen, Halcombe still found himself waking to check on Johnny in the early hours. He hoped against hope that at any time he might find his grandson conscious. But up to now, two long days after the accident, his prayers had come to nought.

The doctor returned, took more blood, and said that Master Johnny should wake up soon. Wyles spoke with decidedly less confidence than he had on his previous visit, Halcombe thought. He reached out to grasp the boy's bandaged left hand. Felt the warmth. His worry made his own skin cold, so he gently released his grip.

One of the maids came in. She curtsied as Halcombe rose from his chair to leave, then felt the boy's forehead with the back of her hand before taking station on the far side of the bed. Halcombe pulled the door shut quietly behind him on his way downstairs.

The hallway was deserted, but there was a sound; soft, like a small bird's wing against a widow pane. The library door was ajar, and Halcombe pushed it away from him to tiptoe inside.

Joshua Lock stood up from the desk. "Mr. Roberts let me in, sir," he said, by way of explanation.

Halcombe smiled. Lock had a book open, and Halcombe crossed to look down at the pages. He turned it so he could see the cover, holding the boy's place with a finger; Shakespeare Plays. "D'you enjoy Shakespeare?" he asked kindly.

Lock paused before answering. "I've never read one of his books before, sir." He hesitated again. "They're…they're difficult to read."

Halcombe chuckled. "The only way is to persevere," he said. "The Tempest, eh? That is apt, though I never thought it much of a comedy." He turned to leave. "Stay as long as you wish, Joshua," he said, then had a thought. "The doctor will be along later. Shall I ask him to take another look at your arm?"

The boy was polite. "Thank you, sir, but it's been dressed today and seems much better."

Halcombe nodded affirmation. "Make sure you let Edward Gaunt know if it should take a turn for the worse."


Lock let out a deep breath. His grandfather had changed the bandage the night before. After smearing some particularly odious-smelling salve on the wound he made the boy drink a concoction of ground herbs and tree bark, which, strangely, seemed to lessen the ache. Even so, his arm was still very sore, and he certainly did not want the doctor prodding and poking it again.

Gaunt was right. Lock found it painful to grip with his right hand and that made lifting any weight almost impossible. At least he tried to convince himself that was good enough reason not to work. But there was something else. Halcombe House had drawn him back. He could not explain the feeling. The sumptuous furnishings, the magnificent stables; it was none of those. The not knowing nagged at him. It was a bugger.

Lock sat down again in front of the book. He had chosen Shakespeare after seeing that name on a volume in the village store, and hearing others speak it, but he found the play's language difficult to master. Old fashioned. And because of that, he found it hard to concentrate on the words. He grew bored. Soon, he stood up, returning the book to its place on the shelves.


Gaunt was not at the stables. Two grooms sweeping the yard told Lock that the Stud Groom had gone to the village, so the boy thought he might as well wait.

The Tempest was still resident in the corner box and pricked its ears at his approach. The black horse put its head over the half-door, allowing Lock to scratch it under the chin. Its coat was short and fine-haired, even in winter, and he marvelled that the animal seemed unaffected by weather which had persuaded him to wear two shirts, as well as his spare coat.

Lock walked into the harness room. As he hoped, the teapot was on the hearth and he crouched to touch it: still hot. He crossed to the cupboard to find a mug, and as he reached for one noticed that the top drawer was open. He felt inside, finding the pistol still there, wrapped in its oily rag.

He drew the gun out. The short barrel had a dull sheen from oiling and its wooden grip was smooth, ingrained with dirt from use. The flint looked new and fitted tightly between the jaws of the cock, half covered with a thin piece of leather to stop it slipping. He tested the edge with his finger. Sharp. Lock re-wrapped the pistol and put it back. It gave him an idea, something he could do to help Gaunt out, but he was not sure if he should.

Pouring himself a mug of the tea, Lock sat down to think his plan out. He would try something he had never done before, though he had read about it in his grandfather's book. After all, the Stud Groom had been good to him, and it would be a way of re-paying the favour. Better than Lord Halcombe getting rid of the horse. He drained the tea mug. Set it down on the table. Then he retrieved the pistol together with a small powder flask which was hidden further back in the drawer but which he had supposed must be there.

Gaunt's two grooms had gone from the stables but he could still hear their voices, so they must be around the corner. Lock fetched a leather halter, hunting around the harness room until he found a rope the right length for his needs; a plough line. At about sixteen feet it was too long, really. Ploughmen used the ropes instead of reins when working a draught horse in the fields; their length meant they could still steer the horse as they stood far back behind the plough. Lock tied one end onto the halter ring beneath The Tempest's chin and led the horse out into the yard.

If the returning grooms thought there was anything odd in a relative stranger taking one of their horses out, they showed no sign of it. Lock waved at them and they waved back as he passed, and he thought how easy it was to get away with the unexpected if you showed enough confidence. He led the horse along the path that curved around the end of the house, then cut down to the right, past the trees which two days before had been pretty with snow but now waited, wet and dark, for spring to burst their leaf-buds.

Behind the trees was an open field, ideal for Lock's purpose. He would be largely hidden from view, and the horse had space to run free if anything went wrong. The Tempest's feet squelched, but the ground would freeze solid during the night. The footprints they made now would bear frosty witness to where Lock and the horse been until morning sun warmed them, but that could not be helped.

The Tempest walked beside him, striding out unworried into the middle of the field, and there they stopped.

Lock faced the horse. He let it drop its head to graze while he took out the pistol. He stored the rag safely in his pocket, so that he could re-wrap the gun when he returned it to the drawer. No-one need know until he chose to tell. The gun would smell of burned powder, and there was nothing he could do about that either but deny he had taken it. The Tempest must have noticed Lock reach into his pocket and raised its head, anticipating a treat, but instead was presented with the pistol. Lock watched the horse carefully. It sniffed the gun, and perhaps its oily smell triggered something in the horse's mind, because it threw up its head and took a step backwards.

"Whoa, boy," Lock gentled. The Tempest showed the whites of its eyes, ears twitching back and forth as if unsure. Lock turned his left hand over so the pistol was underneath and stiffly raised his right so that he could stroke the horse's cheek. He stood still, caressing and speaking gently, until the horse began to relax. Then he turned the hand holding the pistol over, so the horse was forced to sniff the weapon again. This time, there was no reaction.

"Good boy." Lock praised the horse and reached up to stroke its neck, keeping the gun close to its face with his other hand. Then slowly, ever so slowly, he moved the pistol so that he could stroke the horse's nose with its short barrel. The horse ignored the weapon again, so Lock allowed it to graze for a while. So far, it was easier than he thought, but the most difficult part was yet to come.

The plough line was stiffened by mud and lack of use. Lock carefully wound it into loops which would slip easily from his hand rather than wrap around his wrist if he needed to let the rope out quickly. When he was satisfied he took the pistol in his right hand and cocked it.

"Hey, boy!" He got the horse's attention. Then he slowly lifted his right arm sideways away from his body so the horse could see it, and stiffly squeezed the trigger. The hammer sprang forward with a sharp snap, throwing a couple of sparks as it struck the frizzen. But though the noise the action made was barely audible, the horse threw itself backwards in a panic. Lock let the rope pay out and before gradually tightening his grip so he did not completely lose control.

"Whoa, boy: good boy!" The Tempest came to a stop yards away, front feet spread and nostrils flaring. "There's a good boy. Come on then," Lock cajoled. Eventually the horse relaxed again, and he was able to encourage it to walk slowly back to him. He patted its neck and got ready to try again.


Lord Halcombe had tried to prepare himself as best he could, but failed miserably. In his life he had become accustomed to loss. And when his wife died he thought, after the initial blinding grief, that nothing could ever be worse; that now he could deal with anything, anything at all, life might throw at him. But this was far worse than even he could have imagined. The helplessness was the worst. His grandson was dying, and for all his wealth and influence, there was nothing he could do. That simple fact gnawed at his soul.

Doctor Wyles arrived on his rounds, but it seemed he could still find no satisfactory reason for Johnny's unconsciousness.

"Is there nothing at all you can do?" Halcombe begged in desperation.

The doctor pursed his lips. "It is unusual, I grant you, my lord, for a condition of this sort to last so long." He was silent for some time, seemingly in thought. "There is one thing we might try," he said at last, "but it is not pleasant to see. Your lordship might be advised to leave the room."

Halcombe frowned. It could not be that bad, surely? "I will stay."

"Then I must caution you, my lord, not to interfere. I have read that this method has been used with a measure of success by surgeons serving the army, but it brooks no interference."

Halcombe looked disbelieving.

"To do so might cause harm to the boy."

Halcombe acceded, "Very well, doctor, though I cannot see what could make things worse than they already are."

A maid still sat at Killen's side.

"I think you should leave, my dear," the doctor addressed her, "as the sight of this treatment is not for those of a more delicate constitution." The girl looked at Halcombe for confirmation, and he nodded briefly. "Ask Maria to come up, if you would be so kind," he said.

Doctor Wyles coughed and rubbed his nose on his right sleeve. "Do you think that wise, my lord," he asked when the maid had left.

Halcombe's face was stern. "For your information, doctor, Maria has been housekeeper here since before Johnny was born, and nursed him as a baby. I scarcely think anything you can do will upset *her* constitution."


Lock pulled the trigger for a fourth time. The horse, head down to graze, did not even bother to stop chewing. There was no reaction but a flick of its ears. He tugged on the rope, lifting The Tempest's head, and once he had re-cocked the pistol, aimed it at the centre of the horse's forehead. He knew the exact spot. Draw a line, he said to himself, from the right ear down to the left eye, and another from the left ear to the right eye. He pictured it in his mind. Where both lines crossed, that was the aiming point; where the bullet must enter its head. The barrel had to be angled slightly upwards, to destroy the horse's brain, but that was the right spot. He gently pulled the trigger. The flint snapped forward; sparks flew; the horse barely noticed.

Lock patted The Tempest's neck. "Good boy," he said again. "You're a clever lad, aren't you?"

Edward Gaunt dismounted in the stable yard, letting one of the grooms who rushed out take his horse away to be unsaddled and rubbed down. He strode into the harness room. The teapot still stood on the hearth, but no steam curled from its spout and he cursed mildly under his breath. He unhooked the kettle, carefully testing its handle for heat. It felt full enough, so he hung it back on the rail that ran above the fire, shoving it sideways with a poker to boil in the flames.

A gully ran outside the door, to drain rainwater away from the side of the building. Gaunt took the teapot and emptied its contents into the channel. The dark brown liquid trickled slowly on its way ito the drain hole. It would have tasted stewed, as well as cold.

It was when he opened the cupboard for the tea-caddy that the Stud Groom noticed the pistol was missing. Its drawer was part-open, and Gaunt pulled it fully out in surprise. He slammed it back in stalked out to the stables. Two grooms denied all knowledge, which was strange. They must have seen who had taken the gun.

"I'll find out who has it; be sure of that." Gaunt's anger did not surface very often. "You two tell the others I'll expect it back in the drawer by tomorrow morning." That gave the thief a chance to atone with little loss of face. Gaunt turned, satisfied he had said enough, then noticed the corner stable was empty.

"Where's The Tempest?" he demanded. The grooms had not seen the horse leave. "Right," the Stud Groom said firmly. "I want everyone here, now!"

Five men assembled, taking longer than Gaunt expected because some of the jobs being done could not just be dropped and left. And it was the most junior of the grooms who had the answer.

"I've seen 'im, Mr. Gaunt."

"Where, for goodness sake?"

The boy pointed to the path at the back of the house. "Goin' down there. Joshua Lock took 'im."


Doctor Wyles leant over Killen and grabbed his shoulders with both hands. He had removed his coat as a precaution and rolled up his shirt sleeves, but the boy was of slight build so this should not be too strenuous. He began to shake Killen violently, up and down. The boy's head lolled like a broken doll, but Wyles continued, up and down, back and forth, until the effort began to affect his breathing. He let the boy go and, drawing his arm back, slapped Killen across the face. "Johnny, wake up!" he shouted, close to Killen's ear. He slapped the boy again, backhanded against the right cheek this time, and shouted once more, "Wake up!" There was no response. He tried again. Slap! "Wake up!" Slap! "Wake up." And again: slap "Wake up!" Slap. "Wake up!" Then more shaking. Wyles began to breathe heavily.

Halcombe raised his voice, "Doctor, is this absolutely necessary?"

Wyles did not turn his head. "I expressly warned you …my lord… not to interfere," he panted. Letting Killen fall back onto the mattress, he raised his hand to strike the boy once again, but Halcombe stepped forward to catch his forearm.

"I think that's enough, doctor," he said with mild reproof. Wyles staggered, slightly off balance, in mid blow. Turning his head he looked into Halcombe's eyes and saw a warning there. He glanced down at Killen's face. The boy's cheeks were flaming red, but his eyes were still closed; his breathing still shallow.

Halcombe released Wyles' arm. The doctor ran his finger behind his collar. It felt tight, constricting, and he pulled it away from his throat. He took a deep breath, exhaling slowly. "Unfortunately, there appears to be no response," he said, unrolling his sleeves before carefully buttoning each cuff. "It seems we must just wait, my lord, and allow nature take its course." He reached into his bag for the fleam. "I shall bleed him again," he said quickly. "It may well be that his spleen has been emptied by the shaking."


Lock found he had a problem. His injured arm still refused to bend properly, which meant he could not prime the pistol one-handed and hold the horse at the same time. He dropped the ploughline onto the floor and stood on it. The horse, content to graze, lifted its head and moved away, pulling a few yards of rope from under his boot. But it only wandered as far as a fresh patch of pasture.

Lock pulled the powder flask from his pocket. Made from a cow's horn, curved and hollowed, it was capped with a wooden bung at the wide end. Lock wondered how that was fixed until he noticed small rust spots on the horn that betrayed where iron tacks had been hammered through and filed level.

The horn was brown with age but the nozzle mechanism bright, and the lever, which measured out a set amount of powder when pushed, moved easily under his thumb. He pulled the pistol hammer to half-cock and felt it seat against the pawl. Then he flipped the frizzen forward so the pan was exposed, and poured in a measure of powder.

Lock shoved the horn back inside his jacket. He picked up the ploughline, calling the horse at the same time and The Tempest pricked its ears, walking towards him willingly as he reeled in the rope. When it came to a halt, Lock patted the animal again. Then he raised the pistol to the horse's forehead.

Edward Gaunt ran. It was one of his rules not to, for rushing about was guaranteed to upset horses and he had worked with them for most of his life. But he ran anyway, because a horse was missing, together with a pistol, and in his line of work that could mean only one thing. He turned down the path past the house. Behind the trees he could make out a shadow, a dark shape, and he angled off the path towards it, pushing through undergrowth, scattering twigs and dead leaves. The boy must hear him; he must.

The Tempest stood in the middle of the field. Lock was lifting the pistol, aiming at the horse's forehead. Gaunt burst out of the trees. Short of breath, he opened his mouth to shout; but he was too late. Before a sound came out, Lock pulled the trigger.

# Chapter 9

The pistol hammer flew forward. The flint struck the frizzen, flicking it forward so sparks dropped into the pan to explode the powder. The horse, startled at the noise, shot backwards, pulling loops of rope through Lock's hand. He closed his fist, using the rope as a brake on the horse's wild flight, and spoke to it gently; calmly. The horse stopped, nostrils flared, ears pricked; breathing heavily and propped on its front legs, ready for instant flight. Lock quietly lowered the pistol to the ground and began to reel the horse in, little by little, talking to it all the while. When The Tempest stood in front of him once again, breathing normally, he picked up the pistol, adding fresh powder to its pan.

At the second shot, the horse ran back again but not so far. Lock spoke to it using the same cajoling tone before encouraging the animal back to him. He stroked The Tempest's forehead and re-primed the pistol.

The horse alerted him before he heard anything. Lock half-turned to see Edward Gaunt striding across the field. He put his thumb on the hammer and gently squeezed the trigger, easing the pistol safely back to half-cock.

Gaunt reached up to touch the horse's face. "I was wondering where you'd got to." He ran his fingers down to the end of The Tempest's nose and the animal tossed its head, flicking them away in irritation. "I didn't know what to think when I saw you through the trees." The Stud Groom held out his hand. Lock gave him the pistol then fished in his pocket for the oily rag.

"Why didn't you ask me first?" Gaunt pushed open the frizzen to blow the fresh powder charge out of the pan.

Lock shrugged. "It just came to me. You weren't there."

"I'm in charge here," Gaunt said, his tone cold. "I need to know everything that goes on." He pocketed the gun and held out his hand again. Lock gave him the halter rope and the Stud Groom led The Tempest away.

"I'm sorry," Lock called after him, but when the other man ignored his apology he felt the familiar rush. "Bugger you then," he added, under his breath.

Halcombe squeezed his grandson's hand. He had almost lost hope. Not quite, for he knew he would never completely give up while Johnny lived, but the boy had not eaten or drunk for four days now; his pale face lined and shrivelled like a death mask.

Halcombe knew Johnny had not long to live. His wife, paralysed by a massive stroke, lingered for a week, growing gradually weaker and weaker. But Johnny had never been robust and full of life like his grandmother. His end would come sooner.

He turned the boy's left hand over, pressing bony knuckles into his own palm. A faint brown stain at the wrist showed where a dribble of blood from the fleam punctures had dried unnoticed. As he stared at Johnny's hand he saw with dismay that the boy's lifeline was cut short. It stopped halfway across his palm; a cruel twist of fate, perhaps. And though he had never considered himself a superstitious man, Halcombe shuddered involuntarily, closing his eyes in prayer.

There was a tap at the door and a maid entered. Halcombe opened his eyes.

"Doctor Wyles, my lord." She curtsied and left, pulling the door quietly behind her. Halcombe waited until he heard the click of the latch before standing.

"Good morning, my lord," the doctor said brightly, "and how is our patient?" He looked down on Killen's deathbed without meeting Halcombe's eye.

Halcombe was beginning to lose patience. "As you see, doctor," he said stiffly, "there appears to be no improvement."

Wyles picked up the boy's wrist, feeling for a pulse, and stared at him for a long time. "Then we must pray," he said, releasing the wrist and reaching for his bag, "for I have done all that I know." And he drew out the leather case containing the fleam.

As Halcombe watched the sharp blades exposed, Joshua Lock's entreaty came to mind. Edward Gaunt had spoken to him the previous night and told him what Lock had done with The Tempest. "He's a natural with them, my lord," the Stud Groom had enthused, "if a little independent minded. We need someone with common sense like that. Could we not offer him employment?"

And though Halcombe argued that there were enough staff, Gaunt had been persuasive. "The last one we took on is useless. Slow to learn, and the horses don't like him." So they agreed that Lock be given a position. Now, Halcombe decided, for better or worse he would take the boy's advice. It could not, he thought, worsen the situation.

"Wait, doctor, if you please," Halcombe paused, but this was no time for prevarication. "I have decided I do not want Johnny bled again," he said.

The doctor was taken aback. "But my lord," he said, "I beg you reconsider. The efficacies are well researched and..."

"That is as may be," Halcombe interrupted, "but my mind is made up. I thank you for your ministrations doctor, but I wish Johnny to now be left to die...or live, in peace."

"If you insist, my lord," Wyles said sulkily, stuffing the fleam back into his case. "I shall forward you my account directly."

Halcombe ignored the man's social insult. He ignored everything else that day, spending the whole time in Johnny's bedroom. For long periods he stood, staring out of the window across his estate; the estate he built for his son to inherit, and his grandson after. But mostly he sat by the bed, holding the boy's hand and praying, as he had done for his late wife, even though, in the end, that had been to no avail. He fell asleep there with his head on the edge of the bed, Johnny's hand still clasped in his.

He woke in the early dawn and stood, still stiff from the night. One of the servants must have dropped a blanket over his shoulders. He pulled it off, folding it neatly onto his chair. The boy slept on; unknowing, Halcombe thought sadly. The house was waking. Daily routines must continue, and it would be in no-one's interest if he made himself ill and incapable. Guilty at the relief he felt, Halcombe left his grandson's bedroom. He needed to bathe and eat, to make himself ready for whatever this day brought.

And it brought joy, for Lord Halcombe's prayers were answered. Just before noon, and five days after his accident, John Killen woke up.

Halcombe bounced around the House like a new father while his staff, subdued in the days following Master Johnny's accident, went about their daily tasks with renewed vigour.

At first, Killen hardly understood why everyone he saw beamed as if meeting him for the first time. Although his grandfather tried to explain what had befallen him, he could remember nothing after riding away from the house on the fateful day. He tried hard, concentrating his thoughts on a mental picture; of him cantering along on The Tempest. But he would get so far from the stables then nothing else would come. And he was hungry, very hungry, delighting the kitchen maids. Apparently worried that they might struggle to tempt a sickly invalid with small portions and favourites, they found everything they cooked was eagerly devoured, so kept up a continual flow of the most carefully prepared food platters. Eventually, Halcombe was forced to insist they stuck to the usual mealtimes.

Edward Gaunt came to see Killen one afternoon, and brought a stranger with him.

"I am glad to find you recovering, Master Johnny," Gaunt wore an infectious smile, and Killen found himself smiling back although he still felt pretty weak. He pushed himself more upright, elbowing at the pillows behind him so they supported his head and neck.

"Thank you, Edward." He wanted to ask about The Tempest, but was afraid. His grandfather had been angry. The horse would have to go, he warned. The Stud Groom must have seen the question in Killen's eyes.

"The horse is fine," he reassured, "his scratches are healing. And there is someone you should meet." He beckoned Lock forward. "Master Johnny, this is Joshua Lock."

Killen was not sure what he had expected. His grandfather told him that his life had been saved by another boy, and he tried to imagine how this paragon might look. Like one of his friends, perhaps, who mostly came from other wealthy families in the district; tall, with barbered hair and tailored jacket. A young man with a confident air and ready smile. Well, this boy had the air all right, and he was tall, but he dressed like one of the villagers, with face and hands that told of his need for a bath. Still, he deserved politeness.

"Do you wish to sit?" Killen asked, indicating a chair on his left, "I am very much afraid I cannot get up at present." Lock walked around the end of the bed, scraping the chair back. Gaunt was fidgeting, so Killen tried to make it easier for him. "Come back later if you wish, Edward - I know you have things to do."

Killen scrutinised Lock, who had put his hands on his knees and was staring at them. The boy had large hands, he noticed, and dirty fingernails. Where ought he start?

"I must thank you," Killen said at last, "for helping me."

The boy raised his head, answering softly. "I didn't do much." There was a pause as Killen considered what to say next. Lock had very brown eyes, but they looked away, as if he did not really want to be there.

Killen coughed. "I have heard that you did. And that you were injured?"

Lock waggled his right arm. "It's fine," he said flatly.

Killen awkwardly shifted position. "I know," he said slowly, "or heard, rather, that you were training The Tempest. To be steady under fire." Lock stared at him.

"Edward...Mr Gaunt... told me."

"I thought..," Lock was hesitant, "I thought it would be easier for you. When you were better, I mean. So that *you* wouldn't have to do it."

"I thought my grandfather would sell him, after what happened."

"There's not much wrong with him," Lock said firmly, "that time and patience won't cure."

Killen grinned. "I know it!" he said delightedly. "I told my grandfather, but he wouldn't listen! He's from the old school," he confided, "you know, whip and spur; the horse must obey; that sort of thing. I think that they just don't understand, much of the time."

Lock nodded, "They're not stupid; men are."

"That's right! That's right!" Killen was enthusiastic. "How do you know all this," he asked, curious.

Lock shrugged, "Just do, sir."

Killen felt elated. Other boys he knew would have laughed at him. Perkins from the next parish; Wicklow from the Earl of Morton's estate; they would have used the whip and spur. But here, perhaps, was someone who thought the way he did. He lifted his left hand and held it out. "You must call me John," he said. And Lock gripped it. Hard.


Spring arrived. The river level fell, making fords passable again. Even so, water still washed over Lock's boots as he hopped across the weir. Flat rocks that made stepping stones along its crest had re-grown their slick green scum, ready to spill the unwary into mid-stream. The boy held his arms out sideways to balance himself as he crossed.

Lock's wound showed only as a line of puckered scar tissue. A succession of poultices had done their job, drawing out all the muck the sharp branch had driven deep into his flesh. His grandfather removed Doctor Wyles' untidy sewing once the muscle showed signs of healing, slicing through the silk loops with a hoof knife held so close to his face Lock became worried he might accidentally take an eye out. Tiny marks remained where the needle pierced his skin, but they would fade.

Trollope, Lord Halcombe's gamekeeper, discovered Killen's rifle where it had fallen. Used to finding his way in deep woodland, he discovered where the horse's hoof-prints emerged from the trees and backtracked, carefully scanning trunks and boughs until he spotted a sliver of bare wood, where bark had been scraped away. The rifle lay in undergrowth, little rusted despite its spell in the open. But the stock was cracked and the trigger guard bent, so it was despatched to the gunsmith for repairs. John Killen told Lock the story, and Halcombe had thanked him all over again for saving his grandson's life.

Lock sat on a dry rock to pull off his boots. His stockings were wet so he wrung them out, one by one, wrinkling his nose at the smell. He had noticed his own smell more often of late. He also noticed that village girls sought him out more frequently, and while he re-laced his boots he wondered, obscurely, if the two were related. Lock heard the rattle and scrape of hooves on gravel behind him as he started down the drive to Halcombe House. He turned off the road to wait for the rider to catch up. John Killen lifted an arm in greeting, and Lock waved back.

Killen reined The Tempest to a stop. "Were you coming to see me?"

"The horse; I was coming to see him," Lock said, stroking its forehead. He looked up. "You're better!"

Killen did not feel better. If he was honest with himself he felt as weak as a puppy. But he had been determined to get back on a horse - this horse - so ignored his grandfather's pleas to wait. And he had done it. "I'm feeling fine, thank you," he lied. "If you'd care to walk with me to the end of the drive, I think I'll dismount there." The horse moved forward again. Killen's hands trembled slightly on the reins, but The Tempest seemed not to notice his nervousness and strode out with such enthusiasm that Lock, walking alongside, was forced to lengthen his stride to keep up. Killen looked down at his companion. He seemed so strong; so full of life. Killen felt a surge of envy he found difficult to force back inside.

"Whoa." They reached the apron in front of the house and Killen swung one leg back to slide from the saddle, but staggered as he landed. Lock caught his arm to stop him falling. He found his balance and pulled away crossly, then remembered his manners. Leaning against the horse's side he managed, "Thank you." He felt dizzy and out of breath.

"Are you sure you're alright?"

"Forgot to bend my knees when I landed," Killen excused himself with another small lie, "that is all." He straightened up and stood away from the horse. A groom arrived to take The Tempest away to its stable, and Killen gave the horse a half-hearted slap on the rump as it walked away. He thought he noticed a slightly disapproving look on Lock's face, but pretended he had not.

"Come in, why don't you?" Killen set off towards one of the side doors.

Lock was reluctant. "I was going to the stables."

"Oh. Have you decided to take up Edward's offer?"

"I've got plenty to do at home," Lock said, shaking his head. "My grandfather can't do much. He's ill."

"Then come in. Do, please. I have something to show you."

Lock followed John Killen into the house. He carefully scrubbed the doormat with his boots before stepping into the hallway, lest he leave mud on the polished tiles. Halcombe's study door stood open and they both went in.

Window light filtered a mist of smoke growing stale; cigar smoke - Lock thought he recognised the smell. A long package wrapped in brown paper lay on the desk. Killen carefully unpicked the three strings that bound it. He folded the wrapper back and drew out a huge, curved sabre.

"What do you think?" he asked, handing the sword over.

Light glinted from a scabbard so highly polished Lock could see his reflection in the steel.

"Take it out," Killen encouraged. Lock curled the fingers of his right hand around the leather covered grip and drew the sword, the blade scraping through the scabbard's throat.

"Heavier than you might think?" Killen asked, watching him.

Lock let the tip of the blade drop. Placing the scabbard carefully back on the desk he shifted the sword into his left hand, raising it so its broad, flat blade curved upwards; a graceful arc from hilt to point, which, oddly, Lock thought, was not pointed at all. He had never held a sword before. "Why's it feel so awkward?"

Killen enjoyed his discomfiture. "It is the new cavalry sword," he said grandly. "Grandfather bought one as soon as he could. He keeps a collection," he confided, "want to see?" Without waiting for an answer he went to the tall cupboard standing behind his grandfather's desk and threw open its doors. Inside was a row of swords, laid horizontally on wooden shelves, their scabbards racked separately. Straight blades sat alongside curved blades. Some swords had simple cross hand-guards and others complicated arrangements of iron bars that would curl about the fist.

On the bottom shelf was an old lump of rough wood, and Killen took it out, clutching it to his chest. When Lock looked at him oddly he explained. "It is a splinter." He held it out, "Look. This came from the battle of Copenhagen: from the Defiance. A cannonball smashed it out of ship's side. Here, take it," Killen handed the blackened oak over. "If you sniff it you can smell the sea."

Lock shook his head, pointing instead at a sword similar to the sabre he held, but rather than having a polished steel blade this was blued and decorated with gilt-etched designs. The fancy weapon drew the eye, like a painting. "What's that one?"

"It was my father's," Killen said, smiling, "his dress sword. They're kept for special occasions: too valuable to carry into battle!"

Lock grunted. "So, what happened? To your father, I mean?" Killen's face filled with hurt for a moment. "I didn't mean to pry," Lock said quickly. "It doesn't matter."

But Killen smiled wanly. "No, it is fine. He died. In India." He stopped. "You know, it's most odd. I have hardly spoken about it to any of my friends, but then I tell you."

"What happened to him?"

"He was in a battle, I think. Well, that is what everyone says. But I am not completely sure."

He looked slightly puzzled for a moment, Lock thought. "Not sure?"

Killen smiled at him again. "No, he must have been. It was a long time ago, just after I was born."

"So you're an orphan, then."

"My grandfather brought me up."

Lock lifted the great cavalry sword. It quivered, horizontal in the air, before he swept it slowly in a huge arc until the blade-tip was above Killen's heart. He held it there for several seconds before lowering the point so it rested on the floor. "Like me, John," he said, with a grin, "like me."

# Chapter 10

"It's just a stick!"

Lock stared ruefully at the practice sword in his hand. It was a sort of short wooden pole, about three feet long. The hand guard, made from a square of timber, fitted six inches from one end and the remainder formed the handle, bound with thick twine. He stood with Killen on the wide rear lawn of Halcombe House and stabbed the stick's point into the short, springy turf. "I thought we were using proper swords."

"That comes later," Killen said patiently. "You must learn each move and position first, or you might accidentally cut my head off!"

"I wouldn't!"

"Well, perhaps not," Killen agreed, laughing, "but everyone starts with one of these." He brandished the wooden sword in his own hand, and came to stand alongside Lock.

"Now, place your feet like this," he instructed. His right foot pointed forward and he brought the left round behind it at a right-angle.

Lock looked down and copied him. "It feels awkward."

"You will get used to it. Oh, look, you have to hold the sword in your right hand."

"Why?"

Killen spoke with exaggerated patience, as if explaining to a child, "Because it has to hang on your left side, otherwise it will dig in your horse when you mount. And you cannot draw it with your left hand."

Lock sighed. "I suppose so." He switched the training weapon to his other hand and poked it forward as Killen was doing, "Now what?"

"Turn slightly to the left and put your spare hand on your hip. That's it," Killen said approvingly. Lock pulled a face at him. "Do you want to learn properly, or not? Very well, now lean back slightly and push the sword forward. Keep your weight on your back foot. That is called 'making the point'," he said, after Lock had performed a forward thrust to his satisfaction.

"Why can't you lean forward?" Lock asked. He poked the sword forward and his whole body lurched. "You'd get more weight behind it if you were trying to skewer someone."

"Gentlemen do not 'skewer' their opponents," Killen said with mock disgust. "The reason is simple; you are off balance," he explained, "and then if you miss, your enemy's sword will be inside your guard. And he will beat you."

"He'll skewer me?" Lock thought about that for a while before he smiled at his new teacher, prodding him on the shoulder with the end of the practice sword. "You'd better show me how to beat him, then," he said.


After an hour they took a rest. One of the maids walked across the lawn carrying a tray with two glasses and a jug of cool lemonade. A small tree lay at the side of the garden, brought down by winter gales. Halcombe's gardeners had trimmed its branches to short stumps, and now the trunk waited until the ground dried so the draught horses needed to drag away its considerable weight would not damage the precious grass with their huge feet. Killen and Lock sat on the windfall to drink their lemonade in companionable silence.

"I have to work this afternoon," Lock said when the last glass had been drained, "Horses coming to be shod. They bring them after they've been in the fields all day."

To his surprise, Killen found himself feeling disappointment. He had enjoyed the morning. Good food and slowly increasing exercise had given him back much of the strength he had lost while he was ill, but there was something else as well. He could not quite put his finger on the cause, but he felt, well, better in himself. And Lock had proved a rewarding pupil so far. He showed a natural aptitude for the sword, but, more than that, seemed keen to learn.

"It doesn't cause you a problem, does it?" Lock asked.

Killen looked at him enquiringly.

"Your finger." Killen stared at it himself. The index finger of his right handed had mended, but he could no longer hold it straight. He shook his head.

"Why don't you ride back with me," Lock suggested. "I can show you how to fit a horseshoe. Only if you want to, of course."

Killen already knew how a shoe should be applied, but had no desire to upset his new friend. "I'd love to!" he said with enthusiasm.


A few villagers hurried past the two boys, though the main street was quiet. Up on The Tempest's back, Killen smiled broadly at those who looked his way. Some smiled back, but mostly their eyes simply followed the pair dully as they went by. Lock, walking alongside the horse, seemed to keep up with its long stride without effort on the road from Halcombe House, but his dark hair was slicked with sweat and a dribble ran down his forehead. He rubbed at it with his sleeve.

"I need a drink," he said to Killen. "We'll stop at the tavern."

The two boys crossed to where an iron pump stood tall above a stone water trough. Killen dismounted as the horse dropped its head to drink.

"You can leave him there," Lock suggested, pointing to a post alongside the trough with a tie-ring bolted through. A group of youths doing nothing sat in the centre of a grassy patch that passed for the village green. Two girls noticed Lock at the same time he saw them. They got up from the group and wandered over towards the pump.

"Who's your friend, Joshua?" one of the girls called to him.

"Come over here and I'll tell you."

The girls came closer. One hung back, but the one who had spoken was bolder.

"Well - aren't you going to introduce me?" She looked at Killen with interest.

Lock knew them both. "Don't you recognise this gentleman, Daisy Salter?" he teased. "Allow me to introduce Lord John Killen." He said it as grandly as he could.

"I'm not a Lord," Killen hissed behind his hand, "and well you know it." Lock winked at him.

The girls gave deep curtsies. Killen sighed, politely returning the courtesies with a small bow. Lock noticed that Daisy had kept her eyes on Killen throughout.

"Would you ladies care for some refreshment?" Lock reached into his pocket and pulled out a few coins. He stared at the coppers. "Have you got any money?" he whispered to Killen, who reluctantly added silver to the palmful. "Come on then," Lock said, heading for the tavern door.

The second girl shook her head. "I'm not going in there." Her hair was tied loosely with a scrap of brown cloth, Lock noticed, and she twisted the end of the bunch with her fingers as she spoke. "My father would be angry."

Lock murmured sympathetically, "I'll go: you ladies can wait here. Lord Killen shall be your escort."


In his whole life Killen had spoken to very few girls his own age. There were the maids, of course, but he never thought of them as girls; just servants. And there had been girls at parties he attended as a child, prettied in frilly dresses and with hair set in ringlets. But he had rarely spoken to them. Boys were easier. They played the same games; thought the same thoughts. Girls were cissies. And his grandfather sometimes entertained ladies; aunts, supposedly, or other distant relatives, who arrived with servants and stayed for a few days before leaving in apparent disappointment. He never spoke to them, much, either. So he was completely at a loss as to how he should deal with his current predicament.

Daisy Salter, however, seemed totally at ease. "We don't often see you in the village, my lord," she said, staring at Killen with vixen-eyes.

Killen looked downwards and shuffled his feet. "I've been ill," he mumbled indistinctly. Why were girls always so inquisitive? He blushed, but that only seemed to encourage her.

"You're well now, though?"

The tavern door banged as Lock pushed through it with an ale jug in one hand and a fistful of tankards in the other, a small distraction that saved Killen from having to answer. Lock crossed the street and set the jug down on the corner of the water trough.

"You took your time," Killen whispered as Lock poured into four tankards. He was flustered. "I do not know what to say to these two, and those boys have been staring at us." He nodded his head in the direction of the group of young men in the middle of the green.

Lock gave the small gathering a cursory glance. "Ignore them," he advised, "and talk to Daisy. I think she fancies you!"

"She can't! What do I say?"

"Well I don't know; how do you usually talk to women?" Killen's cheeks coloured again, and he stayed silent. "Don't tell me you've never done it before?" Lock asked, shaking his head in amazement when he got no answer. "Look," he suggested urgently, "just tell her how pretty she is and ask her about herself. Girls like that sort of thing."

Lock noticed the other young men strolling towards them just as he emptied the dregs of the ale jug into Killen's tankard. Four boys, there were, and they seemed determined to involve themselves in the party. Lock stood up. Great, he thought; Terrence Tranter and Jimmy Wallis. He had seen the other two around the village, but did not really know them.

Tranter was almost as tall as Lock, and fatter, and it was he who spoke first. He stared down his nose at Killen and the two girls, attempting a disdainful look which Lock thought did not quite come off.

"Not good enough for you now are we, now you're friends with lords and such?" He turned towards Lock, stabbing a forefinger at the ale jug. "I see we weren't invited."

"What d'you want, Terrence?"

Tranter stared at the two girls who ignored him and were vying for Killen's attention. "I want you to stop bringing your high-and mighty friends down here. They're not welcome." His voice slurred slightly.

"Been on the ale have you, Terrence?"

The other boy's mouth hardened. "So what if I have?"

Lock sighed. "Go away and sober up." He turned away, and Tranter shoved him in the back.

Lock turned, anger flaring. "Do that again," he said quietly, "and you'll be sorry."

"You're the one who'll be sorry," Tranter said, and suddenly there was a knife in his hand. "Grab 'im, Jimmy!"

Lock could not quite believe it was happening. Both men stepped towards him and Tranter raised his knife. Whether it was to try to cut him or just threaten, Lock could not tell, and he instinctively threw out his left arm to block the thrust. His wrist caught the inside of Tranter's with such force that the boy lost his grip on the knife. Lock swung at him, right-fisted. That arm was still weak, the blow feeble, and Tranter ducked away from it with ease. Then a pair of arms encircled Lock from behind, pinning his arms to his sides. Jimmy! Taking advantage, Tranter punched him in the stomach, but Lock anticipated the blow.. His body cushioned the punch and he folded forwards over it, at the same time striking backwards with a boot-heel into Jimmy's shin. Pain and surprise loosened the other man's grip, and Lock broke free. Tranter was caught off guard. Lock punched him in the face, knocking him off his feet. He sprawled on the grass, mouth smeared with blood, hands scrabbling for his lost knife.


Killen was shocked at how quickly the fight had started. He had no idea what he should do. He ought to help Lock; there were two against one, after all. But something held him back. He was not afraid, he told himself. He must *do* something.

"I say!" He stood up. "I say!"

The boy on the ground had found his knife and got to his feet. Killen stepped forward to go to his friend's aid, but instead of attacking Lock again, the boy ran directly towards him. Killen was taken completely by surprise, and as the boy ran past he threw out an arm, catching Killen squarely on the nose, pitching him onto his backside.

Killen's eyes watered and his nose hurt like the devil. Blood dribbled down his top lip, spreading over his mouth and chin. Daisy stooped beside him and dabbed furiously at his face with a piece of cloth.

"Oh, my love…I mean, my lord. Keep still now, keep still." Killen snatched the cloth away from her to press firmly over his nose. The rag was soon soaked red with his blood, and the flow seemed reluctant to stop.

Lock held out a hand and, when Killen grasped it, pulled him to his feet. "Tilt your head back," he advised. "That'll help staunch it."

Once Killen's neck began to ache from its unaccustomed position, he dropped his chin. He sniffed once; twice. The bleeding seemed to have stopped. Daisy looked up at him, her big eyes still concerned.

"You've got blood on your coat," she pointed out. Killen scrubbed at the stain with one hand, merely succeeding in spreading it further.

"A lot of use you were," Lock said gruffly. "Still," he admitted, "at least you did try to help." Killen brightened. He had forgotten until then that he had begun to do something. He had not been scared. Not really. It was just the speed it all happened that had put him off.

"You'll have a black eye tomorrow," Lock squinted at his friend, "and you can't go home like that." The second girl hung on to his arm.

"Come with me, my lord." Daisy took charge, "Come on. My house is just round the corner. We'll get you cleaned up there; can't have you walking about all bloody."

Killen was unsure what to do, but Lock winked at him and said quietly, "Never turn down an offer like that, John." He walked away with the other girl in tow. "Come over to the smithy when you're finished." Killen wondered why his friend was grinning at him, but Daisy's insistence was a distraction. He untied the horse to follow her.

Behind the girl's cottage was a stone outbuilding. Daisy led Killen towards it, struggling to push open one of its double doors which dragged on the ground. He tried to help her and she brushed up against him. Killen was not certain if that was accidental or not. He led the horse inside, looping its reins over a wooden beam.

"There's no-one here."

107

Daisy smiled at him, "They're working." She took hold of his coat to examine the bloodstain. "You'll have to take it off," she decided.

Killen made himself comfortable on a pile of straw while the girl worked. She had found another rag, dipping it in a half-barrel of water before scrubbing at the coat front with what appeared a practised hand.

Once Daisy finished she held the coat by the shoulders to shake it out. "It'll have to dry for a while." She hung it on a nail that stuck out of the door frame before walking slowly back over to Killen, unwinding the strip of material that bound her hair so the dark mass cascaded over her shoulders.

She knelt in front of him. "You have blood on your hand." Holding his palm upwards, she took another rag and moistened one corner of the material with her tongue. Killen watched her at work, nervous but fascinated. Her lips were fuller than he had noticed before and he found the pinkness of her tongue as it protruded between them strangely exciting. She wiped at the streak of blood on his palm and he saw that the buttons at the front of her dress were undone; the top gaped open at the neck. He stole a look at her face and saw she was watching him so he glanced down again, embarrassed. God! He could see right inside her dress! Killen flushed and looked away, but she hung onto his hand and drew it towards her.

"There, my lord," she said quietly, her voice husky. Killen felt the material of her dress, then bare skin. He kept his eyes on her face, not daring to look lower. She had placed his hand inside her bodice. He had no idea what he should do: this was way outside his experience. Daisy pushed his hand further down onto something soft and warm. Her breast! Killen suddenly remembered dreams he used to suffer; visions that woke him in the night, hot and dishevelled. For some reason, whenever he tried desperately to go back to sleep, to return to them, he never could. This was just like them. His breeches began to feel uncomfortable. He felt his face grow hot again, and although he told himself he should pull away, he could not.

The girl moved his hand lower until he could feel the whole of her breast. He could not help himself, and now he dared not look her in the face.

"There," she said again, "now - isn't that nice?" Her other hand was on Killen's thigh, creeping slowly up towards his groin.

"Oh, it is nice, then!" She smiled, and giggled.

Killen could stand it no more. He jumped up. "I have to go," he mumbled, struggling to unhitch the horse. He almost ran out of the stable, and would have done but the lump in his breeches made it uncomfortable to hurry. Back outside, there was no sign of Lock, and the girl had followed him. Killen mounted hastily and cast a guilty glance back. Daisy was standing in the barn doorway, but she had re-buttoned the front of her dress. He gave the horse too strong a kick, and trotted off down the road.


Killen felt ashamed of himself. What should he have done? When he thought about it, he realised Lock must have known what was likely to happen. Why had he said nothing? And why was it that however hard Killen tried, he could not get the feel of the girl's skin, or the shape of her tongue, out of his mind. And why did having an, well, an erection, make riding a horse so damned uncomfortable?

Killen heard other horses trotting before he saw them. They came towards him around a bend in the road, screened by trees. Oh, marvellous, he thought gloomily.

The three horsemen halted.

"We've been looking for you," the first said with disapproval, as if Killen ought to always be at his beck and call. Percival Twiston looked at him as one might a disobedient servant. "I say, what have you been up to?"

His companion looked bored. "He's been in a fight, Percy," he said, scathing. "It's blindingly obvious." Killen wiped at his nose with the back of his hand and winced.

"Gave the bounder as good as you got, I hope?" Twiston went on. "Not still about, is he?" He looked around nervously.

Killen shook his head, forcing a smile. "He will be long gone. And in a far worse state than me," he lied to cover his embarrassment.

Twiston visibly relaxed. "Glad to hear it."

His companion became exasperated. "For God's sake get on with it, Percy," he said, "otherwise we'll not be home before dark."

"Of course, of course," Twiston smiled. "Just making sure we'll see you at manoeuvres next week." Killen was puzzled.

"The Yeomanry?" Twiston said patiently, "remember them? Heard you'd had a bang on the head, old boy, but didn't think it would have knocked that much sense from you!" He laughed, and Killen returned his smile half-heartedly.

"I'd not forgotten, Percy," he lied again, "and yes, I'll be there."

# Chapter 11

Lord Halcome pushed away his half-eaten breakfast and stared morosely at the plate of congealing eggs and kidney. "I think it most unwise, Johnny, I really do."

Killen stared across the breakfast table at his grandfather. The bruise on his face was fading to yellow. "But why?"

Halcombe frowned. "He must be officially invited, for one thing." He raised his hand as Killen opened his mouth to speak again. "Yes, I know that you can invite him, but it is not the done thing. He's not family; not even a servant. God knows, I am in his debt, but I cannot allow this."

"You allow him into this house to use the library," Killen countered sulkily.

"That is not the same." Halcombe pushed a cup forward for Roberts to fill with tea. "It would not reflect well. And what would he ride?"

"Joshua has a horse," Killen pursed his lips as he thought of Lock's ancient grey mare, "but I thought he could borrow one of the hunters."

"No. I absolutely forbid it," Halcombe said with finality. "I must consider our position. You will not invite him."

Killen rode through the village towards the forge in high spirits. It was strange, he thought, how his grandfather's attitude towards him had changed since he returned home with a black eye. Before that, he had been allowed almost everything he asked for, but now it seemed obstacles littered his path. Conditions were applied to everything he wanted to do. Do not leave your tutor before *this* time. Return to the house by *that*. Killen pulled a silver pocket watch from inside his coat to check the dial. He had allowed plenty of time for his mission this afternoon but, well, perhaps he ought to hurry a little. He squeezed the horse with his legs until it broke into a trot.

The forge smoked. From outside, Killen could hear the muffled ring of hammer on anvil. He slid down from the saddle and tied the horse to a horizontal rail outside, nodding politely to a farm-worker who sat on an upturned trough with his boots off. Waiting for the work inside to be finished, no doubt. Killen stuck his head in through the doorway.

Lock pulled a glowing horseshoe from the fire with a pair of long-handled tongs, smiling a greeting over his shoulder, "Come on in. I won't be long."

Killen found his way blocked by a bulky draught horse. The animal was tied to a ring in one wall, dozing contentedly. He squeezed his way round towards its head before ducking under its neck so he was close to the fire. Lock had laid the horseshoe face up on the anvil while he tapped a metal spike into one of the nail-holes. He lifted the pritchel, carrying the shoe across to the horse, and Killen saw how the spike kept the horseshoe far enough away to prevent its heat from scorching his friend's hand.

"I'll show you how to nail one on, after, "Lock said, "like I promised." He tugged at the hair around the back of the draught horse's heel and the animal obediently lifted its foot for the hot shoe to be applied. Horn sizzled as the shoe burned it away; acrid smoke billowed upwards. Lock blew it away so he could see what he was doing as he carefully checked that the shoe was seated evenly on the horse's foot. He took the shoe off, squinting at the burn mark it made. Then, apparently satisfied, he turned and tapped the shoe off the pritchel into a half-barrel of water, sending clouds of steam into the already smoky atmosphere.

"So, what happened?" Lock reached into the fire with his tongs for another shoe, but the iron had begun to grey where the heat had gone from it. He frowned. "See that handle?" he said, "just pump it up and down a bit."

Killen took the wooden pole in both hands, heaving on it so the bellows blew air into the coals to make them glow again. After a few minutes the horseshoe was hot enough to work.

"So - did she let you?"

Killen let go of the bellows handle. "Let me what?"

Lock pulled the shoe out of the fire. "Show you her titties." Killen blushed and did not answer, but Lock was already tapping at the hot shoe on the anvil and must have taken his silence for confirmation. "How much did it cost you?"

"Cost?" Killen puzzled.

112

"How much did she charge you? Going rate's a shilling, I've heard."

"She didn't charge me anything!" Killen blushed.

Lock took the second shoe to plant on the draught horse's other front foot. "You lucky devil!" He hissed smoke away. "Must have been your title," he said, grinning. "So what else did she do for you?"

Killen blushed even more furiously. "Nothing like that," he said vehemently, "that's disgusting!"

Lock laughed. "You missed a treat, John, a real treat. Not that I would know, of course."


Tap, tap, tap, tap.

"You listen," Lock mumbled, "for the nail." He crouched beneath the draught horse with one big foot between his knees and nails gripped between his teeth. "The sound gets flatter when the nail's near to coming out." He tapped again. "Did you hear it?"

Killen shook his head. Lock hit the nail head flush with the underside of the shoe before using the hammer's claw to twist off its point, where it protruded from the front of the horse's hoof. "Listen again," he said, starting the next nail.

Killen dropped his head closer. "There!"

"You're right." Lock was surprised Killen had been so quick to notice the difference. "You'll have to spend hours listening before you can get it right every time."

"I believe I would rather pay someone to do it for me."

"I thought you wanted to join the cavalry. What would happen if your horse lost a shoe and you were on a battlefield somewhere?"

"They have farriers do that sort of thing," Killen said grandly. "An officer would not have to."

Lock dropped the horse's foot and straightened up. "So why are you here," he asked crossly.

"I want you to come to the Yeomanry exercise with me next week." It came out in a rush.

Lock wrinkled his nose. "I don't know, John."

"Oh, come on. We can ride over together. It'll be fun."
Killen was persuasive. "Do say you will."

And in the family pew at church on the Sunday morning of
the exercise, John Killen prayed for forgiveness for his deceit.


Lock's shirt collar was buttoned tight and uncomfortable. He
tugged at it with a forefinger as he and Killen rode along, but it
made no difference. Once he had agreed to go with his friend, he
immediately regretted it. He had outgrown his good shirt so wore
the scruffy garment he worked in, and his jacket, though
thoroughly brushed, was threadbare. Lock's grandfather watched
him struggle to dress with a hackneyed eye.

"When the Israelites crossed the River Jordon into the
Promised Land," Abraham observed, "they found it was not the
land of milk and honey they had expected." Lock ignored him.
Abraham was always quoting the Bible.

But it was Lock's horse that was the main problem. Killen,
resplendent in his uniform, was mounted on The Tempest. Jogging
along the gravel track with spurs and sabre jingling, the pair looked
every inch the dashing cavalryman and charger. Lock knew he
looked like what he was; a poor boy on a pensioned-off plough
horse. He had cut the winkers off the old mare's draught bridle
trying to make her look respectable, and it had taken him ages to
stitch the hard leather back together so that the edges were
reasonably neat. And he had no saddle. Lock was used to riding
without, but he felt sure he would be the only rider bareback.


The exercise was held in a huge field. Lock professed surprise at
the number of participants already there when he and Killen
arrived. Groups of horsemen dotted the perimeter, mingling with
spectators. A few open carriages had judiciously parked around the
field edges where trees gave shade, their occupants chatting
beneath parasols. And several small companies of Militia
infantrymen practiced drill on the far side.

Enterprising villagers had set up stalls. Protected from the
sun by awnings or straw hats, they busied themselves selling pies

and pastries or cups of small beer and wine to the well dressed ladies and gentlemen who strolled about the headland.

"I should register," Killen said, "Won't be long."

When he had ridden off, Lock let his reins lengthen, and the mare put her head down to graze. A uniformed man rode past, staring at him. A sergeant, Lock thought, judging by the broad stripes on his uniform sleeve, and not very friendly looking, either. Lock decided to ignore him, letting his gaze stray back to the distant infantrymen. They now seemed to be forming up for some sort of musket drill.

"Hullo, Johnny. I see that you did remember." Percival Twiston rode across to Killen. "I say; that's rather a nice horse you've got."

Killen preened at the compliment. "He's not been to anything like this before, Percy; needs the experience."

"You remember Geoffrey Haverscott? Don't think I introduced you before."

"Pleased to meet you," Killen greeted the other man, who had been Twiston's companion on the road to Halcombe House.

Haverscott merely nodded back without smiling. He seemed more interested in something over Killen's shoulder. "Good God, will you look at that."

"What is it," Percy asked, and Killen turned his head to look.

"Some peasant in the wrong place," Haverscott spluttered. "What on earth does he think he's doing here?"

"That's Joshua," Killen said, realising who the two were gawping at, and when they both swivelled their heads towards him in surprise, added, "He came with me."

The two men looked at each other. "Why the devil did you bring him?"

Killen began to feel a little uncomfortable. "Er...he wanted to."

Haverscott laughed. "Then you should have dissuaded him. Take a gander at those clothes! He's only fit for the foot-sloggers. And that nag!"

Twiston pursed his lips. "Really, Johnny, you might have gotten your servant to dress for the occasion."

But Killen had no time to answer, for just then the trumpet sounded, calling gentlemen to their troops, and the exercise began.


Lock was prepared for boredom. He had thought to dismount; to take his weight off the old mare's back and find some shade under the trees. But the trumpet call changed all that. For a reason he could not understand, its shrill notes made the hair at the back of his neck stand up. So he stayed on the horse, because he could see further than if he had been on foot.

The horsemen lined up. Their uniforms made a brave show, and Lock wondered if they would ever be called upon to fight; if Bonaparte would invade England as gossips and rumour-mongers in the taverns insisted. To their captains' shouted commands, the lines of cavalrymen walked forward. Lock watched, fascinated, as each line split into smaller segments. Formations wheeled, the innermost troops virtually having to come to a halt whilst those on the perimeters hurried their horses to keep in line. Officers screamed instructions, berating those who were too quick or slow and who threatened chaos from order. The cavalry slowed and speeded up in sections, so at one point the whole mass of men and animals appeared to move over the ground in chequerboard squares. And, finally, they came back into line.

Lock was impressed at the precision with which the exercise had been carried out. There seemed to have been few mistakes. A couple of untidy riders, admittedly, kicking and pulling at unschooled or recalcitrant mounts, but all the same, it had been well done. Now though, instead of a sedate walk, the lines moved forward at a trot, and the additional speed threw many manoeuvres into disarray. The captains bellowed even louder, and thanks to the number of horses milling about, dust began to rise. Eventually the cavalrymen became enveloped in such a cloud it was difficult to see them, and many spectators became bored and wandered off. Lock smiled to himself. Controlling a horse was easy. It was controlling it at a fast pace that was the problem.

The afternoon began to drag. The Yeomanry drilled and drilled, until at length, the volume of shouting began to diminish. Lock dismounted and led the old mare to a water trough, where she drank. He was still there when Killen returned with four companions.

Killen was flushed, from the heat as well as the exercise, and pushed up the brim of his helmet so it sat far back on his head. "Well, what did you think?"

Lock glanced at the other three men. "Very good," he said flatly.

"And what would you know about it?" one of them asked brusquely.

Percival Twiston was more polite. "Oh do shut up, Clifford. Aren't you going to introduce us, Johnny?"

"One don't introduce the hired help," Haverscott said out of the side of his mouth.

Killen was contrite. "I'm sorry, Percy. This is Joshua Lock."

Twiston reached down, offering his hand. Lock took it, but found Percy's grip limp. "I am delighted to meet you, Joshua," Twiston said, looking him in the eye with a smile while keeping hold of his hand. "Allow me to introduce Geoffrey Haverscott: the other two fellows are Benjamin Abbott and Clifford Richley." Twiston seemed to realise he had been holding Lock's hand for an indecently long time, and abruptly let it go. Lock glanced at the other two men who stared back at him blankly.

"And what do you do?"

Something about Twiston made Lock careful, but he could not put his finger on the reason. So he did what he often did, adopting a subservient attitude he found was usually acceptable to men who thought themselves his better. It was easy when he was not angry. He inclined his head, "Farrier, sir."

Haverscott, who had looked disgustedly at Twiston's lingering handshake, said "Huh!" loudly.

"Really?" Twiston seemed intrigued. "And you work in Halcombe, I take it?" Lock nodded. "Then I must make it my business to visit," Twiston said with enthusiasm.

"For god's sake Percy, let's get on," Haverscott was impatient, "and stop wasting time with the servant." Lock was relieved, but then Killen spoiled it.

"Joshua's not a servant," he said indignantly. "He saved me from drowning."

Percival Twiston's eyes lit up again, and he stared admiringly at Lock while still talking to Killen. "My dear chap, tell me all!"

"He can tell you while we're riding along," Haverscott interrupted crossly, "or we'll never get damned-well home."

Slowly the five companions travelled back towards Halcombe. Killen rode at the front alongside Percival Twiston and must have been relating the story of his accident to the other man, as he occasionally glanced over his shoulder at a fed-up Lock, trailing along at the rear. All four men kept up an animated conversation for a couple of miles until they flagged. Eventually, Geoffrey Haverscott dropped back so he was riding alongside Lock.

"The problem with Mr. Twiston," he said, pointedly, "is that he's often too polite for his own good." Lock looked straight ahead. "He has a perfectly good farrier, and doesn't need another." Lock glanced across at Haverscott, and the other man stared him in the face for several seconds as if to ensure his point was understood, before kicking his horse into a trot to catch up with Abbott and Richley.

A few miles further on the group split up. Twiston insisted on shaking Lock's hand again, while Killen looked on approvingly. Lock and Killen continued on the road to Halcombe village in a silence broken only by roadside birdsong.

It was Killen who spoke, at last. "I'm sorry, Josh. I thought you might like to go along."

Lock shrugged off the apology, "Why?"

Killen considered. "I just thought it might be good for you to see what happens; that you might enjoy it."

"Why on earth did you think that?"

"Oh, I don't know. You sometimes meet useful people at that type of thing. And Percy seemed to like you."

"D' you know him well?" Lock asked, warily.

"Not really. He's just… around. You know. He likes parties. He goes to balls, hunts, that sort of thing."

Lock picked at the end of the grey mare's mane, twisting strands of hair around his fingers. "There's something odd about him."

"What do you mean, exactly?"

"I don't know. There just is."

"You will need to be more specific than that," Killen demanded.

"I can't be." The horses' feet were loud on the gravel road. "His friend's very protective," Lock observed.

"Haverscott? He's just a pig."

"And I suppose the other two are friends of yours?"

"Not really. I just see them around, at…"

"Balls and hunts?"

"Yes," Killen said with a laugh, "balls, and hunts."

# 1806

# Chapter 12

Edward Gaunt threw down his mallet while Killen surveyed the Stud Groom's handiwork. Three stakes were set in a row down the field, each around twenty yards from the next. And in a slot cut in the top of each post Gaunt had fixed a small wooden ring.

"That's grand, Edward, thank you." Killen checked the ground. Though it was only February, a weak morning sun had driven night-frost from the turf. The Tempest fidgeted beneath him, forcing Killen to close his legs around the horse's sides so it walked forward.

"If you want to trot at first, Master Johnny, I'll re-fit the rings," Gaunt offered. Killen grinned and swung the horse around to set off down the line.

Riding one-handed was difficult. Killen carried the practice sword in his right hand and The Tempest, keen to get on with the job, snatched at the reins in his left. He soothed it with his voice while trying to concentrate on aiming at the rings. His sword-tip caught the side of the first, knocking it from the stake, and it fluttered to the ground. Killen cursed under his breath, trotting at the second. Wait, his Riding Master had taught him. Wait for the target to come to you. But the more he waited the tenser he became. And the horse was wavering off-line, taking him away from the stake. He corrected it skilfully, rein and leg working together. Then his sword went through the ring and it rattled against the wooden hand-guard. The Tempest flicked back one ear at the unfamiliar noise but was reassured when nothing else happened, and Killen trotted at the next.

By now The Tempest had grown familiar with passing close to a stake, so the last ring was easily speared. Killen allowed the horse its head and the animal swung into a canter, leaning slightly leftwards so they arced away from the targets and back up the field. He sat upright, slowing to a walk as they returned to their starting point. Gaunt had already replaced the first ring, and Killen tipped his sword point down so the Stud Groom could remove the two he had collected successfully.

"Well done, sir."

"A little faster this time, I think," Killen said happily, "and I'll have the three of them," so Gaunt walked back to fit the other two targets.

Now The Tempest was ready for the game. Killen lined up with the stakes and asked for canter, but it seemed the black horse was infected with enthusiasm and flew into a gallop. Killen concentrated hard on letting the first ring come to him and his sword drove straight through its centre. His speed made the ring clatter against the hand-guard, the sudden noise spurring the horse on. Its whole body seemed to lengthen as it stretched out towards the second stake. His sword point speared the next ring and then there was just one more, and the horse was galloping even faster. The ring raced towards him but somehow Killen knew he had it even before the sword pierced its centre, then he was turning and slowing and the horse's stride was shortening, and he had done it.

Killen laid his right rein against the horse's neck and it turned to the left as it had been taught, cantering a long, lazy half-circle back up the field. Someone was clapping in the distance, and as the horse straightened up Killen could see that his grandfather had strolled across from the house to watch.

"Bravo," he shouted. "Bravo."

Killen slowed the horse to a walk. The Tempest's chest heaved, but not for long. As its breathing slowed he stroked its neck; it was dry. The animal had not even broken a sweat.

Lord Halcombe walked up to The Tempest, pausing to pat the horse on the shoulder. "You have him decently fit." He looked up at his grandson. "That was well done, my boy, very well done."

Killen was pleased. He jumped off and lifted the saddle flap, loosening girths. "It's Tempest. Not me, really. He just seems to know what to do when he's been shown once."

"Nonsense, nonsense - you have worked hard on him; I know that. Now come down to the house; Roberts is making tea."

Killen turned to Gaunt. "Would you mind awfully putting him away, Edward?" he asked, and the Stud Groom led the horse off. Halcombe had already begun walking back, and Killen hurried to catch him up.

"Do you remember, grandfather, you promised to write to Lord Paget," he asked carefully.

Halcombe slowed for a few paces then strode on. "There is plenty of time for that."

"I'm sixteen now," Killen struggled to keep up, speaking at the same time, "old enough to join a regiment. And you did promise."

"I did."

"Well..," Killen swallowed, "will you write soon?"

Halcombe sighed as he turned sideways to face his grandson. "If you are certain that is what you want," he raised an eyebrow in question, and the boy nodded, "then I shall do it tomorrow."


Curtains were drawn and lamps lit in the house when Lord Halcombe sat down at his desk. He glanced guiltily at a portrait in a small oval frame before opening a lower drawer, pulling out a sheet of white paper. He stared at the blank page in front of him. Not pure white, but creamy. A suitable shade for the letter he was about to write. He had gone over it in his mind dozens of times and knew what he must do. The language must not be too obvious, but the request clear. He dipped a pen in the inkwell to begin.

When he had finished, he re-read the page twice, and was satisfied. He signed it with a flourish, scattering a pinch of chalk over the signature to blot it for the rest had dried. He sat for a while, elbows on the desk, fingers intertwined, staring at the face that smiled back at him from the oval picture frame.

"I've kept my promise," Halcombe said at last to the portrait and dropped the letter into a drawer. It would go on the Mail Coach tomorrow.


It was two weeks before a reply arrived. Killen was fencing with Lock on the rear lawn. They both took a step back away from one another.

Killen smiled, "You've improved a great deal, Josh. You're nearly as good as me!"

Lock brandished his wooden sword with disdain. "When are we going to use the real thing?"

Killen laughed. "Soon; soon." He lifted the tip of the practice sword once more, "Ready? *En garde!*"

The sword tips crossed, then disengaged and Killen swept his wooden blade low from the right. Lock brought his own across his body to block the cut, twisting his wrist to flick the blade upwards. But Killen was ready for that move and his own sword blocked Lock's easily. Then he attacked, cutting down left and right, stepping forward behind the blows. Lock was forced into furious parries but finally managed to work his sword inside Killen's guard. Then it was his opponent who had to defend, and Killen stepped back, forced to give ground.

"Whoa!" Killen held up his hand. He was breathing heavily from the effort. "Let us stop for a minute."

"You nearly had me then."

"You nearly beat *me*," Killen said admiringly, "which is amazing, since you have had no proper tuition."

"What do you call this, then?"

"Oh, I am no expert," Killen said with modesty.

"I don't know anyone who can fight as well as you."

"You do not know any swordsmen!"

Lock shrugged. "True, I suppose. But I'm sure you are good." But Killen was not listening. He was looking over Lock's shoulder towards the house; at his grandfather, who was walking towards them clutching a letter.


Halcombe offered the sheet of paper to his grandson and nodded a greeting, "Joshua."

"Sir."

Killen flexed the single page to flatten any creases. His hand trembled slightly as he read.

*'My dear George...'*

He looked up at his grandfather, whose face betrayed no emotion.


*...I regret that at present the 7$^{th}$ has a full complement of subalterns. Might I advert you, however to the situation of the 20$^{th}$, presently recruiting two squadrons for home service and in need of intelligent young men such as your grandson. In anticipation of*

*your acceptance I have today written to their Colonel a letter of introduction and recommendation.*

*I trust this is satisfactory and wish you continued good health.'*

It was signed, simply, *'Paget'*


"I know it is not the regiment you hoped for," Halcombe said, but Killen was delighted.

"Thank you, grandfather," he said with feeling, "thank you."


When Halcombe had gone Killen brandished the letter at his friend. "Look, Josh, I've got in!" Lock said nothing. "Aren't you pleased? I am! It's just what I've always wanted."

"I'm glad, then," Lock smiled, but Killen saw it was only with his mouth. He folded the letter carefully before stuffing it inside his coat then picked up the practice sword again, swinging the tip towards Lock. "Ready?"

Lock shook his head. "I think I'll go."

"What's the matter?"

Lock kept his eyes down as he scythed the tip of his sword through the grass. "When will you be leaving?"

"Oh, I do not know yet. I shall probably have to wait a month or two. And you need not go; it does not get dark for ages."

"I'm not afraid of the dark," Lock said heatedly.

"I never thought that you were," Killen said, confused. "Why on earth did you say it?"

"I thought your grandfather wanted you to stay at home."

"Do you do everything your grandfather tells you? Your father was a farrier; mine was a cavalry officer."

"And now you'll get yourself killed, like him," Lock said angrily and swung his own sword up, towards his friend's head.

Killen caught the blade on his own sword, pushing the stroke to one side. "I was not ready," he complained, but Lock was attacking again, forcing Killen to parry desperately. Lock's swings seemed to get heavier and wilder, but Killen managed to keep his friend's sword away. He thrust back at his opponent, intending to prod him in the chest, but at the last second Lock unexpectedly twisted to one side. Killen's sword flicked upwards, catching the other boy a stinging blow on the cheek.

Lock stopped and stepped back, and his hand went to his face.

"I am sorry, Josh," Killen apologised. "That was a complete accident...," he began, but abruptly saw Lock's cold expression then he was defending fiercely as his friend came at him with sword swinging. Killen was forced to step back, and back again, from the ferocity of the attack. Then Lock switched the sword into his left hand, and its wooden blade struck at Killen's with more weight than he thought possible.

"Josh, stop! For heaven's sake!" Killen's arm began to ache. He could feel the force of Lock's anger vibrating through blows he only just managed to deflect. He tried to turn away, but his foot caught and he stumbled, losing his balance. Then he was on the ground. Lock's sword came for him. Desperately, Killen put up his own to block his friend's vicious downstroke, and his wooden blade splintered into useless pieces from the impact. Then Lock's sword curved towards him once again.

"God - Josh! No!" Killen shouted; a prayer. He screwed his eyes shut, and the other blade swept past, crashing into the turf. He felt the wind of the sword-stroke on his face and opened his eyes. Lock's sword lay on the ground, and he was striding away.

"Josh!" Killen called after him, "Joshua!" But his friend did not look back.


A stone the size of an apple lay in his path. Lock kicked it with such venom it shot between a pair of trees at the roadside and bounced away out of sight. He was angry. Angry that Killen was leaving. No, that was not it. He was angry he had lost control. That he had behaved badly. It had not happened for a long time, but the anger exploded so quickly he had not even thought to count. God had not made him stop; he had done it himself. But anger still there, smouldered in the pit of his stomach. So what if John Killen got himself killed? He would not care.

And by the time he reached the village, Lock almost convinced himself that was true.


Over the next few weeks, Killen was at pains to deliberately visit the forge, but for some reason Lock never seemed to be there. On the last occasion, he quizzed Lock's grandfather about his friend's whereabouts without success.

"I don't know where he is, sir," the old man wheezed. "Went off and left me, and didn't say when he'd be back."

"Then may I leave a message for him? I shall be leaving in two weeks and my grandfather is holding a ball a week on Saturday. I would be glad to see Joshua there."

"Very good sir, I'll tell him," Abraham agreed. Killen mounted his horse and rode back towards the village.


"You should make it up with him," Abraham came inside, pulling the door shut behind him. "He obviously wants to see you."

"What for?" Lock shook his head. "You heard him - he's leaving."

"I thought he was your friend."

"So did I."

Abraham tutted, "You never told me what you argued about."

"Nothing," Lock said, sullenly.

"I did warn you," Abraham said, and then, when Lock flashed him an angry look, added quickly, "but real friends never leave you for good, boy; just like the Samaritan."

Lock looked through the window after Killen. "Then I don't have any," he said.


Lock was bored. "You're a damned nuisance," he scolded the polecat as he nailed a piece of timber over the hole it had managed to chew in one corner of its cage. The animal had escaped the previous night and killed the single chicken which had gone broody, so was an easy catch. Lock was surprised at how much he missed John Killen's company. He had stopped visiting the library at Halcombe House with its rows of books and he missed the excitement of a new story, a new discovery, even the feel of the stiff white pages and smooth leathered boards.

But it was too late to make it better. He had spoiled things in a moment of stupidity. Futile anger grew inside him again, so that he lost concentration and the hammerhead caught his thumb. He cursed out loud, putting it to his mouth, and, trying to say 'one' at the same time the word became an indecipherable mumble. Lock smiled to himself at that, and his anger died.


Killen flicked the body brush at the stroke's end, raising a tiny cloud of dust from The Tempest's glossy ribcage that hung in the still air. He could not wait to be off. Time dragged as the evening of the ball approached. There was nothing for him to organise; his grandfather and staff had made all the arrangements. His tutor had left early, not wishing to stay for the festivities despite receiving a glowing reference from Halcombe that ran to two pages and which should make future employment a mere formality.

The hunters were roughed off and turned out to grass, so even though Edward Gaunt found him odd jobs to do around the stable yard there were not enough horses in work to occupy him, and he found himself wishing that Lock would come striding down the road to the house.

Gaunt put his head over the stable door. "If you groom that horse any more, Master Johnny, you'll take all coat off," the Stud Groom said, not unkindly. Killen gave a wan smile. "You've not heard from Joshua," Gaunt guessed, and Killen did not answer. "He'll be back." The Stud Groom sounded certain but Killen shook his head.

"Why should he? I'll be leaving tomorrow." He scraped the body brush clean and put the tools down. "Edward, would you do me a kindness?"

Gaunt looked slightly surprised, "Of course."

Killen pulled a lump of dark wood from his pocket. "Would you look after this for me, until I return?" He held out the oak splinter smashed from the Defiance's hull by a French cannonball.

130

"I worry the cleaning-maids will think it rubbish to be thrown away."

The Stud Groom had seen the relic often enough before. "I'll keep it safe, Master Johnny." He took the splinter and hid it in the tack room drawer, tucking it out of sight behind the horse-pistol.

Killen felt relief. He collected the grooming tools he had left in the stable. After being untied The Tempest wandered back to its hay rack.

"You know," Killen observed, staring at the horse eating, "Joshua said if the racks were fixed lower the seeds and dust would not fall into the horses' eyes." He turned towards Gaunt for confirmation.

"He said a lot of things," the Stud Groom admitted with a rueful smile, "that were quite sensible."


Lock stood in front of Halcome House. Two late partygoers clambered from a carriage to scurry, giggling, up the portico steps. Some unseen hand opened the front door in welcome and the guests were ushered inside.

Lock stayed half-hidden in the shadow of laurel bushes. He watched one of his lordship's grooms walk in front of the carriage as it was driven around to the stable yard behind the house. There, the horses would be unhitched and cooled while they waited for the ball to end, and the coachman no doubt refreshed with wine. Lock left his old grey mare grazing on the lawn, tying her front legs together with a hobble made from a short length of tarred rope so she could not stray too far.

He had decided he ought to accept Killen's invitation. Not to stay; he thought that might prove too difficult; but just to wish his erstwhile friend well. Killen deserved that much. But now he was not so sure. Lock's clothes were no match for the finery likely to be on show inside, but tidy enough, he persuaded himself. Over the mare's back he strapped a blanket to prevent the rough cloth of his breeches picking up stray white hairs, but it had not worked as well as he hoped. He bent down, brushing at them with his hand. A few hairs fell off, but still more stuck stubbornly to the material.

After a while he gave up and climbed the stone steps to the front door.

Roberts answered his hesitant tap. "Please come in, Mr Lock." Halcombe's manservant shattered the formality by smiling, and Lock stepped into the hallway. Lamps and candles were lit everywhere leaving no corner shaded, and from deeper within the house came the scratch of musicians playing.

Groups of guests cluttered the hallway in conversation, spilling from crowded reception rooms. A number of heads turned to see who had come in. Lock tried not to catch any eye; to avoid recognition. He just wanted to see Killen, then he would go.

"Good grief; what's this that's crawled in?" Lock recognised the voice. He cursed under his breath as Geoffrey Haverscott swaggered towards him clutching a half-empty wineglass. "What are you doing here?" Haverscott demanded, loudly. Several others of his small group followed him, presumably keen to find out what was going on.

"I was invited," Lock said, keeping his eyes down.

"I was invited 'sir'." If Haverscott was expecting a response, he got none. "So where's your invitation?" he went on, brandishing a printed card in his free hand. "I say, Roberts, there's a gatecrasher here!"

Roberts sounded slightly embarrassed. "I do assure you sir, that Mr Lock is invited."

Haverscott rounded on him. "Allow tramps through the door, do you? I'll see Lord Halcombe about this." The manservant reddened.

"Leave him alone. He's done nothing to you," Lock said in a dangerous tone. Haverscott sounded slightly drunk, but even so the man was a bully. Roberts caught Lock's arm in warning, but he ignored it.

"What did you say to me?" Haverscott blocked Lock's path, surrounded by his friends. "Apologise, damn you."

"Leave it, Geoffrey," one of the others advised, but Haverscott refused to back down. "Well?"

132

"I've nothing to apologise for." Lock felt strangely calm. He had kept his anger well under control. He looked Haverscott in the eye, "It's you who should apologise, to Mr Roberts."

"Damn your apology, then," Haverscott said loudly, and threw the contents of his glass into Lock's face.

Lock did not mean to hit him, but the impulse flared suddenly, giving him no time to start his count. Haverscott sprawled on the floor, the wineglass shattered into shards. Spilt wine blackened the thin lines between tiles; Lock had dripped on them once, he remembered.

Haverscott sat up. "He hit me! Did you see that?" His lower lip was bleeding. "He hit me!" Two of his friends took him by the arms, hauling him to his feet, but he wriggled from their grasp and came towards Lock again. "You'll be sorry for that, you damned peasant," Haverscott snarled, and Lock was ready to dodge away when his arms were pinned to his sides from behind. That gave Haverscott the opportunity to punch him in the stomach.

"Stop it. Now!" Edward Gaunt had grabbed Lock and spat the words at Haverscott over the boy's shoulder.

Haverscott, restrained by two partygoers, pointed at his assailant. "This... this scum started it."

"You're a liar." Lock struggled half-heartedly in the Stud Groom's embrace, but his anger cooled as quickly as it sparked. There was movement behind him, and the murmur of voices, silenced momentarily, began again. Gaunt released him, allowing Lock to turn around. He found Lord Halcombe staring at him with what seemed like...disappointment?

"Why did you come here?" Halcombe asked, but before Lock could answer he carried on, "You have embarrassed me in front of my guests." His voice was cold.

"My lord," Gaunt began, but Halcombe cut him short.

"It will have to wait." He looked at Lock. "I must ask you to leave here," he said, without emotion. "You are no longer welcome in my house." Lock wondered whether he ought to protest the unfairness, but in the end just shrugged and turned away. Haverscott was too busy complaining to his companions to pay any attention; only Roberts rushed across to open the front door. Lock gave him a sideways glance.

"Goodnight…sir," the manservant's voice was loaded with sympathy as Lock stomped out into the night.

The heavy door shut behind him with a bang.

# Chapter 13

There were four beds in the room. At least, John Killen presumed they were beds. The wooden frames strung with hemp straps were unlike anything he had seen before. Even the ships' beds he remembered from a trip across the English Channel as a child had been better made than these. But the sergeant was most insistent.

"Here we are, gentlemen. You will find mattresses in the cupboard at the end," he pointed, "and the orderly will be along shortly with sheets and blankets." The man had a huge, bushy moustache which curved right across each cheek, joining seamlessly with his side-whiskers. Killen, hugely impressed by the display, was too shy to ask the man how long it had taken to grow. "I will come to collect you later on, as the major wishes to see you all at four o'clock sharp."

Killen dropped his leather bag onto the scrubbed wooden floorboards and sat down on the nearest bed. Its webbing sagged alarmingly even under his slight weight, but he supposed it would be the same for all. They had each been provided with a wardrobe and a wooden chest. Killen checked inside his and found both completely empty.


Four new cornets were selected for the squadron. Killen had already met two, who appeared much the same age as he. Robert Millward was a doctor's son from Dorset. Slim and dark, with an air of nervousness, he shook Killen's hand guardedly before retreating behind a large white handkerchief. He seemed to blow his nose with alarming regularity. Charles Harris however, freckle-faced and smiling, held out a calloused hand. 'Call me Charlie, everyone else does,' he said, professing himself delighted to find Killen a fellow foxhunter.

Millward took the cot in the corner furthest from the door. Charlie Harris threw his valise onto that next to Killen's choice and announced he was going to find the thickest, softest mattress. He rifled the cupboard, throwing out a number of bundles, rolled and tied with string. It turned out the mattresses all were much alike, so Harris and Killen spent the next quarter hour pummelling elderly and uneven goose-down to flatten out all the lumps. Killen professed horror at what he was supposed to spend the night on, but Harris seemed completely unruffled.

"Slept on worse than this when I was a baby," he said, patting the mattress. "At least it's not horse-hair; filthy, itchy stuff." He threw himself on to the cot, making the whole thing wobble. "Is your grandfather really a Lord?"

Killen nodded, "Really."

"So, should I call you anything particular; 'Your Honour' or somesuch?"

"Most people call me Johnny," Killen smiled.

"Oh," Harris sat up as if surprised, and to cover his discomfiture reached into a pocket. He pulled an object out which he offered to Killen, "Biscuit?" Killen shook his head, and Harris absent-mindedly stuffed the biscuit into his own mouth then pulled it out again, staring suspiciously.

"Ships biscuit," he said to Killen's query. "They're so hard I'm surprised the weevils can stomach them, but I always like to check to make sure they haven't."


All three cornets stood to attention in front of Major Hughes' wide desk. Killen knew this would be the squadron's administrative office, but to his surprise found it neat and tidy. True, piles of papers stood on the desktop, but they were stacked with neat edges in ramrod-straight rows; a complete contrast to the desk in his grandfather's study. And the wall to his right was racked with storage boxes, each identified by a neatly written paper label.

Hughes put down his pen and slowly stood up. "Good afternoon, gentlemen." Steely grey eyes looked at each man in turn, and then, almost unexpectedly, he smiled. "I am pleased to welcome you to the 20th Light Dragoons. A fine regiment, as I am sure you all know, with a great tradition." He scratched an eyebrow. "You have met Sergeant Armstrong. Mark him well, gentlemen. He is to take charge of certain aspects of your training, and will be of great help to you in the coming months. And I counsel you, also pay heed to the troop sergeants. They are all experienced men whose advice can be invaluable to a young officer." Hughes licked his thumb and forefinger, plucking a sheet of paper from the top of one neat pile. He studied it for a moment before returning it to the stack. "Mr Killen? Mr Millward? You are both allocated to Captain Hackett's Troop. Mr Harris - you are with Captain Butterell. You will meet them and our other officers in the mess. Six o'clock sharp. Come in, sergeant!" he bellowed abruptly. Killen had heard nothing, but sure enough, the door opened and Armstrong marched in.

The sergeant whipped his hand up in a salute that would have done credit to the parade ground.

"You will accompany these gentlemen to the stables," the major ordered, "and be sure to acquaint them with their duties."

"Very good, sir," Armstrong turned on his heel so he faced the cornets and smiled as if anticipating a rare treat. "Now, sirs, if you would care to follow me?"


The familiar smell stuck in Killen's nose well before the four men entered the stable block. Stalls for over a hundred and fifty horses were laid out in neat rows, but not all of them were occupied for part of each of the two resident troops were out on exercise.

Killen found The Tempest's stall. He was worried the horse would not settle in this new environment. The stallion had grown used to the freedom of a loose-box, but now it stood confined in a narrow space between two partitions. Tied with a rope from each side of its headcollar, these were long enough to allow it to eat and drink, and to get up and lie down, but not long enough to allow the animal to bicker with its neighbours.

Killen spoke to the horse, patting its broad black rump.

Charlie Harris was impressed, "A good-looking piece of horseflesh, Johnny." He grasped the horse's nose, expertly prising open its jaws to examine the stallion's teeth. The Tempest snapped at him irritably, making him step back. "A little touchy, isn't he?"

Killen smiled. "Would you be agreeable if I thrust my dirty hands into your mouth? And he's not used to being stalled."

"You gentlemen will be expected to look after your own mounts, as part of your duties," Sergeant Armstrong interrupted with glee. He relented after being rewarded with three crestfallen looks, adding conspiratorially, "of course, any number of troopers will may be glad to earn a few shillings by performing those duties for you. Whether they should or shouldn't, that's not for me to say. May I take it that none of you gentlemen yet employs a servant?"

They wandered down the rows of stalls. Troopers in shirtsleeves dodged in and out between horses, fetching water or carrying away dung. Armstrong seemed to notice every small wrongdoing. A bucket carelessly left outside a stall earned one unfortunate cavalryman a tongue-lashing, and Killen noticed a number of other men quickly make themselves scarce on hearing the sergeant's voice.

"Here's my old fellow," Charlie Harris pointed out his bay hunter. "What do you think?" Killen ran his eye over the animal. It was nothing special to look at but Charlie was stroking its ears, obviously fond of it.

Killen picked on one of the animal's good points. "Plenty of bone, Charlie," he said, reaching down to feel one of the horse's forelegs. "He jumps well, I'll warrant."

"He does! Best hunter in the shire," Harris said proudly. He found a piece of biscuit in his pocket and presented it to the horse, which rolled the rock-hard morsel around its mouth for a while before finally spitting the indigestible lump into the straw beneath its feet.

"Sergeant!" an officer came striding towards Armstrong, and he did not look happy.

Armstrong saluted, "Sir!"

"Sergeant, where the devil has the farrier got to?" the officer demanded.

"Don't know, sir."

"A fat lot of bloody use you are," the officer said rudely, completely ignoring the three cornets standing open-mouthed. "Get off and find him. My horse," he pointed to a scrawny chestnut tied in the space at the end of the stable block, "cast a shoe this morning, and I need the damned animal for later. Be quick about it." He stalked away, and Armstrong sourly watched him go.

"Who was that?" Harris asked.

"Lieutenant Rapton," the sergeant said resignedly. "No doubt you gentlemen will get acquainted with him later."

Lieutenant Melville Rapton read the letter slowly, twice, then folded it carefully in half and tore it into tiny pieces.

"Problems?" Hugo Jamieson asked, putting down a half-empty wineglass.

Rapton shook his head, his long fair hair flapping about his collar. "My father absolutely refuses to send me any more money," he grumbled, "bloody man. I'm certain he sends it to m'wife, though."

Lieutenant Jamieson took another gulp of wine. "I didn't know you were short of cash."

"I'm not," Rapton gave a small smile, "not really. But it never hurt to have more for..." he paused, "...contingencies." He dropped the tiny paper squares onto the table and brushed them carefully into a neat pile, then pulled a second envelope from his sabretache. He peeled it open.

"God, Melville, you're popular today," Jamieson remarked. He drained his glass, waving it in the air to attract the attention of the mess steward. "Bad news this time?" he asked, in a hopeful tone.

"You're damned nosy." Rapton continued reading. "If you must know - ah, here we are - my wife professes her undying admiration for me, it seems her seamstress has taken up with the local lush, and one of the broodmares has just foaled." He folded the letter carefully before stuffing it inside the front of his uniform jacket. "Why she bothers to write such mundane drivel is completely beyond me."

The steward refilled Jamieson's glass, and Rapton gruffly ordered him to leave the bottle. He poured into his own glass before draining it in a single draught.

"Steady on!" Jamieson watched Rapton fill his glass again. The lieutenant gave him a sharp glance. "I only meant...leave some for me! The steward's going off duty."

"So?"

Jamieson looked at him quizzically.

Rapton sighed. "Get one of them to fetch more for you," he indicated the new cornets, sat together on the far side of the mess, "that's what they are here for."

Jamieson looked around carefully. The captains and two remaining lieutenants had all left. He called across the room, "You, there!"

Three cornets stared in his direction, then over their shoulders, then back towards him. He beckoned, "Yes you; over here!"

The three young men stood in a line. Rapton and Jamieson looked each of them up and down. Recruits were usually in awe of more senior officers for the first few days, Rapton thought, until familiarity overcame their nervousness, so this was the best time. "Lieutenant Jamieson requires his glass recharged," he said. "You," he pointed at Killen, "will fetch the decanter, and you," he indicated Millward, "will pour."

Killen froze. He had never, ever, been spoken to like this in his life. Servants fetched and carried, not gentlemen. He was about to say so, but stopped. Perhaps things were different in the army. But he had read Kings Regulations over and over before he arrived, determined he should do everything correctly. And now this. What would Joshua say, he wondered, and a picture formed in his head. He almost laughed.

"Did you hear me sir?" Rapton stared directly at Killen, "I gave you an order."

Killen spoke, but it was his friend who gave him the strength. "I believe, sir, that you may give me any orders pursuant to my duties, but none as befit a personal servant."

Rapton rose to his feet. "What did you say?" he began, but Charlie Harris intervened.

"It's alright sir, I'll get it." Rapton's eyes followed Harris across to the wine cabinet. He licked one index finger, stroking it across both sides of his pencil-thin moustache to lay the hairs before lowering his voice "You must take care how you address a senior officer, Mister Killen," he said in a dark tone, "for you may one day find yourself in dire need of his assistance."

Charlie Harris pulled off his boots to examine his stockinged feet before flopping backwards onto the mattress. He put his hands behind his head, as they had not yet been issued with pillows. "Rum sort of chaps, weren't they?"

Killen agreed. The three cornets had been made welcome in the mess. Their troop captains, in particular, were glad to see them, as more subalterns allowed more delegation, and for each captain less of the day-to-day drudgery of running his troop. "Why didn't you stand up to him?" Killen was disappointed.

Charlie gave a shrug. "It seemed silly to be put on a charge on our first day."

"But he treated us like servants."

Harris did not think that unusual. "It was the same at school. We were fagged by the older boys for a few weeks, until we knew what was what. Weren't you?"

"I was tutored at home," Killen admitted. He looked across the room to where Robert Millward had already gone to bed. The boy had pulled the blankets right up over his head, so his body looked a shapeless lump.

"Lucky old you. They made our lives hell to start with," Harris said ruefully.

"That will not happen here; this is the army, not school."

Harris looked at him sceptically. "I hope you're right, Johnny, I really do."


Lieutenant Rapton stalked up and down the length of his shared double room.

"For God's sake, Melville, what's got into you? You'll wear a hole in the mat if you're not careful." Edward Jamieson was amused that the altercation with the new cornets still bothered his friend. He managed to filch a bottle of wine from the mess on his way out and now held it up. "Have another drink," he encouraged, "and calm yourself."

Rapton stopped pacing to give the other man a sour look. "He won't get away with it," he said angrily. "He disobeyed my order. It's unheard of! Bloody boy thinks he's already a lord."

"It's only unheard of because you've always got away with fagging the Johnny Raws in the past." Jamieson smiled at his own wit, "I say; that's a good one!"

Rapton did not smile back, so Jamieson tried another tack. "You know," he said matter-of-factly, "that it is usual for new officers to suffer a ceremony of some kind when they first arrive."

Then Rapton did smile. It was a brilliant idea. "Edward, of course, you're right. Here," He picked up a pillow from beside his bed and threw it hard towards Jamieson, who caught it delightedly, "have one of these..." He threw another, "...or two - I believe our new friends mislaid them." The cornets must have their initiation, especially Cornet the Honourable Johnny Killen. His would be a particularly memorable occasion. Rapton would make sure of it.

Jamieson had left his wine bottle unattended, and Melville Rapton snatched it up to take a long draught.

"Now then, gentlemen!" Sergeant Patrick Armstrong bawled the words out, even though he stood only a yard in front of the three cornets. His cheeks glowed red, part-hidden beneath luxuriant moustache. "I will call each of you '*Sir*'," he invested the honorific with as much scorn as he could muster whilst just keeping clear of outright insubordination, "and you will call me 'Sergeant'. Is that clear?" A chorus of affirmation provoked a grunt of approval. "Your sabres, gentlemen," Armstrong continued.

Killen, Harris and Millward drew their swords, blades scraping through steel scabbard-throats, holding them out points upward.

"And which of you gentlemen is familiar with His Greatness General Le Marchant's instructions on the proper use of these...lumps of iron?"

No one spoke until Killen stepped forward, "Sergeant!"

Armstrong looked him up and down carefully. "Mr Killen - your sabre, sir, if you please." The sergeant reached out to take Killen's proffered sword. "Mole," he noted the name etched along the blade's spine as he examined it critically, "a fine maker." Armstrong tested the edge of the blade with his thumb and exhaled loudly. "You won't kill many Frenchmen with this, Mr Killen," he said with disgust, "you'd have to batter the poor bastards to death, pardon my language. I suggest you beg the armourers put a proper edge on it." He handed the sabre back before checking the other two curved swords on display, nodding satisfaction at both Harris and Millward. "Gentlemen, you may sheath your sabres." Armstrong picked up a pair of wooden practice swords from the ground at his feet and gave one to Killen. "Have you used one of these before sir?"

"Certainly, sergeant."

"Good. Gentlemen," he addressed the group, "Mr Killen will now assist me to demonstrate some of the required movements. Ready, sir?" he spoke to Killen again, who replied that he was.

Sergeant Armstrong proved a skilled instructor, so though Killen had practiced the cuts, parries and guards hundreds of times in the garden at home, he found a difference swinging his sword under the critical eye of a man who had probably used one in anger on a battlefield. Practising with Lock never made him as nervous as he was now; even his fencing master had not seemed as terrifying.

"Overhead guard, sir," the sergeant ordered, holding the second practice sword as if to cut at him from above, and when Killen lifted his sword so that it was horizontal above his head, Armstrong swept his own down. But instead of hitting the cornet's wooden blade as Killen expected, at the last moment the sergeant twisted his wrist so that his sword turned in mid stroke and struck Killen hard, directly on his elbow. The blow numbed his arm immediately. Killen dropped his sword and doubled over, hugging his elbow to his chest because the stinging pain was so intense.

"As you can see, gentlemen, Mr Killen made a basic error," Armstrong said smugly. "He failed to ensure that his elbow was protected, and the nasty French dragoon chopped off his arm. You must always," he emphasised the word, "*always*, keep your arm straight."

The sergeant tucked his own sword under one arm. "Fortunately for him, in this instance Mr Killen is only bruised. You two gentlemen," he said to Harris and Millward, "will go over there, where we will continue our practice." He pointed towards a wall at the far side of the parade ground on which three large, white circles had been painted. "Mr Killen - you are excused, sir, for this morning. If you are still in discomfort at midday, might I suggest you see the surgeon?"


Two evenings later Killen went into the dormitory to find Charlie Harris unbuttoning his clothes. The smell struck him seconds later. He screwed his face up in disgust.

"They tipped me into the latrines," Harris glumly explained. His stable jacket and overalls were covered with excrement and he was soaking wet. "It wasn't so bad, I suppose." He scrubbed at his face with a spare shirt which just seemed to spread the filth around.

Killen pinched his nose between thumb and forefinger. "You can't stay in here like that Charlie, you'll stink the place out." So they both tramped down to the stables and with the aid of a water bucket and yard broom managed to scrub off the worst of the muck.

Harris looked morosely at his soaking wet uniform. "Have to be laundered I suppose. It'll probably shrink, and it wasn't over-big to start."

"Who was it?" Killen refilled the bucket, working the arm of a big water pump with enthusiasm before sloshing the pail-full over Harris' boots to finish the job.

"Who'd you think?"

"Rapton and Jamieson?"

Harris put his finger to his lips. "Ssh... someone will hear. It was Jamieson and one of the others."

"Who?"

"Oh, I don't know. Smith...or Gaskell," he named two other subalterns, "or both. I couldn't see - they blindfolded me."

Killen considered. "You should tell Captain Hackett. Or the major," he advised, but Harris would have none of it.

"So they can make my life a complete misery for the next seven years? No thank you."

"They ought not get away with it."

Charlie gave a lopsided grin. "It's no worse than school. Sorry, I keep forgetting - you never went." He shivered. "I need to get out of these clothes. You realise, don't you, that it's likely your turn next?"

"And do you realise you still smell?" Killen retorted, but he was thinking about his turn, and he shivered.

It happened three nights later, and Killen was unprepared. He woke only as the sack was pulled over his head, and his protests were muted when something was tied over his face, gagging his mouth. At least he could breathe. The sacking felt thick and coarse against his skin, and he could not see through it. It went down past his waist; his arms bound to his sides. A flour sack; he could taste it. Whatever kept the thing in place was so tight he could hardly wriggle. He kicked out, but a rope must have been looped around his legs, for they were suddenly jerked together and he could no longer move them. Then he was picked up and carried bodily out of the room.

No-one spoke. Killen heard their boots scrunch on the gravel yard. He must have been carried a short distance outside the barracks, for he could feel a breeze on his bare legs, but then, to his surprise, he was lifted up and thrown on his belly over a horse.

"They'll hear us," a voice said, "you should have covered their feet," but the thick sacking muffled the words so he could not tell who had spoken.

The horses walked for about twenty minutes before halting. Killen's chest and stomach ached from lying across the saddle, but now hands grabbed him to drag him from the horse's back. He landed awkwardly, stumbling, and more hands pulled him upright. He felt dirt under his bare feet, the small stones it contained prickling uncomfortably. Then hands grabbed his legs, lifting his feet until they were level with his shoulders, and he felt himself thrown.

Hitting cold water unexpectedly, Killen gasped in shock, but the gag made it difficult to get enough air into his lungs. He fought down a feeling of panic. He was sitting on a solid surface, not out of his depth in a pond or river. The panic subsided until someone pushed his head down, and for a second he was underwater. Killen wondered if this was how it felt to be drowning, for he could not remember. He struggled to sit upright. Then his head was released. His face cleared the surface and, thankfully, he could breathe again. Just about.

"I think that's enough." Even though Killen's ears were full of water he heard the words distinctly.

"Oh, no..."

Killen recognised that voice: Rapton!

"...nowhere near enough. Not yet." Killen's head was pushed underwater again. This time he was more prepared and gasped a breath as soon as he felt hands touch him. It was just as well, for they held him under for longer. When eventually he was released, the saturated sack weighed him down. But mercifully his gag had loosened. He could suck air into his lungs.

A muffled conversation seemed to be going on between the kidnappers. Killen presumed they were deciding what to do next. They were taking their time about it - perhaps a ducking had not been in their plans. The water was freezing. Killen thought he had probably been tipped into a trough for watering livestock, and he started to shiver. The murmuring abruptly stopped, then several pairs of hands dragged him upright before heaving him out of the water. He could feel the breeze again, but now it cut through his soaked nightgown. His shivers grew worse; his whole body shook. But he could move his legs. The rope must have slipped off. He had to get away.

Killen took two steps forward and must have surprised his captors for he broke free from their grip, but then something smacked him across the shins. He tumbled over. Killen had plenty of practice falling from horses; his body twisted, an automatic reaction, so that he crashed onto his shoulder rather than his face. He struggled to free himself from the sack, kicking out with both feet. He caught one of his abductors a blow on the legs for there was a grunt when he felt the impact, then one of them kicked him in the stomach, twice, knocking what little breath he had from his body. He lay still.

"Get him up," Rapton ordered. Again, he was grabbed and lifted. This time they dragged him for some distance, then held him upright against a hard object: a pole? A tree - Killen felt rough bark scrape his back. And one of them must have brought more rope, because he was tied, around the chest, this time, and though he struggled, the bonds would not move. It was hopeless. He shivered harder.

There was a shout. Distant, though. Killen could not quite make it out, but then he heard it again.

"Oi - you!" A coarse voice: common. Horses' hooves scuffed gravel. Saddles creaked.

A voice hissed in Killen's ear, "We don't take kindly to insubordination." Then there was a fist in his stomach. Killen needed to double over, to be sick, but his bonds held him. He heard horses trotting away. They had abandoned him there.

But then heavy footsteps came closer. Hands were untying the rope that held him up; coarse hands, common hands. And when the knots came undone, and the sack was torn off, he collapsed to the ground.


Killen sat in front of a roaring fire cradling a cup of tea when the major arrived. Hughes spent several minutes speaking with the landlord of the Brown Bear Inn before he came over and dropped a canvas bag onto the floor. He dragged a stool across the dusty boards and sat opposite.

"Your uniform, Mr Killen; and boots," the major said gruffly, indicating the bag. He stared into Killen's eyes for a few seconds, seeming satisfied. "I take it you are able to ride?"

"Yes, sir."

"Excellent. I have a spare horse. Be ready to leave shortly." He nodded in the landlord's direction. "I must pay your saviour for his trouble."

Killen said nothing on the ride back. Hughes talked. The landlord of the inn had freed Killen from the flour-sack before despatching an ostler to the barracks, where Hughes happened to be duty officer that day.

"You know who was responsible?" Hughes asked, and when Killen did not answer went on, "I can do nothing unless I know with certainty." Killen stayed silent, and the major gave him a sidelong glance. "I appreciate your reluctance to cause trouble for a fellow officer, Johnny, but think of others who might suffer a similar fate, or worse," he persuaded. "Would you want that?"

Killen was torn. Rapton deserved some punishment; a censure at least. But that would mean he would have to tell. '*Snitch*', the men would call him, behind his back. '*Tell-tale*'; running to the major at the first sign of trouble. The officers would find out initially, but soon the sergeants would hear of it, then the troopers. They would all point him out, sniggering behind his back.

"Well?" Hughes persisted, but Killen remained silent so eventually the major sighed and let the subject rest.

# 1807

# Chapter 14

At first, Lock did not worry when he heard another smith had moved into Halcombe village. He had more pressing concerns.

Abraham began to rise later each morning, retiring to bed earlier; his breathing grew steadily more laboured, and judging from the number of times he bumped into things, his sight had failed. The old man no longer greeted customers, even those he had known for years, and increasingly shut himself away, appearing only for meals. At them he ate very little. Lock sometimes heard his grandfather in the hours before dawn, struggling for breath against a steadily worsening cough.

But Lock was kept busy. Chores must be completed even before he lit the forge. There were animals to feed. Tea to brew: floors to be swept. His days went by in a flurry of activity. Fewer customers called, but he seemed to have just as much to do.

Then one morning, Abraham did not get out of bed, and it was only after he had fed the chickens and collected the few eggs in the coop that Lock noticed. When he pushed open the door to Abraham's room, his grandfather seemed to be asleep. Lock shook his shoulder, but the old man refused to wake. There was blood on his lips; just a smear, but more stained the pillow where he had turned his head during the night.


Doctor Wyles looked at Abraham Lock with disapproval. The old man had patently failed to look after himself. His face was filthy, dirt ingrained in the deep lines around his eyes. The doctor bent over, so his ear was close to Abraham's mouth. The old man's breaths were shallow.

Wyles paused to think. Abraham's lips were bloody; a sure sign of tubercles in his lungs, but the noise from his chest, which the doctor could discern clearly without the aid of a listening-trumpet, suggested much worse. He had a high temperature, too, higher than Wyles had seen for some time. Perhaps he was contagious? The doctor extracted a large handkerchief from his bag, deftly knotting it around his face so it covered his nose and mouth. The old man's pulse was weak, fluttering sometimes, and he had soiled himself. Wyles screwed up his nose at the smell. It seemed Abraham Lock was unlikely to prove a worthwhile investment.

"I am very much afraid it is bad news," Wyles told Lock firmly, closing the room door behind him to shut off the old man from his grandson's view. "There are signs of fever; possibly a contagion."

"I thought it must be the consumption."

Wyles frowned at the boy. Still arrogant and opinionated, he decided. "I believe the fever has made his illness worse," he said, his voice slightly muffled under his mask.

"Can't you do anything?"

"There is no definitive cure," the doctor shook his head, "you may make him more comfortable. Try to feed him some broth. But the fever must take its course." The boy gave him a haunted look but Wyles felt no pity. "That will be three guineas, if you please."

Lock crossed to the back wall of the cottage and wiggled a loose stone until it came free. He reached in the hole, withdrawing a handful of coins before counting out the fee onto the table, instead of Wyles' outstretched hand. The doctor snorted crossly when he saw the number of copper and silver coins. They would weigh heavily in his pocket and spoil the cut of his coat. He checked the amount carefully before shovelling the coins away.

"And do try to keep him clean," he criticised over his shoulder as he left.

Wyles did not take the handkerchief from his face until he had mounted his horse and was riding away. The old man might have the fever; he might not, but there was no sense in taking a chance with his own health. It was well known that the foul air inside sick rooms increased the risk of contagion, and that dingy hovel had the feel of death about it. He gave an involuntary shudder, but soon relaxed. The old man would die, so he would not have to visit the place again. And his next call should be more pleasant; the storekeeper's wife was pregnant. Her progress must be checked and confinement mused upon. It meant the prospect of a gift of provisions, as well as a fee. Wyles pushed the white handkerchief further down into his pocket and promptly forgot it, for he suddenly felt much better.

The parish priest waddled towards Wyles as he rode into Halcombe village. The clergyman led a horse which seemed to match his rotund shape. It was limping slightly, and the doctor saw that one of its front shoes was missing. The doctor raised his hat.

"Good morning, Father."

The priest was red-faced. His horse must have been reluctant to walk and he tugged at its taut leadrope before replying. "I wish it were, my son," he said with some exasperation. "Nothing wrong at the smithy, I trust?"

Wyles looked at the other man carefully before he answered. But he was the village priest, after all. What harm could there be in a little gossip? "I am very much afraid Abraham Lock has the fever."

The priest looked alarmed. "Contagious?"

"It is possible." Wyles shrugged, "These things can be difficult to diagnose." Lord Halcombe's grandson came to mind; he had said much the same thing about that young man's ague. Then, though, the Lock boy had interfered. "I cannot tell with certainty," the doctor continued, his voice growing cross with memory, "and the damned Jewry are oft disposed to a severity of complaint we Christians are not."

The priest gave Wyles a look of surprise, but nodded as if in understanding. "I will pray for him, doctor. It is all we can do." He dragged his horse round in a circle and struggled slowly back the way he had come.


Lock was shocked at how little money remained in the hiding place. He should have taken more notice of how many customers had called at the smithy; of how many paid him. Business was often done with a promise of payment, or even a trade. He opened his hand, letting what coins were left rattle onto the table. Four shillings and elevenpence, three-farthings. He counted again, grimaced, and went out to light the forge.

No-one came. Not a single horse crossed the yard. There was not a scythe to reshape, or a broken door-hinge to fix. Lock crawled into the hen coop and retrieved two eggs. They would have to do for supper. He stared hard at one of the chickens, which was old with tattered plumage, but decided he would have to be very desperate before he rung its scrawny neck. Abraham seemed no worse but still stubbornly refused to wake. Lock wrung out a cloth in cold water to lay across his forehead in an attempt to cool the old man's face. It was pointless trying to feed him anything as he would not swallow, so Lock broke the eggs into a pan and cooked them for himself.

The following morning found Abraham's condition worse. His breathing was shallower, and beads of sweat showed on his face. Lock wiped the moisture away, feeling helpless. His grandfather's skin was clammy and pale. The doctor had been right; the fever was winning.

Lock decided he must try one thing more. Abraham kept jars of medicinal herbs in the smithy, and would sell them to villagers and farm-workers who wanted to cure a horse with colic, or a calf with a bruised foot. He found the jar that contained willow bark and steeped a few pieces in a pan of boiling water. When it cooled he would try to get Abraham to drink it. Then he gathered up the loose coins from where they still lay on the tabletop and took the mare's bridle and a canvas knapsack from where they hung on the back of the cottage door.

The village seemed deserted. Lock slid down from the old mare's back. He left her loose to graze at the roadside, knowing she would not wander very far. He needed bread, and other supplies were running low. Four shillings and eleven-pence would not buy much, but it would be enough. At least until more horses needed to be shod, or ironwork made or repaired.

There were two women in the grocery. Both stared at Lock as he went in then hurried past, out through the doorway. He knew both of them by sight and was surprised they had not spoken, but his mind was occupied elsewhere, so he took little notice. He collected what he needed, stacking the goods on the counter.

The storekeeper stood with his back to the shelves behind. Lock sorted out the correct coins. He offered them, and the man stretched a long way forward to catch them in his palm. Lock thought that a little odd. He pushed the provisions into his knapsack and slung it over his shoulder. It seemed that the grocer's wife had a cold, for she held her shawl across her face. Lock caught her eye as he was leaving, making her look guiltily away.


It was when he went to catch up the old mare that a stranger stepped in Lock's path. A big man: bearded. He stood with his arms folded and feet spread apart. It must be the other smith, Lock decided, holding out his hand to introduce himself.

The stranger ignored it. "What are you doing here?"

Lock was surprised at the man's tone. A few more villagers, men mostly, had sauntered over, but stayed some way behind the new smith. The bearded man repeated his brusque question, and Lock found his anger rising. "Looking for custom." He counted in his head, forcing himself to be civil.

*One.*

*Two.*

"You won't find any here." The bearded man grinned, checking around him. "It seems everyone's my customer now."

Lock abruptly stopped counting. "There would be plenty for both of us," he said hotly, "if you weren't greedy."

The other smith's eyes narrowed. "If Jews bring fever to a village," he said darkly, "they deserve all they get."

Lock was confused. He'd never been called a Jew before, and wondered where the smith had heard it. "You're wrong."

"You're the one in the wrong," the smith stepped closer, "and no-one wants you here." He stood between Lock and where the old grey mare still grazed undisturbed, but Lock's temper was rising and he was not going to go around.

"Out of my way."

"Or?"

Lock strode determinedly forward, intending to shoulder the other smith out of the way, but the bearded man was taller and heavier. He struck Lock in the chest with such force that the boy was knocked backwards and sat down. The impact winded him. The other smith stood over him. Lock looked up.

"Now, go, or next time it'll be worse." The smith turned on his heel and walked away, followed by those villagers who had been watching, talking and laughing like crows behind a ploughman.

Lock picked himself up and shamefacedly beat the dust from his breeches. The storekeeper and his wife were watching, but quickly closed their door when he glanced towards them. His old mare lifted her head when Lock caught her bridle, standing patiently while he clambered up burdened with the knapsack. Then the boy turned away from the village and, giving the mare a kick, headed back towards the smithy.


In the middle of the night, Lock woke. His grandfather had cried out, he thought, but when he went into Abraham's room the old man still lay asleep on his back, his breathing at times hardly strong enough to lift his chest and at others rattling in his throat. It must have been a wandering fox that screamed, Lock decided

Abraham had taken none of the linctus Lock prepared. The boy tried to force it down his throat by lifting his head and pouring it into his mouth, but the old man just coughed, dribbling it out. Soup fared no better, which meant his grandfather had eaten nothing for three days.

Lock felt for a pulse. Slow and unsteady it might be, but his heart still pumped blood around his body. His arm felt cool, but his face burned, sweat beading his forehead. It was strange but, in the lamplight, Lock thought Abraham looked more at ease than he had in days. Again he soaked a cloth in cold water and rung it out to wipe away the salty streaks on his grandfather's face. Then he laid the cloth on the old man's forehead. It would cool his brow for a while, and Lock needed to sleep.


Spring sun was already streaming through dusty cottage windows when Lock woke. It was well past dawn. The chickens called to be let out. Lock rubbed his eyes and swung his feet from under the blanket.

Overnight, the kitchen fire had gone out. He walked barefoot across the flags and after scraping the ashes to one side grabbed a handful of kindling from the bucket alongside the hearth. It took a few strokes of his tinderbox to light, but once a small flame started to flicker and grow Lock added larger sticks and a log. After a while the wood burned fiercely enough for him to fill a kettle and hang it on a blackened hook in the fireplace. He needed tea.

The chickens still squawked annoyance. On his way out to their coop Lock pushed open his grandfather's bedroom door. The old man lay asleep on his back, but his breathing was quiet. That did not seem quite right. Lock went in quickly and looked down at Abraham's face. The wet rag from the night before still lay across his forehead. His eyes were closed, mouth hanging slightly open. Lock reached out to touch the old man's cheek, half-afraid of what he might feel. It was cold.

The chickens would have to wait a while longer.


Hinges screeched a protest as Lock pushed open the church door, startling the priest who struggled to his feet, using the altar rail to haul himself up and leaving a single candle balanced there. Its flame flickered in a draught from the open door.

"What can I do for you, my son?"

"My grandfather has died," Lock explained, without emotion. He had not been inside the church for years. Now he must, for Abraham's sake. "He needs a funeral."

The priest's eyes widened, and to Lock's surprise the man suddenly stepped back, away from him.

"I am afraid that is impossible," the stocky clergyman shook his head, and lifting the maniple from his left arm held it over his nose and mouth. The thick silky material made his voice small.

"I can pay," Lock lied. Perhaps the man needed some persuasion.

The priest shook his head again. "He cannot be buried here."

Lock was puzzled. "I don't understand. Abraham worshipped here all his life."

"The children of Israel follow a separate path," the priest said flatly. "He cannot be buried here. You must leave."

"But..."

"You must leave," the priest became insistent. The timbre of his voice rose; his hands trembled, "Now."

Lock's temper flared, and he did not bother to try to control it. "Damn you," he shouted, and as the priest cowered, the altar cross caught his eye. It carried an effigy of the Christ, stretched in crucifixion, the pain of the crown of thorns carved deeply in its face. Lock snatched up the candle from the altar rail, careless of its flame.

"And damn you," he yelled at the Christ as he hurled the candle. It struck the wooden cross and toppled it from altar to floor, crashing the quiet. Lock gave the priest an angry glare and stalked back down the knave.


Even though the soil had not yet been hardened by hot weather, it took Lock all afternoon to dig a grave. The ground he had chosen, behind the cottage, was stony, and the clay soil stuck stubbornly to his shovel.

His anger which, still blazing, had driven the blade deep, splitting rocks and tree roots with equal ease, spent itself at last, and he sat exhausted at the bottom of the hole. He decided there was something unpleasant about the mud walls that rose towards the sky all around him. From its depths the grave seemed tiny. Lock closed his eyes. He had a sudden vision of the walls collapsing; earth and stones toppling in on him, burying him deeper and deeper until he was completely smothered. He shivered and jumped to his feet, clambering out. The edge of the shovel blade was ruined. Lock stared at the damage before hurling it away, into the bushes. Stupid, he realised. He could fix it.

When Abraham had been carried to the hole, his body covered with earth, rammed down and topped with muddy stones, Lock knew he should say something, but had no idea what.

So he went to the smithy. And after he had stoked the fire, pumping the bellows handle until flames roared angrily inside the chimney, he made a marker for the grave. Lock fashioned a simple cross, hammered from flat iron bars. He rounded each end using different sizes and weights of hammer, carefully filing the edges, returning to the anvil again and again until he got exactly the shape he wanted. Finally he sharpened one long end into a spike.

And after the red iron had turned to dull grey in the cooling tank, he planted the cross at Abraham's head, and hammered it deep.

# Part II

# In the wilderness

# Chapter 15

Next morning, Lock lay on his cot until well after sunrise, staring at the ceiling timbers. There were chores to be done, but, it seemed, no reason to do them. A dry throat eventually persuaded him to get up, to light a fire and brew tea.

No-one came. In the evening, Lock ate the last of the bread he had bought in the village. He pulled absent-mindedly at the stone block over the hole that hid his money and looked behind it; pennies. He would have to earn more soon, or go hungry. But he supposed there was always tomorrow.

He went to bed early. A bright moon shone, and as he stared at it through the window Lock wondered what John Killen was doing. Making new friends, probably; having adventures, meeting girls. Perhaps he should leave the village; find a new life; make a new start somewhere. Now his grandfather was gone there was nothing to hold him here except the smithy. But there was no need to make a decision now; tomorrow would be soon enough. Tomorrow.

No-one came. The sky glowered, overcast, and during the morning it started to rain. At a miserable midday, Lock killed a chicken to roast over the fire. He could not tell if it was the laying bird or not, but he was hungry. He fed its offal to the polecat, which had not eaten for two days. The hungry animal had started making piteous mewing noises every time he passed its cage. He managed to scorch the chicken carcase on the outside, and it was undercooked inside, but he ate it all anyway, and wondered what he should do.


Lock was soaked by the time he reached Halcombe House. He had worn a wide-brimmed hat and long coat to keep off the worst of the downpour, but every so often, when he tilted his head, the hat dribbled a stream of water down his chest. He walked carefully around to the stables, trying to remain hidden from any watchers at the house.

Edward Gaunt opened the tack-room door to his knock. "Joshua?"

"I need to speak with you."

Gaunt stepped back, pulling the door wide. "Come in. You're soaked: go and stand by the fire." Lock shrugged off his coat. "Do you want some tea," Gaunt asked but had obviously not expected a reply as he was already reaching into the cupboard.

"I need some work."

Gaunt put a steaming mug on the table but remained standing. "Smithing work, do you mean?"

"Anything will do at the moment."

Gaunt shook his head. "I'm sorry, Joshua, but even if his lordship would allow it, I don't need any extra staff. The hunting season's come to an end, and with Master Johnny not here most of the horses have already been roughed off."

"Have you heard how he is?"

"Missing him, are you?" Gaunt was unable to suppress a smile. "His lordship's not mentioned anything." His face became serious. "Sorry to hear about your grandfather, though." Lock picked up the tea-mug and sipped the brown liquid. It tasted as disgusting as usual, but he was comforted, though Gaunt still kept back.

He stared at the Stud Groom through narrowed eyes. "Don't think I'm infectious, do you, Edward?"

Gaunt looked embarrassed. "I heard it in the village," he admitted.

Lock's anger flared. "He never had the fever," he said crossly. "It was the consumption. He had it for years."

"So that's why you haven't any work?"

"They can believe what they want. I'm sick of them. Abraham lived here nearly all his life."

Gaunt shook his head sadly. "People don't like things they don't understand. Just like horses, really. They get frightened."

Lock would have none of it. "They don't care. You can't defend them, Edward. They didn't even bother to try to find out the truth," he complained bitterly. "The priest even insisted to me we were Jewish, to avoid having to hold a funeral."

"I heard that, too."

Lock sighed, his anger slowly fading. Gaunt stepped forward a few paces, and he offered the Stud Groom the ghost of a smile. "Thanks, Edward."

"For what?"

Lock drained his tea-mug and put it back on the table "You always manage to help me."

Gaunt looked puzzled. "But I've done nothing."

"Will you lend me the horse-pistol?" Lock asked, nodding towards the drawer where it was kept.

"I still don't understand."

"I'll drop it back tomorrow, early," Lock said. He had made up his mind. He would leave. He could forgive the village for its fear but not its lack of charity. There must be something better, somewhere, and he would find it. Gaunt put the pistol into his hands and looked at him enquiringly.

Lock pulled off the rag wrapped around the weapon and smelled the gun-oil. "If you're not about," he said, "I'll leave it on the step."


Rain still fell, but Lock did not care for there was work to do. He scraped cold ashes from the forge and cleared out the bellows nozzle which was clogged with clinker. Dark corners of the smithy floor seemed not to have been cleaned for years, and when he had thrown the sweepings outside and let the dust settle, he took down all the tools from where they hung around the iron canopy that directed smoke up the chimney, laying them in a long row on the flags. Hammers and chisels; spikes and tongs - the iron was dark with age but their handles were worn; polished silver-smooth from use. Lock first wiped them with oil then rolled them into a bolt of faded canvas he found laid across the rafters. They would stay safe until he came back, whenever that might be.

In late afternoon, the rain stopped. Strangely, the temperature rose, unrolling a carpet of water vapour that swirled about Lock's ankles as he walked up to the paddock. He took the horse pistol. Tucked into his waist belt, the heavy weapon dug into his midriff with every step; a dread reminder of his task. It had to be done, though.

The old grey mare meandered across and nuzzled his hand. Lock had agonised about taking her along with him. Riding her would make his journey easier, more comfortable, but what would happen to her at its end? The horse was older than he. Abraham had put him on her back as a baby, and she had ambled placidly round. Should she be sold on, to work again until the end of her life? She did not deserve that.

Lock pulled out the pistol. He cocked it, loud in the quiet after the rain. The old mare stood quietly, unknowing and unconcerned. He aimed the short barrel carefully and pulled the trigger. And although he had killed horses before, he never got used to the violence; the sudden crash to the ground, legs thrashing though the eye was blank with all life gone. The stillness, afterwards. And something else, deep inside; a hurt, as if part of him died too. He had never got used to that, either.

The old mare looked so small, lying flat. A trickle of bright red blood dripped from one nostril onto the grass. Lock turned away, and a thing happened he had not experienced since he was a small boy. An unexpected emotion; one he could not control, hard though he fought. He cried.

# Chapter 16

After clearing Halcombe's vague boundaries, Lock headed north-west for Gloucester. He was in no rush. The rain of the day before had cleared and the dawn sky glowed pink, not red, with the promise of a fine day.

He had risen well before sunrise. The knapsack contained all he needed to take with him; everything that he owned, and now it hung heavily over one shoulder, bouncing on his hip as he walked. The polecat lay curled up, a lump under his jacket, asleep in the warmth, supported by the string Lock tied around his waist to stop the coat flapping open. He might use the animal to catch a rabbit for dinner, and if not? A tame polecat should fetch a decent price at any market he might come upon.

The sun came up. In front of him a skylark rose into the air, first singer in the chorus that heralded dawn. He watched the tiny speck fluttering higher and higher into the lightening sky, until it was lost from view. Perhaps he could be like a bird. Like John Killen; flying higher and higher until Lock could see him no longer. He laughed at himself, looking down at his big hands and feet. He could no more be a skylark than a mole.

In the distance Lock saw a few big draught horses starting work in the fields. Their breath misted the cool air and clouds of tiny early-birds darted at their feet, hunting insects the giants disturbed, hopping deftly out of reach of death-black crows which pecked and clawed at the fresh furrow behind the ploughman.

He turned off the road onto a drovers' track that meandered slowly westwards. Here, the grass grew longer. Dew washed the mud from his boots, but soon seeped through old repairs. Lock stopped after a while and took off his wet stockings, re-lacing the boots onto bare feet. He tried tying the stockings to the strap of his knapsack, hoping the morning sun would dry them, but their vile smell soon persuaded him against the idea. So he screwed them into a ball and pushed them into a pocket. They could dry out later.

Around midday the polecat began to stir. Lock suffered its sharp claws digging through his shirt for a while, but eventually put his hand inside his coat to dig the animal out. It blinked in the sunlight. "Hungry, are you," Lock spoke to the polecat absent-mindedly, but he was thinking the same about himself. He sought out a flat stone at the side of the track to sit on. Rummaging in the knapsack, he found the cheese he had carefully wrapped in a rag the night before. The polecat refused to touch the small piece he offered it, so Lock tied his string belt around its neck as a lead to let it wander while he ate. It found a beetle in the long grass, batting it around for a while as Lock watched. Eventually the polecat decided the insect was edible and crunched it noisily. Lock pulled a face.

Half a mile further on was a stream to negotiate. Lock had brought nothing to carry water, so drank before he crossed, scooping un-muddied water to his mouth with one hand. Once the ripples he made had cleared, he spotted minnows darting about and walked upstream for a few minutes, searching for a deep pool that might hold bigger fish. But he found nothing so returned to the fording place, taking off his boots and tying the laces around his neck to avoid soaking the leather once again.

Towards evening, he came across a briar patch with a telltale depression in the ground running towards a tunnel through the thorns. The polecat caught one rabbit, dragging it above ground triumphantly. Lock made a small fire in the hedgerow's shelter before he skinned and gutted the carcase. The polecat got the inedible bits and was still happily chewing on stringy intestines as the sun set. Taking his jacket from the knapsack Lock put it on before buttoning his wool coat on top, tying the string belt around his waist. He pulled the collar up around his ears and settled down for the night. If it rained, his overcoat would keep out the worst of the weather.


The following day dawned clear. Lock walked all morning, turning off the drovers' track when it met a well-travelled road. Up ahead a pair of stone cottages stood one either side of the road, but when he reached them they appeared deserted. He soon saw why. Beyond lay a small village crowded with people.. A market, probably, and where there was a market, there would be a tavern. Lock reached into his trouser pocket. Enough coppers jingled there to buy a jug of ale, and all his walking had given him a thirst. He increased his pace.

The beer tasted good. Lock swigged it straight from the jug, not bothering with a tankard, as he mingled with the market customers. There was plenty to look at; stalls selling vegetables; meat stalls; fabrics and haberdashery. Sweetmeat sellers were out in force, catching the eyes of children with unwary parents; there were hawkers, flower-sellers, and even one girl selling kisses. Lock looked at her with a certain amount of admiration, but he was down to his last few pennies and thought that she was probably not worth starving for.

Something flapped to Lock's right, arousing his curiosity. He walked across to look and found a notice, nailed to a sapling.

## RIFLE CORPS!
COUNTRYMEN!
LOOK BEFORE YOU LEAP
Half the Regiments in the service are tying to persuade you to Enlist
But there is ONE MORE to COME YET!!!
## The 95th; or
## Rifle REGIMENT
The first of all Services in the British Army
NO WHITE BELTS! NO PIPECLAY!

The bottom of the page had been torn off.

"Not thinking of joining them, are you?" a voice from behind him asked.

Lock turned his head, "Why not?" he asked over his shoulder.

"Too much like hard work."

Lock twisted around to face the man. He had to look down, for the speaker stood a head shorter, brushing at the front of his blue uniform jacket with both hands as if trying to clean the grubby white lacing stretched decoratively across his chest.

"Why do you say that?"

The other man stared down at Lock's boots and then up at his face. "You've been walking. A good distance I would say?" Lock stayed silent, but the uniformed man seemed to take his lack of a response as normal. He pointed at the poster. "Join them," he went on, "and you'll be doing more of it - a lot more. March everywhere, they do. Farm-boy, are you?" he changed the subject.

"Smith."

"Well, now," the man smiled, "well, now. I should have realised by the size of you. They prefer shorter men in the Rifles, you know, lad. And why walk, when you could be riding. You want to be joining the cavalry." He patted his chest with pride, "We've plenty of work for a good smith."

Lock shook his head. John Killen had left to join the cavalry. The hurt still rankled. Why should he do the same? "I hear they need smiths in the mines." It was true. Coal miners used iron tools, and ponies used to pull the coal-tubs needed to be shod. Mine-owners were always on the lookout for smiths, but Lock had never wanted to work underground. Graves and moles came to mind.

"And why are they always looking? The dust gets them." The cavalryman scrubbed determinedly at the sergeant's stripes on his right sleeve, as if to stop coal dust getting them, too. "Dries out their lungs and kills them, stone dead."

"Not me."

The sergeant shrugged. "'Course, the pay's not bad, but you'll have to find board and lodgings somewhere. Not much left in a man's pocket once you take that out."

Lock was thoughtful, "So how much does the army pay?"

"Come with me, lad," the sergeant smiled, like a poacher tickling a fat trout. "Come with me."


At the back of the tavern, a few tables were scattered, most seating at least one man in uniform. Two serving girls scurried between them replacing jugs of ale that had been emptied down dry throats. A recruiting party, Lock realised. Well, it seemed that the ale was free so there was no harm in finding out what the army might offer.

The sergeant made for a table without any occupants. "Sit here lad," he instructed, "and if any other uniform comes along, you tell him you're with me. Sergeant Kyle, that's who I am." He held out a hand for Lock to shake. "I won't be longer than a few ticks," Kyle grinned. "If you see a serving wench with a full jug, grab her."

One girl brought ale and a fistful of mugs without being asked. Lock poured himself a drink while he waited; twisting in his seat to watch what was going on. It seemed a good number of local men were being persuaded to join up, for he saw silver coins accepted, accompanied by a great deal of handshaking and back-slapping. A woman with two small children stood behind one potential recruit. Lock thought she looked tearful, but could not be sure. He drained his mug, wondering why he still felt thirsty.

Another soldier sat down at the table. Lock turned towards the newcomer and stared, for the man's uniform jacket was bright yellow; the braid a pristine white. "I'm with Sergeant Kyle," Lock said.

The other man nodded, "Pay me no mind." He picked up the ale jug and poured into an empty tankard. After he had taken a long draught, he wiped his mouth on his sleeve, looking Lock in the eye. "You're staring, boy."

"I'm sorry." Lock had not realised. He held out his hand. "Joshua Lock."

The cavalryman made no move to take it, but put his own hand behind his back, drawing out a trumpet. He fished a rag from inside its bell and began to rub at the bright brass.

Lock took his hand back. He lifted the ale jug to refill his glass. "I never met a negro before," he offered, by way of explanation.

The cavalryman put his instrument down. He took another drink, seeming to consider. "We stopped eating white folks years back," he said dourly, "too stringy, often." Then he abruptly stood.

Sergeant Kyle had returned. He carried another jug of beer, and looked at the negro with suspicion. "What are you doing here, Picker?"

"Just passing the time of day, sergeant."

"Well, get your black hide around to the stables and check on the horses."

Picker stood up and slung the trumpet over his shoulder. He raised his eyebrows slightly at Lock. "Don't lose your shilling," he offered, obscurely, as he left.

Sergeant Kyle frowned while he watched the trumpeter walk away before sitting down. He poured ale from the new jug into Lock's still-empty tankard. "So what did Trumpeter Picker say to you?" he demanded.

"I asked why his uniform was a different colour," Lock lied, wondering why the sergeant's tone was less friendly than before, but Kyle seemed to relax at the reply. He smiled again, lifting an ale jug to fill a glass for himself, "Ah, his trumpeter's costume. Did he tell you why it's so bright?"

"Didn't get time."

The sergeant warmed to his explanation, "Because, it makes him easier to spot on a battlefield." He supped more ale. "Ever been in a battle, lad? No," he went on, answering his own question, "don't suppose you have. There are men; thousands of them. Foot, and horse. And cannon. Lots of noise. And there's smoke, from cannon and musket. Half the time, you can hardly see your hand in front of your face. And the trumpeters, they have to call out the orders, see?" He scratched the top of his head, pulling away a couple of loose hairs. "So the Colonel, he has to be able to see where his trumpeters are, in all the muck flying about." Taking a last, regretful look at the hairs he tossed them away, over his shoulder. "D'you know what I'm telling you, lad?"

"I understand what you're saying, sergeant," Lock nodded.

"Now the Colonel," Kyle went on, "Lieutenant-Colonel Taylor, he says we must have a blackie as trumpeter. Other regiments? They have them, so we must have one too. It's the fashion, see? Bloody daft if you ask me, pardon my language." Lock did see. He began to feel some sympathy for Trumpeter Picker.

"'Course, we don't let him fight. Wouldn't do to have blackies fighting for good King George."

Lock thought he remembered John Killen talking about native troops in India, and there was something else he had heard. "But I thought they recruited negros into the Royal Navy."

Sergeant Kyle leant over and spat on the ground. "They allow a lot of things in the bloody navy that gentlemen in the army wouldn't countenance," he said with disgust.

The polecat began to wriggle inside Lock's jacket. He could feel its claws through his shirt. Sergeant Kyle noticed the movement too, and was staring at him oddly. Lock put down his ale to untie the string around his middle, and the polecat poked its head out.

The sergeant leaned forward to scratch the animal's scalp with a grubby fingernail. "Friendly little thing, isn't he?" he started, but had to draw back his hand smartly when the polecat made a grab for the end of his finger with sharply pointed teeth. "They don't allow pets in the army, lad," he observed in warning, but Lock was unworried.

"So how much," he said slowly, "will I get paid?"

All the potential recruits gathered in an empty room at the back of the tavern. Tables and benches were dragged in and they sat, expectantly. Seven men, including Lock, seemed ready to be persuaded that their futures lay in the King's service. Most were scruffily dressed, like he was, and wore brown, weather-beaten faces. Farm workers, probably, looking for an easier life. Lock ignored the conversation around him because for some strange reason, he had begun to feel very tired. The serving girls re-appeared with more jugs of ale, one for each table. Lock usually drank little, but this beer was free. He poured himself a glassful and sipped at it.

"Lads, lads," Sergeant Kyle got to his feet and the room grew quiet. "You all know why you're here; I know why you're here." He looked over everybody's heads and nodded. Two troopers stood up and crossed to the door. They stationed themselves, one each side. Lock fleetingly wondered why, but Kyle was speaking again. "You're sick of your lives; sick of people who treat you like dirt. Sick of having no money. Sick of being ignored by the ladies."

A rumble of agreement encouraged the sergeant to continue, and a there was a guffaw as an obviously married man received a slap across the head. Kyle put up his hands, trying to stop the noise. "I know, I know. I was like you once. You can't believe it can you? That I, Sergeant Frederick Kyle, was once a nobody, with no friends, no job and no money?" He paused for effect. The room stayed completely silent. "But now look at me, lads," he patted his stomach, "well fed, well watered and with gold in my pocket." He shook the leg of his overalls so everyone could hear coins jingle. "And the ladies - oh, the ladies," Kyle sighed dramatically, provoking laughter, "they look up to me; they vie for my attention. The ladies all love a cavalryman; often several times a night."

The audience laughed again. Lock rubbed his eyes. He stifled a yawn, trying to stay awake.

"But the best part, I've saved for last." Sergeant Kyle beamed around the room. "Take the King's shilling, lads, and not only will you avail yourselves of all the advantages I've described, but there's the bounty. Aye - the bounty. Twenty pounds! Twenty pounds for each and every one who takes His Majesty's silver."

"It should be more," a voice hissed in Lock's ear. "I heard it was more."

Sergeant Kyle heard the whisper. "Who was that?" he said frostily. "Who spoke?" The guilty man raised his hand. Kyle marched forwards to stand in front of him. "What did you say, boy?"

"I thought...," the young man looked embarrassed, "...I thought it was more than twenty pounds. Someone told me..."

"I see." Kyle's voice was flinty. "So someone told you I'm a liar. Is that it?"

"N-no, sergeant, I didn't mean..."

"Stand up, boy!" the sergeant commanded. He turned to the other men in the room. "Now, here we have a man who has called me a liar. Me! Frederick Kyle! Servant of the King: man and boy." He placed his hand over his heart, "Frederick Kyle, who could not tell a lie to save his own life!"

The boy's face turned bright red. "I didn't mean you were a l-liar, sergeant" he stuttered miserably.

Kyle turned back to him. "What then?"

"I-I just heard..."

"Well, you heard wrong." The sergeant exhaled loudly. "Sit back down, lad," he said in a calmer voice, "sit back down."

174

Lock heard the exchange but felt as if it was some distance away. He yawned. Kyle began speaking again about shillings and Kings, or something like that, but Lock was so tired he hardly cared. He folded his arms on the table; his head drooped. And when one of the other cavalrymen sat alongside and gave him a coin, he looked at it owlishly, nodding at what the man said though he had not really understood. Then he stuffed the coin into his pocket and laid his head down.


Someone was shaking him. Lock woke slowly. The man spoke, his words indistinct at first.

"Come on. Wake up, it's time to go." Go where, Lock wondered? The shaking grew more violent. Lock lifted his head, but someone had put it in a vice that was turning tighter. He groaned, and dropped it onto the table once again.

"Come on, you lazy bastard: up!" He was lifted by the arms and his feet dragged across the ground. Outside; he must be outside. A breeze fanned his face and the air smelt better. More voices joined in.

"Jesus, not another one. I said it was too strong."

"He's heavy; hold him!" Lock's chin was pulled roughly upwards, and a man looked into his face. Sergeant Kyle. Lock recognised him and tried to smile. The sergeant let his chin drop.

"Stand away, you two."

Lock felt his arms stretched out, and then water hit him in the chest like a punch. Icy cold water; it drenched his face, shooting up his nose. He spluttered it out, gasping.

Sergeant Kyle walked up to him again. "Feeling better now, eh lad? Had a bit too much to drink did you?" He looked into Lock's eyes and spoke out of the side of his mouth. "This one's fine. Get the others ready. We'll march in fifteen minutes."

Lock dripped onto the cobbles. Something else was not quite right but his raging headache made it difficult to concentrate. He put his hand to his stomach. The polecat was gone. It must have got out while he was asleep. He staggered back into the tavern to hunt around under tables, but there was no sign of the damned animal.

"Lost something, lad?" Sergeant Kyle had followed him back inside. Lock explained, but the sergeant shook his head sadly. "I've not seen it. Ask the others if you like, but be quick about it, lad; we'll be off in a few minutes." Lock must have looked slightly perplexed. "Off to town, to sign you up proper," the sergeant explained. He came closer to Lock and looked into his eyes. "Don't you remember?"

"I can't remember anything."

Kyle laughed. "I'm not surprised, the amount of drink you put away. Must have hollow legs, you must." Lock thought about that. He could not remember drinking too much, but the sergeant was convincing. "Begged me to sign you up, you did; begged me."

"I couldn't have," Lock argued, slurring slightly. "I didn't want to join the army." Not like this, anyway.

"You took the King's shilling," the sergeant observed, in a voice that was far less friendly, "so you're indebted to His Majesty now."

That rang a bell in Lock's head. He remembered being given a coin. He had stuffed it in his pocket. "I'll pay him back," he said, reaching into his breeches, but he found nothing. "It's gone," he said, half to himself, and remembered the negro's warning too late.

"If you can't repay His Majesty," Frederick Kyle said with satisfaction, "you'll have to come with me. Now get back outside and line up with the others."

# Chapter 17

Lieutenant Melville Rapton dropped another useless hand of playing cards on the torn baize and bade the remaining players farewell. Throwing a fancy pelisse over his left shoulder he strode towards the stairs, fiddling impatiently with the toggle that secured the garment's strap around his neck. He stamped down the wooden steps, but the customers on the ground floor of the tavern ignored him. Just another wealthy cavalry officer losing his money. Well, damn them all, Rapton thought angrily. And damn the cards. Of late they never seemed to fall in his favour.

The ostler who brought his horse waited hopefully in the lamplight for a tip, but Rapton ignored the man's outstretched palm. The innkeeper was cheating him, he was convinced of that, so he was damned if he would give money to the rogue's employee. He mounted quickly and kicked the horse out of the inn-yard.

There was no lamp lit beyond the gates; nothing shed light on the dark street outside apart from windows on the tavern's upper floor which threw eerie shadows. Rapton abruptly yanked his horse to a standstill, making the animal throw up its head. A wagon had pulled up in an alleyway across the street; one of the carts used to carry forage for the troop horses. That was strange, for it had no business being in town at this time of night.

Rapton pulled out his watch and flipped open the cover. In such poor light it was difficult to see its hands, but he twisted his wrist so that window-light reflected from the polished gold lid onto the crystal. Just before midnight.

There was movement in the alley. Rapton was intrigued. Just what was going on? He stuffed the watch back inside his jacket, quickly glancing around. He and the horse were in shadow, half-hidden by the tavern wall and just about invisible to anyone across the street. He waited quietly in the dark.

"How many have you brought?" a voice asked.

"Thirty."

"I thought we agreed forty."

"There weren't forty to be got," Sergeant Silas Tyloe answered with exaggerated patience, "otherwise I'd have them, wouldn't I? Now, d'you want them or not? I'm a busy man."

"They'd better not be condemned."

Tyloe sounded aggrieved. "What do you take me for? I've got my reputation! Now if you want them, let's see your money." Two burly men appeared. The wagon's tail-board dropped and both began unloading grain sacks, hunching low under their weight. Rapton saw Tyloe take the proffered cash before stuffing it into a money-belt around his waist, hidden beneath his greatcoat.

"What about the other items we discussed," the voice continued.

"They's more difficult; powder and cartridges," Tyloe sniffed. "We need rain."

"Rain?"

"Spoilage. We need rain so that powder can get damp," Tyloe said, "if you get my meaning."

The voice went away. The last two grain sacks were heaved off the wagon. Tyloe replaced the plain tarpaulin which had hidden them before walking round to the rear alone.

"Sergeant Tyloe," Rapton urged his horse forward as the sergeant lifted the wagon's tailboard back into place.

Tyloe spun round at his name, but if he had been taken by surprise he must have recovered quickly for he showed little sign of it. He saluted, "Lieutenant, sir."

"What are you doing here, sergeant?"

"Just dropping off some rubbish, sir."

"It did not look like rubbish to me sergeant. It seemed like perfectly good sacks of corn."

Tyloe looked shocked, "Oh no, sir. Mouldy, it was sir, only fit for pig feed."

Rapton smiled to show that he realised what was going on. "I'm sure Major Hughes would be interested in what I've seen." He paused, as if considering. "But then again, if the grain is, as you say, only fit for pigs, then there is absolutely no point in bothering him with this, is there?"

"No sir, no point at all."

"Especially as your friend paid for what you delivered."

"Paid, sir?" Tyloe frowned.

"Sergeant," Rapton made his voice matter-of-fact, "I witnessed the transaction. And for the favour of not telling what I saw, I shall expect…a present. Fifty percent seems reasonable to me."

"Fifty percent?" Tyloe exploded, but Rapton was already riding away.

"Tomorrow, sergeant," he said over his shoulder, "tomorrow will be quite acceptable."

Rapton's earlier gloom dissipated. He pulled a cigar from his sabretache and lit it as the horse ambled along, reins dropped loose on its neck. What a turn-up! Tyloe would pay him for his silence. It would not be much, because the sergeant would undoubtedly cheat him, but it would help him afford those little extras which made life more bearable. And there was the quartermaster. He must be in league with the sergeant; probably collecting a commission of his own. Rapton thought it probably worth leaning on him, too. At the very least he might discover what else Sergeant Tyloe was pilfering. He dragged deeply on the cigar and kicked the horse into a trot.

Bloody hell, Silas Tyloe thought to himself: bloody hell! It had been difficult enough persuading the quartermaster of the benefits of his scheme. Now bloody Lieutenant Rapton had found him out. Still, there were advantages. The lieutenant would never get fifty percent of the real price. Even after paying the quartermaster, he would still make enough money for the risk to be worth taking. And having the lieutenant in his pocket: now, that might be a huge advantage in the future. He carefully backed up the two draught mules, wary lest the cart should scrape the alley walls, then turned their heads towards the barracks and flicked the reins at them.

Major Hughes slapped The Tempest on its glossy rump, making the horse swish its tail in annoyance.

"A fine horse, Mr Killen," he opined, "a thoroughbred?"

"Yes sir."

Hughes nodded. "The best stamp of horse for a cavalry officer, in my opinion. Is he trained?"

Killen scraped a body brush across the metal curry and tapped the dust the comb collected onto the floor. It would be swept away at morning stables. "Not to cannon-fire, sir."

"I don't believe many of the troop horses have been." Hughes pursed his lips, in thought. "I think we must organise something. I shall speak to the colonel about it." He was silent while Killen just waited. "Have you thought any more of our discussion?" the major asked at last.

Killen had, of course. He knew it was Rapton who had organised the cornets' ordeals, but nothing untoward had happened since he was blindfolded and dumped in town. Cornet Millward seemed to have got away scot-free, though he had been absent from barracks for the last two days.

"I have sir," he was definite, this time, "but the answer is still the same."

"Very well," Hughes sounded disappointed, "I shall say no more about it." He turned to leave.

"Mr Millward sir. Is he still with us?" Killen asked.

The major shook his head. "Transferred - to an infantry regiment. Why the devil his father commissioned him into the cavalry I'll never know." He chuckled, "Couldn't ride, and sneezed every time he went near a damned horse!"

"But he will have to ride as an infantry officer."

"Then he can sneeze all over them, and bloody good riddance, I say," Hughes nodded curtly. "I shall bid you goodnight, lieutenant."

# Chapter 18

On a door laid across two trestles to serve as a desk, the sergeant placed both hands palm down and leant forwards to look up at his new recruit, "Name?"

"Lock."

"My name," he said quietly, "is *Sergeant* Blackmore." Lock straightened up, dropping his arms to his sides, "Yes, sergeant."

Blackmore grunted. "Christian name? I presume you are a Christian?"

"Joshua, sergeant."

The sergeant scratched the boy's answers on a printed form in loopy handwriting. "Occupation?"

Lock was unsure what to say.

"Well?"

"Farrier, sergeant."

Blackmore paused, quill hovering over the paper. "We have a full complement," he said. He fiddled with his moustache. "Not indentured are you? We're not allowed to steal apprentices." Lock shook his head. "That's fine, then." He wet his pen and wrote 'Smith' in the space. "You'll have to join as a private. Now take off your shirt." He stood up.

"Sergeant?"

"Take your shirt off, son." He pointed to the paper. "It says here, 'identifying marks,' and you've still got a clean face."

Blackmore took a good look at the scar on Lock's right arm. "How'd you get that?" he asked with suspicion.

"An accident."

The sergeant gave him a sceptical glance and the pen scratched again. "It looks like a knife wound to me. In a fight, were you?"

"Honestly, sergeant, it was an accident."

"If you say so," Blackmore sniffed before handing Lock the pen. "Make your mark there," he tapped the bottom of the paper, "and on your way to the doctor, send the next man in."

Lock sat on the grass under a tree, hugging his knees. For once he felt he was not in control. The doctor had prodded first his scar, then his stomach, and finally tugged at his scrotum. Satisfied the recruit was neither unfit through injury, nor ruptured, and showed no signs of venereal disease, he had simply nodded at the orderly taking notes before moving on to the next man

Another recruit dropped to the ground beside him and offered a wry smile.

"Got you too, did they?"

Lock did not answer.

The recruit shook his head sadly, "Should know better at my age." Lock thought the man did not look that old.

"Too fond of a drink, that's my trouble." He seemed to notice Lock's stare. "You didn't realise, did you? Christ, you must be just out of the crib." Tilting his head closer to Lock's, "They doctored, the ale, didn't they," he said in a hoarse whisper. "Oldest trick in the book, and I fell for it."

Lock was horrified. "They wouldn't!"

"Huh!" The other recruit lay back on the grass, shirtless. His ribcage showed through pale skin. "That Sergeant Kyle would probably recruit his own mother to turn a guinea."

"I lost my shilling," Lock said, feeling anger stir inside.

The man rolled to onto his side. "They stole it," he said. "Got you dopey-drunk, and stole it back. Same with me. Stands to reason; if you can't pay it back, they've got you."

Lock's jaw tightened. "They won't get away with that." He made as if to get up, but the older man grabbed his arm.

"And what are you going to do?" He took a deep breath and let it out slowly. "Look, son, you can't touch Kyle; the troopers would be all over you like fleas. You'll get yourself flogged for assaulting a sergeant. It's done now; get over it."

"My polecat went missing, too."

"Now that's shame," the other man seemed more sympathetic, releasing Lock's arm, "a real shame. A good animal's worth money. They probably stole that as well. Bastards," he said with feeling, and held out his hand. "The name's Francis. Francis Kittoe."

They marched soon after. Sergeant Kyle took the lead. The recruits were made to walk along the crown of the road, with mounted troopers riding the verge on each side. Like guards, Lock thought. He fell into step beside Kittoe but spoke little. After half an hour, they stopped to rest for five minutes. Lock understood the reason for their frequent short breaks only after they had been on the road for several hours. A number of recruits, unused to walking such distances, had already begun to get sore feet.

At midday they halted again, and Sergeant Kyle rode back through the group.

"Twenty minutes rest!" he shouted. "Picker! Over here!" Lock noticed that the trumpeter was relegated to the rear. "See if you can find somewhere to water the horses," the sergeant ordered, and Picker obediently trotted away down the road.

Kyle turned his attention to the recruits. "My men will come around with canteens. Don't drink them dry; you might be thirsty again later!" He laughed, to show it was a little joke.

"When do we get to ride, sergeant?" One of the younger men sat down to pull off his boots and stockings. He winced as he prodded blisters.

"When we get to the other side of England, Tollit," Kyle said with a smile.

Nathan Tollit grumbled, "I didn't join the cavalry to go marching everywhere."

"But you have joined the cavalry, so you'll do as I bloody well tell you. Now stop complaining; you'll have your bounty money tomorrow. Enough cash to buy yourself a bloody horse!" Kyle passed down two circular wooden canteens to the men. Kittoe took one and uncorked it.

Picker must have found a well or a stream. When he returned, three troopers dismounted with un-holstered carbines while Picker and the remaining cavalrymen rode away, leading the spare horses.

"Making sure we don't run off," Kittoe wiped his mouth on his sleeve and nodded towards their guards.

Lock took a drink from the canteen the older man offered before passing it along to Tollit. "You want to wrap your feet in some cloths," he suggested, "until they get used to the walking. Those stockings are too thin."

"I will buy myself a horse," Tollit gingerly flexed his toes a couple of times before tipping water on them, which drew an oath from Kittoe, "then I'll look down on the rest of you, dragging along in the dirt."

Kittoe laughed drily. "With what's left of your bounty," he said, "you won't buy a donkey."


They spent the night sleeping in a barn. The troopers made themselves comfortable with blankets, but there were none for the recruits, which elicited a few protests.

"Lads, lads," Kyle was calming, "please - be patient. There'll be tents and blankets for all tomorrow. Just imagine you're on campaign," he said soothingly, "and must rough it for a night or two. Consider it a part of your training." He put his hands on his hips, staring belligerently at the recruits, and his attitude had the desired effect. Grumbles lessened and the men gathered heaps of straw to lie on. Lock had often slept in barns in bad weather rather than out in the open, so he had experienced the comparative discomfort and knew his clothes would likely be crawling with fleas by morning. And he thought that from the way Francis Kittoe was packing down straw in alternate layers, he was no stranger to roughing it either.

Kittoe gave him a sidelong glance. "Got anything of value in that knapsack?" he said quietly.

"Only my clothes."

"Use it as a pillow," Kittoe advised. He pointed towards the two troopers delegated as guards who prowled in front of the barn door, "Less chance of those bastards going through it."

Kittoe was proved right. The recruits never got their bounty: it seemed that most ended up being poured down the cavalrymen's throats. And one night, on the long march south-east, Lock lost his good shirt.

# Chapter 19

As the recruits stomped towards the square, Lock looked up at the barrack gates. Their heavy iron plate-and-pin hinges folded back without a squeak and were newly blacked. The timber even had a fresh coat of pitch, which seemed a dubious idea to him; it would burn fiercely should the cavalrymen ever upset the local populace by assisting the constables.

Twenty-nine men marched in, Sergeant Kyle having made good use of his silver tongue at each town and village on the way. The recruits were tired and dirty, many of them lame from blisters. And even though Lock was used to walking, so had not suffered as much, he desperately wanted to yank off his boots and plunge his feet into a tub of cold water.

The men halted, forming up in two ranks, their trooper-guards shoving them roughly about so that they stood in reasonably straight lines. Then they were commanded to turn to the left, so both lines faced one of the large stone buildings making up one side of the barracks. The guards left them there.

Lock wet his lips with his tongue and scraped at some chapped skin with his bottom teeth. "What now?" he said out of the side of his mouth. Alongside him, Francis Kittoe shrugged. Lock picked at a piece of skin on his top lip he had managed to loosen, "I could do with a drink." But they all had to wait.


John Killen marched onto the barrack square from the direction of the stables, glancing at the new recruits' backs. Like most other small groups brought in recently, they were grubby and unkempt.

Rumours abounded. Bonaparte was making preparations for a new invasion of England after his first was aborted; Admiral Nelson had seen to that. Or the army was being sent to South America, to wrest French-held dominions from their masters in Paris. Killen believed neither, though judging by the number of recruiting parties he had seen whilst on the road exercising troop horses, the size of the army was being increased dramatically. He carried on past the recruits, heading for the mess.

A figure in the first line caught Killen's attention. This man was taller than the others, but it was the way he stood; broad-shouldered, with a set to his stance that seemed, somehow, familiar. Killen increased his pace, striding around the end of the row, ignoring those men who stood to ragged attention as he passed. He stopped in front of the tall recruit and felt a great swell in his chest.

"Joshua!" Killen held out his hand, and Lock smiled and took it. Killen held on with both hands and shook Lock's arm excitedly. "Joshua! What on earth are you doing here?"

"Hello, John," Lock smiled lopsidedly. "It was something of an accident, really."


"Silence!" Silence in the ranks, damn you!" Sergeant Tyloe was not sure what to make of it. An officer shaking hands with a recruit? Unheard of, it was; unheard of. And the cornet was an 'Honourable'. That would make him a lord, one day. Tyloe was missing something here; he was sure of it, and that fact annoyed him, but he would find out. He marched up to the cornet, saluting smartly, "Sir!"

Killen's face fell a little, and he released the recruit's hand. "Sergeant?"

"Mr Killen, sir. Come to take charge of the recruits." Tyloe gave the cornet a beaming smile. "Sort them out, sir; you know, let them know what's what. What their duties are, sir, etcetera."

"Right. Of course, sergeant."

Cornet Killen blushed, the sergeant noted.

"I'll leave you to get on." Killen gave the recruit a quick glance and nodded at Tyloe before marching away.

This was one duty Silas Tyloe enjoyed immensely. He scowled at the tall recruit before marching to the far end of the lines. "Atten-shun!" he bawled. "Front rank; one pace forward – march!" The recruits made a reasonable effort to obey both instructions. Tyloe was pleased. This lot seemed reasonably intelligent, compared to some he had dealt with in the past. He turned smartly and marched mid-way down the lines before turning to face the men again.

"My name," he shouted, "is Sergeant Tyloe. Remember that name. From now, you'll do nothing unless I tell you to; or one of the other sergeants: unless, of course, an officer orders you." He scanned back and forth, but no-one seemed to have moved, and none spoke. "Now then," he continued loudly, "let's be having a look at what we've got."

Tyloe marched to the far end of the front rank and began to slowly work his way back. He stared into each man's face, trying to read it, seeking out the strong-willed who might be difficult to deal with, or the weak; those he could bully or bend more easily to his will. Every recruit avoided his gaze.

One man moved, shifting his weight from one foot to the other. Tyloe strode to his position in the line and stared into the recruit's face, "Name?"

"T-tollit, sergeant."

Tyloe grinned. "What's the matter, Tollit; fleas in your breeches?" He lifted his right boot over Tollit's left, leaning his weight down.

The young man winced, "No, sergeant."

Tyloe pressed harder. "Crabs, then? Doctor missed the buggers, did he?"

Beads of sweat began to form on the Tollit's brow. "No, sergeant!" he insisted.

"I'm glad to hear it." Tyloe stamped his boot down hard before stepping back. The recruit obviously suffered sore feet. "Nothing worse for a soldier than crabs. Stay away from whores and strong drink, that's my advice to you, Tollit. And stand bloody still!" He moved on.

This was the one. Tyloe looked up at the recruit who had shaken hands with Cornet Killen. He was big alright; looked strong, too, but looks were not always the best judge.

"Name?"

"Lock."

Tyloe suddenly raised his hand and slapped the recruit hard across the face. "Lock, *sergeant*," he growled. The boy's jaw tightened. Tyloe tensed ready for some response, but then saw a twitch in the corner of the recruit's eye. He was going to cry! A big cry-baby! Tyloe relaxed. This one was asking for it; a cry-baby officer's pet. "Mind you call me Sergeant Tyloe in future, sonny," he instructed, putting the emphasis on '*Sergeant*'. "And there's no need to blubber, lad; it were only a tiny little slap."


Lock controlled his anger only with great difficulty, mindful of Francis Kittoe's warning about confronting sergeants. His count reached six. A few recruits chuckled at Tyloe's baiting. Well, they could go to hell; let them think what they liked. Out of the corner of his eye, Lock saw the sergeant was further down the line, prodding another recruit in the stomach. He touched his jaw where Tyloe's ring had scraped the skin. A tiny smear of blood came away on his fingers, but nothing much. Lock relaxed. He could deal with it.


Sergeant Tyloe beamed at his men. A little sport to start the day always put him in a good mood. He turned to bawl across the parade ground at a uniformed trooper, who hurried across and stood beside him. "Now, you men will follow Trooper Smithers, here, to the stores, where you will be issued with your necessaries," he announced. "Right turn! Off you go!" He had a sudden thought, "You! Lock! Come here." The tall recruit turned out of the ranks and halted in front of him.

"Sergeant?"

"Major wants to see you," Tyloe said quickly. "Down there," he pointed at the building, "third door down, then first right, off the corridor – got it? Away with you then; sharpish, boy." He smiled to himself watching Lock march off. A meeting with Major Hughes was enough to put the fear of God into the hardest-bitten veteran. A cry-baby would likely piss in his breeches. Tyloe expected to get a good laugh at that.


Lock knocked gently on the office door which was half-open. No answer. He went in, boots virtually silent on a patterned rug which stretched from the threshold up to a large desk, piled with neat stacks of paper. The rug reminded Lock of Halcombe House. He checked around carefully, and had just made up his mind that the office was empty and he ought to leave, when a voice froze him to the spot.

"Who the devil are you?" It was not only that the voice was loud; there was menace in its tone. Lock came to attention, staring straight ahead.

"Well?"

The voice came from his right. There must be another doorway he had missed. "Trooper Lock, sir."

"You're not a bloody trooper until you're passed out, private." Hughes stalked into the main office from a side room. "What the hell do you want?" he demanded.

Lock was at a loss. "Sergeant Tyloe said you wanted to see me, sir."


Major Jonas Hughes stared critically at the young man in front of his desk. Just the type of recruit he was pleased to see. Tall, the boy was; strong-looking. A little too big, perhaps, for the Light Dragoons, troops who tended to ride smaller-framed horses than their heavyweight counterparts, but welcome nonetheless. And the boy had a confident air. A good many who had stood on the rug in front of him appeared paralysed with fear.

The major stepped behind his desk, leafing through a stack of enlistment papers until he found the right one. "Did he say why I wanted to see you?" he asked with less heat.

"No, sir."

"It says here," Hughes tapped the paper Sergeant Blackmore had filled in, "that you're a smith."

"Farrier, sir," Lock corrected. "My grandfather taught me."

"I see." Blackmore obviously realised that there was little to be gained from signing on another farrier, but did not want to lose the commission he would earn from an extra recruit. Hughes frowned. "But you've worked iron?" Lock nodded, and the major raised his eyebrows, "And do I take it you can ride?"

"Yes, sir."

"Good." That would make less work for the instructors, Hughes thought. He was beginning to despair at the number of men who signed up with no idea even that one end of a horse could bite and the other kick. "You're dismissed, Private Lock," Hughes turned away, "and if you happen to meet Sergeant Tyloe, tell him I wish to see him."

Hughes sat down behind his desk and picked up the stack of enlistment papers, tapping the edge of the pile on his blotter until it was all square. He had a form for everything. Store requisitions. Requests for forage and horseshoes. Standing orders. Daily orders. Leave sheets. Patrol reports. Every piece of paper neatly arranged in its proper place. The army ran on pieces of paper, and Hughes knew how good he was at organising them. Yes, it was monotonous - boring, even - but it was his efficiency that had raised him to his present rank; that had allowed him to transfer from a sweltering post in India to a regiment at home.

The major picked up a quill, dipping the already prepared nib into one of his inkwells. He looked at the frieze carved in miniature on the small ivory pot, where tiny men riding an elephant threw spears at a rearing tiger. Hughes sighed. It brought back memories of the heat and smell. But it was the blood and death he had finally grown sick of, often dreaming of home service until the opportunity of such a posting arose. The 20th had given him that chance, and he was grateful.

Taking a cigar from the top drawer of his desk Hughes lit it, inhaling deeply to savour the smoke-taste as he turned in his seat to look out of the window. Lock was walking across the parade ground, but suddenly halted as an officer approached, slapping him on the back. They began a conversation. Hughes was intrigued. Why the devil would an officer risk being seen to be so friendly towards an enlisted man? Regretfully he stubbed out his cigar and crossed to the outer door.

"Private Lock," he screamed across the square. Both Lock and the officer looked in his direction. Cornet Killen was the other man; that was even more odd.

"A word with you, private," Hughes called, but a tiny movement behind made him look around. "What are you doing, skulking around corners," Hughes demanded of Sergeant Tyloe.

190

The sergeant looked blithely innocent. "Nothing sir," Tyloe managed to sound surprised. "On my way to check the new men are settling in sir."

"Well get on with it," Hughes barked irritably, "and you will report to me afterwards."


Lock found himself on the rug once again. Major Hughes looked at him expectantly but he kept quiet, wondering what was to come.

"So you are acquainted with our Mr Killen?" Hughes began.

"Yes, sir."

Hughes walked around Lock in a small circle, hands clasped behind his back. "The army," he said, "works a little differently to civilian life. It is not usual for privates to consort with officers. And vice versa." He stopped in front of Lock. "The officers don't like it, nor do the troopers. Spoils the natural order of things." He put his face close to Lock's so the boy could smell tobacco on his breath. "Might make life difficult for Mr Killen - discipline and all that. D'you understand what I'm getting at, private?"

Lock nodded. "I..." he started to explain, then thought better of it. "His grandfather was my landlord," he said instead.

# Chapter 20

"Call this a saddle, sergeant," Joshua Lock laughed, "I'd rather ride bareback."

Quartermaster Sergeant Joseph Archer might agree that the four pieces of beechwood strung with a piece of thin leather did not look comfortable, but he gave Lock a hackneyed stare. "The Duke of York has decreed that's what you'll ride on," he said dourly, "and so you will." He dumped a tangled bundle of leather straps on the table in front of him. "Bridle, breastplate, leathers and girth. You can sort it all out. Draw the ironmongery yonder." He pointed further down the storeroom. "What horse have they given you?"

"Sexton."

"Know why they called him that? 'Cause he buries his riders!" The sergeant laughed loudly at his own joke. "Buries them, he does!"

Lock grinned lopsidedly. "Not me, he won't."

Archer's eyes narrowed. "A guinea says he does," he whispered behind his hand.

"Done." Annoyance quickened Lock's pulse. He did not have a guinea but was confident he would not have to pay out.


A blanket went on each horse's back first. It needed to be folded enough times to prevent the saddle frame rubbing the animal's skin to sores. Sergeant Blackmore demonstrated the technique to the recruits.

"And woe betide anyone," he finished warningly, "who gives his horse a sore back. Flogging offence, that is - so Major Hughes believes." He went around each horse, checking the recruit's efforts, ordering a refolded blanket here; a tightened girth-strap there. When he was at last satisfied, the horses were bridled and led from the stables.

The school was simply a tall, open barn with sand on the floor. Blackmore strode to the centre while eight recruits lined up.

"Prepare to mount," he bellowed, and Lock vaulted up into the saddle. "Lock, you're too bloody early. That's just showing off." Lock turned the horse in a circle. "Now dismount and wait for the order!" They lined up again. "Prepare to mount," Blackmore called, and each of the recruits put his left foot into the stirrup. Lock felt Sexton tense.

"And...mount!" Lock sprung up and the horse took off, from a standstill to gallop in a half-second. Lock was in mid air, both hands clinging grimly to the saddle pommel. He managed to scramble his right leg over the animal's back just before it started to buck, not with a light-hearted humping of its back, but with a gut-wrenching violence that threw Lock forward and back against the pommel and cantle plates. He wrapped his legs around the horse's body, ignoring the stirrups, hauling on the reins to slow Sexton down. And gradually the bucking grew less violent, and the horse slowed from mad gallop to a canter. Finally, he managed to slow it to a walk.

Lock rode Sexton to the centre of the school. Most recruits were still there, staring wide-eyed, while a couple of horses which had been startled by the fracas were brought quietly back.

"Enjoy that, did you?" Sergeant Blackmore's eyes were amused.

Lock took a deep breath and exhaled, letting the tension out. He reached forward to pat the horse's neck.

"Right, you useless bastards," the sergeant bawled, "Now the entertainment's over, let's get down to some work!"


Lock never collected his guinea.

"You cheated me," Sergeant Archer complained loudly. "Never told me you could ride, did you? Not fair, that isn't."

"You never asked me." Lock held out his hand. "Pay up sergeant; he didn't bury me."

"Haven't got it," Archer evaded. "Pay you again, alright?" He put his face very close to Lock's, "Alright, *private?*"

Lock counted in his head. He held the sergeant's gaze for a while then dropped his eyes. "Yes, sarge," he said, and abruptly walked away.

Half-way across the square, Kittoe caught him up. "Wouldn't pay, eh?" He must have overheard the exchange.

"No."

"Huh," Kittoe exclaimed. "We'll know next time, won't we?"

"Yes," Lock was deep in thought, "we will."


Dung picking. Piles of the stuff lay scattered over the school's sandy surface from the previous ride. Lock scraped at them with brush and shovel, throwing the mess into a basket. It was one job all the troopers hated; trust him to be chosen again.

A horse came into the school, but he ignored it.

"Yes, sir." The vast empty space gave the confirmation an echo, but it was Tyloe's voice. Lock glanced up. The sergeant was dragging a heavy pole into the middle of the school where two beer kegs stood on their ends. Whoever was with him must be trying to teach his horse to leap an obstacle.

"Lock!" He straightened up as Tyloe approached. "You're in the way," the sergeant grumbled. "Hurry up with that, for God's sake."

Lock heard the slaps. He turned to see the horse shy away from the whip-strikes. Lieutenant Rapton was riding, his face flushed with anger.

"Drag another pole across, sergeant," Rapton yanked at the horse's mouth to prevent it running off. "I'll damned well beat it over them." He cantered up to the pole once more, digging the horse's sides with his spurs, and again it stopped. The animal threw up its head as Rapton sawed on the reins to keep it from bolting. Skittering sideways its eyes rolled white, anticipating another blow. Rapton raised his arm, but Lock was already crossing the sand towards him.

"Don't!" Lock shouted a warning, but he was too late. Rapton's whip slashed across the horse's flank. The animal leapt into the air and Rapton raised his arm again. The horse half-reared as the whip came down, but the blow never landed.

Lock caught the whip on the downstroke. "Don't," he repeated, and yanked the whip from Rapton's grasp.

The lieutenant recoiled as if he had been hit. And there was something else in his face; Lock would have sworn to it. Fear.

195

"Sergeant!" Rapton screamed, upsetting the horse even more, "Sergeant; did you see that? Arrest that man; arrest him!"

Lock felt anger rising again. He stepped forward, but a weight hit him in the back; someone pinned his arms to his sides.

"Josh; no!" Killen hissed in his ear. Lock abruptly stopped struggling. He threw Rapton's whip onto the floor.

"Sergeant Tyloe, I want that man arrested!" Rapton was insistent. "He struck me! You saw it."

Killen released his hold and stepped back. "He never struck you, lieutenant. I saw what happened." His voice was thick with outrage.

Rapton ignored his inferior. "Sergeant," he commanded, "you will do your duty. Arrest him immediately!"

Tyloe took over. "Mr Killen? Step aside, sir, if you please. Private Lock, you will come with me. Now!" He barked the last word as if afraid Lock would disobey. Lock merely turned his head and looked towards his friend as he was marched off.

Rapton seemed to have recovered himself. "I strongly suggest," he spat angrily at Killen, "that you stay out of this." He dismounted to retrieve his whip from where Lock had thrown it down, offering the cornet a look of dislike. "I suggest it most strongly." He led the sweating horse away.


At the enquiry, Major Hughes listened hard. Long ago, he had discovered a talent for listening. He had come to believe it was often not so much what was said, but the way in which it was said. And even what was not said might provide the key to an issue. So he listened carefully to Rapton's vehement accusation and Sergeant Tyloe's corroboration, and nodded as if in agreement with their arguments. But something did not quite ring true.

"Mr Killen," he said at length, "since you appear to have appointed yourself Private Lock's advocate, you will kindly appraise us of your view in this matter." Killen glanced nervously at his friend, but since Lock was held on one side of the room, wearing irons and flanked by two guards, he could be of no assistance.

Killen's Troop Captain tried to help him out. "Just say what you saw," Thomas Hackett encouraged, "in your own words."

Hughes looked sideways. "I'm sure Mr Killen is quite capable of doing that without any help, Hackett" he admonished. "Well, cornet?"

"The bloody man struck me!" Rapton butted in, and Hughes shot him a cold glare.

"Private Lock did not strike Mr. Rapton," Killen found his voice at last. "In fact," he had sudden inspiration, "I thought that the lieutenant struck him."

Rapton looked daggers at his adversary. "That's not true, sir," he said to Hughes, who now gazed at him enquiringly, "it's a lie."

Hughes sighed. "Thank you, lieutenant, for your most lucid account. You and Sergeant Tyloe may go." Once the door closed behind them, he spoke directly to Lock "You realise, private, how much trouble you are in? No, I don't suppose you do. The penalty for striking an officer is to be flogged; not a punishment I much care for but, by God, I will pass that sentence should it prove necessary." He banged on the table with his fist. "Now, what *exactly* happened? The facts, if you please."

Lock told him. "I might have struck him, sir," he admitted truthfully, "but Mr Killen stopped me."

Hughes stepped out from behind the table. "A damned good job he did." He stopped in front of Lock. "Free his hands," he commanded the guards, holding out one of his own. "Give me your hand, private." Lock raised his left hand, and Hughes took it, turning the palm upwards. The weal Rapton's whip had raised stretched right across the middle joint of each finger. That must have hurt, Hughes thought, but the boy's face betrayed nothing. He let the hand go. "But why?" Hughes puzzled, "Why did you do it?" Lock mumbled a response.

"What did you say?"

"It didn't understand." Lock blurted out, as if he thought it sounded stupid.

"What?"

"The horse; it didn't understand." Lock looked Major Hughes in the face. "It was the lieutenant who needed a beating, sir, not the horse. It just didn't know what he wanted."


Hughes thanked Captain Hackett for attending. Lock was marched off flanked by the two guards. "But I'd like you to stay, cornet," the major said to Killen.

"Sit down, Johnny." Hughes made himself comfortable, leaning back in his chair. He plucked a cigar from a desk drawer and lit the end, drawing on it deeply. "So tell me," the major could be disarming when he wanted to, "all about Private Lock."

Killen was not sure where this was leading. "What do you mean, sir?"

"It is quite obvious you have...a relationship," Hughes puffed delicately on the cigar. "I merely wish to ascertain what effect, if any, that fact may have on the regiment."

Killen was stung. "Sir," he said heatedly, "I have no idea what you imply. Joshua Lock is my friend." He paused, and saw that it was not enough. "He saved my life, sir."


Killen told Major Hughes the story; at least, the parts of it that he knew, or had been told by others, because he and Lock had never spoken of that night. And from time to time, the major interrupted.

"So, he carried you how far?"

"And, you say, this was through a blizzard?"

"With an injured arm?" Good God, Hughes thought to himself, good God. It was almost unbelievable. The problem was the major found himself believing every word.

At length, Hughes stood, and Killen followed. "Thank you for being frank with me, Johnny," he said kindly. "I trust we can keep this little chat between ourselves?" Killen nodded, looking relieved. "Good, good." He indicated the door. "On your way out, please tell Sergeant Tyloe, who will, no doubt, be behind it," he gave a small smile, "to fetch Private Lock back to me."

Lock stared down at the rug. This was the third time he had been on the major's carpet, and he decided he did not much care for the experience. He expected the worst so was surprised to find himself the only other man in the room.

The hour hand on Hughes' mantel clock was approaching four. Afternoon stables. Lock willed its water-drip tick to stop, but the mechanism carried on its relentless hammering.

Hughes was silent, hands behind his back, staring out of the window onto the parade yard. "I was like you, once," he said quietly, and Lock thought at first he must be talking to himself. But then he turned round. "Young, strong; full of myself." He picked up one ivory inkwell and looked at it as if he had never seen it before. "That was a long time ago," he admitted, carefully replacing the inkwell. "You lied to me, boy," he stared Lock in the face, accusing.

"No, sir!"

"You told me Mr Killen's grandfather was your landlord."

"But he was."

"You knew that was not what I meant." Hughes turned back to the window. He sighed. "Mr Killen told me what he knows of what took place in the river." Lock felt shocked at that, but the major held up his hand. "I have assured Johnny that it stays between ourselves, and I can understand why you too might wish to keep it quiet. Get on well with the other enlisted men, do you?"

"Yes, sir."

Hughes nodded. "We must do our best to keep it that way. Understand me, private. Your actions toward Lieutenant Rapton amount to insubordination at the very least, and I will not stand for ill-discipline within my squadron. If I believed for one moment that you did strike him..." his voice tailed off. Lock's heart dropped close to his bootlaces. "However, neither will I stand for abuse of any horse. We are a cavalry regiment, for God's sake. We need as many sound, sane animals as we can muster."

The major sat down, reaching into his desk drawer for a cigar. He lit it, while Lock watched and waited.

"Know what the Arabs say about horses, Lock?"

"No, sir."

The major drew deeply on the cigar, letting smoke dribble out of his nose, "God's work; that's what." He leaned back in the chair. "They say Allah took a handful of the north wind and moulded it with his own hands. Shaped it, into a creature. Then he called to his Prophet and said, 'I give you this animal called Horse. You shall have dominion over it, and all lands that tremble beneath its feet.' What d'you make of that?"

Lock thought it best to avoid his own view of God's work. "A good story, sir?"

Hughes took the cigar out of his mouth, contemplating a tiny wisp of smoke that drifted from its glowing end. Then he stabbed it fiercely in Lock's direction. "Look after your horse and it will look after you, private. That's what I make of it."


Jonas Hughes found himself in a quandary; not a situation he was used to or much liked. Disciplinary matters were straightforward. The offender was guilty, or not; the punishment for insubordination clear. But Hughes was a practical man. This private had acted with the best of intentions, if wrongly. Lock's swordsmanship was reported as excellent for a raw recruit, and Hughes himself had seen the boy ride. Exactly the sort of man the regiment needed. His self-confidence must be curbed, though.

"What the hell do I do with you, private?" Hughes wondered out loud, rising from his chair. "Sergeant Blackmore tells me you swing a sabre decently."

"Mr Killen taught me sir."

"Payment in kind, eh?" The major came to a decision. "The muck-pit needs to be emptied. You will do it – alone, starting tomorrow, at first light. I shall organise a wagon for its disposal." He turned his back on Lock to stare across the parade ground. "Now get out. Ensure I have no reason to see you before me again."


Back out in the yard, Lock leaned back against a cold stone wall and sighed with relief. He had avoided not only a flogging but another night in a damp cell, for Hughes had followed him through the office door to dismiss his guards.

A pair of boots appeared in front of him. "Lock?" Sergeant Tyloe was incredulous, "how the hell are you free?"

200

But before Lock could answer, there was a great bellow from inside the doorway. "Sergeant: in here!" Tyloe threw Lock a furious scowl and scurried off.


During the night it began to rain heavily. The downpour swirled across the cobbles, puddling where, here and there, a rounded stone was missing. Just after dawn, Lock stood in front of the muck-pit. His boots were already soaked with stinking brown slurry, and the rainwater that slicked his hair ran freely down his bare torso. He had not realised how big the muck-pit really was until he paced it out. Filled with dung and rotting straw to just above Lock's height, it would take him two full days to clean it, he reckoned.

A tall-sided cart drew up. The two steaming wet draught mules jerked up their heads when the driver reined them to a standstill. Silas Tyloe climbed down, giving Lock a look filled with venom. Rain ran in streams down his woollen cloak, and he had pulled his watering-cap down over his ears.

"Good morning, sergeant," Lock said pleasantly

"No it bloody isn't." Tyloe drew one hand from beneath the cloak to wipe rain from his cheeks. He poked a long finger in Lock's face.

"This is all *your* bloody fault," he boiled with anger, "officers' bloody pet."

"I don't know what you mean, sergeant."

"You'll find out, soon enough," Tyloe snarled. He pointed at a muck-fork, buried half-way up its shaft in the mound. "Get on with it then; I've got better things to do than stand in shit all day." Lock yanked the fork out, but as he did his feet slipped in the manure and the tines swung towards Tyloe. The sergeant stepped back hurriedly, eyes widening.

"Sorry, sergeant," Lock put up the fork in meek apology. But now he knew where he stood, and smiled to himself.


John Killen stared through one of the exercise-hall windows. He could see Lock, blurred by rain-streaks, still throwing forkfuls of muck into the cart. They had not spoken after the enquiry; duties kept Killen away from the horses at evening stables. At least his friend had not been sentenced to a flogging. Killen shuddered at the thought. He had sometimes watched the estate workers castrating lambs and wondered what that would feel like; the knife blade slicing deep and warm blood running down his skin. Flogging must be like that, except you never saw the slash that cut you.

"Come on, Johnny." Charlie Harris straightened up from where he had crouched to re-buckle one of his shoes. He raised his rapier. Killen dragged his eyes from the window, lifting his own sword before stepping forward. The two blade-tips touched then he feinted right. Harris was taken in, allowing Killen to simply flick his own blade back over a clumsy parry. He touched his opponent's torso.

"No, no!" Captain Hackett shook his head in exasperation. "Give me your sword, Charlie." He took Harris' position. "Now look closely," he instructed, "Johnny was only teasing you. I've told you before; watch his eyes, not his sword; like this." He nodded at Killen, "Again, Johnny."

Killen put up his blade once more, and once more feinted right, but this time Hackett faked a block and was ready to parry Killen's cut. The captain lowered his sword and stepped back. "You see?" Harris nodded miserably, his cheeks pink. "And once you've parried, you can attack his next stroke. Again, Johnny, if you please."

Killen repeated the performance, but this time Hackett moved forward after his initial parry. Killen was forced to block the captain's stroke, stepping backwards to give himself room.

"You can do exactly the same, Charlie," Hackett told him, still keeping a wary eye on his opponent, "then move in for the kill," he joked; but Killen did not smile, he concentrated. Hackett's blade reached forward and Killen slashed at it, feigning panic. Hackett flicked the cornet's blade away, ready to swing his own underneath, but Killen parried that stroke, immediately launching his own attack which forced his captain on the defensive. It was so unexpected Hackett had to take two quick steps backwards. He lowered his sword-point with a faint look of surprise.

Killen was deadpan. The other three pairs of practicing swordsmen had stopped to stare at him. He wondered why.

"I think," Hackett said, "that for now you shall practice with me, Charlie." He offered Killen a small inclination of the head. "You fence well, Mr Killen," he said with formality. "Get changed. That will be all for today."

# Chapter 21

Killen shook out his cloak in the hallway. The rain had eased to a drizzle; still not pleasant for Lock, he thought. He slung the long garment over his shoulder and began to climb the stairs to his dormitory.

The front door opened behind him. "I say; you there!" Killen turned his head towards the caller who beckoned, "Come here!"

It was a boy. Wearing uniform, but still a boy. Killen slowly descended, and the door opened a second time. Another man appeared, backwards, dragging a large wooden trunk. Once clear of the doorway he let his end of the chest crash to the floor. The boy glanced at him with irritation.

"Where is the subaltern's accommodation," the boy demanded, turning his attention back to Killen.

"You are Mr…?"

"Blake-Weston," he answered stiffly. "Lieutenant Blake-Weston. Upstairs, I assume?" Killen looked at the boy's jacket which bore the insignia of a cornet, but Blake-Weston correctly guessed his thoughts. "I merely await confirmation of my purchase from Horse Guards," he looked down his long nose as if Killen had just crawled out from beneath a stone, "though why on earth they must take such an inordinate time about it is beyond my comprehension."

Killen was unsure whether the lieutenant would be pleased by what he said, but went ahead anyway. "There are no spare rooms, sir," he said, "but you would be most welcome to share the cornet's dormitory."

"There are what?" the boy began, but the front door burst open to admit Lieutenant Rapton. His foot caught one corner of the trunk, tripping him so he almost fell.

"Who the devil left that damned thing in the way?" Rapton roared. Blake-Weston's servant stepped back uncertainly, but the boy held out his hand.

"Blake-Weston: Julius. Pleased to make your acquaintance, Lieutenant…?"

"Melville Rapton." Rapton took the outstretched hand with reluctance.

"I was asking this...cornet," Blake-Weston indicated Killen, "about rooms. He seems to believe there are none available."

"Usually pointless asking Killen a sensible question," Rapton was scathing, "but on this occasion he is correct. Your servant?" he pointed at the other man in the hallway, and when Blake-Weston nodded, continued in a more friendly manner, "then I suggest it would be advantageous to take rooms in town. I can offer introductions if you wish?" Blake-Weston agreed. "Then follow me, Julius," Rapton started upstairs. "I have a rare claret in my room which you shall share while I write." He gave the boy a conspiratorial look, "Killen can help your servant stow the chest. That will suit his abilities admirably."


"Are you certain, Melville?" Edward Jamieson leaned forward, elbows on the mess table, and spoke in a whisper.

Rapton smiled, delighted with himself. "He's ripe for plucking. God, Edward, you should have heard the sprog. Brain the size of a pea, I shouldn't wonder, and dripping gold from his purse." He sat back to draw on a long cigar. "We'll introduce him to our pleasures gradually at first. Let him settle in. You know; win a few hands; buy a few bottles of port." He raised his wineglass to Jamieson, "With luck, we'll not have to worry about our mess bills again. I give you Lieutenant Blake-Weston."

Jamieson burped loudly. "God bless him," he responded to the toast.

# 1808

# Chapter 22

"Troop!" Captain Hackett turned in the saddle to shout at the top of his voice, "Troop will form line by threes! Two ranks!" The three cavalrymen riding immediately behind their troop commander halted. The three behind them angled left to ride up alongside the first three, and the following three angled right. Lock's three had the furthest to go, being the last file on the far right of the line.

Sergeant Tyloe rode on the wide outside next to Lock. "Keep up, you bastards," he admonished, and Lock had to nudge his horse into a trot.

Killen was the officer charged with marking and holding the centre of the second line, bringing his three to a halt in just the right spot, a horse's length back from the front rank, so the files following could form on his. He checked left and right, waving at a trooper whose horse had moved forwards out of position. The man tugged on the animal's mouth to get it to reverse. Killen grimaced, making a mental note to rebuke him later.

At the same time, farther to the right, Captain Victor Butterell was giving his own troop identical commands. The danger was that if the two captains were even slightly out of position, there would be insufficient room where the two front lines met. As it was, Tyloe moved his horse to the left to allow the left-hand three of Butterell's troop to complete their line, forcing Lock to side-step his mount into that of the adjacent trooper. Sexton ground its teeth and swished its tail in annoyance. Lock gently ran his fingers up and down the horse's neck, to sooth it.

The whole squadron formed a magnificent dark blue ribbon of flickering helmet-crests and fidgeting horse-heads; a two-deep line of horseman a hundred and sixty feet across. Both captains walked their horses three paces forward. They halted raising their swords in salute.


"Well done, I thought, eh, major?"

Major Hughes thought that Butterill had almost made a pig's ear of it. Averagely well done, the colonel should have said. "Yes, sir."

"Obviously, they've been kept up to their drill; your doing, major, I'll warrant." Lieutenant-Colonel Charles Taylor generally absented himself from barracks, arousing Hughes' curiosity. Why had he unexpectedly appeared that morning to order the usual afternoon parade be carried out in full dress, most often reserved for special occasions? There was the Prize Tournament, of course, which began the following day; the colonel never liked to miss that. But there was something else

The major inclined his head modestly at Taylor's compliment, "Squadron inspection, sir?"

"Of course, of course," Taylor smiled with enthusiasm, picking up his horse's flapping reins. "Lead on, Jonas."


Lock watched the officers' approach out of the corner of his eye. The colonel's horse kept tossing its head, as if restrained, even though he allowed it a loose rein. The troops stood to attention, swords drawn. Lock's right hand rested easily on his thigh, sabre pointing straight up, but the colonel was taking so long with Captain Butterell's troop that many troopers' wrists must have begun to protest at their sabres' weight. Some sloped arms, letting the swords fall backwards so the rear edges rested against their collarbones. But Lock's arms were strengthened by years of controlling the fall of a hammer and working a bellows handle; he was more concerned that Sexton was trying to bite an ear off Sergeant Tyloe's horse. The sergeant gave Lock a black look, prompting him to growl at the animal to behave.

The colonel's party grew closer. Captain Hackett rode over to join them as they reached his troop. Then Taylor was reining his horse to a halt. Bloody hell, Lock thought, as the colonel came to a stop right in front of him.


Colonel Taylor was pleased with what he had seen. Horses gleamed with good health. The men; well, they looked superb, in pristine uniforms and with polished arms. They would be delighted at the order in his sabretache; it was what they had trained for.

He spoke to some of them, most replying nervously. That was understandable, for many had never seen him before. But this trooper seemed different, though Taylor could not put his finger on the reason. Perhaps it was the way he sat in the saddle. A tall man anyway; his straight back seemed to accentuate his height. And he looked confident. A stubborn man, perhaps, the colonel thought. Taylor halted his horse and smiled. "What's your name, trooper?"

"Lock, sir."

The trooper's neutral expression never faltered. Taylor pointed downwards. "I see you still carry the old pattern carbine, Lock. You do not find Lord Paget's design an improvement?"

The trooper looked his colonel straight in the eye. "Easier to load, sir, but more difficult to kill with."

Taylor felt excitement rise inside him. By God, he was a fighter, too, this one. The colonel imagined leading a whole regiment of men like him into battle.

Major Hughes interrupted. "Trooper Lock is one of our better marksmen, sir," he explained. "I have encouraged him to use the new carbine, but…"

"Poppycock, major," Taylor replied, still holding the trooper's gaze. "Our task is to kill Frenchmen. If Trooper Lock finds his familiar weapon more effective in that respect, I am not inclined to insist he change it."

The trooper flicked his eyes towards where Major Hughes sat, but then they came back. "Thank you, sir," Lock said.

His inspection finished, Colonel Taylor walked his horse to the middle of the line so he faced the squadron. "Gentlemen," he raised his voice so all could hear, "I congratulate you. Your performance and turnout have been exemplary. I now look forward with great anticipation to the Prize Tournament, which begins tomorrow. And allow me to tell you why." He reached down to his sabretache and pulled out a sheet of paper. Lifting his arm high, he waved the order above his head. "Yesterday, I received this from Horse Guards, from His Highness, the Duke of York." The colonel cleared his throat to read an extract.

*"His Majesty's government, mindful of its obligations to the peace-loving peoples of Portugal, and of its treat with the emissaries of Spain, has determined to offer them every assistance*

211

*in their struggle with the usurper, Bonaparte."* He paused, scanning the handwriting, *"To this end, you are commanded to embark two squadrons of the 20th Light Dragoons at Portsmouth, to join the remainder of the army for Spain; this force to be under the command of..."* he looked closely at the document, *"Lieutenant- General Sir Arthur Wellesley."*

Taylor stuffed the letter between leg and saddle and beamed at the squadron. This was what he had waited for; what he always prayed for - to command a cavalry regiment in battle. "Next month, we leave for Spain. Napoleon, gentlemen, I am certain, will learn to fear the edge of our steel."


The horses had cooled off by the time they walked back to the stables to be unsaddled. Lock took off his jacket, turning it carefully inside out to protect its white braid and bright yellow trim at collar and cuffs. He placed the bundle in one corner of Sexton's stall before starting to brush off the sweaty marks where the horse's saddle and bridle fitted.

Sergeant Tyloe was rushing about, admonishing men who were slow; upsetting the horses. "Hurry up, you bastards. Morris! Walters! There'll be no supper for you unless you get a move on."

Francis Kittoe strode past Sexton's stall carrying a wooden water bucket. "What's got into him?" he asked. Lock had no idea. "I'll fill your bucket if you pass it over." Lock thanked him and carried on brushing. He picked up the horse's feet one at a time to dig out any earth or small stones trapped in each hoof.

Tyloe still ranted. "Walters, what in God's name d'you think you're about? Get that bloody saddle off now."

Lock let Sexton's hind foot drop and straightened up. Trooper Luke Walters was one of the less able men. Not stupid, exactly, as Kittoe explained, just slow. For some reason his horse remained saddled. Lock double-checked his own animal's tie-rope before ducking out of the stall.

"D'you want to be on a charge?" Tyloe shouted at the unfortunate Walters, who still seemed reluctant, but finally started to undo the girths. Lock soon saw why. Walters' horse had a redraw patch of skin on its back where the saddle had rubbed through its blanket. Walters dropped the saddle outside the horse's stall

"What's that?" Tyloe pointed at the sore and turned on the unfortunate trooper, "Walters, you useless bastard. How long's it been like this?" he accused. "I'll have to report it to the captain. He'll go mad! You know how fussy the major is about the horses. You'll be on a charge, you bloody fool."

Walters hung his head, "Sorry, sergeant."

"Sorry? You'll be bloody sorry. How many punishments have you had already?" Tyloe ranted. "You've really done it this time."

Lock lifted Walters' saddle, running his fingers along one side of the frame. "Sergeant?" He felt sorry for Walters. "Sergeant, let me help him."

"I don't recall asking you to interfere, Lock," Tyloe was brusque, but Lock stepped past him to look at the horse's wound. It did not seem too severe. Saddle-sores often looked worse than they were, just like a blister.

"I can treat that, sergeant. It'll be good as new in a couple of days. You said it yourself - Walters doesn't need to be in any more trouble."

Tyloe glared at him, then back at Walters who was cowed, staring at the floor.

"Very well," he decided at last, "I will not report this to Captain Hackett. He won't want to get the veterinary, anyroad." He pointed a forefinger in Lock's face. "Just make sure it gets better," he said, and marched out of the stables.


Killen usually enjoyed making an inspection after evening stables. Simple things reminded him of home: the sound of horses chewing contentedly; the occasional stamp of an iron-shod hoof. And the smell, of course. He would dawdle, stopping every now and again to watch and listen, just for the pleasure of being around the big animals.

Not this evening. He marched up the aisle between rows of stalls with a purpose, hoping he would find nothing wrong.

His heart sank. Lock glanced towards his friend. "Hello, John."

"What are you doing, Josh?" Killen asked, disappointment heavy in his voice. "What's that?" he pointed at the tub in Lock's hand, but he already knew the answer. "You know I'll have to report this," Killen said sadly. "Why on earth did you do it? Why not report it to the veterinary surgeon yourself?"

"Because Walters would have gotten into trouble," Lock sighed, "that's why."

"And now, you will," Killen said. "Sergeant Tyloe said you would be here and..." his voice tailed off. "He knew!" Realisation dawned. "He knew I would have to report you. Why would he do that?"

Lock grimaced. "You'll have to ask him, won't you," he said bitterly, then flashed Killen a quick smile as he patted the horse's neck. "Come on then, sir, let's get it over with."


Major Hughes came down to the squadron office in a dressing gown. "This had better be worth my while, captain," he grumbled frostily to Hackett, then saw Lock stiffen to attention alongside Cornet Killen. He scuffed wearily over to his desk and sat down. "Tell me the damned story, captain." Hackett explained.

"I assume," the major addressed Lock, "that you'll not deny this?" He raised his eyebrows.

"No, sir."

Hughes rubbed his eyes. He was missing something again. Perhaps, he thought, he was getting old. "You have good reason?"

"It's Walters' saddle, sir; sharp edge on the side-board. It wasn't his fault, sir..." Lock stopped. "It wasn't fair to punish him," he said slowly.

Hughes jumped up. "I'll bloody well decide who it is fair to punish, trooper," he roared. "And I warned you not to find yourself in front of me again!" He abruptly sat back down. "I'll have the saddle checked," he threatened. Lock kept silent, while the major fixed him with a fierce stare, "Can it be mended?"

"Yes, sir."

Hughes sighed. "Hackett, you will ensure that Trooper Lock reports to the saddlers' workshop in the morning. I want every damned saddle checked, and since Lock has identified the problem, he can solve it."

"But sir," Hackett protested, "the tournament. This man is…"

"I know what he is, captain" the major's voice was cold, "but perhaps you do not." He spoke directly to Lock. "You will confine yourself to quarters until tomorrow morning, when one of the sergeants will escort you to your task. You understand me?"

"Yes, sir," Lock said, surprised. He had expected worse.

Hughes flapped his hand. "You are dismissed." He waited until the trooper left. "You thought Lock would win the tournament for your troop, captain," he said to Hackett. "There is no point in denying it. But Trooper Lock thinks only for the moment. That is his fault, as well as virtue. Perhaps, captain, if you insisted on more self-discipline from your men, this situation might have been avoided." That was unfair, Hughes knew, but he was tired. "Mr Killen, you will advise the quartermaster and saddlers they must present themselves to me at eight sharp. Perhaps they have an explanation as to why we are issued with damned inferior equipment. Now, if that is all?"

"Trooper Walters, sir," Hackett reminded the major, "It was his mount."

Hughes rose from his seat, "For God's sake, captain, you can deal with that yourself. For what it's worth I recommend a week's latrine duty." He stomped over to the door, holding it open in curt dismissal, "Goodnight, gentlemen."


Blake-Weston spread his cards on the table. "I do believe I have won again."

Rapton stared at the coloured pasteboards in mock disbelief. "Damn it, Julius, so you have. I shall have to ask you for a loan shortly, if the cards continue in your favour." He threw his hand down theatrically. "Will you look at that, Edward," he said to Jamieson, "the man must be cheating." He gave Lieutenant Jamieson a tiny wink.

"I most certainly am not," Blake-Weston was outraged.

"My dear Julius," Rapton soothed, "a jest, merely a jest. Another hand?"

Silas Tyloe appeared, saluting with a flourish. Rapton shuffled the deck. "What do you want, sergeant?"

"I did what you said, sir," Tyloe was obviously bursting with news.

"And what, pray, was that?" Tyloe looked carefully at the other two officers, but Rapton waved his worries away. "You may say what you wish, sergeant; you are among friends."

"Lieutenant Killen has reported Trooper Lock for..." he paused, "...an offence. He wasn't happy about it, sir," he warned.

"Keeping your options open, sergeant?" Rapton was thoughtful. "So Lock is under arrest?"

"Confined, sir, confined. He won't be in the tournament," Tyloe could not keep the satisfaction out of his voice.

"Sergeant, your insight occasionally amazes me, it really does. So now," he went on sarcastically, "a man who could have won the trooper's tournament, one we might have persuaded not to, is out of our reach."

"I thought you'd be pleased, sir."

Rapton ignored him. "Then I suppose we must concentrate on the officers. Who is likely favourite for that, Edward?"

"Cornet Killen, I believe."

Rapton gave a twisted smile. "We shall just have to ensure Mr Killen loses."

"You certainly won't bribe him, Melville," Jamieson insisted.

"I can beat him," Blake-Weston interjected with confidence.

"Oh, you shall, Julius," Rapton answered, his thoughts elsewhere, "I am convinced of it."


Awards were presented two days after the competition. Harold Hunt from Captain Butterell's troop was adjudged best swordsman from the rank and file, and modestly received an arm-badge.

"Well done; well done indeed," Colonel Taylor was effusive, "Proud to have you in the regiment." Hunt seemed slightly overwhelmed by his commanding officer's compliments, blushing scarlet.

"And you, Mr Killen." Killen had beaten all opponents for the officers' title. Taylor drew the prize sword from its soft leather cover and the heavily decorated blade flashed bright. He handed it to Killen, drawing polite applause from his fellows. Killen turned the fine sword in his hands, raising his head to thank the colonel, and just for a second imagined he saw his father, which left him tongue-tied. Taylor seemed not to notice. He nodded affably at the cornet before moving away in the direction of a proffered wineglass.


"A capital idea, lieutenant; capital." Rapton caught the colonel alone in the mess, expertly steering their conversation. Having failed to find another capable of defeating Killen, betting on the tournament had raised him a pittance. But that did not matter. If this wheeze came off, the profit should pay his mess bill for months.

"And think what it will do for the morale of the men, sir," Rapton continued, "that one of their own should even take part in such a contest."

Colonel Taylor nodded. "Yes; yes." He beckoned Major Hughes. "What think you, Jonas. A competition: best officer pitted against the best of the troopers. What spectacle, eh?"

Hughes was unenthusiastic. "I don't believe Mr Killen would be keen, sir." But Killen, when asked, surprised his major by agreeing.

Taylor was exultant. "What about your trooper, Butterell?"

"I'm afraid, sir," Butterell reported dourly, "that Hunt does not wish to take part. Insists Mr Killen would beat him easily."

"Damn," Taylor expressed disappointment. "Oh well, a good idea gone to waste."

"There is another who might be persuaded," Rapton suggested.

Taylor brightened again. "Well, fetch him, man."

"Sir," Hughes interrupted, "I believe I know to whom Mr Rapton refers. That trooper is on a punishment duty, on my order." He shot Rapton a look like the tip of a bayonet.

"Hah!" the colonel was exultant, "All the better. Tell him his punishment will be commuted if he agrees. Bound to, don't you think?"

Rapton smiled like a cat.

Hughes excused himself. He strode across to Killen, grabbing the cornet by the arm so he spilled his drink. The major propelled Killen to one side of the room where they could not be overheard.

"Can you beat Lock with a sabre?"

Killen, ignorant of the colonel's conversation with Rapton, was confused. "I...I think so."

"You're going to have to," the major scowled. "Bloody Rapton's persuaded the colonel. He's going to let your friend off his punishment if he fights you." He had a sudden thought, "D'you think he'll agree to it?"

Killen knew all about Lock's temper. "If he's angry with me for reporting him, sir, he probably will."


They used the exercise hall, scattering its wood-planked floor with chalk to prevent leather-soled shoes slipping. A row of chairs was set up on one side and Colonel Taylor seated himself right at the centre, Hughes on his left. Captains and subalterns filled the remaining seats, but Rapton was absent.

"I still think it a damn bad idea, sir," Hughes was grumpy. "What if Killen should lose?"

Taylor laughed, "Of course he won't. A trooper defeating an officer? Who ever heard of such a thing?"


Lock knew he was in trouble when two men from Butterell's troop grabbed him. They dragged him backwards into an alley between the buildings so swiftly he had no time to put up a struggle. One of the men planted a short right hand into Lock's midriff; a boxer's punch that knocked the wind from his lungs, doubling him over.

The second pulled him upright, and the first punched him again.

The blow made him retch. Lock sagged against the wall, forcing both assailants to hold him up. The boxer made as if to punch him again.

"Wait." Another man had come into the alley. A commanding voice; one Lock recognised at once. Lieutenant Rapton. He grabbed Lock by the hair, yanking his head up. "Well, well." Rapton stared into Lock's eyes as if searching for something. "You look a little under the weather, Lock. Perhaps you should retire to bed. Yes; that's it. Forget about fencing with Mr Killen."

"No," Lock dragged the word out.

"Oh dear me," Rapton continued. "I think Trooper Lock is feeling a little worse." He nodded at the boxer, who hit Lock once more. "I do realise," Rapton said conversationally, "that you believe you can beat Mr Killen. I am persuaded most of the squadron think so too. Personally; I don't believe you will." He pulled Lock's head up again as if wanting to see the pain he had inflicted. "In fact," he went on, "I know that you will not. Not, that is, unless you wish Mr Killen to find himself alone in an alley such as this."

Lock looked into Rapton's face and believed him. The lieutenant turned away, and again the boxer's fist was in Lock's gut. This time he dropped to the ground, feeling wretched.

"Who's there?"

"Shit!" Rapton swore under his breath. "Come on."

"Who is it?" the voice called once more. Boots scrabbled on the stones, and the three men must have gone, for Lock could hear only one set of footsteps.

"What's going on?" Hands grabbed him again, but only one pair, and they hauled him to his feet. Lock groaned, partly in relief.

Matthew Picker brushed at the dust on Lock's jacket. "Been upsetting someone, have you?"

"I didn't think so."

"You must have," Picker said reasonably. "Last time I saw a man get this much of a lesson, it was me."

"And what had you done?" Lock grimaced as he spoke.

"Don't rightly know," Picker considered, "just be me, I guess."

Lock leaned back against the stonework, clutching his sore stomach. The punches had hurt, but it was bearable. He stood upright; stretched. He would be fine.

"I hear," Picker said, "you're fighting Mister Killen. I hear you're favourite to win." He looked Lock up and down. "Trying to nobble you, I reckon."

"Heard that too did you?"

Picker shook his head. "The sergeants have been making a book, so it stands to reason. Mr. Killen must be worried you'll beat him."

Lock saw that his jacket was still filthy despite Picker's efforts, and that made him angry. Rapton would pay, somehow. "It wasn't his doing."

"You sure?"

"Anyway, there's no harm done. Thanks to you." Lock held out his hand. And this time, Picker took it.


Killen frowned. "Josh! What on earth has happened to you? Your jacket's covered in dirt." He looked Lock up and down. "You are unwell."

"It's nothing," Lock shrugged off his friend's concern, "I'll be fine."

"I shall have the contest postponed," Killen decided, and made to walk over to where the officers sat, but Lock held him back.

"No," he insisted. "Look at that lot."

Killen glanced over his shoulder. The double doors at one end of the hall had been opened, allowing troopers to file in.

"Do you want to spoil their afternoon?" Lock grinned to mask a wince. "They're expecting to watch me beat you."

Killen could see a row of officers seated on the far side. Colonel Taylor, right in the centre, gave a small smile which the lieutenant acknowledged with a nod. He felt nervous. Lock would not defeat him; he was sure of that. Of course, his friend was bigger and stronger. But he, Killen, was good. Hadn't his German fencing master always said so? And Lock was ill. That gave Killen an advantage. He felt badly about it, though; the contest really ought to wait until Lock was recovered.

A whistle blew. "Gentlemen, if you please?" Sergeant Armstrong had agreed to referee. There was a pause while Lieutenant Rapton pushed through the crowd of troopers before making his way to an empty seat next to the colonel. He said something to Tyloe as he passed and the sergeant disappeared back into the throng. Killen felt a knot tighten in his stomach.

"If we are quite ready," Armstrong huffed, looking pointedly at Rapton. The sergeant then produced a pair of wire mesh head-guards. Lock and Killen looked at one another. Lock hated the things. Clumsy and ill-fitting, whilst they might protect a man's face from a wayward sword-cut, they reduced his field of vision.

"Do we have to wear them, sir?" he asked his opponent.

Killen was relieved. He never felt comfortable wearing a guard, either. "I shall trust to your skill, then," he said graciously.

Lock gave his friend a small bow, "And I to yours, sir."

Colonel Taylor whispered to Hughes, "D'you think that wise, major?"

Hughes shrugged: he knew the two men's background. "That's up to them, sir. The surgeon is present, if either should be injured." He doubted that would happen, though.

Taylor nodded. "I must say it makes for a more exciting entertainment."

Armstrong called the two men together, prompting a flurry of activity in the ranks. The colonel commented on it, frowning at Lieutenant Rapton.

"Last minute bets, sir, I'll warrant."

"Have you had a wager?" Taylor raised his eyebrows.

"Of course, sir. On Mr Killen, you understand."

"I'll have a guinea. On Mr Killen, of course. See to it, there's a good chap," Taylor said quietly. Rapton managed to catch

221

Sergeant Tyloe's eye. Beckoning him across, he whispered in the sergeant's ear.

"Very good, sir," Tyloe remembered to salute before rushing off.

"Of course," Rapton said to the colonel, "I gather Trooper Lock is an outstanding swordsman. Killen may have found his master."

"Lock?" Taylor suddenly remembered the tall, confident cavalryman he had spoken to on parade. "Lock," he repeated thoughtfully. Perhaps, unlikely as tradition suggested, he had backed the wrong man. "Then we must just hope for the best, lieutenant."


Lock crossed sword-tips with his friend, and the contest began. Killen made the first attack. He came forward, feeling Lock's responses to his sword-strokes, and finding little resistance, tried to press home his advantage. Lock back-pedalled, but not furiously. He was content to parry; to bide his time; wait for an opening.

Killen stopped. Lock had almost reversed as far as the horde of watching troopers. The cornet lowered his sword slightly, but realised his mistake. Lock saw the slight hesitation and immediately went on the attack. This time Killen was forced onto the back foot. His shoes squeaked on the floor.

Then Lock made an error. Stomach muscles protesting, his next cut went fractionally high. Killen twisted his blade below the stroke, but somehow Lock managed to twitch his sword back to block his friend's thrust. Both men stepped away from one another, Killen breathing hard. He wiped his forehead on his sleeve, but his friend seemed unaffected by the effort. Lock merely smiled, and his sword snaked forward again.


"Honours even, so far, eh, major?" Colonel Taylor spoke to his left but did not take his eyes from the contestants. Despite initial reluctance, Hughes began to enjoy the duel. The two men were evenly matched. Lock was the taller and stronger, but Killen's build gave him the advantage of speed.

"The longer it goes on, sir, the better chance I believe Trooper Lock has," he said quietly

"How so?"

"I'll bet Mr Killen has never wanted for much in his life. The other man? He has probably always wanted. Want breeds stamina, sir."

"And what do you want for, major?" Hughes, surprised by the question, shook his head. What he wanted he seemed unlikely to get.


Lock's frustration increased as both men began to tire, and even he found his sword arm beginning to ache. Whenever he launched an attack, Killen dealt with it easily, so although up to now he had prevented his friend breaching his defence, he could not find a way past Killen's sword.

Lock noticed that when they both broke off, Killen always seemed to restart with a double feint to the left before making his real attack the other way. It was the only weakness he might exploit. Throwing off an overhead cut more forcibly than usual made Killen step back to keep his balance, and the contest paused.

They restarted, and this time Lock attacked his friend's second feint. But Killen was too quick, his sword point flicking up towards Lock's chest. Lock twisted his shoulder back and away, but was almost too late. Killen's blade caught in a loop of white braid on Lock's jacket slicing it through.

A murmur ran through the crowd.

"Was that a hit?" Colonel Taylor jumped up, but Sergeant Armstrong was paying close attention and waved the two men on. Lock looked down at the braid. He was proud of his uniform; it was the best set of clothes he had ever owned. He fingered the broken loop, and anger bubbled.

"I'm sorry, Josh," Killen came forward to inspect the damage. "That was a complete accident."

Lock lifted his sword tip again, and his friend seemed to shrink backwards, but he did not care. His temper rose and somehow reason flew with it. Lock barged forward, the sword light as a feather in his hand. He swung this way and that, forcing Killen backwards, blocking and parrying. Lock's blows grew heavier, but it seemed that their weight did not spoil his control or his accuracy. Killen could not find away through. Lock beat at the cornet's sword, and his friend had no answer.

Then Killen's foot slipped on the chalked boards. He went down on one knee and Lock pressed home his attack. Killen defended desperately, but the weight of blows was too much. He fell backwards, and Lock gritted his teeth in a snarl as he brought his sword down; a vicious, swingeing arc to finish his friend off. To win the contest: to be the best.

"*Josh, no!*" a voice cried loud in Lock's head. He was back in the garden at Halcombe House, and John Killen was on the grass.

"*Josh, no!*" Killen's surprise and anguish shouted at him as if it were now, not years before. He had walked away then, anger still seething, and regretted it.

Lock twisted his wrist midway through the killing downstroke, sending the blade to Killen's right. The rage left him suddenly, like mist in sunshine. He stepped back a few paces with lowered sword, inviting his friend to continue.


"By God, I thought Killen had it lost," Taylor exclaimed. Sergeant Armstrong stepped forward, concerned, but now the cornet was back on his feet.

Lock saw strain in his friend's face. It was unthinkable that an officer should not beat a trooper, even one as good as Lock. Rapton had tried to ensure Killen's success, but for his own ends. From what Picker said, it seemed highly likely the lieutenant was behind Tyloe's bookmaking racket, and merely hoped to insure the outcome. It was a pity the troop would lose their money, but Lock really had no choice.

The swords crossed once again. This time Killen warily stayed back. Lock had to encourage his attack: it must look genuine. He fluffed a simple parry so Killen's sword ran down his blade, clanging on the hand-guard. Lock threw it off before he wiped his sleeve across his forehead, making it look as if he were tiring. Killen's confidence grew. He began to press forward once more. At his next thrust, Lock twisted his sword over his friend's to get inside his guard, but then let the point slide downwards. He saw a look of triumph on Killen's face as his sword came free and the point flicked upwards. It dug into Lock's jacket, just above his heart.

Lock opened his hand; his sword crashed to the floor. He had lost.


"Bravo!" Colonel Taylor jumped to his feet, applauding. The rest of the officers joined him. Only curses and grumbling came from the far end of the hall, but Lock expected that.

"Why?" Killen strode up to him. "Josh, why did you do it? You had me beaten. You..." He shut up suddenly, standing to attention.

"My congratulations, Mr Killen," Jonas Hughes was effusive, "a most impressive performance, if I may say." He shook Killen's hand. "Colonel Taylor wishes to offer his regards, I believe," he added, packing Killen off to where the officers gathered around a steward bearing a tray of wineglasses.

"But you were more impressive, Lock," the major lowered his voice. "I don't believe I have seen a fight thrown in a more professional manner." He held up his hand before the boy could deny it. "Don't tell me I'm wrong," the major said, "I take it you have good reason?"

Lock rubbed his stomach. "Honestly, sir - I couldn't have lasted much longer," he said. "I've not been feeling too well."


Melville Rapton was in an unusually good humour. Thanks to his arrangement with Sergeant Tyloe, and the good sergeant's influence over his peers, it had been he who had made most profit from the book Tyloe ran on the contest. The vast majority of the troop bet on Lock, and the silver they lost weighed comfortably in the lieutenant's pocket. Not a huge sum, but enough to placate the mess steward for a couple of weeks. He bounded up the stairs to his room two at a time and found he had a visitor.

"Julius!" Rapton exclaimed. "We missed you earlier."

Blake-Weston ignored the greeting. "I shall be leaving the regiment tomorrow."

Rapton laughed. "My dear chap, but you've only just arrived!"

"Father," Blake-Weston sniffed, "has purchased me a commission in the Guards."

"Shame," Rapton shook his head sadly, "just as we are about to set off on a great adventure."

"Exactly. I certainly have no desire to suffer the inconveniences of a foreign posting. Hot weather disagrees with me." There were more footsteps on the stairs: Lieutenant Jamieson.

"Ah, Edward," Rapton greeted him, "you will be mortified to hear that Julius is leaving us."

"No!" Jamieson had also pocketed a few of Blake-Weston's golden eggs.

Blake-Weston shifted from one foot to the other while the two lieutenants towered over him. "There is a matter, er..., I wished to discuss," he said hesitantly to Rapton. He looked at the floor. "It is the loan I afforded you, Melville."

"Well, why didn't you say so before, Julius," Rapton clapped him on the shoulder. "We are all gentlemen here. As you know, I am presently unable to settle. Next month, well, that will be a different matter. But please do allow me to give you my note."

"That will be quite acceptable, Melville" Blake Weston said, sounding relieved.

Rapton knew it would be; that Blake-Weston would find a gentleman's agreement preferable to confrontation. And next month, the squadron left for Spain. By the time they returned, the promissory note might well have been forgotten. And if not? Rapton thought the odds of him ever having to cover it were slight.

He fetched three glasses and a bottle from the chest beneath his cot, pouring for each of them.

"Your very good health, Julius," he toasted Blake-Weston. "Personally, I can't wait to feel the sun on my back. And I hear the *senoritas* are very beautiful." He drank the glass of wine straight down, sighing, "I think I shall enjoy Spain."

# Part III

# Hammer of

# the Levites

# Evora, Portugal

## July

# Chapter 23

On the morning of the sixth day, here was proof, the Frenchman thought, that there was no God. Dust: so vile, so useless a substance no deity could have even imagined its creation.

It spread in ripples, an incoming tide over the flat plain of the Portuguese heartland. Kicked up by infantrymen's stamping boots, dirt rose around the marching army like a sea mist. It coated their uniforms and clogged their weapons. It stuck to their sweaty faces, so that if they spoke, or smiled, the skin cracked.

Louis-Henri Loison, General of Division, hero of France, leant from his horse to spit a gritty gob of saliva into the maelstrom at its feet. His left shoulder, where a good arm once hung, ached with fatigue. Dropping the horse's reins to pull a handkerchief from his sabretache, he moistened the cloth with his tongue to pat chapped lips. The animal was trained to stop when the reins were released, and he gave it a smart kick to keep it moving.

Loison's week-long journey was nearly over. The Portuguese must know by now his army was near. Seven thousand men marching with three thousand horses and mules threw up such a dust-cloud that even the damned Spanish, over their border fifty miles to the east, could probably see it. Loison did not care. He would march his veterans into the city of Evora to tear out the heart of partisan resistance in the south. Then every peasant would know that Napoleon Bonaparte, damn him, was master of all Europe.

A single plume of dust sped towards the French army. A dragoon: galloping hard. The rider's cross-belts, that on the parade ground would have been startling white against his olive jacket, were lost in drab brown. Loison rode his horse out to one side of the column of marching men, waiting. His infantrymen strode past, driven on by beating drums.

A bandsman stared up at the general as he passed, drumsticks moving rhythmically up and down. A small boy, Loison saw: just a child. He must have been startled by something in the general's gaze, for he suddenly looked away. Loison sighed, thinking of his own family, safe in France. He watched the drummer-boy swallowed by the dust. An automaton; a conscript, like many of his men, forced to march, shoot, rest, then march again. Or die.

The dragoon yanked his horse to a stop, wiping dirty sweat from his face on the back of one long glove. Loison dropped the reins onto his horse's neck once more. The animal halted. The sun had begun to rise and he used his hand to shade his eyes.

"They are waiting, sire, in front of the city."

Loison grunted, "Horse? Guns?

The dragoon removed his helmet and shook long hair free. "Five or six guns? We saw Spanish gunners. And cavalry," the man gave an embarrassed smile, "the Maria-Luisa Hussars."

Loison grimaced, "So, they have gone back to their own side? I think you have no need to worry about them, *Captaine*. They served Bonaparte badly, and no doubt will do the same for their new masters." He gave a small nod of thanks, dismissing the messenger. So the enemy had cavalry and artillery, but only a small force. This should be easier than expected.


Francisco de la Paula Leite squinted at the dirty-grey dust cloud hanging low in the western sky and felt the fear beat hard and fast in his chest.

He closed his eyes, and for a moment he was back at sea. The cloud became a distant sail. The rough, planked deck of a great oak warship pitched beneath his feet. Her bows drove deep into the troughs between waves, speckling his face with salt spray as she tore through the swell towards the enemy vessel. He heard the snap as breeze filled her studding sails; the creak of spars under strain as the great ship fought to race the wind. Gun-ports crashed open below decks in preparation for battle. He smelt black powder in the wind, the sharp tang of wet timber and canvas, the stink of unwashed men. Captain Leite took a huge breath, as if to save the memory deep in his lungs, and opened his eyes. The colour of his coat had not changed, but now his deck was the back of a horse; his ocean the vast, dry plain, and he wore the insignia of a soldier on his arm. Once more he was General Leite, commander of the Army of Southern Portugal; an older man now, and wiser.

Leite stared westwards again. The dust cloud still hung there, but his fear had vanished. His country needed him to fight.

Something else came from the west; another horseman, travelling fast enough to kick up his own small cloud. Late the previous night, Leite had sent a trusted man to scout the approaching French army. Peasants from the surrounding countryside had been arriving in the city all week. They told of seeing thousands of French dragoons, or hundreds of infantry battalions on the road. Leite listened impassively, for privately he believed few of their tales. In the end he had been forced to send an old friend into danger, to find out the truth.

The rider pulled to a halt and swept off a wide brimmed hat. He flapped it against his right leg, beating dust from the leather; showing his balding head to the early sun.

"General!" The man smiled as he bowed, his sweating horse jogging a semi-circle around Leite with tight, elevated steps. Its neck was soaked dark, and its flanks heaved.

"Well?" Leite asked.

The other man looked grim. "It is as you thought, Francisco," he said, "four battalions of infantry, at least."

The general nodded. "Cavalry?" he asked.

"Dragoons; I counted six hundred. But there will be more, scouting and foraging."

Leite sighed. Four battalions of French infantry meant they brought five thousand men against him. He had only half that number of regular troops, plus a few thousand peasants; enthusiastic, but with hardly a musket between them. "Did you see any guns?"

The other man shook his head. "They will be back down the road with their baggage train. The draught horses will struggle in this heat."

"We will all struggle," Leite worried. "I cannot hold them here, Josef," he admitted, "they are too many." He looked back at the city wall, at the old timber gates guarding its entrance. In ancient times, the Moors had made the massive boundary proof against all intruders. Until at last, a hero came; a Christian knight who stormed the barrier, slaughtering all followers of the Prophet to reclaim Evora for the faithful. Leite shook his head sadly, for though he would lead the fight, he was no hero, while a devil marched toward them: a devil with one arm. "Only God can help us now," he said.

Small stands of cork trees and rocky outcrops dotted the plain in front of the city. They made fine hiding places for the Portuguese, since the old wall had neither deep ditch nor sloping glacis to protect it or offer men shelter. Leite rode out to the very front of his defensive line to look at his army again. The partisans were few; the gaps between their hiding places worryingly wide. Experienced French infantry would have little trouble forcing a way through, he thought. Many of the men stopped what they were doing to smile up at their general as he passed, but Leite could not bring himself to smile back.

The partisans wore no uniform, at least, none that could be recognised as such. Dressed in bedraggled shirts and pantaloons thick with dirt, a few wore hats against the sun and only one man in three carried a serviceable musket. The rest armed themselves haphazardly with knives and swords. Leite saw that some even wielded long, iron tipped pikes. That weapon had been in use for more than a century, and many of the gnarled shafts and rusting spikes the partisans proudly carried looked their age. They might be of some use if the French attacked with cavalry, but against infantry muskets?

At least the Spanish were well armed, Leite conceded, if just as poorly dressed. A *Junta* from across the border had sent him a battalion of infantry recruited from the countryside around the grim fortress of Badajoz, as if to prove that historic hatreds between two peoples could be put aside in the struggle against a common enemy. It was a gracious gesture, he knew, but one which looked doomed to futility.

A Spanish officer, more gaudily dressed than a cavalryman, rode up to the general before saluting. Much of the braid on the front of his jacket was tarnished and torn, Leite saw, and glanced over the man's shoulder. An artillery troop galloped their horses across to a flat area south of the city before beginning to unlimber five cannon. The raucous shouts of the gunners and the thump of gun-trails being dropped to the ground carried clearly in the still air. And Leite had cavalry. Spanish light cavalry, their uniforms untidy but still resplendent from a distance, took up a position on the flank of the guns. Leite watched them sourly. The men might seem impressive, but a closer look would reveal their horses unkempt and underfed. He knew Bonaparte had recruited them, these Hussars of the Queen of Spain, keeping them idle. But even though they had deserted their erstwhile employer when the Spanish people rose in revolt against the French, would they fight now?

The Spanish officer led the way to where his small infantry company waited. How different to his own men, Leite thought. Although a few Spaniards found cover amongst bushes and rocks, far more stood confidently out in the open. Some sat relaxed, smoking and talking; others busied themselves sharpening bayonets, scraping flat stones along the bright steel to keen the edges. It seemed as if every man knew what was expected of him. And Leite could find no gaps for the French to exploit.

A Portuguese spotted the enemy first. His shouts and arm-waving caused a flurry of activity along the defensive line. Ramrods rattled in barrels as men loaded muskets. Artillery officers shouted orders at gunners, who levered at the heavy gun carriage trails with long steel handspikes so their barrels pointed straight at the enemy. Dismounted hussars climbed back aboard their horses and the whole troop formed up in two lines behind the gun battery. Leite looked on with approval. He took out his telescope, peering westwards. Let the damned French come now. But they were still too far away, hidden in the dust, with only the occasional flickering reflection of sunlight from one of a thousand bayonets to suggest how large a force approached.

. Leite lowered his glass. The enemy had advanced to about three-quarters of a mile from the city, he guessed. By now, more Portuguese peasants had spotted them and begun to leave their hiding places. In ones and twos they slipped away, heads down, not looking at those men who stayed behind, and scuttled back towards Evora. Leite could not blame them. Who would not be afraid for his life, facing up to the army of the conqueror of Europe?

But the Spanish infantry seemed completely oblivious. Groups of men still sprawled in what shade they could find, talking amongst themselves, unwilling, it seemed, to tap out their clay pipes or extinguish thin cigars until the last shred of precious tobacco was burnt. Officers walked or rode casually about behind them. The general hoped they would have the heart to fight when the time came.

Then more shouting erupted from Portuguese throats, prompting Leite to raise his telescope. Now only a half-mile away, the first French column emerged from the dust cloud and appeared to be shaking itself into a line. Troops behind the centre of the column moved outwards on each side whilst the men in the middle marked time, stamping down feet to the march-time without moving forward. Leite imagined what must be happening. The drummers in each column would beat out the rhythm while sergeants shouted commands. He glanced back at his artillery battery. The French were in range. Powder and shot ought to be loaded and ready, but the gunner-officers stood unmoving, their guns empty.

The hussars still waited impassively behind the Spaniards, horses swishing their tails at early flies. Should *he* have given the order to fire? Leite was about to ride to the guns before more shouts made him pause. Through his glass he watched the French infantrymen spread out, right across the plain. They formed a single line, wider than the whole frontage of his small army, and as he studied the manoeuvre with reluctant admiration the drums suddenly stopped. Leite was bemused; he had not seen this tactic before. The French were too far away to use their muskets effectively, while none of their cavalry galloped to attack his force. A few Portuguese fired muskets, but at that distance the shots were wasted. Lead balls bounced harmlessly in the grass well short of the enemy.

But then the whole of the French front line raised their muskets and, to an unheard word of command, fired a single, massive volley. The sound was like a crash of thunder across the plain, echoing back off the city walls. Then Leite did understand, for his Portuguese volunteers began to leave the field in scores, no longer caring who saw them go. The musket fire had wrenched their courage away and they ran for the city like hares. Leite cantered his horse amongst them, shouting admonishment, but they ignored him and ran on.

Even worse was to follow. The whole regiment of hussars turned away, trotting off to the southeast. Deserted by their protectors, the Spanish artillerymen whipped horse teams forward and began dragging the heavy gun carriages towards them. They heaved the wooden trails up, dropping them onto securing pins at the rear of each limber. Then the gunners hurled themselves on board horse and limber to gallop off after the hussars. Not one of the guns had fired a shot.

Leite despaired. Those cannon had been his one small hope of delaying the French advance. Their iron shot could cut bloody swathes through columns of infantry or cavalry, and grapeshot, the smaller rough iron balls packed in a canvas bag that would disintegrate in a cannon barrel and spread like a shotgun blast, could halt an attack in its tracks. He had once seen a whole boarding party, crowded on a rolling ship-deck, swept into screaming, twitching oblivion by a barrel-load of grape. Without guns Leite knew he would have to retreat. They must go eastwards: head for Olivenza, deeper inland, then make for the border with Spain. He turned back towards the enemy, his mind made up.

Two hundred yards away, the French had reloaded in the smoke of their first volley and were marching forward. Leite knew he had one minute yet. The enemy would not open fire again until they were about sixty yards from his men, because muskets were woefully inaccurate at a longer distance. It would be a different matter if they faced a solid line of defenders, for then even a poorly aimed shot might hit home. But the Spanish and remaining Portuguese were spread out, gaps between each small group making them awkward targets.

Leite trotted unhurriedly to where a number of Spanish officers waited. They stood behind their men when they ought to have been in front, but Leite held his tongue.

"We'll be overwhelmed." A captain spoke for them all, a note of panic in his voice, "Sir, we must retreat."

Leite shook his head. "We came to fight," he said firmly, "and we will. What will people say if we merely turn and run, like those cowards?" he pointed to where ruts in the dirt were all that remained of his artillery. "That there is no heart left in Portugal and Spain. That God has deserted us. That Bonaparte will be our master, and we his slaves. No, gentlemen, we will fight!" Sweat pricked his forehead. Here he was, a sailor - telling soldiers how to behave! Leite wiped his face on his sleeve. "But then...then we will retire." And the general calmly explained how it would be done.


A hundred yards away, the French came to a halt, dropping their musket butts to the ground. Bayonets were dragged from leather scabbards and slotted onto warm muzzles.

Leite stared through his telescope. The first line of infantrymen had the number '58'clearly stamped into the badges on their tall shakos. This time the general recognised what the French were doing. Fixing bayonets in full view was another simple tactic to spread fear and despondency through the ranks of an unsteady enemy. It worked, frightening the few Portuguese who remained. Muskets banged wastefully from their hiding places, but the Spanish sensibly held their fire. Like professional soldiers should, they waited for their enemy to come closer still, so that when they finally pulled their triggers the hail of lead balls would kill and maim as many as possible.

Drums rattled behind the leading French companies. Young drummer-boys, deliberately concealed amongst more experienced troops, must be nervous. Leite heard them clearly, testing drum-skins, preparing to beat out the march-time.

The Spanish and Portuguese troops waited as the sun rose higher. Leite's horse fidgeted, so he walked it quietly in a circle.

French officers began shouting commands. Muskets were raised, bayonet-points forward. Then, as one, the drums began, and the long line of Frenchmen started forward.

*Boom-boom, boom-boom!*

Dust rose again as they stamped their boots down in time with the drumsticks. Ten paces forward. The Spanish troops still held their fire. Twenty paces. Leite felt sure that a nervous Spaniard must pull his trigger too soon, but the officers kept their men in check, waiting, waiting. Thirty paces forward. More Portuguese deserted, scuttling back towards to safety, but still the Spanish infantry did not fire. Thirty five paces. Leite collapsed his telescope, pushing it back into its leather saddle-holster. He could see perfectly well without it that the French were not going to stop, and he would have to run. Shortening his horse's reins, he prepared for retreat.

Sixty paces away, the French line halted. Officers screamed; muskets were raised. The grey-coated infantrymen were close enough for Leite to see grime on their unshaven faces. Their muskets all pointed straight at him. But in the few seconds after their halt, Spanish officers ordered their own men to present arms, and as French infantrymen jammed musket butts into shoulders, the Spanish gave the order to fire.

Leite's battle-line seemed to explode flame and smoke. Hot lead balls slammed into the leading French companies. Men fell or staggered back as they were struck. Sergeants frantically pulled injured soldiers away or pushed others into gaps left by the dead. Then the French fired. Bullets whistled past Leite, frightening the horse, but none was close enough to cause him injury. And he saw that because the Spanish fired first and were masked by smoke from their own guns, they seemed to have taken few casualties. Most were feverishly reloading.

More shouts came from the French. Muskets tipped with bright steel bayonets inclined forward and the drums began again, forcing men onwards to the march-rhythm. Those Spaniards quickest to reload fired again at the mass of grey-coated bodies advancing toward them. Others were mustered into companies, readied to retreat. The French marched stolidly forward, enduring the musket fire, but became more confident as it slackened. Many Spaniards were hurrying to form ranks.

Then all at once the French began to run; shouting, stumbling sometimes; keeping their line intact. Most of the remaining Portuguese took to their heels, fleeing back towards the city, leaving dead and injured men behind. Thankfully, Leite saw, they did not abandon their weapons.

Two companies of Spaniards formed a new line fifty paces to the rear. Officers screamed at the men to check their muskets were loaded. The French advanced, the Spaniards fired and the grey-coated infantry flinched, a respite that gave time for yet more

Spaniards to run back and form up, then turn to fire a fresh volley at their attackers.

"East, go east!" Leite screamed. His officers understood and chivvied their men across the plain. The Spaniards fought grimly, loading and firing their muskets in the teeth of a determined French advance, running back to reform again and again; giving covering fire so their comrades could do the same. And, faced with such stinging volleys, and with their enemy retreating, the French attack began to stall.

General Leite stared over his shoulder at the city walls; at the peasants who climbed to the ancient battlements only to watch their army leave. The French would not take long to smash their way in, he thought. Perhaps they would be merciful, but he doubted it. At least most of his tiny army was saved. The hills around Olivenza would protect them for a while; they could rest there and regroup. He felt badly about the city, but there was nothing to be done. As he rode eastwards, Leite bowed his head and prayed, because, to his shame, he had been right: only God could help Evora.


General Loison clambered from his horse. The left sleeve of his jacket caught on the nearside stirrup and he tugged it free in irritation. Men of the 58th *Ligne* leading the advance now sat with their tall shakos on the ground beside them as they lit clay pipes. They swigged at canteens, soothing throats parched by bitter gunpowder from musket cartridges, ignoring the bodies of dead comrades. Thankfully, they had taken few casualties, Loison thought, against an unusually well-organised body of troops. But they had cleared the damned Portuguese from the field, so although his infantrymen had not given chase Loison had no desire to force them on. Ambushes might be laid in the eastern hills to trap an unwary pursuit, and taking the city had always been his objective. So the general let his troops rest. He would find more work for them soon enough.

"*Trépied!*" Loison shouted back at a crowd of dismounted officers gathered behind him. A scrawny lieutenant pushed his way out of the group, walking sullenly forward.

"Why do you call him that?" one of Loison's aides whispered.

Loison grinned. "Because, my dear LeMande, they say he's hung like a donkey!" the general laughed.

The lieutenant scratched at a spot on his cheek, drawing blood, and scowled at the aide. Loison ignored his insubordination. Taking a telescope from one of his saddlebags he pulled the tubes apart one-handed, gripping the eyepiece between his teeth. He motioned the lieutenant to stand in front of him, facing the city, and rested one end of the glass on his right shoulder. "Keep still!" Loison commanded as the lieutenant picked at his face again.

Loison twisted the eyepiece so an image sharpened into focus. Two huge wooden gates were set into the city wall. That was the weak spot, but the gates were protected by bastions, semi-circular towers which jutted out either side. There were no windows or loopholes piercing the masonry, but he knew that from their crenellated summits defenders might catch attacking infantrymen in a vicious cross-fire. He panned the telescope further. Stonework both sides of the gates looked ancient; massive blocks, smoothed by centuries of weathering. But the general was not fooled. The wall might be old, but firing at it with the small six-pound field guns that travelled with his army would be like trying to bring down an elephant with a sling-shot. It would take weeks to smash a way through. So it had to be the gates.

Loison raised his voice. "Robert!"

An artillery captain stepped forward, "Sir?"

"How long before your guns arrive?"

Robert was reticent. "Two hours, sir," he said apologetically.

"Two hours?" Loison took his eye from the glass, turning angrily on the hapless captain.

"The horses are tired, sir."

"Tired? My God, we're all tired!" the general shouted. "I need them here now!" The artillery officer stared at his boots.

Loison shook his head in exasperation. "Double up the teams. You have whips; use them! Christ, do I have to do everything myself?" Robert fled.

Loison stared after him; the idiot was a slacker. "And someone bring me food!" the general yelled as an afterthought.

In the end, Loison's impatience made him rash. Fortified by a hastily produced bottle of claret and bread his servant scrounged from a grenadier's knapsack, he determined to attack without the damned guns. His infantry would take the glory. And when news of Captain Robert's tardiness reached General Junot, Robert's hoped-for promotion would be blocked. It would serve the imbecile right, Loison decided.

His plan was simple, but simple often worked best. The meanest foot-soldier could understand such orders. The *tirailleurs*, his light infantry, would go forward to snipe at Portuguese defenders; covering fire for the column he would launch at the gates. Muskets showed above the battlements, and pikes, but that was all; no cannon. Perhaps they had been unable to hoist guns high up to the fire-step running behind the top of the wall. Success was certain.

Officers formed the column with grenadier companies in its front ranks. The tallest and strongest infantrymen were positioned in the centre, each man carrying an axe to hack and smash at the ancient timber gates. It should all be over before the guns arrived. Bonaparte, once a lowly artilleryman, would not approve, but why should Loison care? He called his commanders to give final orders.

In pairs, the *tirailleurs* went forward. Trained to crouch low to the ground and use what cover they could find, one man of each pair searched for a target while the other kept watch, swiftly re-loading his own musket at the same time. The tactic usually worked well on a battlefield, but close to the city wall the ground had been cleared. The *tirailleurs* had nowhere to hide so very soon Portuguese musket balls began to kick up dust around them. The bombardment forced them to dodge and run, and made it awkward for them to shoot up at the battlements with any accuracy. Much of their fire went over the defenders' heads.

Then the column began its advance, a huge block of infantrymen, thirty soldiers broad and twenty deep: six hundred men thrown at a city wall protecting ten thousand. The gates must be breached.

"What's happening?" Something was wrong. Loison, mounted again, could see that much. He heard the clattering sound of musket balls striking stone, but the attacking column seemed to have come to a halt. A captain cantered his horse back towards the general and Loison repeated the question.

"The peasants are fighting back," the officer reported with disgust. Loison dropped the reins on his horse's neck to pull open his telescope. It was difficult to keep the damned instrument steady on horseback, but he concentrated, focussing on the gates.

Defenders must have massed on the battlements above. A veil of musket smoke hung over the gateway, like fog on a hilltop, and he saw that the Portuguese were throwing things! Rocks, tiles, even what looked like iron pots and pans; just about anything that could be used as a missile, it seemed, was hurled down onto the attacking column. And even though his infantrymen were firing back they must be unsighted by smoke from their own muskets.

Loison reasoned his *tirailleurs* had to be doing some damage, but it was not enough. Grenadiers reeled away from the column, holding their bloodied heads in agony. Others fell where they were hit; the tall shakos most wore offering little protection from falling rocks. Men farther back in the column still marched forward, unaware of the carnage at the gates. Stepping over fallen comrades they merely added to the crush right at the front. The column slowed; stopped. And then, all at once, the great mass began to inch its way backwards prompting a faint cheer from the city walls.

"Shit!" Loison cursed. The attack would fail. "Where are the damned guns?" he yelled at his aides. LeMande shrugged a response; there was still no sign of the artillery captain, damn him. Now he would be forced to wait.


Just as Robert predicted, the guns took two hours to arrive. There were not enough horses to double up the teams without leaving half the battery behind, and the artillery officer reasoned that would

243

incur far more of his general's anger than being late. And even though the horses had been whipped until blood ran from the weals, they were too worn out with tiredness to make up any time.

In the event his decision was the right one. Having worked himself into a fury watching wounded men dragged back to the French lines, his general ignored the delay. Surgeons worked at a feverish pace, bandaging heads and splinting limbs. At least there were more wounded than dead, but those men unable to walk would be a burden on the return march. Loison would make the bastards inside Evora pay for that.

Six-horse teams, dog-tired, swung their field guns into position, where gunners swarmed around them like flies on dead flesh. Some men lifted heavy carriage-trails from their caissons and dropped them to the ground. Others scoured the area, clearing rocks that might snag fragile wheels as yet more hauled on axle-ropes, dragging each gun into position. Artillerymen hand-spiked the trails around so every long barrel pointed in approximately the right direction. A sergeant finalised the adjustment of each gun, squinting down the barrel at his target while he turned its elevating screw one way to lift the barrel, or the opposite to depress it, until he was satisfied. Shot and powder bags were stacked within easy reach, and leather buckets of water fetched to wet wool pads fixed on the ends of the long, timber rammers. Each soaking fleece must be thrust down a hot barrel to snuff out the glowing remnants of burnt gunpowder before a new charge could be loaded. At last, the horses were led away to the rear, out of enemy range. Only then could the gunners stand easy, ready when they were needed.

Loison waited until the light began to fail. Approaching dusk would make a defence more difficult for the enemy. This time he would order two attacks, one launched at the wall on the French left flank; a feint, designed to draw defenders away from the big gates on his right which were the main target. Now the city would fall. A major of engineers had told his general he believed the gates so old and fragile only two or three cannon shots might smash a way through. Two companies of grenadiers were ordered forward, one each side of the right-hand battery's line of fire. They would attack any breach the guns made. And this time they would be protected by lines of infantry firing up at the defenders.

Loison ordered the guns to begin. The left-hand battery fired first. A huge gout of dirty grey smoke spewed from the nearest cannon's mouth, the recoil slamming its carriage backwards. Men heaved against wheel rims and lifted the trail, dragging the gun back into position. Loison tried to see how the shot fell. The gun-barrel was cold so the six-pound iron ball dropped short, but bounced up, striking the base of the wall. Grazing, artillerymen called that. The sergeant who fired the shot nodded with satisfaction. As the gun barrel warmed, each ball would strike the old stones without grazing first.

Then the right-hand battery fired. Loison concentrated on what was happening on this flank: the important one, where the real attack would happen. Gun-smoke masked the grenadiers as they began to move forward, pale dustcoats turning them to ghosts in a smoke-haze.

The nearest gun of the three that made up the battery fired again. Loison could not see whether the gates had been hit yet; the acrid fog blinded him to almost everything. Musket shots rattled the stonework and must be making the top of the wall an unhealthy place. But there were no shouts yet, no yells of victory. Just the concussion of guns and a distant crackle, like a raging fire, as hundreds of lead balls flayed the city wall.

And then the sound changed. It was not the roar of victory the general expected but a quietening. Musket fire slackened. Word must have passed back, though no-one came to tell him, for more infantry companies began moving forward into the smog. The right-hand battery stopped firing. Loison called for his aides and his horse was brought forward. To his left, the guns still hammered away uselessly at the wall on that flank, but it was not important. Someone else could order them to cease firing because the gates of Evora had been breached, and now the city would be his.


Smashed and smoking, fallen timbers were still being cleared from the archway as the general rode in. The old gates must have taken several direct hits, Loison thought with satisfaction, before the grenadiers' huge axes cut through what remained. French troops poured inside to rampage through the streets. The cobbles in front of him were a teeming mass of inhumanity.

The screaming had begun. Those inhabitants who put up any sort of resistance were shot or bayoneted unceremoniously. Groups of infantrymen ran from building to building, smashing down doors and kicking windows, seeking women, wine and plunder. Some small houses were already in flames.

Loison ignored all of it, for more important matters demanded his attention. "Bateleur!" He called one of his most trusted captains forward. Loison pointed out a street which snaked towards the centre of the city. "Find the *Alcade*," he commanded. "The mayor always carries the keys to the treasury. And set a company to guard it." A sudden crackling from across the narrow street made all the horses start, and a tongue of flame licked up a window frame, spitting smoke into the night. Loison nodded at the captain, who saluted, turning away, but the general called him back. "And when you've done that, find women," he ordered. "You know what I like."

"And if none can be persuaded, sire?"

"Offer them money." Bateleur gave him a quizzical look. "Just tell them they'll be paid," Loison said. They would not be, but who would care? If they complained, death was a simple enough punishment. The captain forced his way through the crowd to his horse. "No ugly bitches like the last time," Loison shouted after him, "and make sure no poxed dragoon has screwed them first!"

A tall man dressed in a cassock shouldered his way through the crush. He squeezed past infantrymen still swarming around the general and his aides, and miraculously it was not until he had almost reached Loison's side that he was grabbed roughly by a pair of sergeants.

*"General!"* the priest shouted, in perfect French, startling the sergeants enough to loosen their grip. The priest shook them off. "General!" Loison turned his head towards the man. "You must stop them!" The priest's hair was wild. "They are killing everyone!"

Loison shrugged, "If they fight my men, they will be killed."

"But, women and children? Old men? They cannot fight!"

Loison stared at the man's black clothing with distaste. Priests! Vultures - preying on the young, the old and the sick. They should all be exterminated.

"Please, general, call off your men!"

"I am tired of you, priest," Loison turned away. "Get rid of him!" he ordered the sergeants, and the priest was immediately caught up by a dozen hands before being dragged off into the crowd.

Then a stray Portuguese, chased by bayonets, ran blindly into the side of Loison's horse. With panic-stricken eyes he caught sight of the general's empty sleeve, pinned up like the stump of a wing. "*Maneta!*" he screamed in terror, "*Maneta!*"

Loison frowned. That was the nickname the peasants had given him, '*Penguin*'; he supposed because the jacket sleeve reminded them of a flipper.

A pair of infantrymen caught the Portuguese to carry him off. "*Maneta,*" he still screamed, until a musket-butt smashed into his face and shut off the noise. Loison closed his ears. He had heard too many screams. The damned peasant reminded him of his own shame; his own screams, while the surgeon sawed off his shattered left arm. He called to his aides and rode on, deeper into the city.

Meanwhile, on the streets, the population died. They had killed to keep the French out, so now they must die in their turn. Men were stabbed, or shot, even though they might plead for quarter. Women raped before their throats were cut, their children tossed carelessly onto bonfires. They screamed and died as Loison's veteran troops took a terrible revenge for their own casualties. Streets were left littered with the dead and the dead-drunk. Gutters and drains overflowed with blood. Flames reddened the sky. Evora cried, long into the night.

From the top floor window of what must once have been a wealthy merchant's house, Loison looked down onto the streets, into the chaos he had made, and saw that it was good. He was hot and tired, and the stump of his arm ached like the devil. Tomorrow would be the seventh day of his march, and he would rest; but now? "Marcel!" Loison shouted for his servant while he tugged thick velvet drapes across the window. "Marcel! Find out where the hell Bateleur's got to! And for God's sake, find me some food!"

For the heat of victory had made his groin itch, and his stomach was empty.

# Part VI

# Jericho's walls

# Mondego Bay, Portugal

## August

# Chapter 24

A wave caught the longboat obliquely, rolling the small vessel heavily to port. Balanced in the stern, the boatswain leaned hard on the tiller, fighting the swell.

"Row, you bastards," he yelled, as eight brawny oarsmen dug their blades into swirling water.

Joshua Lock gripped the gunwale with white-knuckled hands. A voyage across the Bay of Biscay had shown him he would have made a poor sailor, but this was proving the worst part; approaching the beach, where the sea grew shallower and the waves malevolent.

Since the early hours he had watched the army disembark. The green-jackets quit their rotting transport ships first. They were to be the advance guard, these men carrying rifles - trained skirmishers who would spread out into the countryside surrounding the beach to protect the army's landing site. One of their boats was upset in the breakers, but through a borrowed telescope Lock saw the men struggle ashore, soaked but alive.

The boatswain kept watch over his shoulder. Another wave was catching them. He must judge his moment finely; launch the longboat just as the wave-crest rose beneath it. The oarsmen hauled a steady rhythm, awaiting his order.

"Get ready, boys," the boatswain called, glancing back once more, "ready now." The wave was almost upon them. Lock shut his eyes and hung on tight.

"Now! Now!" the boatswain's voice rose to a scream. The stern lifted as the wave took the boat, hurling it shoreward. Eight oars dug water. Lock felt the bow drop into a wave-trough and spray soaked his uniform. He wiped salt from his face, half-opening one eye. The nearest oarsman's mouth gaped as he panted, neck sinews bulging taut from his efforts. Oar-blades forced the sea back, drizzling it on the upstroke before they sliced into foaming water once more.

Abruptly, the pace of the boat slowed. The swell gently lifted her bows. The oarsmen stopped rowing.

"Out, out, you dogs!" the boatswain cried, as the two forward rowers shipped their oars before vaulting out into waist deep water. Each man took a line from the prow to drag the longboat towards the beach. Lock felt the once bucking craft steady, then the longboat seemed to stagger as its keel ground into sand.

"Time for you 'lubbers to disembark," the boatswain grinned, "and the Good Lord help you all!"

The remaining oarsmen splashed overboard, heaving on the gunwales so the longboat stuck more firmly. Even then, the swell began to twist the stern so the craft swung broadside to the waves.

With five other troopers Lock clambered over the side, dropping almost gratefully into the sea. Knee-deep water filled his boots and soaked his woollen overalls. The longboat's side swung at him but a seaman grabbed him by the shoulder to stop him falling. He thanked the sailor profusely, wondering if his legs would ever recover from the pitching, rolling transport ship. Even wading to the beach was hard work. The undertow sucked sand from beneath each step, twisting his ankles, but eventually Lock reached the water's edge before turning to look back out to sea.

Mondego Bay was full of ships. Big three-masted transports were attended by smaller sloops and brigs. Tiny sailboats tacked here and there, skilfully avoiding oar-driven longboats and punts that tracked back and forth from shore. And far out, in deep water, sat the guardians; massive ships of war bristling with cannon, ready to intercept any plundering privateer that might try to disrupt the landings.

Lock watched two more longboats pull away from his transport, ferrying another dozen cavalrymen through the gauntlet of wave-crests and hidden rocks. From the ship alongside, more horses were being offloaded, and he worried for them. The army had brought so few. For a reason Lock was unable to fathom, not enough transports were available for all, so only sixty troop-horses had been loaded. Sixty! Between three hundred men! He was told more horses would be procured at their destination, but the artillery were allowed to embark far more. Surely it would be easier to buy draught horses than cavalry mounts?

He saw two horses lowered over the transport's side. Tied together, with canvas slings beneath their bellies, a long rope trailed from each animal's halter. The horses' legs began to paddle as they dipped in the ocean, then a seaman clambered down pulley ropes to release their slings while another stood in the stern of a small rowboat, grabbing for the halter-ropes. Lock shook his head in disbelief. The animals were forced to tread water whilst another two were lowered and their lead-ropes caught up. Only then did the rowboat begin its slow progress towards the shore, with all four horses swimming along behind.

"Lock!" Major Hughes had come ashore earlier. As he walked his charger up to Lock a spent wave washed over his boots. The horse hurriedly backed away, and Lock watched the major sooth the animal, noticing Hughes' uniform was wet, the back of his jacket plastered in sand.

"Bloody stupid way to get them ashore," the major complained. "Mine was on a punt. Like that one," he pointed at a flat-bottomed barge approaching the beach. Apart from oarsmen it carried two officers, standing upright to steady their horses. The barge grounded gently on the beach, allowing each soldier to simply clamber out still holding his horse, which hopped high over the gunwale before paddling onto dry land.

"Did you see that, damn it? I had to bloody well vault onto mine when we got close to shore. Had to jump out of the bloody boat into the sea! The horse couldn't stand up straight for ten minutes; its legs had gone." Lock smiled. That would explain the state of the major's clothes.

Hughes pointed out a boat landing further down the beach. "Christ, look there!" The vessel tilted on its side as it hit the sand, tipping oarsmen and soldiers into the surf. Four horses staggered out of the sea after it. One fell onto its side, and in the confusion the sailor in charge let go of all four halters. Finding themselves free, and on dry land at last, the soaking troop horses careered off down the beach, leadropes flying.

"See if you can catch them, Lock, before they end up in Lisbon."

Lock gave his major an uncomprehending look.

"For god's sake, don't look to me for an explanation," Hughes growled, "I thought we were supposed to be in bloody Spain."

"I have heard," John Killen told his friend, "that the Spanish did not really want our help. Something like that, anyway." Lock put his weight behind a brush-stroke. All the troop horses stood tied to one long rope line strung high through a row of trees. Their coats were full of sand and salt. Lock's brush bumped across Sexton's ribcage. Bones showed through the horse's skin; it had lost weight on its long sea voyage.

"But I thought that they were the ones who asked." Lock dragged his brush through the curry, tapping the metal comb on the sole of his boot to knock out grease and loose hair. He packed the tools back in his valise before taking out an iron hoof pick.

"God knows. The Portuguese had also sent emissaries to London, apparently, so we are to help them instead." Killen perched on a rock. He watched Lock lift one of the horse's forefeet. "I thought you might have one of the troopers do that for you, now you are a corporal."

Lock had been promoted after the Prize Tournament, on Colonel Taylor's recommendation. Now he glanced sourly at the single white stripe, newly sewn on the sleeve of his jacket by Sergeant Armstrong's wife. "And how would I pay? An extra 3d a day doesn't go very far. Of course," he feigned envy, "that doesn't seem to be a problem for you, lieutenant."

Killen bristled. "Grandfather purchased the commission," he said tartly, "and well you know it." Lock was only teasing, but the newness of his rank made him sensitive. "And it was my good fortune that Blake-Weston chose to sell, and I had seniority."

"By a few hours."

Killen sighed. "There is no need to be horrid, corporal," he countered, "especially as I have something for you." He reached inside his jacket and brought out a small package, carefully bound with twine.

Lock was surprised. He could never remember having a present before, certainly not one that had been wrapped. "What is it?"

Killen looked smug. "You will have to open it. Go on," he encouraged but seemed slightly shocked when Lock leant down to extract a small knife from inside the cuff of his boot. He carefully cut the string, peeling off the brown paper.

"What is it?" Killen asked. Lock examined the gift in the fading daylight; a crucifix, carved from dark wood. A hole drilled in the top of the cross allowed it to be strung with a leather thong to wear round the neck. Lock twisted it in his finger, noticing that the edges had been carefully smoothed so it would not chafe the skin. Killen must have known.

"Edward Gaunt made it for you," the lieutenant explained. Killen had wangled a few days leave before the squadron sailed. Travelling home, he brought back a spare horse for himself as well as the gift. "He carved it from that piece of the Defiance I collected. He hoped it might help keep you safe," Killen went on. "They all did."

"Not your grandfather."

"He would not wish you ill, Josh," Killen said. "I am disappointed you might think so."

Lock shrugged. He stuffed the crucifix in his pocket.

"Put it on, won't you?" Killen pleaded, but Lock left it there.

"Maybe later," he said gruffly. "I'll see."


Jonas Hughes unrolled a large map onto the trestle table at one side of his tent. He weighted one end with its leather carrying-tube and fetched a pair of books for the other two corners, to stop it curling. Hughes' desk was already set, the squadron ledgers stacked squarely at one end. At its centre he placed his two ivory inkwells, afterwards rummaging in his travelling chest until he found quills to join them. When all was in order he sat, contemplating elephants and tigers while awaiting his guests.


"We are in dire need of accurate intelligence, gentlemen," Hughes indicated the map as his captains and lieutenants gathered around. "This is the main road to Leira," he tapped the thick, wavy line with a forefinger. "A couple of engineers with the Rifles have reported on its condition, and God help the artillery if they prove correct." He stopped, expecting some reaction, but there was none. They were all paying close attention. "We believe we know where the enemy is concentrated, but Portuguese reports have been conflicting. They..," he paused, lowering his voice, "they cannot altogether be relied upon." The major unbuckled a flat leather case drawing out four sheets of paper. "These are copies of the main map. They are hand drawn, and as you see," he waved his hand over the trestle table, "we have very little detail. We must fill in that detail. Sir!" He stood to attention as Colonel Taylor entered the tent.

The other officers followed suit and Taylor nodded at them in acknowledgement. "Carry on, major." The colonel seemed in jaunty mood. "Just came to wish you luck, gentlemen."

Hughes held out a map. "Captain Hackett, you will take this road." He pointed at the drawing. "We need rivers, villages, houses, roads; everything, in fact, marked on it. And we especially require information about the French. Ask the villagers. We must hope they understand some English."

"What if they don't sir," Lieutenant Jamieson piped up.

Hughes gave him a withering stare, "Then you must use your initiative, lieutenant. Mr. Rapton," he held out another copy, "you will take this road, to the south-east. Notice that it stops here," he stabbed his finger down, "but the shape of these hills suggests the road may continue between them, curling back towards the main road, here." He traced the shape of the valley on the large map. "If that is indeed the case, it would make an ideal spot for the French to hide a brigade ready to hit this army in the flank as we march. We *must* know what is hidden there."

The major passed the other two maps to Captain Butterell and one of his lieutenants, pointing out the routes they should follow. "General Wellesley has instructed we go forward no farther than a few leagues," he said. "As we can muster so few horses, he does not wish any lost in needless skirmishes with the enemy. Look after them well, gentlemen, or you will answer to me." Hughes took the large map and began to roll it up, "And allow me to wish you joy of the morrow."

Four patrols left well before first light. Lieutenant Rapton led one, choosing Sergeant Tyloe as his shadow. With no concession to his new rank, Lock brought up the rear. Once the army's encampment fell behind them, the horses' feet were loud on the dirt track, for apart from the occasional rattle of a scabbarded sabre the night was silent.

Half a mile on, they were stopped. "Halt!" A voice rang out. "Who goes there?"

Rapton looked about, but could see no-one. "Who is that? Show yourself!"

Lock thought his night vision pretty good. He stared to the front but could make out no shadow, no movement: nothing.

"Where the hell is he?" he heard Rapton whisper nervously to Sergeant Tyloe.

A figure appeared from a stand of trees at the roadside; a big man, wearing a green uniform that had made him almost invisible in the darkness. Carrying a rifle across his chest, he stepped into the middle of the track where the cavalrymen could see him.

"Who the devil are you?" Rapton demanded.

"I might ask the same of you," the rifleman said, and added, "sir," after looking the lieutenant up and down.

"Patrol: 20th," Rapton snapped. "Isn't it damned obvious?"

"Advance piquet, 95th, sir, and well now, sir, it is, and it isn't." The rifleman spoke affably, with an Irish twang. "You could just as well be a Frog patrol, so you could, all dressed up in your fancy blue coats."

"Speaking English?" Rapton exploded.

"You'd be surprised, sir, you'd be surprised," the Irishman said calmly. His bulk still blocked the road, and now he raised his rifle. "And you haven't given me the password, sir."

Rapton looked askance at Tyloe, who shrugged hopelessly. "Obviously no-one thought to provide me with a password, private," the lieutenant looked down haughtily. "Now let me through."

The rifleman hesitated, as if deep in thought. Eventually he lowered his weapon. "Very good, sir," he allowed at last, "but I'd be careful if I were you. Frogs are about somewhere, sure as I'm standing here…" He stepped back quickly to avoid Rapton who rode on, straight at him.

Only Lock noticed a second rifleman slip out of the shadows to stand alongside the Irishman.

"Bloody cavalry," the other man opined, "think they're God's bloody gift."

"That, they do, Dan," the big Irishman caught Lock's eye and held it as he rode past, "that, they do."

# Chapter 25

Captain Maurice Pinot was lost. He had long ago discounted the map he had been provided with as a work of fiction, relying instead on his instinct and the tracking skills of one of his sergeants.

But now it seemed both had let him down. He led his thirty men up a steep tree-lined track that grew narrower and narrower until the small field gun that travelled with them caught a wheel and became stuck fast. It took an hour to carefully manhandle the gun and its limber over boulders threatening to shatter its fragile spoked wheels - the same wheels that helped make the cannon so manoeuvrable on an open battlefield. Pinot considered abandoning the gun. Without it his *chasseurs* would be able to move faster across this wooded terrain, but the loss would make him unpopular with his commanding officer. He mashed the burned-out butt of a cigar on the tree he leant against and straightened up.

*Sous-Lieutenant* Tirenne trotted back to the troop. Pinot had sent him forward, down the hill, to scout the valley floor.

"I found buildings," Tirenne dismounted as he spoke, "and a stream. We can water the horses."

"Did you see anyone?"

The lieutenant shook his head as he loosened the horse's girth. "Every door is open. It looks abandoned. I went as close as I dared, but I could not be sure."

Pinot thought Tirenne was probably right. His troop had come across any number of farms, and even some villages, from which every occupant had fled.

"We will go there," he decided. Men and horses could rest until dawn. Or at least until he could work out where the hell they were.


Pinot selected five good men. Carrying loaded carbines they moved swiftly down to the valley floor, crouching as low as their long boots would allow. The captain cringed inwardly each time a sword scabbard clanged on a rock, but no-one woke in the farmstead. At last he poked his head through the doorway of what he assumed was the main house; little more than a cottage. But Tirenne was right - the inside had been gutted; any furniture hauled away. Pinot straightened up and let out a deep breath before calling the rest of his troop out of hiding.

"Christ, what's that stink?"

"Lefebre's cooking!" A few *chasseurs* laughed, but others admitted they could smell it too.

Their sergeant became serious. "What are you giggling for, Roget? Bugger off and do something useful; check the horses have all had a drink." He sniffed the air again, "Something's died somewhere." Pulling a face, the sergeant marched off to investigate.

Pinot clambered along the wall surrounding the farmstead, taking care at those places where the stonework had collapsed. It would be so easy to fall and break an ankle. In the blackness before dawn he could not see far down the track leading away from the buildings, along the valley floor, but instinct prickled the back of his neck. One of his men handed him a mug of coffee. The captain blew steam away from its brim while he considered.

"You."

The *chasseur* who had brought the mug turned back, "Sir?"

"Fetch me Lieutenant Tirenne," Pinot commanded.

Rapton first decided that patrolling in darkness was too frightening, and second that it was too easy. He was, in fact, bored with it. Early on, the track crossed straight over a broad plain, but because it was dark and he could see very little on either side his nerves were on edge. But as they rode further he relaxed. If he could not see the French, then they could not see him, he reasoned. He was in no danger. Just the same, he pulled one pistol from its holster in front of his saddle and double-checked he had primed the pan.

"Think we'll run into trouble, do you sir?" Sergeant Tyloe also sounded nervous.

"I hope we do, sergeant," Rapton tried out his new found confidence. "Think how envious the infantry will be if we are the first to engage the enemy."

"But…I thought the major said we weren't to get into a fight."

"Jealousy, sergeant," Rapton said the first thing that came into his head, "simple jealousy. Wishes he were out here himself, no doubt. He will find fighting the French a very different proposition to the savages he faced in India."

Pulling a watch from inside his jacket, Rapton flipped open the cover. He could just make out the hands against its white face; they had been riding for half an hour. "Ten minutes rest, sergeant. Then we move on."


"There's a dead Portuguese in one of the outbuildings, sir," Pinot's sergeant untied the scarf masking his nose and mouth. "Looks like an old man. Been rotting for some time, I should imagine."

The captain grunted, but paid little attention. Tirenne had not returned yet.

"Sir?" the sergeant expected a response.

"What? Oh, just ignore it," Pinot was offhand. "Block the door, if you must." He waved the sergeant away, for he had seen movement in the darkness. Tirenne was coming back.


Lieutenant Rapton pulled his horse to a stop at a fork in the road and took the map from his sabretache. He studied it carefully, rotating the paper this way and that.

"I can't remember there being a junction marked," he said to Tyloe. "What do you think, sergeant?"

Tyloe took the paper. "Nothing on here, sir," he agreed, handing it back. The lieutenant pondered for a while. Which track to take? Then he came to a decision. He called Lock forward.

"Ride up that way, corporal," Rapton ordered, indicating the left fork. "Find out if there is a way through. Sergeant, you go to the right. Ten minutes only; clear? The rest of you," he twisted in his seat to address the remaining troopers, "may dismount. Ten minutes rest."

Lock found it strange to be riding alone after so long a time spent in crowded barracks or cramped on board ship. The horse trotted with an even rhythmic stride he found easy to post to. One of the mounts the Portuguese provided, the stocky grey stood smaller than most troop horses. But it possessed a mind of its own and since Lock liked its spirit, the usually reliable Sexton had been allocated to a less able rider.

The track seemed to go on indefinitely. After a while Lock halted the horse so he could listen. Tiny scuffles broke out in the undergrowth. The breeze, barely noticeable earlier, began to blow harder. He heard nothing unexpected though, and his five minutes were just about up. Reluctantly he turned the animal back the way they had come.

Tyloe told a different story. Apparently, his track had petered out after a few hundred yards.

"This way then," Rapton commanded, indicating the left fork. "Mount them up, sergeant." The lieutenant marked the dead-end trail on his map, as he had been instructed. "No water down there, I suppose?" he asked Tyloe.

"No, sir."

"Very well." He rode back to the head of the patrol. "Sort them out, sergeant, and follow me," he said grandly.


"Cavalry patrol." Tirenne dismounted in front of his captain and tugged at the horse's girth straps. He was fastidious where his mounts were concerned, Pinot had noticed.

"How many men?"

"Couldn't see, sir," the lieutenant admitted. "A small one, anyway."

Pinot scratched his head. "How in God's name can you tell that?"

"No talking, sir. The men at the back always talk amongst themselves if they think they're far enough away for the officer not to hear. You know that."

Pinot scowled. "You're damn right." He took two cigars from his sabretache, offering one to Tirenne who accepted gratefully.

"How long before they get here?"

The lieutenant considered. "I came back fast, once I was out of earshot. Around twenty minutes?"

"Well done, Paul." Pinot struck a flame in his tinderbox and offered it up for the lieutenant's cigar. He jerked his thumb toward the farmstead, "Now get some food before those bastards eat it all."

The captain had a few minutes, he decided, before he must move. The tinderbox flint sparked once more, and Pinot thrust the end of his cigar into its tiny flame. He sucked until the end was well alight then blew a long plume of smoke into the darkness.

And planned his ambush.


On both sides of the track the ground began to rise, gently at first, but then more steeply, forming a narrow defile. Odd trees sprouted here and there, making strange shapes in the gloom. Some branches overhung the road, forcing the troopers to brush them away from their faces, or duck underneath. Francis Kittoe fell back to ride beside Lock.

"Does he know what he's doing?" he leaned across, hissing the question in Lock's ear.

Lock shook his head. "Should have a vedette out in front," he whispered back. "It's obvious. In this light you'd never see a French dragoon until you ran into him."

Tyloe turned in his saddle. "Silence in the ranks," he shouted harshly. Kittoe shrugged at Lock and returned to his place.


"Here," Pinot instructed the gun crew, "I want it here." He had walked the small valley until he found the right spot; a flat area of ground on the left of the farmstead, where the hillside began to rise. Their artillery horses could get the cannon close enough for its crew to manhandle into position without a great effort, and bushes lower down should conceal it from the approaching cavalry.

Two artillerymen brought rocks big enough to chock the carriage-wheels and stop the gun rolling away down the slope. Ropes were placed around the axle, one either side of the carriage, and with three men hauling on each the six-pound cannon was slowly inched downwards until its wheels rested against the stone stops.

There would be no need for the ammunition limber. Pinot reckoned the gunners would only get off one shot before the enemy scattered; any who still lived, that was. He stood at the gun's trail to check the barrel pointed in the right direction.

A sergeant appeared with a long iron hand-spike. Pinot stepped out of his way to allow the artilleryman a clear sight down the barrel. The sergeant grunted satisfaction. He stabbed the end of the hand-spike through an iron ring on the cannon's trail, levering it an inch to the right before sighting down the barrel again. Seemingly happy, he stepped aside, inviting his captain to check the aim.

"Canister?" Pinot suggested politely. The sergeant nodded agreement, ordering three rounds brought. The thin, tin containers would split apart as they left the cannon's muzzle to spray a hail of musket balls across the road, like a huge shotgun blast.

One of the gun crew filled a water bucket from the stream, ready to sop out the barrel between shots. The sergeant unnecessarily checked the aim again before ordering his men to load. First a canvas bag containing the powder charge was pushed into the muzzle before another artilleryman wielding a long timber rammer thrust it down the barrel. The canister followed. After staring along the barrel one last time, the sergeant pushed a spike into the vent-hole to pierce the powder-bag. A priming tube was inserted last, to flash flame to the powder when lit. The sergeant grunted again.

"On my order, sergeant," Pinot confirmed. His trap was ready.


Pinot returned to the farmstead wall The rest of his troop, apart from those men delegated to watch the horses, were stationed behind it, long carbines loaded ready to pick off any men who survived the cannon. He collected his telescope and found a position from where he could watch the road and see the gun

The English were already in sight! He ducked down, cursing himself for not being more careful of the time. As dawn approached the sky began to lighten. Pinot's telescope had a tubular hood at the front, and now he pulled it out, in case a stray reflection should betray his presence. The enemy rode in column; there was no scout. Amateurs, he thought to himself. He kept the lens focussed on the two front men, walking their horses, seemingly unconcerned. This was going to work exactly as he had planned.

Then they stopped. Pinot glanced at the gun crew and saw with horror a tiny, yellow glow, from the end of the slow-match in the sergeant's hand. Damn; he should have thought of that. But it was difficult to spot, and too late to worry about now. He looked back at the cavalry patrol, silently cursing again. A single horseman was riding forward.

"Column: halt!" Rapton raised his hand. 'Column' sounded much more impressive than 'patrol'. "Sergeant," the lieutenant pointed ahead, "what do you make of that."

Tyloe stared into the gloom. "Looks like a cottage sir, or a farm."

"Take a look, will you?"

"Begging your pardon, sir," Tyloe said quietly, "but wouldn't you be better off sending one of the troopers?"

"You are right, of course. Lock!" Rapton called the corporal forward, "find out what's up there."


Lock could make out a building and the outline of something surrounding it: a wall, probably. And the noise on his left was water running; a stream. It made sense to build a house close to water. And now they would be able to let their horses drink.

But there was something…odd; not quite right. Lock stopped, listening. He tried to imagine he was back in Combe Wood at night. The horse pricked its ears, staring into the darkness for a second, then just as quickly relaxed. Lock could hear nothing. He squeezed the horse forward. Again, the horse pricked its ears, and this time was reluctant to move. Not wanting to leave the others too far behind, Lock thought. He gave it a tap with his heels; then a kick. The horse gave in and stepped forward.

Fifty yards from the farmstead wall, Lock halted to check about him again. He could hear horses coming from behind; Lieutenant Rapton had evidently decided not to wait. The buildings seemed deserted. He listened, but apart from the stream the night was quiet.

There was something - to his right. Lock thought he saw a movement out of the corner of his eye. He concentrated, staring into the darkness. There it was again; a small yellow light. Like a firefly, but this one swung back and forth. And then he could make out a shape. Like a tree limb, but more regular. Unnaturally round. And he realised with horrified certainty what it was.

Lock yanked his horse's head round savagely and booted it in the ribs.

"The French!" he screamed at the approaching horsemen, "The French!" Then his world exploded.


"*Tirez!*" Captain Pinot screamed, "Fire!" but he was too late. Flints sparked and barrels roared, but none of the *chasseurs*' carbine balls found a target. As he predicted, the English immediately turned tail; galloping out of range.

He loudly cursed the artillery sergeant for firing early. When the horseman stopped in front of the farmstead, Pinot held up his hand as a signal for the man holding the slow-match to wait. The gunner had taken it as the order to fire. The lone Englishman was caught in the blast's spread. His prone horse kicked weakly once, twice, as life leaked from its body. He was the only casualty.

Pinot had no idea whether the patrol was part of a larger force, but if it was, and the patrol reported back, he had no desire to be trapped in the narrow defile when reinforcements arrived. They must move. He called for Tirenne, but before the lieutenant reached him a musket ball whined past, striking the farmhouse wall. Pinot dropped to the floor. A gunner shouted a warning as another shot clanged against the cannon barrel and ricocheted into the trees.

Shit, Pinot thought. "Where are they?" he yelled to the *chasseurs* further along the wall, crouching low behind it for protection. "Sergeant; shoot into the trees. Scare the bastards off!" Only two shots had sounded. That suggested only two men, both of whom were probably re-loading: damned peasants, most likely. He should send men up the side of the valley to flush them out, but it would take too long.

Lieutenant Tirenne scuttled towards him, bending low to keep his head down.

"Get the men out," Pinot instructed. "I don't want to be caught here if there are more cavalry behind that patrol."

Tirenne nodded. "What about him?" he cocked his thumb over the top of the wall.

Pinot straightened up warily to peer across at the dead Englishman. "His friends will be back," he said. "They can bury him."

# Chapter 26

At first, Killen could not believe Lock was missing from the returning patrol. It must be a mistake. Something had happened to his horse; a sudden lameness, or a cast shoe. Perhaps he had got lost. That was it; he had taken a wrong turn on the way back. Killen refused to give in to the gloom that seemed to settle over the rest of the troop.

The patrol had galloped back into camp on tired, sweating horses. Rapton, white faced, dismounted, throwing his reins to another trooper before he dragged Sergeant Tyloe with him to report to the major. Killen went round each man, asking questions, but all seemed shocked. Every story was different. Even Francis Kittoe, the most lucid, kept repeating the same thing. "They ran away."

"What do you mean?"

"They ran away," Kittoe's horse was still saddled. He tied the animal in the horse-lines, slumping to the ground beside it. Looking up at the lieutenant with blank eyes he repeated, "Rapton and Tyloe....they ran away."

"What happened to Joshua?" Killen demanded plaintively. "Where is he?"

"They left him," Kittoe said. "They left him there. We all did," he sounded as if he could not believe what had happened, "after the cannon fired."

"You did not go back?" Killen tried to take in what he was hearing. "No-one went back to check if he was alive?"

Kittoe gave a guilty shake of the head. "He's not coming back, sir," he said sadly. "He must be dead."

"He is not. He is not dead." It was not possible. Killen felt a swell of anger. They had left his friend to the mercy of the enemy, so *he* would have to fetch him back. "He is not dead," Killen repeated loudly, and stalked off towards Major Hughes' tent.


Hughes put down the chicken leg, from which he taken a single bite, with a glance of regret. How on earth Trumpeter Picker managed to conjure up such a delicious snack in these conditions was entirely beyond his comprehension, and now the bird would go cold. He chewed quickly and swallowed.

"So you say there was a farmstead about here?" His large map lay unrolled on the desk in front of him. He pointed with a pencil at the spot, and when Rapton confirmed, scribbled a note. "How far up the road would you say, lieutenant, eight or nine miles? Good." Hughes thought Rapton looked unwell. Being shot at could do that to a man, but whether the lieutenant's pallor was from fright, or the sudden realisation of how swiftly death could come, Hughes had no idea.

"So you sent Corporal Lock forward?"

"The French must have known we were coming. We did our best, sir," Rapton spoke more confidently now, "but there were too many of them."

That was odd, Hughes thought. "How far away from the farm were you?"

"Two hundred yards."

Sergeant Tyloe chipped in. "Two or three hundred, sir," he said quietly.

"It might have been more," Rapton re-considered, "Yes - three hundred."

They had been lucky, Hughes realised. The French must have laid their gun at an angle to the road, firing diagonally across the patrol's path. If the cavalrymen were any closer, they would have been massacred.

Voices sounded outside; the tent flap abruptly drawn back. Hughes stood, "Sir."

"Sit down, major, sit down," Colonel Taylor strode in, but Hughes disobeyed, for he recognised the colonel's companion.

"Sir Arthur," Taylor turned to his guest, "allow me to introduce Major Jonas Hughes."


Killen tore back the tent flap. He burst inside, halting abruptly at attention as six pairs of eyes swivelled his way. Killen's ears began to burn; he could feel his face blazing hot.

"What do you want, Mr. Killen?" Hughes asked, cold but polite.

The lieutenant brushed a strand of hair from his forehead. "I…er"

"Well, sir?"

Calm, Killen told himself: stay calm. "I request permission to lead out a patrol, sir"

Hughes glanced at his other visitors as if for permission before sitting down heavily. "Your request is denied, lieutenant. You are dismissed, for the time being."

Killen turned away - an automatic reaction. As soon as he had done it he felt angry with himself. He had come to help Lock, and he would not, simply *would not,* be dissuaded. So he spun back, again standing to attention. The major ignored him.

"Lieutenant," Hughes continued to quiz Rapton, "you assert the force opposing you had cannon. How many men, do you suppose?"

"It must have been around a hundred," Rapton stroked his jaw as if thinking.

Hughes raised his eyebrows, "Can you be sure?"

"No, sir, but they fired a volley after us: a large volley."

"And were they dragoons, lieutenant, or *chasseurs*?" Sir Arthur Wellesley spoke for the first time. "It is important, sir, I know what troops we face."

Rapton was stumped. He turned to face the general, "I could not say, sir."

Wellesley frowned. "Well, did they wear fur caps or helmets? You must have seen that."

"They were in hiding, sir. We turned to face them again, but I judged it best not to charge the devils."

Wellesley's expression changed; Killen watched his face grow cold. "How very wise, lieutenant."

"I almost ordered the charge, to avenge Corporal Lock," Rapton warmed to his subject, somehow managing to ignore the general's look of disapproval. Killen could hardly believe it.

Wellesley turned away, absentmindedly pulling the remaining leg from Major Hughes' cooked fowl and lifting it towards his mouth.

"But some of the men were afraid for their lives, ain't that so, sergeant?"

Before Tyloe could agree, Killen's anger overcame him. "The men say you ran away," he blurted. Wellesley froze, the pilfered chicken leg in mid-bite.

"That's an absolute lie!" Rapton stormed. "Major, Lieutenant Killen was not present, so he can be no judge."

Hughes jumped up, angrily raising his voice. "Gentlemen: enough! Mr. Killen: I believe I ordered you to leave. No, stay there; I will deal with you in a moment." He turned to Rapton. "I shall expect your full report," he considered, "shall we say... by lunchtime? Thank you, lieutenant, and you, sergeant; you may go."

Hughes sighed wearily. Wellesley at last managed to take a bite of chicken before turning to Colonel Taylor. "The major and I have already met," he mumbled through a full mouth, "In India. I must say, Hughes; this is very good. Who's your cook?"

Hughes stood again, facing his two superiors. "Good to see you again, sir," he addressed Wellesley, "and the colonel's orderly trumpeter's a passable cook. He seems to have a way with fowl."

"Indeed?" Wellesley nodded before swallowing. "So what did you make of that, major?"

"They bumped into a French patrol - small, most probably - were fired on and fled."

"You give no credence to numbers?"

"No, sir," Hughes shook his head, "nor the troops involved. I suspect they saw none. Any commander worth his salt would have made sure his men were well hidden."

Wellesley nodded. "I agree. Waste of a patrol. And a horse, by the sounds of it."

"The mounts the Bishop of Porto promised have not arrived?" Taylor asked, worrying.

"They will be here, have no fear of that," Wellesley sounded frustrated, "but these damned people seem to have no sense of urgency. The horses will arrive," he shrugged, "but they cannot, or will not, say when."


For the moment, Killen seemed to have been forgotten. Anger cooling, he relaxed, and his small movement caught Major Hughes' eye. "Mr Killen," he said offhandedly," I thought I had dismissed you. Off you go."

"No, sir," Killen stifled his urge to leave. But it was a direct disobedience.

"What?" Hughes sounded as if he had misheard.

"I want to take a patrol out, sir. I...I have to."

"The answer is still no, lieutenant," Hughes said, more kindly, "I understand your reasons, but..."

"Major," Wellesley interrupted smoothly, "let us not be too hasty." He turned to the lieutenant. "Are you by chance related to Lord Halcombe?"

Killen stiffened to attention, "My grandfather, sir."

"If you are in agreement, Charles," Sir Arthur skilfully drew Taylor in, "I see no reason to deny Lieutenant Killen his request. We are desperate for accurate information: desperate. Major?"

"The other patrols have not yet come in, sir." Hughes shuffled through several sheets of paper to double-check he was correct.

"As I thought. Lieutenant Killen," Wellesley addressed him directly, and there was something about the general's eyes: Killen felt they might see deep into his soul. "It is essential, lieutenant, that I have information, but without risking a confrontation with the enemy. None at all, do you understand?" Killen nodded. "We shall meet the French at a time and place of my choosing, and not before. There will be no possibility of 'revenge' until I give the command." He stopped. "This corporal," Wellesley recalled the name, "this corporal...Lock. What was he to you?"

"He...he saved my life, sir." It sounded trite, but Killen looked the general in the eye, and just for a second his expression seemed to soften.

"In battle?" Wellesley asked quietly, but Killen shook his head.

"We were boys, sir."

Wellesley grunted. "Just remember, lieutenant, I will have information. And you will not engage the enemy; is that clear?"

"Will he do, d'you think," Wellesley asked of both men, once Killen left.

"Johnny's an excellent officer," Colonel Taylor was full of praise. "Best swordsman in the squadron. Good family, of course; I gather his father was killed in India." He looked questioningly at the general, but Sir Arthur shook his head.

"I never made his acquaintance." Wellesley noticed Hughes, busy scribbling. "Still on top of the paperwork I see, eh, major? Major Hughes was always efficient, in my estimation," he confided to Taylor. "Bonaparte's view is that armies win battles. Mine," he waved an arm in the major's direction, "is that efficient staff work is the key. An army must be fed, clothed, armed. I will not rob the populace as do the French, so how will I achieve this? Better organisation and accurate paperwork. D'you see, Charles?"

Taylor nodded as if he understood, "And I am sure Lieutenant Killen will do splendidly. He speaks several languages, you know."

Wellesley was thoughtful. "Does he indeed?"

"And the men seem to like him."

Hughes interrupted. "The men like him because he is too easy on them. I hope I am wrong, but I don't believe Lieutenant Killen will make a good officer, sir. He seems too…" he searched for a suitable word, "…too *cautious*."

"A degree of caution in a cavalry officer," Wellesley observed, "is not always to be discouraged."


An orderly trooper, one of those men still without a horse, led The Tempest out before legging Killen up into the saddle. The lieutenant had wanted to take Tyloe out again, but the sergeant made all sorts of excuses to avoid extra duty. In the end, commandeering a fresh horse, Francis Kittoe offered to lead, professing himself still angry they had left Lock to his fate. Killen accepted his help with gratitude, so six men set off.

"Don't worry, sir," Kittoe encouraged, "we'll bring him back."

"Thank you, Francis." Killen smiled with his mouth, but his heart wore mourning black.

# Chapter 27

The rising sun had just pinked the morning sky with the promise of a fine day when the vulture came. It seemed to grow from a distant speck, tracking across the sky in a zig-zag path as it sought rising currents of warm air to keep it aloft, the vulture headed unerringly for a mist-wreathed valley. Though the ground was, as yet, invisible from above, a scent had drawn the bird, a scent so faint no man could detect it. But the vulture's senses were honed over millions of years, and this scent was a promise of plenty. It was the smell of death.

The sun rose higher. Mist receded like some monstrous spirit returning to its lair, exposing the line of a track that followed the valley floor. Treetops emerged; the outlines of a few stone buildings, but the vulture, with a patience born of long experience, still waited, circling on thermals that grew in power as the countryside warmed. And very soon its wait was rewarded. On the ground below, bodies lay: a man and horse. The bird drew in its wings to drop lower.

Gliding slowly towards the ground, huge feathers at the vulture's wingtips opened to act as brakes before it stretched out its scaly legs. The bird stuttered to a landing, raising its wings to keep its balance, and hopped warily towards the carcases. For though blessed with powerful beak and talons, the vulture's wings were fragile, and to keep them from harm the bird needed to be certain its prey was fully dead.

The horse's face had been smashed by a canister ball, its chest torn bloodily open from the same cause. The soldier lay trapped beneath his mount, head twisted to one side. Nothing moved, yet still the bird was wary, torn between its desires to feed and for safety. It crept closer.

Just as it was about to peck at the horse's open eye, the soldier moved. Almost imperceptibly, he shuddered, startling the vulture which flapped its broad wings, lifting off. The soldier did not move again. Even so, the watchful bird flew to the farmstead wall where it settled to wait. But it must not wait too long. Each second the sky grew brighter, and daylight would bring other scavengers to the valley.

Hidden in the tree line, crouched in leaf mould, Marco waited. He had approached quietly and kept so still even the vulture's sharp eyes missed his presence. A big man, he hid in front of a tree-trunk, knowing it would break his outline, though bark dug uncomfortably into the small of his back.

Dribbles of sweat ran down Marco's darkly stubbled cheeks, but he dare not move to scratch the itch; the French might have left men behind, waiting for him to show himself. Perspiration dripped onto the oiled stock of the musket he held across his knees like a child's toy. A single shot from that, and one from his companion's weapon, had been enough to unnerve the *chasseurs*. But the gun was primed and cocked, just in case.

Half an hour passed. Marco saw no movement down the valley apart from the vulture. Small birds settled into the green canopy above while unknown creatures rustled through fallen leaves. A stream burbled on its way; but out on the valley floor nothing moved.

It was time. He rose from his crouch, grimacing as cramped muscles and tendons creaked. He stretched. Still the vulture sat unperturbed, but then Marco took a step forward out of the tree-shade. Startled again, the bird jumped into the air from its stone perch, this time flapping slowly up to the ridge of the farmstead roof.

Marco checked up and down the track once again. Deciding he was indeed alone, he marched swiftly to the dead soldier, prodding him with the muzzle of his musket. A soft rattle made the big man start, but it was just the vulture shaking its feathers. Satisfied, Marco put his fingers to his mouth and gave a low whistle. Very soon another man emerged from the tree-line leading a mule and two horses.

"The French are gone," the big Portuguese informed his companion. "We will check the buildings. Maybe they left something behind in their hurry." Marco looked down at the soldier's unfamiliar uniform noticing the short musket slung from his saddle was not French. He had heard that an English army was coming to fight the invaders, but who believed rumours?

From up ahead, the other man gave a sudden shout. Marco left the dead soldier; they would collect his equipment later.

Marco's companion beckoned urgently, his nose and mouth covered with one hand. "In there," he pointed at one of the outbuildings. The doorway had been blocked with timbers which the big man yanked to one side.

The body must have been dead for some time, Marco thought, judging by the stench. He made the sign of the cross before he knelt down to examine the corpse. An old man: Portuguese. He might have died naturally, or not. The big man cursed. God and decency demanded he be buried, but Marco did not want to stay in the valley any longer than necessary.

"Bring shovels," he ordered. Marco gripped the old man's coat, dragging him out by the shoulders. He ignored the stinking wet trail the body left behind it. "Bring shovels," he repeated, "we will bury him." He looked around. "Over there," he twitched his head towards a patch of ground where no rocks showed.

It took the two men over an hour to dig a deep enough hole. Now the sun was rising fast. Marco began to feel anxious, but no French came. They piled what loose rocks they could find on top of the earth mound, to stop foxes digging the body out, and Marco said a prayer over the old man's grave. Then he crossed himself again.

Because the dead horse trapped the soldier's leg beneath its body as if he were still astride, it would be difficult to get its saddle off, but not impossible. Marco pulled the bridle over its head. Blood on the leather had already dried, he noticed. The girth straps undid easily enough, but to remove the saddle he needed to move the dead man. Marco's companion grabbed the soldier under the armpits while Marco took hold of the horse's tail, heaving on it in an attempt to roll the animal's weight off the corpse's leg. Then his companion abruptly let go.

"He moved!" he said in a frightened voice, "he moved!" He made the sign of the cross.

"He is dead," Marco scoffed at the other man but released the horse's tail, reaching across to feel the soldier's neck. He found a pulse. Weak, but the man was alive.

"We must take him with us," Marco decided, "or he will surely die."

His companion shook his head. "He is nearly dead, anyway," he said. "Leave him here. Someone will find him. Or kill him now," he suggested. "That will be kinder."

Marco rummaged through the soldier's pockets; somewhere he might find a clue to who he was. In the leg pocket of the soldier's woollen overalls was a small lump. The big Portuguese drew the object out; a crucifix, carved from wood and strung with a leather thong. Marco held it up. "He is a true believer," the big man said. "We must take him with us. Only God will decide if he lives or dies."

With a struggle the two Portuguese dragged the soldier clear. Marco hauled him upright, finding the young man both taller and heavier than he expected, but the pack mule could cope. They slung him over the animal's back, head hanging one side and feet the other. Marco knew it was not the best way to carry an injured man, but he had no other choice. The remaining equipment, stripped from the soldier's mount, was shared between each riding horse.

Marco and his companion left soon after. The soldier's dead horse remained in the valley. Marco was sorry to leave fresh meat behind, but he had no time. The injured man must be got to a doctor, so the carcase was left to feed the scavengers.

And the vulture, long wait at last rewarded, unfurled its huge, black wings and returned to the feast.


"The farmstead is over that rise, sir," Kittoe said, "about a half-mile off."

Killen pulled out his watch. It was just before midday. He was angry that they had not arrived earlier, but it was sensible to be cautious so close to the French. Rapton's trail had been easy to follow; the hoof-prints bunched together as his patrol approached the farm then spread far apart, showing where they had galloped wildly away.

"Scout, sir?"

Killen's thoughts were far away. "Er...yes, thank you Kittoe." The man was quite right, Killen realised; stupid to make the same mistake as Rapton. The trooper trotted ahead, leaving the lieutenant to lead his remaining men slowly forward.

Quite by accident, Killen noticed two crows fly up in the distance. They sped away from the valley, startled. The lieutenant turned his horse. "Into the trees," he pointed left, "swiftly now!" It might just be that Kittoe had disturbed the birds, or it might be something more insidious. Killen heard no carbine fire, often the danger signal, but he was taking no chances. He would bring his patrol back intact.

Kittoe returned a few minutes later. Killen saw his surprise at finding the track deserted. Though he scanned both sides of the valley, the cavalrymen were hidden in shadow.

Killen rode out. "Over here!"

Kittoe halted to salute. His face was drawn. "It's deserted, sir."

"I saw the birds," Killen explained. "That is why we were hidden."

"Oh," Kittoe gave a wan smile, "a fox, it was, sir, sitting on the track. Put them up when it ran off." He gave Killen an odd look, "Surprised you noticed, sir."

"I am not a complete dunce, Kittoe," Killen said curtly and straightaway wished he had not.


Lock was dead; that much was obvious. Killen stared at the horse. From the look of its face, scavengers had already chewed at it. The French must have stripped its harness, wanting loot. The grave told its own story. Kittoe expressed surprise the French would bother to bury a fallen enemy.

"They are not animals, Francis. They have officers who are gentlemen, as we do," Killen gave a small sniff. "We would have buried a casualty of theirs; I doubt they are very different."

Disappointment soured the other troopers' faces. Only Kittoe did not seem upset. "Seen it before, sir," he said. "Nothing a man can do, 'cept get on."

Killen stood at Lock's grave for some time, staring down at the rocks. He remembered the boy who first sat in his bedroom and seemed so big and strong. The confident young man he taught to fence. The friend he missed badly when he first joined the army. Now, that was all he had of Joshua: memories. For the first time in his life Killen felt completely alone.

# Chapter 28

Astride a horse the colour of sunrise, Francisco da Souza Carvilho wept as he gazed down from a mountain ridge at the wreckage of his beloved country. Lurking deep in that fog of destruction, his enemies prowled: rabid dogs of the revolution, curs of France. They had marched through his land unmolested, offering the people visions of a new future, a better life; the dream of a republic. But their fine proclamations of hope were lies. Instead they had pillaged and burned, raped and murdered, until the last embers of his people's dwindling faith threatened to die in a wasteland of despair. For that, he must destroy them.

All at once, it seemed the invaders spied him. Apparitions swirling in the murk solidified into soldiers. Chaos became ordered lines; battalions. The whole French army drew itself into one huge, unstoppable mass. Then, screaming heresies, with swords and muskets raised in defiance, the horde turned uphill and charged towards him.

Carvilho knew he would die, his bright blue and silver coat torn and trodden in the dirt of his homeland. But his resolve was firm. And perhaps, drawn to the Portuguese cause by the manner of his death, others would come, their numbers growing and growing until no army on earth could stand before them. And the French would be driven back down into the black pit of hell from whence they came.

His enemies' screams grew louder. Now he could make out faces, contorted with anger, baying for his life. He drew his sabre, and gently touching spurs to his horse's side he rode gladly towards his fate. His mount's pace increased. "Almighty God," the old man prayed, "give my sword-arm strength. Speed my resolve; that your people will suffer no longer." He urged the horse on to a gallop; the final charge - one man against the forces of the devil. And as he shouted his challenge, and swung the curved sabre above his head, a stray shaft of sunlight struck its bright blade, reflecting into the faces of the enemy, blinding them with its brightness. Slowly, at first, the French tide seemed to slacken. Shock replaced their spite and anger; then fear. The enemy line slowed to a walk: stopped.

And then, incredibly, the whole French army broke. They ran for their lives.

For the mountainside trembled beneath the hooves of hundreds of white-clad horsemen. A regiment of angels, sprung from the clouds, sabres whistling wind-song, charged alongside him. And from every golden lance-head fluttered a pennant marked with the cross of the Lord.

The galloping horsemen smashed into the fleeing French, cutting and hacking at the enemy until their flailing sabres dripped scarlet blood.

Carvilho's body shook violently, "Grandfather!" It shook again, "Wake up!"

Carvilho opened his eyes, trying to keep his dream alive. "What is it, Isabella?"

"Marco has returned. He has brought a soldier."

Carvilho sat up and rubbed his eyes, "A Frenchman?"

The girl shook her long black hair, "An Englishman. They have taken him upstairs. Miguel has gone to fetch the doctor." Her brown eyes were huge, "They think he will die."

The old man slowly got to his feet. There had been so many deaths. He put his arm around Isabella's shoulders, hugging her to him. "Perhaps he will live; there is always hope," he encouraged. It was all they had.

She looked at him reproachfully. "You always say that. Hope did not save the others."


Carvilho looked into the soldier's face. Before the doctor began to scrub at the dried blood with a wet rag, they had stripped the young man of his jacket and shirt. The old man picked the coat up, seeing how the fancy white braid across its front was stained down one side where the boy bled. A dolman, the English called the short jacket, Carvilho was certain: a cavalryman's uniform. That gave him an idea; a small idea, true, but hope fed on such things. "Will he live?"

The doctor wrung the rag out, watching the cold water in his bucket turn black as he considered the question. "Who can tell?" he answered at last, continuing his work.

Carvilho took Marco to one side. "What did you discover?" he asked quietly.

"The English do not move. They send out patrols. The French? I cannot tell. We only saw the ones who did this. They rode away, to the south-west."

The old man understood. From other reports he had been brought, it seemed likely the French were trying to gather their scattered forces. "They will attack the British when they are joined. Then we will fight them," he said firmly.

"All of the French army?" Marco blurted in disbelief, making Isabella and the others in the room turn towards him in surprise.

Carvilho took his arm, leading Marco back through the door so his words could not be overheard. "We will attack them when they are preoccupied with the British," he kept his voice low, "so they will not expect us." Carvilho's anguish was still very young, so bitterness thickened his voice. "We will have our revenge; trust in God."

It seemed Marco trusted in Carvilho. He gave the old man a small bow, "I will, Francisco; I will."


Lock was drowning. His head was beneath the surface, and though he fought desperately something held him there. A face; a face floated above, glowing with a bright light, just visible through swirling water. Forcing his head towards the light, he reached towards the face with both hands. Anger gave him strength and his head broke the surface. Now he could see more clearly. It was a girl's face. "Mary," he mumbled, and her long hair brushed his cheek. She would save him; the river would not win. He closed his eyes again.

Isabella carefully picked up the wet rag she had laid on the soldier's forehead, touching his skin with the back of her hand. Below the bandage that swathed his scalp his face seemed cool; there was no fever. "I thought he woke, just for a moment," she told her grandfather. "That is a good sign." Carvilho hoped it was, for the doctor was vague.

"He may die," he said morosely, "he may live. Even if he survives, he may be an idiot; I cannot tell. The ball did not enter his head; that is all I can say for certain."

"But he is young and strong," Carvilho allowed, "so we should know soon. If he lives, perhaps he will stay."

Isabella pursed her lips. "We must send him back. The English have come to help us. We must not keep him from them."

"We will take him back," Carvilho agreed, staring through the window, his mind elsewhere. "Now you should rest," he ruffled the girl's hair. She had kept watch over the Englishman all night. "I will stay for a while."

After Isabella had gone, Carvilho sat watching the cavalryman sleep. His idea might work if the soldier could be persuaded to help. That would not be popular with the older men. But they would do what he, Francisco, commanded, for his family had owned and worked this land for generations.

Of those who sought refuge in the valley, many had served Carvilho for years and would follow his lead with little hesitation. Younger men might be more difficult to convince. Respect for their elders waned as they saw the French destroy their homes and ravage their country. They craved action, any action, but youthful rashness was not what Carvilho had in mind. Once they saw the long sabre scar on the soldier's left arm, then perhaps they too would believe, but if not Carvilho would have his revenge on the French without their help. And the young cavalryman would play his part, whether he wished to or not.

The old man took the Englishman's crucifix from his pocket. Kneeling beside the bed, he held it aloft, feeling the wood's smoothness. He bowed his head in prayer, to thank God for delivering his instrument into Carvilho's hands. The Lord's horsemen would be more than just a dream.


Isabella sat on the edge of her bed, brushing her hair. When she fled into the hills with her grandfather she managed to bring a small hand mirror amongst her meagre luggage, but since the only lamp upstairs burned in the soldier's room she could not tell how she looked.

It was clear her grandfather was planning something. Isabella had no idea what except that it involved the English cavalryman, and would keep him with them. And although she knew he must return to his army, even now she felt she did not want him to leave. When she thought of him, lying helpless in bed, the want seemed to grow stronger, perhaps because now he was an injured fawn; a fawn hiding from a lynx. That must be the reason, she decided, for Paulo was her young man. And though he might pretend otherwise, she was his master.

Isabella smiled to herself. Perhaps she could be this English soldier's master, too. She smoothed down her nightdress and lay back on the bed, staring up at the ceiling where spiders spun their webs in dark corners.

Lock woke slowly. Gingerly, he opened one eye, but bright daylight hammered at his skull so he slammed it shut. He tried again but the hammering refused to stop. From the soft cloth against his cheek, and the sag as he flexed each limb, he surmised he was lying on a bed. Stiffly, he rolled onto his back.

"You are awake, then." A soft voice: a girl. Lock half-remembered the shadow of a face; but no detail would come.

"Close the curtains," his voice croaked.

"Shutters…they are shutters. And have you forgotten your manners?" the girl asked.

"Please?" There were scraping sounds and the room darkened. Lock tried again to open his eyes. One refused, so he gave up for the time being. "Thank you."

"And you are welcome." Lock could hear the smile in the girl's voice, and forced both eyes open. The left side of his face hurt like hell. The girl stood over the bed, watching him.

"You were shot in the head," she said, by way of explanation. "The doctor thinks you will live, but you may be mad." She stooped closer to look into his eyes.

Lock thought her the most beautiful thing he had ever seen.

"Are you mad?" The girl raised her eyebrows, but her eyes still smiled. Lock thought he should say something complimentary, but nothing came. He pulled the sheet up over his naked chest.

"Thank you; and I don't..." he croaked, "...I don't think so."

The girl sat down on the edge of his bed to pour water from a jug. "You must drink," she insisted, offering Lock the cup. He turned sideways, sipping at it carefully. The water was tepid, but it unstuck his tongue and soothed his dry throat. He coughed, finding that a bad mistake. His head throbbed unmercifully.

"You will have a headache for a few days," the girl must have seen him wince. "It seems your wound is not so bad," she reached out to touch his bandage but he jerked his head away. "I am sorry," she said contritely, "but the dressing must be changed." Again she reached out, but this time Lock grabbed her wrist, holding on when she tried to snatch her hand back. Her eyes were huge.

"Don't be frightened," Lock said in apology. "Change it later?" He let her arm go and she stood immediately, stepping away from him.

"I'm sorry," Lock realised his mistake. "Tell me where I am?" But the girl turned and fled from the room without speaking.

"My name is Joshua," he called after her, but it was too late. Damn, Lock thought to himself. Then pain stabbed again, and he closed his eyes.


In the last weeks, Carvilho's faith had been sorely tested. He prayed for a sign; some small confirmation that the course of action he set himself was just. Now God had delivered this English soldier, another Christian; not only that, but a horseman; a warrior bearing a great sabre scar on one arm. A man who shared his name with the greatest of all the Israelites: Joshua.

Carvilho opened his hand above Lock's, dropping the wooden crucifix onto the boy's palm. "My men discovered it in your pocket. Please, corporal, put it on. You are among friends, here." Francisco brought a plate of food, and waited patiently while Lock ate ravenously. He had also ordered the cavalryman's jacket be washed, and it hung on the back of the chair the old man dragged forward, its single white stripe of rank clearly visible on one sleeve.

Lock hesitated before pulling the cross carefully over his head. That was understandable, Carvilho thought. He had heard Catholicism was still persecuted in England.

"I have a favour to ask of you, when you are well."

The corporal nodded acceptance. "But I think," Lock said slowly, "I might have frightened Isabella."

Carvilho did not understand that, for when he spoke to the girl after she rushed from the soldier's room she had seemed, well, distracted. Excited, even, but certainly not frightened. He waved the apology away. "I think it would take a good deal to scare my granddaughter, corporal. Rest, now. We will speak more of this later."

The old man felt his spirits rise. Now his followers would truly understand the power of God. He clattered downstairs and out into the courtyard.

"Find Marco," he called to one of his followers. "Tell him to bring in every man we can spare. No," he changed his mind, "tell him to bring everyone. Tell him I will have news." It would not be the sort of news any of them expected, though. Carvilho rubbed his hands together gleefully at the prospect.


Isabella pulled Lock's sabre from its scabbard and the curved blade wobbled dangerously. Its odd weight was concentrated towards the tip, and when she slashed it sideways, cutting air, the huge weapon threatened to take control of her arm. Crossly she dropped the point. The cavalryman's sword was nothing like her own, a slim-bladed lightweight rapier, made for thrusting and stabbing.

Footsteps sounded outside the barn. The girl hastily tucked sword and scabbard back where Lock's saddle and harness were stored. But it was only one of the men, come to fetch a horse. Four animals were stalled along one side of the building.

The Portuguese nodded affably at Isabella as he ducked out of the doorway, trailing his mount behind. A sentry, she realised, off to relieve one of those her grandfather stationed all around the small community to bring warning if the French should approach.

Once the man had gone, Isabella moved swiftly to one end of the barn. There, a rotten roof timber had slipped downwards, creating a cavity behind it. She felt inside for her bundle, well wrapped in oilcloth. It seemed no-one had disturbed its hiding place. The girl decided she would wait until afternoon, when the valley grew hot, and men dozed in the shade. Then she would practice again with her sword.


Carvilho returned after midday. Lock was feeling a little better, though his head still hammered and much to his annoyance the bandage kept slipping down over his left eye.

"Ah, corporal," Carvilho was all smiles, "your wound is improved, I hope?" Lock felt grateful to his saviour, and said so, but Carvilho held up his hands. "You have no need to thank me. Your help will be enough." Lock wondered what help he could possibly offer, so Carvilho explained. "We hide in this valley," he said sadly, "from the French. They drove us from our homes and families. We could not fight them, because we were too few."

"But don't the Portuguese have an army?" Lock puzzled.

"Once..." Carvilho sighed, "...once, we did. When the King left for Brazil, many sailed away with him. Then the French came. They destroyed what was left."

"You could still fight," Lock objected. "I've heard the Spanish set ambushes with very small groups of men."

"The Spanish..." Carvilho spat the words, "those dogs colluded with Bonaparte, until the people finally realised their mistake. Now they hide in bushes throwing rocks, and run away when the French turn on them." He gave a small shake of the head, composing himself. "There are some who have arms. Some have fought the French; some have even beaten them. But they are far from here. My people need a man to lead them, by example. To give the French..." he searched for an English phrase, "...a bloody nose."

It was a long speech, and when the old man finished Lock pushed up the drooping bandage to stare at him, "You?"

Carvilho gave a wry smile. "I am old. They would follow me, yes, but to do what? My men will fight, but they are untrained." He leaned forward. "That is why I need your help," he said earnestly.

"For what?"

"We will not," Carvilho said with determination in his voice, "stab at the French from behind bushes, like animals. My men have pride. They are horsemen. They can shoot; swing a sword." He looked Lock in the eye, "But they are not... soldiers. I want you to show them how they can beat the French, with honour. I will lead them, but you must teach them how to be cavalry; how to charge. That will be your thanks."

"And you will lead them?" Lock grew more incredulous.

"Once, I too was a cavalryman," Carvilho admitted modestly, "but it was years ago."

Jesus Christ, Lock thought.


Roof tiles baked under the afternoon sun. Lock's bandage irritated him so much he determined to pull it off, but it had stuck to the wound. Even though he peeled the fabric away very carefully the pain, which had dulled to a nagging ache, now stabbed at him with a vengeance. And the bleeding restarted; he could feel it dribbling down the side of his face. He folded the bandage into a pad, wincing as he pressed it against his skull.

Sunlight streamed between folded-back shutters. Curious of his surroundings, Lock looked out, gazing down across the courtyard. His lodging seemed a far grander building than those scattered amongst the trees. Mostly small cottages, some were almost derelict, with threadbare tarpaulins tied over their roofs to keep out the weather. A single narrow track crossed in front of the house, and as Lock watched, Isabella made her way through the courtyard towards a small barn on its far side. Something about the way she moved caught his attention. She looked around furtively, as if worried she might be seen. He felt disappointment when the girl went straight into the barn, but a few minutes later she emerged leading a saddled horse, vaulting up easily before disappearing into the trees. Lock wondered where she was going, and, strangely, felt a stab of annoyance at his ignorance.

"I will translate, if you wish." Late that day Isabella stood at Lock's side in the long barn where Carvilho's men gathered. They must have slipped back from the hills during the night and early morning, for the cavalryman had seen no-one arrive. He examined them critically. Thirty or perhaps forty strong, the peasants mostly dressed in scruffy, almost worn-out clothing. A number sported wide-brimmed hats which they did not bother to remove indoors. They formed small groups, chatting unintelligibly. Some stared in his direction, or pointed at him, but no-one approached. They waited.

Lock was unimpressed. These must be the men and boys he was to turn into soldiers. He sighed; he might as well give up before he started. There was one man, though; a huge figure, his long brown coat struggling to encompass massive shoulders. Lock pointed, "Who's that?"

"Marco."

"The man who found me?" Isabella nodded. "Then I'm glad he's on my side." The girl looked at him questioningly, but Lock simply smiled at her. "I must thank him," he explained.

Carvilho arrived, and the barn quietened. He looked younger, Lock thought, and taller, as if a weight had suddenly lifted from his shoulders. Isabella stirred beside him, and her grandfather looked across at the two of them with a smile.

He began to speak. Lock had no idea what was being said, but then Carvilho pointed directly at him.

"He is telling them who you are," Isabella whispered. A few in the crowd looked towards the young Englishman, but Carvilho dragged their attention back.

"He says that God sent you to us," Isabella translated. "That you will teach them how to fight in the modern way; that you will show them how to beat the French." She stared at him, "Did you promise to do this?"

Lock shrugged. "Your grandfather asked me to. How else am I to show my gratitude?"

The girl narrowed her eyes. "You are a fool."

Lock thought she was probably right. Carvilho, though, spoke again, and this time Isabella raised her eyebrows. "He says that God loved Joshua for his bravery, and broke down the walls of

Jericho so that Joshua's people might return to the Promised Land."
Lock remembered the story from long ago, and was silent. Isabella
turned to face him. "He says God will give them the strength and
courage to succeed," she said. "Do you believe that?"

What Lock believed was that a troop of regular cavalry
might be more useful. But this was not the time for doubt. "Your
grandfather does," he said helplessly.

Now Marco spoke with vehemence, provoking fierce
argument. Isabella began to look worried.

"What's going on now?" Lock hissed.

"Oh, Marco does not agree." Isabella blushed, "He says you
are just a boy; how can you teach a man to fight?" Lock heard
others join in; a chorus of agreement. Marco had obviously struck a
chord. Carvilho spoke with desperate passion, but more voices
were raised against him. Lock began to feel sorry for the old man.

"Grandfather cannot persuade them," Isabella said,
sounding relieved. "They wish to fight in their own way."

"Then they will all die." The girl gave Lock a horrified
look. "Look at them," he waved towards the Portuguese. "If they
ride to war a disorganised rabble, the French will first laugh, then
slaughter them."

"I will speak to them," Isabella said sternly, but Lock
stopped her before she could take a step.

"Tell Marco," he said quietly, "he has insulted me, and that
I demand satisfaction."

"Tell him what?"

Lock rephrased the duellist's challenge. "Tell him I will
fight him, to prove I am a man, and he is a fool."

Isabella gave a small gasp. "He is no fool. He will kill you!"

"Tell him," Lock insisted. "And no, he won't." He hoped he
was right.


They brought Lock his sword. Isabella twice asked him to
reconsider. He was wounded, she insisted; everyone could see that.
It would be no disgrace to back down.

Lock refused. He had made his bed, and as his own
grandfather had often reminded him, now he must lie in it. Besides,

he thought, as he drew the curved sabre slowly from its scabbard, the practice would be useful.

Carvilho talked urgently to Marco, but the big man kept shaking his head. "No!" he said at last, walking away.

The old man crossed to where Lock waited. "I have asked him not to fight you, corporal, but he refuses," Carvilho sounded worried. He looked at Lock, tilting his head on one side. "He is no fool, you know."

"I never thought he was." Lock wondered why no-one seemed worried Marco might be injured. He must prove himself to them all, then.

Marco stripped off his long coat.

"Sir," Lock smiled at Carvilho, "we shall need a referee."

The old man gave a small bow of acceptance. "I pray, corporal," he said seriously, "you will have no need of a priest."


The two protagonists came face to face. Lock was forced to look up at his taller opponent, bringing a smile from Marco's yellow teeth. Lock stared blandly back. He had no need of his anger - yet.

"*Eu tantarel nă o matar*," the huge Portuguese muttered as he stepped back, raising his sword in salute. Lock glanced at the weapon which was both long and broad-bladed, matching the man who wielded it. He lifted his own sword. "What did he say?" he asked Isabella, repeating the question when she did not immediately answer.

"*'I will try not to kill you.'*" She said it so softly, Lock caught her translation with difficulty, but then he stopped worrying about words because Marco came forward.

The big Portuguese swung his sword in a huge arc, at chest height. Had his powerful stroke landed it would have disembowelled a bullock. The watchers gasped in awe, but it was an easy blow for Lock to avoid. He kept his sword low, merely stepping backwards, and the blade tip missed him by a foot.

The cavalryman raised his hand. His request for a pause confused the Portuguese; this was not how a contest usually started. Lock sidestepped across to where Isabella sat with one hand over her mouth.

"How do you say…" Lock whispered in her ear, and once she had told him paced back to the middle of the barn, beckoning Marco to continue. The big Portuguese swung his sword again, and again Lock retreated. Let the man tire, he thought. That huge waepon would be hard work.

Lock was getting very close to the barn wall, so when Marco swung next, he put his sword up in a block. The jolt as their blades clashed jarred his shoulder. God, the man was strong. Marco stepped back, and this time he signalled the cavalryman to come forward. The Portuguese grinned, showing off stained teeth again. It was time to end it.

The massive sword swung once more, but this time, as he parried the stroke, Lock twisted his wrist. Marco's blade was deflected downwards and the cavalryman's sword swung back over the top, aimed for the big man's throat. At the last second Lock twisted his wrist the opposite way, pulling the stroke. The flat of his blade slapped the Portuguese hard on the cheek, snapping Marco's head sideways.

"*Você é matado*!" Lock said, loudly enough for everyone to hear, and he smiled, "You're dead!"


Marco dropped his sword to the stone floor, and in the silence the clatter was deafening. The big Portuguese put a hand to his cheek, but no blood stained his fingers. Lock lowered his sabre, not even bothering to raise it again when Marco stamped towards him with a face like thunder. The Portuguese stopped short. He stared at the curved cavalry sword in Lock's hand, then back into his opponent's face, and, much to the cavalryman's surprise he smiled broadly.

"Jericho - hah!" the big man clapped him on the shoulder. Lock cursed under his breath; the shock of the blow made his headache return, seeking vengeance. But he had not lost his temper; not for a second.

# Chapter 29

Killen led his men back into camp, tired and hungry. The loss of his friend weighed heavily throughout the patrol; even the excitement of spotting a distant squadron of French dragoons and trailing them for several hours failed to lighten his mood. Matthew Picker stood in his way as he walked dejectedly back to the horse-lines.

"I'll take The Tempest, sir."

"What?" Killen suddenly realised Picker must be another of the troopers without a horse. Until fresh mounts arrived the men were being used as orderlies. "Oh, thank you, Matthew. I must report in."

Two sentries posted outside Major Hughes' tent saluted. Killen bashed his uniform all over to get rid of as much dust as he could, but thought he must still look like a vagrant. That could not be helped. The sentries allowed him to pass without challenge and he dropped the tent flap behind him.

Inside, the floor-space was crammed with officers. Killen spotted Wellesley and Colonel Taylor, both deep in conversation with another general officer, judging by his uniform, and an infantry colonel. Captain Butterell, his dolman just as grubby as Killen's, was speaking to Major Hughes, who spotted the lieutenant and beckoned him to join them.

"Just relax, Johnny." Killen stood to rigid attention in front of the major's desk, which looked as neat and tidy as ever. Hughes exuded calm. "What did you find?"

The lieutenant reached down to his sabretache, retrieving the map he had been given. Now it was crumpled and littered with copious pencilled notes. He placed it on Hughes' desk, smoothing out the creases.

"We discovered where Lieutenan Rapton's patrol was attacked, sir," Killen began. "The French were gone. Trooper Kittoe believes they mounted thirty men with one light field gun, judging from tracks they left behind. They moved off this way," he put his finger on the map to trace a line already drawn on it. "They appeared to have circled around here," his finger stopped, "we believe they were lost."

"We?" Hughes queried.

"Er…I thought it likely, sir," Killen said, surprised, "and my men concurred. The country was mostly thick brush and scrub. We found their trail heading off to the south-west, but then we spotted another squadron, so followed them instead." Killen stopped talking. He thought it odd that other conversations had also quietened, but Hughes had sat down and was looking at him expectantly so he ploughed on with growing confidence. "Dragoons, we believe. Green coats with cross-belts. Their helmets were covered up, so the brass would not reflect sunlight." Killen thought it an eminently sensible idea of the French; a stray reflection might easily betray their position. "We counted a hundred and fifty. We followed for a couple of miles along…" he leant over the map again, pointing, "along this road, taking care to keep out of sight. Then I judged it sensible to return; the horses had had enough, sir, though the men would have continued." Killen stood to attention, "I am pleased to report no injuries or losses. Oh," he had a second thought, "sorry sir, Trooper Fletcher's horse cast a shoe, but not too far from home. The animal is still sound."

Hughes sat back in his chair, fingers intertwined across his chest. "A concise report, Mr Killen, I must say."

"Indeed." Wellesley's voice cut in. He strode across, leaning over the sketch-map Killen had scrawled notes on. "You are certain that they were headed south-east?" his eyes stabbed at Killen who nodded meekly.

With a forefinger, Wellesley traced the line the lieutenant had marked. Then he straightened to address all three officers he had spoken with earlier. "There, gentlemen; I was correct. I am convinced of it." Taylor and the other two came to the table. "General Junot is concentrating every man he can find in this area," Wellesley pointed at the map, "and once he believes he has sufficient, he will march north to meet us." He turned back to Killen, "And you saw no other troops on your patrol? Be advised you must be certain of this."

"None, sir, nor sign of any."

Wellesley inclined his head, but still did not smile. "Thank you, lieutenant. You have more questions for Mr. Killen, major?"

"Just one more thing, sir," Hughes raised his eyebrows at Killen, who shook his head sadly.

"We found a grave, sir," he said, feeling Lock's loss anew. "They had the good manners to bury him, at least."

Hughes had lost men in action in the past, discovering long ago that it never became any easier to bear. "Very well, Mr Killen," he said, his voice flat, "you may go back to your men. Get some sleep."

Wellesley became more animated after Killen left. "Gentlemen, I think we may dispense with further cavalry patrols. At least, they need go no further than the perimeter held by our piquets. It seems wasteful to tire out what horses we have when we now know what the French are up to. Major: the map, if you please."

Hughes unrolled his large drawing with exaggerated care. Wellesley questioned Taylor, "I recall you said your lieutenant is reliable?"

"I believe so," the colonel affirmed.

"My instinct agrees. Sometimes we must allow the heart to guide us, eh, major? And so, gentlemen, we march tomorrow. All our troops are landed. Heavy baggage will stay in the rear, though as you are aware, I ordered most left on board the convoy. I have received word that your remounts will be with us in the next few days, colonel. Good news, at last."

Taylor agreed, "Most certainly, sir."

"Now, if you will excuse us, gentlemen," Wellesley became polite," MacAllen and I need a word with the major, here."

Uh-oh, Hughes thought.

"I find myself in something of a pickle, Hughes," Wellesley confided. "You well know my feelings with regard to any lack of organisation, and it would seem my Commissary suffers greatly from this malady." Hughes stayed silent. "I have it in mind to requisition your services from Colonel Taylor. You would have no objection, I assume?"

"I would rather stay with my regiment, sir, but of course," Hughes stood, "I will serve in any capacity you deem fit."

"Good, good. I must have men who will get the job done. Like your lieutenant. It would seem your concerns were misplaced."

"With respect, sir, I did not doubt his competence; only his ability to lead men."

"Hmmph," Wellesley sounded unconvinced. "Now, you must excuse us, major. I have orders to write, and no doubt Colonel MacAllen has duties which I do not care to think about."

McAllen winked conspiratorially at Hughes, "I do, sir." The major scowled back.

"A shame our first casualty should be one of yours, Hughes," Wellesley commiserated, "a damned shame."

"Yes sir," Hughes said. It was a shame; a damned shame. But for Lieutenant Killen it might be worse than that.


At least the officers had set up a mess, of sorts. Killen trudged across to the building; four mud-brick walls roofed with canvas, bringing a tiny piece of England to foreign soil. For some reason he craved a drink. An odd feeling; he drank wine with dinner, of course, but rarely during the day. Now he needed one.

A steward filled his glass and with admirable foresight, waited while he drained it, then filled it again. Killen sipped the second glass slowly, the taste acid in his mouth. It did not make him feel any better. He put the refill down, half drunk.

A voice spoke from behind him. "I was so sorry about your friend," Rapton sounded gloating. He seemed recovered from the shock of his first meeting with the enemy. And he did not sound at all sorry. Killen turned to face him. "Such a pity," the lieutenant went on, "as he was particularly helpful to me when he allowed you to beat him for the tournament's prize."

Lock had never explained to his friend why, on that day, he left himself open to Killen's final thrust. "I beat him, fair and square," Killen lied, wanting to know the truth.

Rapton lifted his wineglass towards the light, examining its murky contents. "Do you really believe so? Oh, no, my dear fellow, I paid him well for the favour."

Killen could not believe his ears, "He would not have!" But, he conceded to himself, it made some sort of sense. Why else would Lock have deliberately lost the contest? Killen's emotions wrestled with Rapton's words. Emotion won. "He would not have taken your money."

"Who said anything about money?" Rapton leaned forward, so his face was very close to Killen's. "I paid him in kind," he hissed, "beforehand."

Killen tried to take in Rapton's words. Lock complained of a stomach ache before the contest, he remembered. Guilt surged through him; shame, that he had doubted his friend even for a second. Rapton was responsible for that, and Killen's remorse turned in an instant to pure hatred. He grabbed the hilt of his sabre, desperate to yank the sharp weapon from its scabbard and thrust it into this vile monster; to twist it, mercilessly, until Rapton screamed for quarter.

But that was not his way; the rage passed. Killen took his hand away from the sword-hilt. He glared at the other subaltern, and his voice cracked. "Stay away from me, Rapton."

"Or, what? What will *you* do?"

Killen turned to leave, but somehow words he would not normally have uttered forced their way out of a place locked deep inside, "or you'll be sorry."

# Chapter 30

In the middle of next afternoon Isabella crossed to the barn again, at the time of day when men sheltered from the sun's shimmering heat behind cool stone walls. Lock watched from his upstairs window. The girl soon emerged, leading the same horse and carrying the same slim bundle as the day before. He carefully noted which path she took into the trees before strapping on his sword belt and hurrying downstairs. Outside, the air dried his mouth as he stepped from Carvilho's doorway; the courtyard was stifling. He hurried to the barn, conscious he might be seen, but nothing else stirred.

Lock found his saddle propped on a bundle of willow sticks in one corner. He threw it up on one of three remaining horses, choosing the quietest-looking because there was no point in taking risks. His bridle would not fit; this horse had a smaller head than the Portuguese remount he had lost, forcing him to fiddle with buckles and straps until it was right. Then a recumbent pig seeking shade blocked the doorway. Lock encouraged it to move with the toe of his boot, praying it did not make too much noise. When he led the horse outside its footsteps were so loud on the cobbles he looked around, fearful he would be noticed. But no-one came to investigate; they must all be asleep.

The track Isabella had climbed was easy to follow at first, but very soon vegetation on both sides thickened and her route began to twist and turn up the steep valley-side. Several times Lock stopped at shade-dappled junctions where paths or animal trails veered away, but fresh hoof-prints were easy to recognise even over rocky ground. At each halt, Lock picked up the girl's tracks again.

He spotted her horse first. Tied to a tree by its reins, the animal turned its head towards Lock's mount, even though low branches must have blocked its line of sight. Lock circled it warily, but the girl was nowhere to be seen. She must have gone deeper into the trees. He dismounted, tying his own horse alongside.

Now, tracking the girl was more difficult. Being lighter than a man, Isabella's boots made shallower impressions. Lock started up one trail but turned back as soon as he realised the undergrowth showed no sign of being disturbed. Then a noise alerted him; a scraping sound, like a grindstone on a sickle blade. He cautiously headed towards it.

The small clearing was completely hidden from view. Lock would never have found it had he not heard the girl draw her sword. Isabella stood right at its centre and Lock watched as she thrust her sword point forward then drew back, twitching the blade to one side as if to parry an imaginary opponent. He stayed hidden for a while. The girl was light on her feet, and quick. But she always reached too far forward, he noticed, upsetting her balance.

When Lock finally showed himself, Carvilho's granddaughter whirled to face him at once, sword raised. She dropped the point immediately in recognition. "You followed me," Isabella accused, but her voice was not angry.

Lock indicated her sword. "I wondered what you were hiding." The girl reversed the weapon to hand it over. Like a rapier, with a slim, straight blade, Lock found its edge sharp when he tested it. He sucked a cut thumb as he handed the sword back.

"Grandfather would not approve," Isabella offered an explanation. "He does not believe a woman should carry any weapon."

"And what do you believe?"

The girl gave a small shrug. "I am no different to a man. I work; why should I not fight also?"

"If you fight like that," Lock criticised, "you will die too easily."

Isabella drew herself up. "If you are so clever, you should show me."

Lock smiled at her bravado. He drew his long curved sabre, holding it out towards her, and gave a deep bow, "If you are ready, then, *Senhorita*?"

Lock let Isabella attack him, mostly, for that was where her technique was weakest. She threw her weight too far forward, losing her balance ever so slightly, so that if her stroke was parried she struggled to recover in time to block her opponent's counter. Lock tried to correct her mistake, and it was not that she did not understand what he taught, but that she allowed her emotions to intrude too much. It showed in her face. When Isabella failed to fence past Lock's guard, in frustration her strokes became faster and faster: more and more wild. Lock stepped back, lifting his hand. "Look," he explained, "you must treat your opponent as a puzzle to be unlocked, not a pig to be butchered as swiftly as possible." He raised his sword, touching hers. "Try again. And this time," he gently scolded, "try to keep your temper."

Their swords clashed. Lock saw concentration furrow Isabella's forehead, but again, when she failed to breach his defence, her strokes grew uncontrolled and her face flushed with frustration. Lock parried one wild slash, catching her sword with his own. He stepped forward so her blade ran the full length of his down to the hand-guard. The two swords locked, forming a cross between their bodies. She pushed hard, grunting through bared teeth, but he stood his ground. "Steady, now," he said quietly. Their faces were close. She looked up at him, fiercely angry, and Lock leant forward, between the blades, to kiss her on the mouth. Later, he could not say for certain why he had done it, but now, for just a second she returned his kiss, forcing her lips hard against his. Then, abruptly, she broke away. She stared blankly at the cavalryman before turning her back to trot out of the clearing.

Isabella had forgotten her scabbard. Lock bent down to retrieve it, cursing himself for a fool. He had set a fire; it would be his own fault if he was burned.


At first light, Lock was ready to begin, though he was forced to kick his heels in frustration until morning was half gone before all the Portuguese gathered. It was a motley collection of men and horses, but Francisco Carvilho introduced them proudly.

"But they don't all have swords," Lock objected.

"We will find more," Carvilho glossed over the problem. "They can use sticks for now. It is only in practice, after all."

Away from the settlement, they rode up one side of the wooded valley, ducking overhanging branches. At the top a small plateau opened out, a field of animal-pasture bounded on three sides by more hills. Lock had to admit that it was an ideal spot for what Carvilho had in mind.

"Now, corporal, you will show them."

Lock got the men to form their horses into a rough line. Isabella, who had followed the group, stood beside her grandfather. Lock beckoned her forward. "You'll have to translate for me."

The girl nodded. "Thank you," she whispered to him, "for my scabbard." Her eyes smiled. Lock had left the scabbard back in the barn, tucked beneath his saddle so she might find it. The two walked their horses until they faced the middle of the Portuguese line.

"If you wish to battle the French," Lock told them, "you must fight in the French way." He paused, while the girl translated, "Otherwise, they will beat you. Before the charge, first you must walk." Lock drew his sabre, holding it point-upwards and leaning to the rear, so the back of the blade rested against his shoulder. His right hand rested on his thigh. "You draw your swords and hold them like this," he instructed, "then trot. When you gallop, you may hold the sword forward," he demonstrated again, first holding his arm horizontally then dropping the sword-point while lifting his elbow. "The charge is ordered only when you are very close to the enemy. Otherwise, the horses will tire too quickly."

There was some nodding – the men had obviously understood that last instruction. A couple of the peasants looked relaxed and competent, Lock thought. Marco was present, sitting a horse big enough to pull a field gun without help. He recognised a few the young men; those who had watched him fight the big Portuguese to prove his worth.

Isabella seemed particularly interested in one young horseman, responding to his glances with shy smiles. "Who's that?" Lock indicated the dark haired boy.

"Paulo," she blushed, lowering her eyes.

He changed the subject, not wanting to hear more. "Do you think they all understood?"

The girl nodded, "Of course," but Lock thought her unsure. He would soon find out.


Only when the men tried to trot did things begin to go wrong. A number of horses, excited by their companions' proximity and the significant change to their usual routine, began cantering. That set them all off and many of the men, riding one handed with drawn swords, lost control, careering away across the plain. Lock pulled his mount to a walk, watching the shambles with exasperation. Horses were everywhere but where they should be.

They tried again, Lock cursing and shouting at the men to get them back into line, but with much the same result. Fewer horses galloped off out of control, but still too many. He rode back to where Carvilho and his granddaughter stood watching.

"It's hopeless, sir," Lock shook his head in defeat. "It will take months to train them." He waved his arm in the general direction of the melee, "See for yourself."

Carvilho frowned. "They are all horsemen, corporal," he chided.

"Oh, they managed to stay aboard," Lock agreed bitterly, for none of the men had actually parted company from his mount, "but they must use their swords as well, without chopping their horses' heads off. Can you see any of them doing that?"

"They will do it," the old man was convinced, "with practice. You will train them."

"I can't do it, sir," Lock said. "In weeks – perhaps. Not in a few days." He sought a way out, "And I must get back to the army."

"Very well, corporal," Carvilho's face betrayed his disappointment, but Lock knew there was not much he could do about it, "Very well."


A small noise woke Lock. The bedroom was pitch-dark, and he could see nothing. Then he heard it again, and he very slowly let his left arm trail from the side of the bed, reaching toward where his sabre lay.

But it was Isabella's bare feet Lock had heard as the girl tiptoed across the boards. She leant over him, smiling when she saw his eyes open. Lock opened his mouth to speak but she pressed her fingers over his lips, trapping his words. She stepped away, back into darkness. Lock wondered mutely what she wanted, but then there was a rustle of material, and the bedsheet was pulled back. Lock moved to one side of the mattress and Isabella slipped in beside him. She was naked; he could feel her skin hot against his chest. He should say something, but once again her fingers stopped him. Neither of them tried to speak, after that.


Lock propped himself on one elbow to look into the girl's face, but she stared straight ahead, refusing to catch his eye. With a forefinger he traced a line, along her collar-bone and down between her breasts. "Why did you come?" He thought he knew, but wanted her to say it. When she stayed silent, he told her himself, "Your grandfather?" There was no answer. "You want me to stay for him."

Isabella studied him through narrowed eyes then turned away, shutting them tight. She shook her head, "Not for him; no. But you would think that. You are a man." She sat up in bed, hugging her knees. "There is something you must know about my grandfather. He hates the French for what they have done. He will do anything he can to…," she paused, "…to hurt them back. I do not agree with what he intends," she looked into Lock's eyes once again as if searching for something, "but I cannot fight what is in his heart."

The girl stood up, crossing the bedroom to where her nightdress made a shapeless mound on the floor. "You must do what you will, Joshua," she stooped to collect the thin garment on her way out, "as I must."


Lying sleepless on his back, Lock stared at the ceiling, his head filled with a jumble of emotions. Carvilho's dream of leading his men against the French was just that; a hopeless dream. There was no chance Lock could turn them into an effective cavalry troop; the partisans would never be able to work in unison. His regiment would be concerned where he had got to; no, they would not, but John Killen would worry. And then there was the girl. Why had she come to his bed if not to persuade him to stay?

Lock gave up trying to sleep and instead sat up to pull on shirt and overalls, tugging canvas braces over his shoulders. His boots would be loud on the floorboards, he decided, so he left them. Creeping carefully out of the room across the landing, he padded downstairs barefoot.

Though the rest of the kitchen was in darkness, a fire still burned on the hearth, illuminating one corner. Its brightness drew his eyes, so he pretended he had not noticed a shadow sitting at the table.

"There is tea," the shadow said, in Carvilho's voice, "in the cauldron."

Lock found a mug and dipped it in the dark brown liquid. He sat down opposite the old man, carefully lifting out another chair so it did not scrape on the flags. Isabella's grandfather stared past him, into the flames. Lock waited patiently for Carvilho to speak, which eventually he did.

"I will provide a guide, corporal, to take you back to your army," the old man did not take his eyes from the fire. "My men tell me they are not far; a day's ride; two perhaps?"

Lock was surprised Carvilho had not tried harder to persuade him to stay. Perhaps he too realised the task he had set himself was impossible. He had given up. That thought annoyed Lock; he was missing something still unsaid. "Why did you ask me to help you?"

"I have told you," Carvilho said, tiredly.

"No. No you have not. Not all." In the firelight Lock saw the old man's face gouged with deep lines, his eyes sunk in black hollows. "What will you do when I leave?" he asked.

"Whatever God wills," Carvilho answered, and Lock's anger flashed like powder.

"And is it God's will that you and all your men be killed? Is it his will the French ravage your country?" He put his hand inside his shirt and pulled out the wooden crucifix, holding it up where Carvilho could see it clearly. "You see this? This is what I think of your God's will!" Lock tore the cross from his neck, snapping its leather thong, and hurled it into the fire

"No!" the old man cried, "no!" He strode to the hearth and fell to his knees, raking through burning embers with a poker. "No," he wailed again in desperation, but the crucifix had disappeared.

Carvilho jumped to his feet, taking a step towards Lock with the poker raised, but abruptly the fury in his eyes cooled. He turned back towards the fire, dropping the poker with a clatter. His shoulders sagged with defeat. "There is," Carvilho said at last, "a man...a devil." He clenched his fists at the memory. "A few weeks ago, he led his army to a city called Evora. Many important men were there; those who would lead my people in revolt against the French. They were overwhelmed. The French broke into the city and...butchered them: men and women, babies; all of them." Lock saw tears in the firelight, but Carvilho would not look at him. "My son was there," he said, trembling with anguish, "with his wife. And my grandson. He killed them." The old man raised his hands to stare at the marks on both palms where his fingernails had dug in. "And with God's help, if not yours," he glared at the cavalryman defiantly, "I will kill him."

Lock thought of his own grandfather, the man who had brought him up. He had managed the task alone, asking nothing in return. And when he died, leaving Lock with no family, others had turned their faces away, uncaring. He would not be like them, *never*. "I will help you," Lock decided, knowing God would not, "but you won't find him; not one man, amongst the whole French army."

"I will know him," Carvilho insisted stubbornly, "because he has lost an arm. My people call him *Maneta;* penguin. His name is Loison; General Louis-Henri Loison." He screwed up his face and spat into the fire. "And I *will* kill him."


"The problem" Lock grumbled in frustration next morning, "is not the horses, it's the men. They're too bloody keen to get on with things. They don't listen." He racked his brains for some way to encourage Carvilho's followers to be more disciplined. Then he had an idea. "Get them to bring a bundle of willow-sticks up here," he told Isabella. It was a childish game, he thought, but it just might work.

Lock lined the Portuguese up again, close together, but this time every man held one end of a willow stick in his left hand. The horseman to his left held the other end, so each was effectively joined to the next in line. The game might force the partisans to control their horses.

This time, trotting in line worked well, but the formation still broke up when the men attempted to gallop. It was an improvement. Lock repeated the exercise again and again, until they could canter for almost half a mile keeping their line intact, and both men and horses sweated from their efforts.

Carvilho was delighted. "You see, corporal; I said you could make them do it!"

But Lock still saw problems everywhere. "They haven't had to carry swords yet," he said gloomily. "That's when we'll see if they are really any good. And we still haven't enough weapons. We can't beat the French to death with sticks."

"There are no more swords," the old man told him disappointedly. "We searched everywhere. We did find lances."

Lock was doubtful the Portuguese could manage such long weapons. He had once practiced with a lance, finding it difficult to wield with accuracy. The French mounted squadrons of lancers, though, and their pointed spears certainly struck fear into any enemy. "Where are they?" A lance might be better than no sword at all.

"Marco knows," Carvilho patted him on the shoulder. "Soon, we will show the French a thing or two, eh?"


"Jericho! Here!" Marco dragged a pile of sacks to one side and beckoned. Ever since Lock's sword slapped his face, he had taken to calling the Englishman 'Jericho', and now the other Portuguese were beginning to get the hang of riding in formation they started using the nickname. Lock was pleased because it at least gave him some sort of status; made him one of them for a while, but right now he had more important things to worry about. Grabbing one end of a bundle of wooden poles, he began heaving them out into the open.

Covered with a thick layer of dust, the weapons must have been stored in the building for years. Their shafts proved very long; too long. Lock stopped what he was doing to pull a single lance from the bundle.

"What's this?" he asked Marco, but the big man just shrugged his shoulders. The poles were not lances but pikes, over sixteen feet in length and mounted at the ends with broad iron blades. Such old-fashioned weapons were far too long and heavy to be carried by a horseman but, Lock wondered, what if they could be made smaller?

Carvilho set a number of the older men to work. The pike shafts were shortened. Nine feet, Lock thought, would be plenty long enough for the partisans to handle. Poles were laboriously shaved to reduce both thickness and weight, and, finally grindstones were treadled through the night, spitting bright sparks as they cut the old blades to half their original width. Lock worried that a French patrol might ride close enough to hear the noise, but Carvilho seemed blithely unconcerned. In the event, nobody came to investigate, and in the morning Lock was presented with twenty serviceable lances.

"I need a pig," Lock had asked Carvilho the previous evening, "if you can spare one. And Marco's help," and the old man was so pleased with the progress the Portuguese were making that he did not bother to ask why.


Lock brandished his sword. Earlier in the day he and Marco had driven a cart up the winding track, loaded with the slaughtered pig. Now it lay on the ground, dressed in a greatcoat and with a pack strapped to its back which Lock had constructed from a straw-stuffed knapsack.

"When you charge at infantry," Lock told the watching men, "they will usually run away. They'll be scared of you." He waited for Isabella to translate and saw grins appear on many swarthy faces. "It will seem easy to cut them down, but it's no use striking them like this," he brought the sword down on the pig's back as hard as he could, several times. Then he stripped off pack and greatcoat and held them up. His sabre's keen edge had cut right through the pack, slitting the thick wool coat. "But look," Lock pointed at the pig's bare back, "you see - the skin has not been marked."

Lock summoned Marco and the two of them lifted the pig, hooking it over a post they had hammered into the ground earlier, so its snout pointed up in the air. The corporal retrieved his horse from the man holding it and vaulting up, turned a circle before cantering towards the carcase. Just before he reached the post, he back-swung his sabre, slicing the pig's snout clean off as he galloped past.

"That is what you must do," Lock returned to the watching Portuguese, thankful he had not made a fool of himself by missing with his sword-stroke. "Cut backwards, at their faces. Do you all understand?"

From the ensuing chatter it seemed they did. This was more like real fighting; swords slicing into flesh, blood flying. Lock thought they would enjoy it more than practicing staying in line.

Isabella smiled at him. "They are all to try that, one at a time," he told her, "and tell them not to cut off their horses' ears," then motioned at Marco before riding across to where their home-made lances were thrust point downwards into the ground.

The Portuguese began trying to sabre the pig. Lock watched them for a few minutes. The boy, Paulo, obviously had a good eye, making his backswing accurate and fast, keeping his horse under control.

Uprooting one of the lances, Lock tested his grip, finding the balance point. He had trained with one at barracks, tilting at pegs driven into the ground. That taught him how far forward to lean; when to thrust; how high above the ground the tip must travel to prevent an accidental dip catching the turf. Where you held the lance was critical; just past its centre of balance, so the point travelled below the horizontal when it was carried. And the weapon really needed a strap to go around a man's elbow, to help support its weight, but these had none.

Lock held the lance upright, the end of its long shaft resting on the toe of his right boot. He cantered the horse up and down the field a few times, re-accustoming himself to how the weapon felt in his hand. After a short time he realised the sword-practice had stopped. The Portuguese were all watching him. He turned away from them to face the target.

Marco had set a willow stick in the ground some way down the field, topping it with a cabbage. It would have to do. Lock asked the horse to canter, and let the lance point drop.

Approaching the target, he kicked the horse into a gallop, tucking the lance shaft under his elbow; praying for a hit. The cabbage disintegrated in a satisfying explosion of green leaves as the blade struck it square on, drawing cheers from the watching Portuguese. Lock felt something of a fraud; running the lance point into a live opponent was far more difficult because you must pull the sharp blade back out or risk being unhorsed. Or what was worse, being left without a weapon.

A scrummage developed around the lances. All the Portuguese wanted a turn, and Lock found it interesting how some older men were deferred to, but others forced aside by the younger. Paulo seized a lance and turned his horse out of the melee, brandishing the weapon above his head. Riding across to where Isabella stood dismounted the boy spoke to her, his face flushed. Lock noticed how the girl rested her hand on Paulo's thigh, her eyes sparkling when she laughed. So that was it; she had used him merely to make another man jealous. Oh, well.

They practiced tilting at the pig's carcase. Lock showed the men how to stand up in their stirrups when delivering a thrust, then sit down to pull and twist the shaft backwards so the blade would come free. There was great hilarity when one man drove his lance into the pig with such force the blade lodged in the wooden post, the impact throwing him sideways off his horse.

Marco yanked the lance out of the post to hand it back. He glowered at the unfortunate partisan, saying something in his own language that made the man flush with shame so he returned to his jeering compatriots suitably chastened.

Marco strode towards Lock. "Hey, Jericho," the big man pointed at Paulo, and then at his own sword. Lock nodded understanding and called the boy over. Isabella followed, wondering what this was about.

"You can practice with the lance," Lock told him, "but you won't be carrying one." Isabella translated. Paulo scowled and spoke harshly to Marco, who shook his head fiercely.

"Why can't he?" the girl was instantly on Paulo's side. "He fights just as well as the others."

"That's exactly why," Lock explained patiently. "We'll need swordsmen to protect the men carrying lances. Paulo can use a sword better than most of the others."

Isabella translated again. The boy seemed to take the compliment as his due. He looked towards Marco for confirmation, and the big Portuguese gave a curt nod. Paulo inclined his head haughtily towards Lock and rode away, still carrying the lance.

"He will do what you wish," Isabella watched the boy trot towards the other young men.

"Then you can go after him and tell him I wish him to keep that lot," he pointed at the group, "under control as well." He sounded arrogant, even to himself. He not had intended that, but the girl looked at him crossly.

"You can tell him yourself," she said, stalking away.

"She is strong willed, like her mother." Carvilho rode up from behind the Englishman and spoke as if in apology, but Lock thought he detected a sneaking admiration in the old man's voice. "She will not make a good wife." Lock believed him wrong, but did not say so. He watched critically as another Portuguese galloped at the pig.

"They are doing well," Carvilho observed. "They understood what you taught."

"But can they hold a line? What will they do in a real charge?" Lock gently rubbed at his temple where his healing wound itched. "We still need to practice that. A couple more days; then we'll see."

Except there were no more days; no more time. A messenger reached the sleeping valley that night. The British were moving. Junot had gathered his scattered French battalions and was marching from the south to confront them.

"Tomorrow," Carvilho told them all, "we will leave tomorrow."

To avenge a dead city.

# Chapter 31

High above, where dark specks wheeled through clear air, a mist of feather-like cloud unfurled across the blue. Killen stared at the birds but they were too far up to identify. And even if they had flown low enough for him to hear, their plaintive calls would have been drowned by the cacophony resonating through the dust-shrouded valley.

Killen had never heard anything like it. Men shouted and cursed; mules and donkeys brayed. Wagons and guns rattled and thumped, and from the rear came the infernal squeal of hundreds of un-greased axles turning beneath hundreds of Portuguese ox-carts. A fat worm of humanity and animals stretched miles back down the valley: an army on the move.

"That racket's enough to scare the French away, don't you think, sir?" Francis Kittoe observed loudly, riding up alongside his lieutenant.

Killen's mind was elsewhere. "I doubt it; I gather they have far more men than we," he said curtly, "so it will merely advertise our army's position."

Kittoe checked his horse, "Rather be up here," he took a deep breath, "the air's cleaner."

Killen wished Lock was alive to see this. And he would likely have taken Kittoe's side; argued the point just for the hell of it, or told Killen not to be so damned stuffy.

"Sir?" Kittoe had spoken again and his lieutenant missed what he said. Killen halted.

"Ahead, sir; can you hear it?" Killen tugged his helmet's brass-linked chinstrap forward, pulling the whole fur-crested contraption off to brush back sweat-slicked hair. The Tempest fidgeted under him but abruptly stood still, ears pricked, and Killen could hear it too; the distant crackle of musketry. "Advance companies must have found the French, sir," Kittoe said unnecessarily, for Killen's heart had already begun to drum faster. His group of cavalrymen was strung out along the hillside, patrolling the marching army's left flank; on the lookout for danger.

"We will continue as we are." Killen decided. They would meet the enemy soon enough.


From in front of the patrol another horseman approached. The man bounced loosely in his saddle, Killen observed critically, but as he got nearer recognised Charles Harris. The cornet's face glowed bright pink, and he gasped for breath as he pulled to a stop.

"You're in a hurry, Charlie," Killen observed mildly.

Harris uncorked his waterbottle to take a swig, washing his mouth out with the lukewarm liquid before leaning sideways to spit it clear of the horse. "Colonel's called everyone in, Johnny," he started, then noticed Kittoe only a few paces away, "er…sir."

"What is going on?"

"There's been some fighting." Harris's breathing was slowing back to normal. "Apparently, the French were holding a hill in front of us and we've pushed them off it," he said excitedly. "The colonel wants every man to the front. There've been reports of hundreds of French cavalry."

Killen's heart, which had begun to steady, now thumped again, "Hundreds?"

"Five hundred at least; that's why we're all ordered forward. The colonel expects we'll have to fight them soon."

"And we are less than two hundred," Killen spoke this thoughts, but Harris was dismissive.

"Don't you believe that one Englishman is worth three frogs?" he asked, in a confident tone. "We're God's Own - how can we not win?" He moved closer to the lieutenant. "Not frightened are you, Johnny?" His voice was just above a whisper.

"Of course not," Killen hissed back crossly, then raised his voice again, mindful that other men in his patrol would be catching them up, "so who will be left to guard the column?"

"There'll be no need for guards. The general believes the French are all to our front. He's sent the Portuguese out that way," Harris pointed east, "and someone, can't remember who, sorry, towards the sea, to make sure they can't get past."

Killen had a sudden thought, "Have you brought orders?"

Harris patted his sabretache, "In here; d'you want to see them?"

"I trust you, Charlie," the lieutenant smiled, "but you will need them for the following patrol." Harris gave him a quizzical look. "Lieutenant Rapton is leading them," Killen explained.

Harris rolled his eyes, "Oh, marvellous. So I shall have the pleasure of his company all the way back. And that damned sergeant of his."

"At least you can relax. He will not be in any hurry to get to the sharp end, you can be sure of that."

Harris looked alarmed. "He'll have to be! The colonel will go mad if anyone is missing." He gave his horse a kick and began to ride away. "You'll have to get a move on, Johnny," he grinned over his shoulder, "don't want to miss it!"

"Mind the rocks at the base of the slope," Killen warned, but Harris was already galloping.


For a battlefield, Killen thought, it was oddly quiet. The thinly wooded hillside they mustered on seemed to muffle the great explosions of cannon fire, so only dull thumps could be heard. The crackle of muskets was sporadic. There was no shouting; no cheering. In fact, Killen thought, not much appeared to be happening at all.

Colonel Taylor addressed his officers. The French had been chased from the hill in front of the regiment, but only as far as the next.

"It would seem, gentlemen," Taylor sounded oddly subdued, "the enemy have the best of the ground. The general intends to outflank them, and we must be ready to support a push from the centre of our position." A stray cannonball crashed through trees behind them, making some of the horses skitter about nervously, but the roundshot fell harmlessly to the ground before rolling to a stop. Taylor waited for the horses to settle. "Their dragoons," he scanned the officers' faces, "their dragoons outnumber us, but I am certain we shall not be found wanting." He seemed satisfied by the expressions he saw, "To your troops then, gentlemen."

Killen turned The Tempest away, but the colonel called him back. "You're with me, Mr Killen," he said, and when the lieutenant looked surprised, added, "we may find the Portuguese coming on from our left. Don't trust 'em myself, but... you speak the lingo?"

"Yes, sir!"

"If we get mixed up with them, you'll tell me what they're chattering about." He turned away, yelling, "Picker! Picker! Where the devil has he got to."

"Here, sir..." Taylor's orderly trumpeter walked his horse slowly towards the colonel and saluted them both, "...lieutenant."

"Where've you been, man," Taylor said impatiently.

"Well, sir," the trumpeter tugged at the golden cord over his shoulder as if to settle the slung instrument more comfortably across his back, "General Wellesley wanted to speak to me. Asked if I was happy in the 20th, sir."

"Ah," Taylor nodded. "I do recall Sir Arthur mentioning something...."

"Sir," Killen had seen the Staff officer approaching, and that meant orders, "I do believe you are wanted."


They took a track that rose up the left hand side of the hill. The squadron was formed up in column, three men riding abreast, but after a short distance the dirt road narrowed as its sides banked steeply upwards. Killen glanced back, watching men change formation into a column of twos, the path forcing horses closer together. In front, though, Colonel Taylor seemed not to notice any difference, urging his horse along as if on a brisk hack.

The guns sounded closer. Not many shots from the French side cleared the ridge. Killen presumed that was because they were being forced to fire from a downhill slope, making it difficult for the artillerymen to elevate their barrels high enough. It was a comforting thought.

Another Staff officer galloped up from behind them, Taylor halting the squadron once more to allow the messenger to catch up. He saluted the colonel before presenting a piece of paper.

"The general's compliments, sir, and will you form at the top, to await further orders." Taylor glanced at the note, nodding confirmation to the aide. He stuffed the paper into his sabretache and they went on. Once at the summit, the order to form line was passed back and cavalrymen spread out along the crest. Taylor went forward. He un-holstered a telescope and trained it towards the enemy, who occupied the hillside opposite.

"By God!" Killen heard the shock in his colonel's voice, "...by God!" but he soon spied what had prompted Taylor's outburst. For the enemy hill seethed with horsemen, sunlight reflecting in bright flashes from their metal sword-scabbards and polished harness.

Colonel Taylor rode back to the lieutenant and offered his glass. "What d'you think, Mr Killen, will they come up here?" A tremble distorted the colonel's voice, but whether from excitement or fear Killen did not know. He twisted the telescope's brass tubes until green-coated French horsemen came into focus. Not dragoons, after all but *chasseurs à cheval*, the same light cavalry Killen's patrol had tracked for a time while he was searching for Lock. They seemed to be milling about aimlessly, though several groups had gathered near the foot of the slope. The men's tall fur caps must be damnably hot, Killen thought, glad his helmet was leather.

Something was going on further to the west, but even with the telescope Killen could make no sense of it through the mist of powder smoke that had spread from the cannon-duel. He collapsed the glass before handing it back. "I don't know, sir." That was not a very useful comment, Killen decided. Lock would have said 'yes' or 'no', his confidence making him sound correct, even if he was not. He looked around for inspiration, and the answer suddenly became obvious. "I don't think they realise our true strength, sir," Killen offered. "They cannot see if we have more men behind the crest."

Taylor looked back at the squadron in surprise, then down again toward the French. "I do believe you are right, Johnny," he said, sounding relieved. "Ask the other officers to come forward, if you will," the colonel smiled. "Might as well let the hounds see the fox, eh?"

Captain Hackett stared at the *chasseurs* for some time before closing his telescope with a snap. "Plenty of them there, sir," he said to Colonel Taylor.

"Handsome looking devils, aren't they?"

Hackett agreed, "But we have the beating of them, sir."

"I am certain we do, captain." Taylor sounded far from convinced, Killen thought.

"Colonel doesn't like it," Picker had wandered closer to the lieutenant and spoke quietly, "not one bit."

"But they won't come up here, Matthew?"

Picker shook his head. "Would you? The horses would be beat before they got halfway up this hill. And see the rocks yonder?" the trumpeter pointed down the slope, "You'd have to walk them through that lot; they'd be sitting ducks." He stopped, and leant closer. "Look at him," he whispered, indicating another cavalryman.

Melville Rapton lowered his own telescope. His face had turned as pale as the braid on his jacket. Colonel Taylor noticed the change as well.

"Melville," he said with concern, "you look ill, man."

Rapton dismissed the idea. "It's nothing, sir. The food has not been agreeing with me..." but he never finished the sentence. Abruptly he leaned down from his horse, retching up whatever he had eaten for breakfast. Taylor rode across, concerned, as Rapton sat up to wipe at his mouth with a handkerchief.

"Get off to the surgeon, lieutenant; that's an order." Taylor smiled. "You'll be right as ninepence in an hour or so, and I warrant we'll still be here."

"Very good, sir," Rapton reluctantly agreed and turned his horse away from the squadron.

"Fear does that to a man, sir," Picker said quietly to Killen, "seen it before: gets you in the guts first, head later."

"And you are not afraid?"

The trumpeter shook his head, "What's to be afraid of? You won't see the ball that kills you, so it's pointless being scared of that. Now, if one of yonder froggies comes at you with a sabre, that's the time to be scared, sir."

Killen was impressed. He had not really thought of battle in such simple terms. "That is very profound, Matthew."

"Don't know about that, sir," Picker shrugged, "just common sense."


The day grew hotter. The squadron, formed in line on the ridge and facing south, sweated and burnt in the sun. Judging from the noise and smoke which wreathed the valley far over to their right, the battle was going on without them.

Colonel Taylor grew impatient. "What good are we doing here, eh, Johnny? We ought to be over there," he stabbed a forefinger westwards. Killen said nothing. He thought it should be obvious they had been ordered to this spot to watch the *chasseurs*, lest the French horsemen advance onto the flank of Wellesley's infantry. Sweat dribbled down one side of his face and he wiped it away with the back of a glove.

"Sir, a break? For the horses?" he suggested. They had stood exposed on the sweltering hilltop for over an hour.

Taylor considered. "Yes, of course," he agreed at last. "Ten minutes? Have the men dismount and lead them about; ten at a time."

Butterell sent his first ten men to the rear where they dismounted with evident relief, stretching cramped legs and chatting amongst themselves while they uncorked canteens. Killen ran his tongue over dry lips. Knowing the horses should have water, he rode back down the track they had just climbed in search of supplies. But the water-carts must be still stuck with the baggage train, and the stream-beds were dry. The horses would have to suffer.

Killen dismounted. His waterbottle was full, but he had no bucket so instead took off his helmet and, holding it upturned, poured in half his water. When he offered it to The Tempest the horse slurped the mouthful noisily. Such lukewarm liquid must taste pretty foul, he thought, but the horse seemed not to mind, and his helmet felt blessedly cool when he refastened it. He sipped a little canteen water himself, pulling a face because it tasted of the candle-wax used to keep the wooden drum watertight. There was no telling how long it would be before more water was brought, so he supposed he should save some. He forced the canteen's wooden stopper in tight.


Back on the hilltop, nothing much had changed. A different group of troopers walked their horses about below the crest. Taylor frowned at Killen as he rode up alongside his colonel. "You took your time, lieutenant."

"Sorry, sir; I was searching for water for the horses."

"Well?" Taylor raised his eyebrows.

"There was none."

The colonel grunted. "The frogs are spying on us." He pointed at the bottom of the slope opposite, where Killen could see a group of *chasseurs* gathered around the occasional flash of light; sunlight on a lens. "They think we're up to something. Must have seen our men going back and forth."

A gun fired from the opposite hill, sketching a tiny smoke trail across the sky. The lieutenant watched it, fascinated.

"Shell," Taylor had seen it. "Too far to the right, though." He turned his attention back to the French, but Killen followed the missile's arc. It fell lower and lower until there was a puff of smoke, and a second later the sound of an explosion. The colonel had been correct; it fell too far to the right.

But then there was a commotion in the squadron's rear. Killen tried to see, but horses blocked his view.

"Find out what's going on, there's a good chap," Taylor asked him.


One troop horse was down on its side, legs paddling aimlessly. Sergeant Tyloe's mount. Fortunately, it seemed that as the animal collapsed, horses on both sides had backed away, clearing a space so the sergeant was not trampled.

"Jesus!" The horse had tipped him clear as it fell, but Tyloe trembled as he climbed to his feet, "Jesus Christ!"

"Are you hurt, sergeant?" Killen forced The Tempest through the crush. The animal was wary of stepping too close to the fallen horse, forcing Killen to use his legs more strongly than usual. Tyloe seemed stunned. "Are you hurt?" Killen repeated, and finally the sergeant responded.

"No, sir," he looked up, "I don't think so, sir." He examined his hands, which were shaking, "Bloody hell!" Tyloe took a deep breath, "what happened?"

Killen looked carefully at the fallen horse. Flies were already gathering around its parted lips, and one paddled across its dead eyeball, but there was no blood to be seen. He dismounted, letting The Tempest's reins trail on the ground.

"Get your saddle off, sergeant." Tyloe was still staring at the carcase in shock. Killen walked around the sergeant's horse, eventually spotting a tiny wound that had dribbled a short, bloody line on the animal's neck, just below its mane. It must have been the shell, he thought. Though the projectile had burst some distance away, part of its casing must have travelled fast and far enough to strike the horse. Nothing else could have made that mark. Picker was right; you never saw the ball that killed you, so there was no need to fear it.

Colonel Taylor rode round to the rear rank to find out why his lieutenant had not returned. His face registered distaste as he stared at the dead horse.

"Damned howitzer," Taylor was grim when Killen pointed out the wound. "That's the only thing that can have thrown a shell so high; must have cut through its spine, poor devil."

Tyloe clutched his helmet tight to his chest. "Went down without any warning, sir," he explained to the colonel, "dropped stone dead, it did. Nothing I could do, sir."

Taylor nodded in understanding. "Lucky it was not you, sergeant. Nasty things, shell splinters - might have taken your head from your shoulders." He said it in a matter of fact voice but Tyloe paled visibly. "Still," the colonel went on, "no harm done to you, eh? Good man."

Killen remounted to follow Colonel Taylor back to the crest. The squadron stood silent. "Given them a scare, I'll be bound," Taylor said quietly. His horse began to fidget, and he stroked its neck. "Wait till the next one comes over, then we'll see how badly it has shaken them."

But there were no others. The battle further down the valley seemed to have reached stalemate. Taylor again grew frustrated as time went on, complaining repeatedly that the regiment had not been called. His men began to relax. A troop horse at the back staled noisily. "I'm not scared," one wag observed in a loud voice, "but the 'orse is pissing hisself!" The joke prompted nervous laughter before Captain Hackett shouted at the men to be quiet, but Taylor admonished him to leave them be.

Eventually the *chasseurs* moved off. Killen, scanning the battlefield through Taylor's telescope, spotted movement down the valley to the east. He pointed it out to the colonel who pulled out his watch. "That will be Ferguson and Trant," Taylor commented, "late, as usual. Sir Arthur won't be best pleased." He must have known, Killen realised, that the approaching brigades had been sent around the army's left to outflank the French. The *chasseurs* must have seen them too, for two companies galloped off in that direction. Those that remained went right, retiring towards the stalemate.

*"We are up here!"* Taylor yelled after them angrily. "It never hurts to try, lieutenant," he gave Killen an embarrassed smile. "It never hurts to try."

Cavalry trumpets blared in the east. Killen could make out the cloud of dust kicked up by horsemen advancing toward the French cavalry, but then it seemed they must have wheeled about, reluctant to engage the enemy. Taylor pointed out those *chasseurs* who had turned westwards. Four squadrons were formed up, stationary; seemingly inviting attack. "The blasted frogs are retreating," Taylor read the battlefield as a professional should. "Look there," he pointed, "our infantrymen dare not attack their cavalry, and we are too far away to be any help. Damn it, Johnny" he complained again, "we'll get no exercise today."

But he was wrong. A messenger arrived soon after with orders for the squadron to advance. Still in formation, they picked their way down into the valley, where once again they halted to wait.

While the French, cleverly handled by their commander, escaped to the south.

# Chapter 32

Lock yawned as near-dawn lightened his room. He sat upright on the bed and stretched tiredly, having lain awake for hours in hope. Now he realised the girl would not come. He would not be with her again; a miserable thought, but her grandfather would forbid her to ride with his men. He sighed, and stood up to dress.

When Lock got downstairs he found the kitchen already crowded. Grabbing a tin cup he dipped it into a cauldron hung over the fire. Someone had made a soup, thick with lumps; not the tea he hoped for, but it would do. Lock reached down to draw out the short knife hidden in the top of his left boot. He stirred and prodded at the lumps without making much improvement and afterwards carefully sucked the blade clean in his mouth.

Peasants greeted one another in their own language. Lock felt excluded, but he supposed that even now he was an outsider; a foreigner. He watched from the room's edge as Marco bustled in and other Portuguese moved out of the big man's way. One day, Lock decided, he would command that sort of respect from his fellows.

He sipped at the hot soup. Most lumps had sunk to the bottom so Lock stirred the mugful again, and an idea came into his head; something he should have thought about before now.

"Jericho!" Marco singled the Englishman out as he crossed the room. He beckoned, "Come; come," and Lock followed him out into the dawn. He found a horse, saddled with his regimental equipment, and, hung from the saddle pommel, his Tarleton helmet. Marco lifted it off and presented it to him almost shyly.

Lock turned the helmet over in his hands. Canister had mashed one metal boss where the chinstrap attached; that must have been what saved his life. The fixing had been beaten back into shape and scuffed leather blackened over. A little blood still stained the helmet's fur crest, but it would brush out. Marco was smiling at him, so Lock pulled the helmet on. The big man grinned, and Lock slapped him on the shoulder as thanks.

"Now we go," Marco said happily.

But Lock shook his head. "I've forgotten something," he said to the puzzled Portuguese, before hurrying away.

They left late, in the end. The sun had risen by the time Francisco Carvilho finally appeared, and Lock immediately realised why the old man had waited. For he stepped from the front of his house dressed in the pale blue uniform and flashing braid of a Colonel of Hussars, the gaudiness of his jacket contrasting starkly with the dull clothing the peasants wore. Lock stared at the partisan brigade and saw belief shine clearly from each man's face. Carvilho would lead; the colonel would be their banner. They could not lose

He shook his head in admiration, and Carvilho saw. "Are you not impressed, corporal," he said, teasing.

Lock stood to attention and saluted. "You ought to have told me, sir."

"Ah," Carvilho caught the Englishman's accusing tone, "but then you might not have helped me."

"You could have ordered me to."

"But would you have obeyed?" the old man gave a small shake of the head, "I think not, corporal, I think not. Why should a colonel need a man like you to help him?" He pursed his mouth, considering, "perhaps I will tell you, when I have the time. But you can tell me," Carvilho pointed to one of the Portuguese horses, "what is the purpose of that?" A tin mug was lashed to its right-hand stirrup with thick cord.

"Perhaps, colonel," Lock said seriously, "I will tell you." Then he grinned, "When I have time."

"You will have time for this." Carvilho unstrapped a long package from one of his saddlebags, pulling off its cloth covering. Underneath was a trumpet; bright brass and silver, strung with a golden cord. "A retirement gift," he explained, "from my regiment. You can play?"

"Badly," Lock admitted. Picker had tried to teach him trumpet calls, to wile away time on board the transport ship that had bucked and reared its way across the ocean from Plymouth.

Carvilho handed the instrument to him. "That is more than I can do," the old man said. Lock slung the trumpet over his shoulder, preparing to mount. But Carvilho had brought something else. He held out his hand and from it dangled a wooden crucifix, a little charred at the edges but still intact, strung with a new leather thong. "Fire could not destroy it," Carvilho chuckled, "so it must be the gift of a true friend." His eyes crinkled, "Now I give it back to you."

The group left soon after. Carvilho leaned down from the saddle to kiss his granddaughter while she held onto him with fierce determination, the old man eventually having to push her gently away. Lock felt strangely jealous, especially when she did the same thing to Paulo. The boy gave the Englishman a hard smile as he rode by.

Carvilho led them off in a column two men wide, but Lock hung back. Isabella stared at him with big eyes.

"Be careful, corporal," she said, clutching at Lock's arm. "He will not wish to be careful," the girl added, meaning her grandfather. "Look after him - please?"

"He can look after himself."

"I mean it." She dug her fingers into his flesh. "He is," she dropped her eyes, "he is all I have left, now."

Lock put his hand under her chin, tilting her face upwards. "I will do my best," he said as her eyes filled his own, "that is all I can promise."

A narrow track meandered up the wooded hillside, slowing the column so that Lock caught the Portuguese up. He squeezed past the other horsemen. Those with lances held them vertically, butt-ends resting in the cups Lock had fixed to their right-hand stirrups. Holders made the weapons more comfortable to carry on a long march. Most of the group seemed happy enough to squeeze over, allowing the Englishman to the front, but Paulo and a couple of the other young men deliberately blocked his path. He forced his horse between theirs, hearing their laughter when he broke clear.

"Hey, Jericho," Marco moved over to make space for the Englishman's horse between himself and Carvilho. It was his favourite greeting; others used it too and Lock, once pleased, found himself growing heartily sick of his new nickname. Carvilho apologised for the young men's behaviour, but Lock waved his words away.

"They're nervous; bound to be. It's just bravado." Lock might have done the same thing himself, once. "A battle will take the wind out of their sails," he warned.

"We will defeat the enemy," Carvilho was convinced his men would chase the French from the field. "God is on our side; I told you."

"I'd rather a regiment of regular cavalry on our side," Lock retorted, "as I once told you."

"Corporal," Carvilho emphasised Lock's lower rank, "you are not thinking of deserting? Going back to your army when we meet the French?"

Lock stared to the front. It was true; he had thought of it. Rejoining the 20th would be the most sensible course of action; safer, probably. He had done everything Carvilho had asked. The Portuguese had saved his life, and he had kept his bargain; showed them how the French should be fought. There would be no dishonour in leaving the group now, except that it did not feel right. And he had made a promise, to a girl with long dark hair and huge eyes.

"I am disappointed you would think that of me, sir," Lock answered, making his voice sound hurt.

Carvilho seemed pleased with the Englishman's reply. He smiled and spoke to Marco in his own language. The big man laughed, shaking his lance. Lock noted it was much larger than the others; the Portuguese had chosen to use one of the huge ancient pikes just as it was. He shrugged to himself. Marco was certainly strong enough to wield the pike, but its sheer size would make it a clumsy weapon to use. And a slow man would be easy meat for French dragoons, however strong he was.

When they stopped at a stream to rest and water the horses, Lock took Carvilho to one side.

"Marco would tell you to save your concerns for the French," the colonel was obviously fond of the big man, "but he must take care of himself," he said, "as must we all."

The country became more thickly wooded, prompting Carvilho to call two Portuguese forward to take the lead. Lock had grown used to following narrow trails as a boy, exploring woods and copses around his home, but these men seemed to possess a sixth sense. Following tracks which only looked fit for rabbits to travel, they pushed bodily through dense clumps of undergrowth that opened into wide glades. They found water in unlikely places. Even so, the small group travelled what appeared an unnecessarily tortuous path across the countryside, arousing Lock's curiosity.

"The French have spies," Carvilho told him sadly, "even amongst my own people. They would tell of us, for money." Lock could understand that; most peasants seemed to live in penury. "Tonight we will stop," the colonel continued. "There is a town: Obidos. The French were there, but they have left. We will stay hidden in the hills and my men will talk with the people."

"There are no spies?"

Carvilho shrugged. "My men will find out. If there are..?" He drew his finger across his throat, but Lock remained sceptical. The colonel's men were farmers, not murderers.

"I told you, corporal that others would come? Marco knows men who are," the old man hesitated, searching for a word, "not like us. Not...decent. But they wish to fight the French. They will meet us at Obidos, and I will not refuse their help."


The Portuguese picketed their horses in a small clearing halfway up the hillside before gathering armfuls of dry bracken to sleep on. Lock felt slightly nervous after Carvilho's warnings. He was sure their cooking fires must be visible from Obidos, and that the group would be easily discovered. But the colonel's men showed their woodsmen's experience. Saddle-blankets were pegged with swords to shield open fires so the flames would not be seen from town, and the Portuguese pedantically selected only the driest sticks as fuel. The tiny smoke-wisps their fires produced filtered to invisibility through the leafy canopy above.

Darkness fell. Marco had left the camp at dusk, posting sentries before he went because he would not return for several hours. Lock ate the soup he was given, slurping straight from the bowl. He poked a finger through the greasy scum floating on top to stir a few unidentifiable lumps about. The lukewarm liquid was heavily flavoured with garlic, which he did not much care for. The army had spoiled him, he thought. Before he enlisted, any meal would have been welcome.

Partisans gathered in small groups, talking. They grumbled that Carvilho had banned them from smoking their short clay pipes, but the colonel strode determinedly from group to group, careless of twigs that cracked beneath his feet, dispensing encouragement and confidence. Lock watched for a while. He saw how easily Carvilho made the men smile; made them relax, and the deference they offered him in turn. A pity his regimental officers were not all like that, he decided, before a more important thought intruded. He badly needed a pee.

Lock walked uphill, away from the cooking-fires, past where their horses were picketed, wandering deep into the trees. From here he could barely hear the camp, and certainly not see it, so townsfolk further away should be oblivious. He had just unbuttoned the front of his breeches when he glimpsed a movement in the undergrowth. He froze. Nothing. Lock held his breath, and was just beginning to believe it must have been an animal, when there it was again. He turned his head very slowly, staring hard into the darkness.

It was a man. The figure moved silently from behind a tree on his right to another, further down the slope, and then Lock lost sight of the intruder against its black trunk. A spy! Lock crept forward, placing his feet with care. He must stay silent. When he was a boy, he stalked animals through the woods at home, but this species was far more dangerous.

The figure stepped from hiding again. Lock stopped instantly, waiting until the spy moved on downhill. Again, the man paused, and this time Lock heard movement ahead. They were close to the horses. Perhaps the spy had been sent to release them; to leave the group stranded. Lock needed to move quickly, risking that he might be heard. Then the figure disappeared.

Lock crouched, drawing the knife hidden inside his boot top. The spy suddenly reappeared from behind a tree just yards away. The corporal stood, took two quick steps, and his right arm

332

was around the intruder's neck; his knife blade pricking flesh beneath the man's ear. The spy struggled violently, ignoring the discomfort. He kicked back with a heel hard into Lock's shin.

*"Eu tantarel nă o matar,"* Lock growled angrily, pressing harder with the blade. And unexpectedly the intruder relaxed, leaning back against him.

*"Joshua!"*

Lock released his stranglehold and spun Isabella round by the shoulders. "What the hell are you doing here?"

She pulled off a wide-brimmed had she had worn to hide her face and her long hair cascaded down. "Joshua, there are men..." the girl began, but Lock pulled her towards him and kissed her fiercely. The knife fell from his hand, forgotten. After a short while she pushed him away. "There are men here," her big eyes were serious, "prowling the woods. I have seen them."

Lock was instantly wary, "Where?" he whispered. Isabella pointed. Lock took her hand, motioning her to follow, and they started downhill.

A glow-worm flew in the woods, its tiny light flickering in jerks. But it flew too slowly; Lock knew about strange lights and ducked behind a tree, pulling the girl with him. He could hear a voice, a mumbled monotone. He put his mouth close to Isabella's ear, feeling wetness when his cheek touched her skin. His knife must have cut her. "Can you hear what they are saying?" She listened, but shook her head. "We must warn your grandfather."

Isabella shook her head again. "He must not know I am here," she insisted.

Damn, Lock thought. "Stay here, then," he told her, "and be careful. I'll come back for you."

Carvilho stomped about in irritation when Lock strode back into camp. Marco had returned earlier than expected, bringing with him a half-dozen men Lock did not recognise. "Where have you been, corporal?" The old man's voice was heavy with disapproval.

"Went for a walk," Lock saw no reason to explain his absence.

One of the newcomers stepped forward, speaking to Carvilho in Portuguese. Lock did not like the tone of his voice.

"This is Guillermo Alonso," Carvilho offered a cursory introduction. "He wonders what an Englishman is doing, wandering in woods he does not know, late at night."

"Tell him I went for a piss," Lock said flippantly. He stared fixedly at Alonso, "and you might ask him what *his* men are doing, creeping about back there."

Carvilho looked surprised, but spoke firmly to the other man. "He says they were merely making sure he had not been followed."

Lock took Carvilho's arm, drawing him to one side. "How well do you know this man?"

"I do not," the old man admitted, "Marco brought him." In the firelight his face looked troubled. "Some say he is a bandit."

"Get him to call all his men in," Lock advised. "I don't like the look of them. We want them where we can see them."

"But he has *volunteered* to help us," Carvilho could see the sense in Lock's argument, but his very nature seemed to rail against it, "and what is it you English say? Do not look a horse in the mouth?"

"A gift," Lock corrected. "Don't look a gift horse in the mouth." But if Alonso's men were a gift, they looked to have been delivered by the devil. Dirty and unkempt, they matched their spare, underfed horses. Every man carried sword and pistol, and all looked as if they would have no hesitation in using them. But would they hold steady against French cavalry? "And they've had no training at all."

Carvilho sighed, "No; but I told you, corporal, I will not refuse them."

Lock's shin began to itch. He bent down to scratch under his overalls but found his fingers came away sticky; the little bitch must have broken the skin when she kicked him. He had accidentally cut her, so that made them even, he decided. Not quite even, though, because he had left her alone in the woods.

Lock collected the bowl he had drunk his soup from. There was still a little broth left in the bottom of the pot hung over one cooking fire, so he scooped it out. Then, taking care no-one was watching, he slipped quietly away from Carvilho's camp into the trees.

# Chapter 33

An urgent summons to his squadron commander's tent was an unusual enough event for Killen to wonder if he was mistaken. Perhaps, by some miracle, Lock had survived. Hope flared, but died instantly when instead of Major Hughes he found two infantry officers inside the canvas walls; one, a general at that.

"Sir Arthur tells me, lieutenant, you speak Portuguese?" General Fane raised his eyebrows in expectation.

Killen swallowed disappointment. "I shall be a little rusty, sir." He had not spoken any of the language for more than two years. The patrol he took out early on had met none of the natives, so he had no opportunity to practice.

"I doubt that will matter a great deal," Fane said, "like riding a horse, I shouldn't wonder; it soon comes back to one." He turned away from Killen for a few moments. "You see, Mr Killen, I have a problem. We constantly receive reports concerning the whereabouts of the enemy; from peasants, most often. They cannot speak English and our patrols rarely have a good Portuguese speaker. Even if they should be understood correctly, stories may get…," he paused in thought, "let us just say that they get confused, if you understand me."

Killen understood. No-one really had an idea what on earth the French were up to.

"We believe they are advancing to offer us battle," Fane went on, "and most reports so far suggest there are somewhere here." Hughes' map was spread out on the table and the general sketched a circle on it with his index finger. The British army occupied the town of Vimeiro, but the area Fane had indicated was a good way to the south. "I personally instructed one patrol. Your fellows; stout chaps. I want you to ride south - catch them up. This area," he tapped the map, "is just too large. The frogs could come at us from any direction, and Sir Arthur insists we be ready, in the right place to meet them." General Fane pulled out a gold watch. "Meet me at…five, say, at the church. I shall put you on the road the patrol took. Find the French for me, lieutenant, and for Sir Arthur."

The other officer stayed when Fane left. A colonel, from the insignia on his scarlet uniform, but Killen could not identify his regiment. The colonel hitched his backside onto Hughes' map table, letting his legs swing back and forth.

"You can relax, lieutenant." He appraised Killen with piercing blue eyes. Like Wellesley's, Killen thought, determinedly staying alert. "My name's MacAllen," the colonel offered. "I was sorry to hear about your friend."

Killen was taken aback. How did he know about Joshua?

"You are wondering," MacAllen continued, "how I know he was your friend?" He stared into Killen's face; a disconcerting experience. "Because I make it my business to know, lieutenant. Knowledge is power; but I think you must know that," MacAllen stood up, "so I have been keeping my eye on you." He turned as if to leave, but the tent flap flew open and Major Hughes strode in.

"What do you want, MacAllen?" Hughes made no effort to salute but gave the colonel a look in which wariness seemed to struggle with politeness and win.

"Just leaving, Jonas," MacAllen offered Killen a disarming smile, "just leaving." He ducked through the tent flap, but checked to look back. "It came as a great surprise to me," he said to the lieutenant, "how very much like your father you are."

"Wait...," Killen stepped forward urgently, "...sir!" but MacAllen had gone.

Hughes grabbed the lieutenant's arm, to prevent him following. "What did he want?" he asked urgently.

"I...I'm not sure." It had been an odd conversation. Killen felt interrogated, though he had said nothing.

Hughes scowled. "Take my advice, Mr. Killen; steer clear of him."

"Why? He said he knew my father."

"Your father's dead?" Hughes demanded brutally. Killen nodded. "Then take my advice, Johnny," the major released his arm, "take my advice."


Shadows had begun to lengthen, but bathed in evening sunshine the air was still uncomfortably hot.

"I am afraid I know very little of him, Johnny," General Fane took off his bicorn hat, at the same time pulling a large white handkerchief from his pocket to towel his face. "In fact," he replaced the bicorn, pulling it square, "I thought you must know him, since it was he who put forward your name. Are you certain he is no relation?"

Killen shook his head. Both horses' feet clip-clopped on the cobbles, matching time as the two men rode along. "Colonel MacAllen shows his face above the ramparts now and again, before disappearing to who knows where." Fane took out his handkerchief again, patting his cheeks. "It's deuced hot for the time of day."

Killen thought hard about MacAllen, but found no answers.

"It seems to me," the general confided, "he secretly advises Sir Arthur, but on what matters I have no idea." He twisted in his saddle to face the lieutenant. "I gather Wellesley's appointment was ill received in some quarters." Killen did not really understand what the general was getting at, and eventually Fane gave him an apologetic smile. "Rather MacAllen than me, I must say. Sir Arthur can be...frightening."

They continued downhill, past a white-washed church set on rising ground and bounded by a high, white wall. A red-coated soldier lay sprawled at the bottom of a flight of stone steps which rose, through a gap in the stonework, towards the church doorway. Seeing another red jacket, this time on horseback, the man scrambled to his feet. He dropped the bottle he was holding to pick up his musket before standing to attention. The man's shako was tilted at a crazy angle, Killen noticed.

"Back to your company, young man," Fane called benignly to the redcoat, "there'll be work for you tomorrow."

"How do you know that, sir?" Killen was curious.

"Oh, the French are close," Fane confirmed, "we have ascertained that much. What we do not know is from which direction they will attack." He halted his horse and pointed. "Follow this road for half-a-league until you reach an old chapel. I have directed a piquet be set there. Find out what the peasants in the village beyond know; what gossip there is. If the French march up this road, Sir Arthur will be delighted. But they may head farther east in an attempt to outflank us. It is critical we know which." Fane rummaged in his sabretache, finally pulling out a small piece of paper. The general scanned it carelessly before handing it across.

'*Provide any assistance this officer may request,*' Killen read the scribble. It was signed simply '*Fane.*' He looked at the general, who smiled. "You know where to find me? Then I shall look forward to seeing you later, lieutenant."

Stars pricked the sky after sunset. Killen slowed The Tempest to a walk, staring heavenwards. The stars reminded him of home; of summer evenings, like this one, when he lay on his back in the middle of the lawn, imagining himself on some great adventure. The problem was he kept seeing Joshua at his side. Killen shook the daydream from his head and rode on.

The moon rose, casting dark shadows from roadside bushes to disguise ruts and deep holes. He picked his way carefully around the obstructions until he saw the chapel in the distance, its roof stained blood-red by moonlight. Killen hoped it was not an omen.

A piquet challenged him soon after; a cornet and three troopers. Other men would be hidden nearby. Killen presented the general's paper.

"The patrol is forward, sir," the cornet advised him. "My sergeant's with them. He's a German." Killen showed no surprise. Plenty of Germans had joined the army; men displaced from their own countries by Bonaparte, and who wished retribution.

"How far is the village?" A small stream burbled alongside the road; the loudest sound in the night. The Tempest fidgeted at the delay, forcing Killen to turn the horse in a tight circle.

"Don't know sir," the cornet answered him honestly. "About fifteen minutes ride, I think." Killen thanked him, and went on.

Eventually, the road split into three. Two tracks led one each side of the village and the third passed straight through. Killen halted The Tempest. He could still hear the stream, louder now it tumbled downhill, but that was all; no sign of the patrol. He chose the central path, closing his legs against the horse's sides to encourage it forward.

Killen found his compatriots at the tavern. Even without a signboard, the hostelry was easy to spot; six horses stood tied outside and its windows bled light, where every other building seemed dark and deserted. The trooper left in charge of the cavalry mounts lowered his carbine once he recognised Killen's uniform, taking The Tempest's reins after the lieutenant dismounted.

Inside the tavern, the German sergeant rose to attention as Killen stepped through the door, but he waved the man down, dragging a chair across to sit at the same table. It turned out there was no need for his mission, for the sergeant spoke some Portuguese.

"The landlord says," the sergeant had a wineglass in front of him and swirled its remaining contents around, "that one of his friends from Lisbon came through town not a couple of hours ago, and he had passed the French army on this road." He lifted the glass, swallowing the wine in a single gulp.

"You believed him?"

"Seemed no reason not to, sir," the sergeant shrugged his shoulders. He spoke good English, though his accent was still strong.

Killen pressed him, "But you've not advised General Fane?"

"No, sir; we've not seen them, yet. I would pretty look stupid if I rousted the whole army out when the frogs had turned off the road and suddenly appeared somewhere else." He raised two fingers towards the innkeeper and as if by magic more wine was brought, with an extra glass. Another trooper approached the sergeant, whispering in his ear. He nodded and the man left, but very soon the cavalryman guarding the horses entered without his carbine, and joined his comrades.

The sergeant grunted, satisfied at the sentry change, before pouring wine into both glasses. "I've left two vedettes posted further down the hill. The frogs will have to cross the bridge over the river if they want to come up this road, so we'll hear them." Killen was impressed, and said as much. "Just doing my job, sir," the sergeant sipped at the wine, but Killen left his alone. An enlisted man drinking on duty was one thing, but an officer? He looked across at the other men, engrossed in a game of dice, and the sergeant seemed to read his thoughts. "Don't worry about them, sir, they'll have me to deal with if they overdo it."

Voices were raised, suddenly, outside, and a cavlaryman burst in. The sergeant looked up but did not get out of his chair, though Killen could see the tension in his face.

"Horses, sarge', on the bridge," the man reported. He glanced at the lieutenant without recognition and his eyes went back to his sergeant. One of the vedettes, Killen supposed.

"And how many were there?"

"Dunno, sarge'." The trooper took off his helmet, scratching his head, "Ten? Twelve, maybe?"

The sergeant relaxed again. "Frog cavalry patrol, I'll bet. Checking the bridge. They'll have to be sure," he told Killen, "it'll take the weight of their guns. Get back down there and keep your ears open," he ordered the trooper. "Relief in one hour, got it?"

But the trooper returned in less time. "You'd better come, sarge'," he said, poking his head through the door.

It was the news Killen hoped for. The bridge rattled and creaked beneath hundreds of pairs of boots, the noise carrying clearly to the cavalrymen hidden high on the hill.

"Heard enough, sir?" the sergeant whispered.

Killen turned The Tempest back towards the village, then stopped. He must be certain. If the troops they could hear were not Junot's main thrust, he would appear an utter fool to Fane and Wellesley for reporting that they were. "Er...no, sergeant." Killen thought hard. "It may just be a stray battalion. But their guns will support the main attack; we need to know where they are." He prayed the marching infantry were the vanguard and the artillery would be close behind, for if the French had deployed forward cavalry patrols, they must be close.

They waited. Time seemed to drag; French dragoons would be creeping nearer.

"We should go, sir," the sergeant began, but then all heard it; the unmistakeable rumble of iron-shod wheels over timber. 'Bonaparte's daughters', Killen thought - heavy guns that would supposedly destroy all France's enemies.

"Mount up; mount up," the sergeant hissed. "You go on ahead, sir," he suggested, "they'll likely take more notice of you than me."

Killen agreed with the idiotic truth of it. He held out his hand, and the sergeant, after his initial surprise, took it. "Look out for their cavalry," Killen advised, then turned The Tempest's head northwards.


General Fane danced a little jig of delight when Killen reported what he had heard. After Major Hughes' warning, the lieutenant was dismayed to find Colonel MacAllen present, but even more disconcerted when Fane sent the lieutenant straight on to Wellesley.

"I shall accompany you, Mr Killen," MacAllen insisted. "Show you exactly where Sir Arthur has secreted himself."

They rode in silence. "Jonas warned you off, has he?" MacAllen seemed to be able to read Killen's thoughts. "He and I never hit it off, more's the pity. He has the right sort of mind." Killen did not like to ask what sort of mind that was. He agonised whether he should risk asking the colonel about his father, but in the end failed to find the right words, so they reached the large house Wellesley had chosen as headquarters in silence. "Stables around the back," MacAllen offered, "and you will find Sir Arthur upstairs."

The general was indeed on the top floor, cloaked in almost total darkness. The buzz of conversation quietened as Killen entered.

"Ah, lieutenant," Wellesley sat on the edge of a table, swinging his feet off the floor, "you have news for me?"

Killen cleared his throat nervously as other general officers gathered around. In the dark it was difficult to make out features, but he recognised Brigadier-General Anstruther, and the man with the rotund face must be General Hill. "The French have crossed a bridge to the south, sir; they are heading straight up the road towards us." A tinderbox flared suddenly as one man lit a cigar.

Wellesley's eyes gleamed in the dim light, "And you are certain this is their main thrust?"

"We heard their guns, sir, crossing the bridge."

Wellesley jumped up. "Gentlemen - to your regiments. You must be in position at first light, as we discussed." He sounded excited.

Colonel MacAllen came into the room just as the others were leaving. "I shall be with you directly, MacAllen," Wellesley acknowledged his presence before turning to the lieutenant. "I thank you, Mr Killen. You will find my orderly in the kitchens. Get him to prepare you some food; you look all in."


Killen climbed back downstairs, feeling his way along a corridor leading to the back of the building. He hurried, guilty that in his rush to report he had left The Tempest still saddled in the stables. Edward Gaunt would have apoplexy, he thought. Rounding a corner, he almost bumped in to the orderly.

"Picker!" Killen exclaimed in surprise. "What on earth are you doing here?"

Matthew Picker smiled back. "Sir Arthur asked for me," he said proudly. "His cook took ill, so I does for him, now."

"What on earth did Colonel Taylor say?"

Picker frowned. "He wasn't best pleased, the colonel. Not a lot he could do, though."

Killen turned towards the back door. "I have to see to The Tempest, Matthew," but Picker held up his hands.

"Already done, sir; already done. Eating his hay, quiet as you please. I recognised him, soon as I saw him there. Thought it must be you, gone upstairs."

Killen thanked him, but Picker shook his head, "There's stew on the stove, sir, if you want some?"

"I would rather a bed, Matthew, if there is one," Killen yawned, suddenly feeling very weary, but the trumpeter disappointed him.

"Only the stable, sir, but there's plenty of straw."

So Killen spread out his saddle blanket in an empty stall and lay down, still in his uniform. He went straight to sleep.

342

It was after dawn when he woke. "Matthew?" he called out to Picker but got no answer. Killen trotted back to the kitchen only to find it empty; the house deserted. Then he heard it; a distant crackle, like a fire consuming its first twigs, hungering for more.

The lieutenant recognised that faint sound immediately: damn it; the battle had started! He shook straw from his saddle blanket, hurriedly folding it to fit The Tempest's back. He was going to be late.

But not too late, he hoped.

# Chapter 34

"This is undercooked," General Louis-Henri Loison grumbled to his servant through a mouthful of fat bacon. The French army had marched all day and most of the night until a halt was called in a small village south of Vimeiro. A rest; hah! They might just as well have carried on for all the rest he would be getting. His servant answered a sharp rap on the door, but it was only Kellerman.

"Louis-Henri!" General Francois Kellerman spotted the bacon. The cavalryman strode across to Loison's table, helping himself to two rashers. "Andoche wants to see us," Kellerman mumbled through a mouthful, "he's called a council." Grease ran down his chin.

Loison swallowed the remains of his breakfast. "What does the old woman want now?"

"Probably to inform us the Emperor has made him a Marshal of France," Kellerman suggested, "as if a Dukedom is not enough. I think *I* deserve the promotion." He puffed out his chest, "Marshal Kellerman, Duke of...Porto. The title would sit well, don't you think."

Loison knew his friend was teasing, but could not help himself. "Kiss my arse, you pompous windbag," he spluttered. He, Loison, should be a Marshal. After all, he was already a Count. But Bonaparte ignored his magnificent record, damn him, promoting lesser soldiers, lesser *men*, over his head.

Kellerman's cheeks glowed bright red from trying to contain his laughter. He managed to swallow the last of his bacon before a bout of coughing struck him.

"Marcel!" Loison wiped his face on a napkin before calling the servant, "bring my sword."

Kellerman rubbed his chin on his uniform sleeve, noticing ruefully that the bacon grease stained its gilded embroidery black where the thread had worn. "Damned cavalry uniforms are too fancy to fight a war in," he observed, "I've always said it."

"But my dear Francois," Loison had his flash of temper under control and determined to get his own back, "how on earth will the ladies choose between two magnificent beasts, if you have none?"

Kellerman grinned at his friend's counter, bowing extravagantly from the waist. "You have insulted me, sir, but I believe a draw a fair result," he conceded.

"Agreed." Loison's servant knelt in front of him. "Haven't you finished yet," the general demanded.

"Your sword-belt, sire," Marcel confessed. "The slings have almost rotted through. Might I bring your dress belt?"

"And how will you do that? The baggage is miles back down the road to Lisbon." Loison pushed the man away impatiently. "I've worn this belt for years; it will probably outlive me. Just fetch my coat, and be done."


"Ah, gentlemen, thank you for coming." General Andoche Junot smothered the statement with a generous helping of sarcasm when the two generals entered. Loison took no notice. He found a spare chair and sat, while Kellerman stood at the back of the room.

"As I was about to say," Junot seemed unwilling to let the perceived slight to his authority rest, "our scouts report the English have two brigades in hills to the west of town, and more to the east. Their centre is thinly defended," he smiled, "perhaps they believe peasant cottages will stop our columns!" Most officers present smiled, Junot's comments eliciting confident murmurs. The general held up his hand for quiet. "Thomieres' and Charlot's brigades will attack the centre. Brennier? You will march east before turning to outflank them. We shall push them back against the Maciera river so they have nowhere to go but the ocean." Junot seemed to exude confidence that his simple plan would work. Loison understood his optimism. No army had yet stood against French columns and won, and this time would be no different. The British were outnumbered and out-gunned.

"General Loison," Junot addressed him directly once the murmur of conversation died, "you will take responsibility for Solignac's brigade. He forms our reserve on the left."

Loison scowled. Junot must have given orders to the brigadier direct, ignoring him, the *General de Division*. It was a slight; unheard of! The bastard must want all the glory for himself.

"And General Kellerman; your grenadiers will be held in reserve to support the centre brigades."

"And my dragoons?" Kellerman wondered out loud.

Junot gave him a withering look, obviously still smarting at the cavalry commander's lateness. "I have instructed Brigadier Margaron to support the centre, in case he should be needed, but our scouts report the British have few cavalry. They did not engage you at Rolica, Delaborde?"

Loison glanced across at General Delaborde. Outnumbered, the man had managed to delay the British advance just long enough for Junot to assemble his scattered army. Delaborde's head was bandaged, and he shook it, tiredly.

"*Bon*," Junot stood, rubbing his hands together. "Let the men rest, for now, gentlemen. We move at dawn. God willing, we shall eat a victory lunch."

God willing? Loison laughed inwardly. There was no god on a battlefield but the man who made himself one. He had done it, years ago, smashing an Austrian army to bloody ruin across the bridge at Elchingen. But not today; today he would twiddle his thumb in command of the reserve. It was ridiculous.

Kellerman crossed to clap Loison on the shoulder. "The reserve, eh?" he seemed unconcerned. "So there will be no Marshal's baton for either of us this time, my friend."

Junot was talking to Delaborde on the far side of the room, and Loison gave his commander a poisonous stare. "He will go to hell," he said.

# Chapter 35

The Tempest's feet slipped and skidded on the cobbles as Killen clattered through town. A few brown faces peered at him from half-shuttered windows, but he ignored their stares. He would get into trouble for being late. The road past the church was blocked by a mass of red-coated infantrymen so he turned left, almost running into Colonel MacAllen who was riding up from that direction. He hurriedly saluted.

"You have not missed much," the colonel touched his cocked hat, "though you gave Sir Arthur pause."

"Sir?"

"First thing this morning," MacAllen explained, "the French failed to show up. Sir Arthur was most put out. He hates to be kept waiting." He paused, and when Killen stayed silent gave a small shrug. "I told him you could not have been mistaken in your judgement; you can thank me for that."

"I can thank you?" Killen said in puzzlement.

"Why do you suppose the French arrived late, lieutenant?"

"Breakfast, sir." Killen said the first thing that came into his head, but when he thought about it that had to be the reason. "They must have stopped for breakfast. They had marched through the night."

"Exactly what I told Sir Arthur," MacAllen smiled. "Then, of course, once we could see the devils advancing he forgot all about reducing you to the ranks. He admitted it a close run thing, though." He held up a hand, "Only joking, Johnny."

Killen began to think that perhaps Major Hughes was right about the colonel. "Thank you then, sir."

MacAllen inclined his head. "You'll find your fellows skulking round the back of the hill," the colonel, guessing at Killen's purpose, pointed back the way he had come, "and allow me to wish you joy of the day." He rode away, past the lieutenant's stiff salute.

And in the west, guns sounded.

"We are too late," Carvilho's voice was clouded in disappointment. They dismounted to descend a steep tree-shrouded slope, a long line of men in silent single file, horses slipping on dead leaves. Gunfire rumbled; a distant thunderstorm.

"You don't know that." Lock was encouraged by the sound. He knew artillery usually fired first, as each army attempted to weaken its opponent. Eventually, one side would attack while gunners continued to hammer roundshot after roundshot at the marching ranks, smashing men and horses into shapeless lumps of flesh and blood and splintered bone. And when the survivors were close enough, the artillerymen would forgo solid iron balls to charge their barrels with canister. The containers filled with musket balls tore themselves apart as they left each blackened muzzle, spreading like duck-shot to kill and maim. Only when the enemy were near the defenders' lines would the guns be silenced, for fear of hitting their own. That was the time for musket volleys to commence, and the terrible rain of death would begin again. Hell must be like that, Lock thought, but instead he said, "The battle has begun, that's all."


"Can you tell what's happening, Johnny?" Colonel Taylor squinted through his telescope, "I cannot make out a damned thing through all this smoke." Killen twisted the eyepiece of his own, smaller, glass, but the adjustment made little difference.

"It looks to me, sir," he answered, "as if the French are running." It was difficult to see clearly, downhill through dirty clouds. Though Killen was already some way in front of the regiment, he urged The Tempest on a few more strides before steadying the telescope again.

French infantry were going backwards. Torn by artillery and with its front ranks decimated by sustained musket fire from the British redcoats, the first column's early bravado seemed to have exhausted itself. Killen watched one of the grey coated men turn to fire at the defenders only to be thrown backwards as a ball struck him. He swallowed. "They are retreating, sir," he called over to Taylor.

"Then get yourself off to General Fane," Taylor urged excitedly, "and beg leave the 20<sup>th</sup> be allowed to advance."

Loison smiled to himself, because the battle did not go as his commander planned. He stood with his back to Junot, smoking a cigar, listening to an increasing number of breathless messengers. The first two central attack columns had, much to Junot's chagrin, been beaten back. The British must have strengthened that position without it being noticed. And to make matters worse, a cavalry patrol reported more troop movements to the east of Vimeiro. Junot beckoned Loison over. "You sent Solignac's brigade after Brennier, as I ordered?"

Loison removed the cigar from his mouth, "Of course."

Junot turned away. He scribbled a note in a small leather bound book and ripped out the page, handing it to a messenger. "Tell General Kellerman to ready the grenadiers; they must gain the centre," he said urgently. Loison walked away in disgust. The old woman had panicked already!

"Your request is noted, Mr. Killen," Fane smiled grimly, "but I cannot allow it without orders of my own. And besides," he pointed across the battlefield to where two fresh columns of French infantry had already begun their advance, "I do not believe you would wish to tangle with those fellows until mine have first softened them up."

Fane's riflemen waited in small groups, sitting down. A private of the 95<sup>th</sup> regiment climbed to his feet, brushing dust from the front of his dark green uniform with both hands. He removed his shako respectfully before calling out to the general, "We'll get after them now, sir, if it's your wish." There were murmurs of assent from many others, but Fane kept a hold on their enthusiasm.

"Now, now, men; don't be too eager," he called back, "I shan't allow the cavalry to steal your thunder."

"T'would make a change from them stealing our women!" another voice remarked and there was a burst of laughter, soon drowned in thunder. British guns had targeted the two columns.

Fane's horse stood like a rock, but The Tempest fidgeted at the noise. The general pointed at the approaching French. "Stay, lieutenant; let me show you something."

"I should like to, sir, but I must get back."

"Very well," Fane nodded, turning his horse to face the new attack. "Up: up then, lads. Here come our friends again." The greenjackets stood, expectantly. "We shall welcome them warmly, as before," Fane roared at them all, "then send them on their way with our steel."

"You took your time, Mr. Killen," Taylor grumbled his constant complaint without much heat. Killen knew the colonel must have realised how hopeless a task his few horsemen would face against such huge infantry formations, for he did not ask Fane's reply. Let the artillery do the donkey-work, Killen thought; let the infantry flay them with musket fire. The cavalry could pursue the vanquished: secure a victory.

Charlie Harris waved at the lieutenant, riding forward to join him. "What's going on, Johnny?" Harris whispered, glancing warily towards the colonel who seemed not to have noticed him break rank. "Couple of the men are getting restless, and why are *they* here?" Charlie pointed back at a troop of Portuguese regular cavalry, late arrivals of the day before.

"Because there are so few of us, I suppose." Killen wondered why the Portuguese horses had not simply been requisitioned, for even after the Bishop of Porto's draft, many of the 20th still languished as orderlies. But he supposed he would have been reluctant to give up his own mount had the boot been on the other foot. "Just be glad of them," he said. "There are probably hundreds of dragoons over the next hill."

"There can't be," Charlie argued. "I haven't seen any."

"Where's Lieutenant Rapton? " Killen wondered why Cornet Harris, Rapton's subordinate, had been the one to ask the question.

Harris grinned, "Still up-chucking his breakfast. Looked as green as a gooseberry the last time I saw him. It couldn't have happened to a nicer fellow!"

Both men flinched at an explosion to their right and the horses skittered nervously. French guns fired at the town, but so far seemed to have caused little damage, and this shell merely sent Charlie Harris back to his place in the squadron. Killen had never seen an army attack in column, watching awestruck as the massive block of French infantrymen marched slowly forward, heading straight at the British. The column must win, Killen thought, though for some reason he felt no fear. The redcoats' thin defensive line seemed too frail to withstand such an onslaught. He half-wished he had accepted General Fane's offer to stay in the front line, but his place was here, with his regiment.

Above the column's head a small puff of smoke appeared. Killen watched the breeze snatch at it. A shell must have gone off too early, wasting its killing power on the already dead bodies of Frenchmen butchered in previous attacks. But another exploded, closer to the column this time, and Killen saw men thrown down, screaming and thrashing as if attacked by some invisible force. Colonel Taylor rode forward to stand alongside, training his telescope on the column.

"Spherical case shot," Taylor observed loudly. "The French don't have them, thank God. It cannot be a very pleasant experience for those poor fellows." Killen tried to imagine such deadly missiles falling amongst his own men, and the vision made him feel sick.

The snap of small arms fire told Killen that Fane's riflemen had begun sniping at the column. Skirmishers hurried forward, in twos and threes, crouching or lying down to aim their weapons. The column was still so far away he thought it unlikely firing from such a distance would have any effect, but men still fell as the greenjackets' spinning bullets, more accurate than any musket ball, took their toll.

As the column marched closer, whistles recalled the riflemen. They hared back to re-join the thin line of redcoats waiting patiently with musket-butts grounded.

The French came on. Fallen men in the column's front ranks were simply stepped over by those following and swallowed by the great mass. Now Killen began to grow nervous. The column was unstoppable; it must be!

A flicker of light from the British lines made the lieutenant turn his telescope towards them. Sun flashed bright on bayonets as hundreds of muskets were levelled at the approaching French. Cannon fire from both sides petered out now the opposing infantrymen were close to one another.

The attack changed so quickly. Perhaps seeing what a pathetically fragile line of men opposed them, the French gave a roar and began to run. Then the redcoats opened fire; one terrible crash of noise. The whole of the column's front line seemed to stagger from the blow. For an instant the mass wavered - a bulldog bothered by a wasp - then like some unstoppable juggernaut it shook itself and ran on. More gunshots rang out, ragged this time, as those redcoats who had been quickest to reload pulled their triggers again.

The French tried to fire as they ran, but their shots had little effect on the British infantry whose volleys rose in a crescendo of noise as slower men fired their second shots. Each company soon settled into a rhythm of firing and loading; firing and loading.

Killen watched, mesmerised. Unbelievably, the French column had begun to slow. The redcoats' defensive line was wreathed in smoke. They must be taking casualties, but Killen could not tell how many, and their musket-fire had not slackened. In the face of such sustained ferocity, the French slowed to a walk, front ranks forced to repeatedly step over the bodies of dead and dying comrades. With bravery ebbing, the column came to a halt. Fought to a standstill, men at the front began to edge backwards, no longer willing to face the deadly hail.

And abruptly, for the second time that morning, the French broke and ran.


Keeping to shaded woodland, using old, half-remembered paths and tracks, the Portuguese horseman had travelled through the countryside largely unseen. But now they were forced to a halt. They must cross the river.

Lock rode forward to find Carvilho staring ahead, where a stone bridge spanned the banks of the Maciera.

"They have guards!" It was true. Four redcoats armed with muskets were posted as lookouts; two sentries on each bank. To warn of an attack from the rear, Lock thought, or stop curious locals getting too close to the fighting.

"They can't stop you," Lock said, "you're a colonel, remember?"

"There is a ford, further west," the old man suggested. "We could go around?"

Lock was not listening to him. The guns had stopped. He wished he could see what was happening, and Carvilho's overwhelming desire to stay hidden was costing them time. Could it be that now the French were so near, the colonel's determination for revenge was failing?

Lock decided for him; it must be now or never. "I thought you were in a hurry?"

"You are right of course, corporal," Carvilho agreed. "The time for caution is past." He rode from tree-shadow into sunlight.


The two redcoats on the far bank of the river were swiftly summoned as reinforcements.

"'Morning, sergeant," Lock followed Carvilho to address the man in charge, "Colonel Carvilho, here, needs to speak with the general."

The sergeant gazed at the group of armed peasants with suspicion. "Can't let you cross, sir," he spoke directly to Carvilho, "got my orders."

Lock was about to interrupt, but the old man held up his hand. "Sergeant," Carvilho stiffened in his saddle, "it is imperative I meet with General Wellesley. As you can see, I could force my way across."

The sergeant let his gaze wander down the line of dour Portuguese, taking in the swords; the long, wickedly pointed lances. He swallowed, nervously, "You could, sir."

"But I ask you, as a friend of the Portuguese people," Carvilho persuaded, "to allow my men across."

Caught between a rock and a hard place, the sergeant swallowed again, looking for help at the only man wearing a uniform he recognised. Lock simply raised his eyebrows.

"Very good, sir," the sergeant gave in. His redcoats moved to one side, and Lock suddenly remembered Isabella. Well, if she had followed them this far, she could certainly manage to charm the sergeant into allowing her to cross.

"I believe," Carvilho said happily as they clattered over the bridge, "that it all begins to come back to me."

And once more guns thundered up ahead.


General Andoche Junot affected a confident air despite the failure of his second attempt to break the British centre. That position had to be taken for his original plan to succeed, and by now his artillery must surely have fatally weakened what seemed at first such a frail defence.

The general checked his watch. "Any news of Brennier?" he quizzed a group of aides but was rewarded with shakes of their heads. The two brigades Junot had despatched eastwards on a long flank-march should reach their objective very soon. His reserve battalions would attack the centre again; Wellesley must have strengthened it with troops from his left, and once Brennier attacked there, the centre would collapse. Then he could let loose his cavalry to hunt down survivors.

Junot scribbled a note, passing it to an aide. "Take this to General Kellerman. He is ordered to lead the First Reserve Grenadiers to assault the centre." Kellerman would not fail. Junot had been annoyed with him that morning, but there was no doubt men followed where the cavalryman led. And after all, what battles had this General Wellesley, this *amateur*, won? Skirmishes in India; fighting men with bows and spears. Hah!

Loison had disappeared, so Junot signalled to a second messenger. "Find General Loison," he instructed, writing out the order so there could be no possibility of a misunderstanding. "Tell him it is vital he reform his men." Two infantry battalions in the second assault were from Loison's Division, and Charlot, who led them, had not returned.

Junot frowned. Loison was insubordinate but undoubtedly a brilliant soldier, and Kellerman his friend. "Tell him he is to support General Kellerman." The general gave a grim smile. This time, the attack would succeed.


From his vantage point above Vimeiro, Sir Arthur Wellesley allowed that, thus far, his theories had been proved correct. Massed columns of infantry, employed by the French to smash through opposing armies like gigantic battering rams, had one fatal flaw. No other field-commander seemed to have grasped the fact that only the first two ranks of men could fire their muskets, and since they marched as they fired, their aim was inaccurate. Accordingly, Wellesley ordered his red-coated infantry stand in a two-deep line, instead of their more usual three-deep. That meant every musket could bear on a target; every ball kill or maim. Provided the line stood firm, even as the French drew close enough for a footsoldier to see fear in his enemy's eyes, the line should never be overcome. And so far, it had not.

"More of them, sir: starting down the hill." A young Staff lieutenant spotted the grenadiers first.

Wellesley swung his telescope around. "I see them, I see them." Sir Arthur was disappointed; yet another frontal attack. He could not understand why his opponent preferred to use the same tactic which had already failed twice, when logic must surely dictate it would do so again.

He expected the French would attempt to turn his left flank, since with his right he held the high ground between Vimeiro and the coast, but so far no message had come from the east to indicate imminent peril. Should he reinforce his centre? He held battalions in reserve, but they might be needed if the French attacked in force on the left. No; Fane and Anstruther had coped admirably up to now, and must do so again. But a little encouragement never hurt.

"With me, gentlemen," Wellesley turned his horse downhill towards the town. "You are welcome to join us, MacAllen, since it would seem you have no other business to attend to today," he chided gently.

"I should be honoured sir. Time spent observing the deployment of troops is never wasted."

Wellesley pursed his lips. McAllen was teasing him. The man could be a confounded nuisance but sometimes, just sometimes, was deuced useful to have around. Sir Arthur gave a short bark of a laugh, and cantered away to find his generals.

The third French attack was dying. Kellerman's First Reserve grenadiers, sent further eastwards so a small rise in the ground masked their approach, forced their way into town as far as the church. Held there, flayed by the fierce firepower of Fane's men who defended the churchyard wall like demons, they were now set upon by General Anstruther who enterprisingly ordered one redcoat battalion angle forward to fire at the column's left flank. Brave as they were, the French were again brought to a standstill by vicious musket volleys.

By sheer weight of numbers, marching men at the rear of the column forced those at the front to climb growing piles of casualties. It was too much. Advancing grenadiers, slowed by the obstruction, were forced to stop. Then all at once, and for the third time that morning, the French could take no more punishment. The column dissolved into chaos as Kellerman's men fled back down Vimeiro hill in confusion.

"Now, 20th," General Fane's voice boomed, "We want you now!"

Killen's heart began to thump.

"At last," Taylor muttered under his breath. "Mr Killen: threes about and forward, if you please. Trumpeter, sound the advance!"

Killen repeated the command over his shoulder where it was picked up by the troop captains, who repeated it to the lieutenants, who passed it down to the sergeants. The cavalrymen sorted themselves into three-man ranks, wheeling to form a column able to swiftly spread into a long, killing line when the time came.

Trumpets blew. Colonel Taylor drew his curved sabre, cutting the still air. The squadron moved off at a walk, drawing a few sarcastic jeers from tired infantrymen. Riding alongside his colonel, Killen gave a shocked gasp as the regiment came out from behind the town onto the field of battle.

Bodies lay scattered everywhere, their dust-coated uniforms making it impossible to discern friend from foe. Killen shut his ears to the cries of wounded men and hardened his heart when a loose horse crossed his path, hobbling along on three legs Taylor glanced at him. "You'll soon get used to it, lieutenant," he said with approval, and Killen supposed the colonel was right. He must ignore the carnage to concentrate on his task. This was what he had wished for, standing in front of his father's portrait; this had been his dream, and he must not let such feelings of revulsion tarnish his vision.

"Form line! Form line!" The first three troopers halted where they were, allowing others to spread out on both sides, each rank of three horses and men angling in the opposite direction to its predecessor. A well trained troop could move from column of threes to line in under a minute. Killen checked behind him and was stunned. He had assumed the Portuguese cavalry would hold back, forming up behind the 20th as a reserve, but instead they lined up on the formation's flanks. Should he risk checking with the colonel? A reserve was usual, in the event the first line got into trouble and was forced to retreat. Perhaps Portuguese cavalry manoeuvred differently? But then it was too late; Taylor raised his sabre.

"Draw swords!" Five hundred sabres scraped from iron scabbards. Killen's stomach turned over, but whether from joy or terror he could not tell.

"20$^{th}$ will advance! Walk-march!"

The horsemen started forward.

# Chapter 36

Colonel Francisco da Souza Carvilho peered out across the battlefield with horrified eyes and made the sign of the cross. His group of hurriedly trained men emerged from the woods south of Vimeiro into a gap between two British infantry brigades. A few redcoats passed the Portuguese, scurrying northwards away from the fighting, but after the partisans crossed the river no one tried to stop them, or ask their business.

Once more making his way to the front of the column, Lock stood alongside the old man. Carvilho's face paled at the destruction already wrought on his country's enemies.

"I did not realise," he said, awestruck, "there are so many." British guns and muskets had littered dead on the slope down which French infantry now raced towards safety. Artillery fire still hampered their retreat, but it had slackened. The gunners must be tiring, Lock thought.

Then, in the distance, a trumpet called horsemen to order. Its shrill notes raised hairs on the back of Lock's neck. He pushed his horse past Carvilho's through scrub bordering the tree-line, hoping for a glimpse of his comrades. The old man's silvered trumpet snagged on a low-hanging branch, and Lock impatiently tugged it free.


"Trot-march!"

Killen risked another glance over his shoulder. The regiment had spread out, its single squadron forming a two-man deep line. Portuguese cavalry still hugged the 20th's flanks. Professionals, he heard they were; escapees from French rule. The remnants of once fine regiments of hussars and dragoons; even mounted police who patrolled Lisbon. Killen's assumption they would act as a reserve was proved wrong; they must be too proud to loiter in the rear and either his colonel had failed to notice or did not care.

Something buzzed past his head. Killen realised with a start the French must be firing at them.

"Whoa, damn you!" Colonel Taylor had difficulty controlling his horse, which flung its head around, eager to be off. "She's keen, today," he flashed a grim smile at Killen, yanking at his reins left-handed whilst keeping his sword upright in the other, "too damned keen."

Killen had no such concerns about The Tempest. Calmer now the cannon-fire had stopped, the horse lengthened its trot to keep in position ahead of the squadron. The lieutenant struggled desperately to see what lay ahead, but they were jogging through cannon-smoke. Grubby white drifts of the stuff hung stubbornly over the battlefield. Gunfire stilled the wind, it was said and while Killen knew that modern science held many old beliefs impossible, clipper-ship masters continued to toss barrels of lamp-oil over their sterns in a storm. And the wind had dropped!

"Ready, lieutenant?" the colonel interrupted Killen's thoughts. He stabbed the point of his sabre forward in confirmation. "Regiment will advance at the gallop!" Taylor shouted to his left, "Trumpeter, gallop-march!"

Past the edge of town, the flat land turned downhill. There were bodies to avoid. Scattered, at first, in ones and twos, corpses lay thicker on the ground where the last French column had been stopped. Killen was forced to swerve past three dead grenadiers piled where they fell, one on top of another. Each neat line of cavalry horses began to break up as men sought clear paths for their mounts. Their speed increased. Pressed by the ranks behind, The Tempest easily kept its place in front of the first line, but they were going too fast. Killen shouted to Colonel Taylor and said so.

"The hell with it!" Taylor looked back at his lieutenant with excited eyes. His horse seemed to be pulling his arms out, but the colonel did not appear to care. He waved his sabre, and the mare accelerated again.

"Trumpeter," the colonel yelled breathlessly, "sound the charge!"


Lock could hardly believe what he saw. The 20th came round from behind Vimeiro hill and before he knew it charged downhill at the fleeing French grenadiers. It was much too early to gallop flat-out;

what was the colonel thinking? He must realise the horses would tire once they began the climb on the far side?

"Magnificent! Magnificent!" Carvilho clapped his hands, making his horse jump forwards in startled surprise. "Look at my countrymen!" The old man had spotted regular Portuguese troopers on each flank of the charge. "That is what we must do, corporal," he pointed enthusiastically, "follow them! Ready the men, if you please."

But Lock hardly heard. The 20th were in amongst French fugitives. Most infantrymen continued running for their lives, but some, more disciplined, had stopped, he saw, turning back to face their pursuers with raised muskets. There was some sort of barrier in front of the horsemen; Lock could not see clearly because of the smoke, but least it might slow their headlong gallop. He breathed a sigh of relief just as the first muskets opened fire at the horsemen.


"Cowards: damned cowards!" Taylor yelled impotently at the Portuguese cavalry as he saw them turn away.

The retreating horsemen never heard his condemnation. Terrified of galloping hooves, and realising they had but one course of action left, French grenadiers began to form small groups for protection. They held their muskets bayonets-outward, for few horses would charge directly into such a deadly barrier. Those on the very edge of the battlefield saw that the British charge would miss them completely, and emptied their muskets at the line of horsemen. Few cavalrymen were hit, but one Portuguese trooper fell, a tangle of blue and scarlet, and several wounded horses slowed as they bled. The Portuguese wavered, then as one they unexpectedly pulled away from the 20th; away from the charge. And they galloped madly back towards Vimeiro, leaving the horror of smoke and noise and death far behind.

Killen had no time to concern himself with deserters. Taylor led the 20th's charge towards what looked like a stone wall; low and broken in places, but still tall enough to hide a kneeling man. Some French must have crouched behind the barrier, for muskets suddenly sprouted over the top. Killen saw their bayonets waiting. The Tempest sidestepped abruptly, throwing him off balance. He grabbed the horse's mane with his rein-hand, hauling desperately to keep himself in the saddle. A man had stood up, right in front of them. Killen got the impression of a dark green uniform. Rifle-green; his own side! The Tempest narrowly avoided running the confused man down. And they were almost at the wall.

"Yaaaaaaa…!" In front of Killen, Colonel Taylor let out a scream that his troopers echoed along their whole line. A musket came up on the lieutenant's right, bayonet seeking him out, and he slashed his sabre wildly towards it in a panic. With good fortune his blade slammed against the end of the muzzle, knocking the weapon away. Then he was at the wall. He aimed The Tempest for a gap to his left, where some of the stones had fallen. Another musket flamed from in front, but the ball came nowhere near him, and then the horse leapt at the wall, scrabbling in loose stones that had fallen beyond. The Tempest twisted its body, struggling for balance, and a grenadier bounced off the horse's shoulder, his bayonet thrust going up and over its neck. Killen stabbed his sword down. The man screamed, falling away.

Then the horse was galloping, and Killen saw why the French had been running back so determinedly. Coming slowly towards him was a line of green-coated dragoons; sabres sloped back against their shoulders and brass helmets gleaming.

"God, help me!" Killen prayed. But that day, god was with the French

*"'Ware dragoons!"* The old hunting call travelled right along the 20th's broken front line. Killen could still see Colonel Taylor, galloping in front but over to his left. He should be right at the colonel's side. He turned The Tempest's head that way in an effort to narrow the gap.

The French dragoons advanced, big men on even bigger horses. But why were they only walking? Killen lifted his sabre horizontally, aiming at the nearest. His hand trembled. This was a moment a cavalryman should dream of; sword against sword; horseman against horseman. But the dragoon still did not move; surely he must have seen his danger?

The Frenchman left it far too late. At a walking pace, he must not have realised how fast his galloping opponent would reach him. Killen's sabre slash disabled the man before he had even lifted his own blade. With the dragoon's screams ringing in Killen's ears, The Tempest lunged through the line of enemy cavalry, creating panic amongst fleeing grenadiers whose apparent saviours had failed them.

The ground began to rise. Now they charged uphill, horses breathing harder with every stride. Taylor still led, slashing backhanded at every Frenchman within a sword-length. Killen had again drifted wide so angled The Tempest back towards the colonel, who suddenly kicked his mare forward. The lieutenant saw with horror that Taylor had spied a group of Frenchmen being shoved roughly into line by a sergeant. While they feverishly rammed their muskets with powder and ball, the sergeant shouted, gesticulating; urging them to hurry. Killen booted The Tempest in the ribs and the black horse seemed to fly across the hill, but the lieutenant knew he should have been alongside; that he would get there too late. Taylor raised his sabre: muskets exploded.

Killen threw his horse at the French, cutting and hacking like a maniac until his sabre was slick with blood, and The Tempest reared up, smashing at heads and bodies with razor-shod forefeet. Assaulted by this screaming madman, the grenadiers first hesitated; then ran, cut and bleeding, for the rolling smoke clouds. But others of the 20th had seen them go. Un-blooded troopers raised their swords and crouched grim-faced in their saddles to spur flagging horses onward.

Sir Arthur Wellesley lowered his telescope. From his station above the town he watched his cavalry scatter the dragoons. It was true that the Portuguese were a grave disappointment, but then just about everything involving their army, such as it was, disappointed him.

He dropped his eyes to a leather-bound notebook strapped to the front of his saddle. Sir Arthur had designed its mount himself, to make his writings on horseback easier, and was absurdly pleased at how effectively the idea worked. He dashed a note, reminding himself to congratulate General Anstruther on his initiative. The man had advanced a battalion against the flank of the last French attack at just the right moment, and without specific orders. That stroke had turned the fight in his favour.

"Still writing, Sir Arthur?" Colonel MacAllen rode up alongside the general, lowering his own glass.

"I have found, MacAllen," Wellesley replied coolly, "that notes taken on the field of battle make reports after the event less taxing and more accurate. I commend the practice to you." He bent his head forward to continue.

"I think, sir," MacAllen raised his telescope again, "that you may consider this of greater significance."

Wellesley put down his pencil and looked at the colonel sharply, "I hope you are right." He extended his telescope again and cursed inwardly. For although Taylor's men had got among the French infantry, as Sir Arthur intended, he could see that instead of maintaining their position they had galloped on, deep into the smoke. Damn the man!

"And look there," MacAllen pointed higher up the far hillside. "Are those more green devils?" Wellesley found them: dragoons, and more numerous than he anticipated. Junot had not sent cavalry to protect the battalions Wellesley expected would soon fall on his left flank but had concentrated them here, in the centre. Taylor and his men would be caught squarely between a fresh wave of horsemen and the squadrons they had just overcome, but which were even now being hastily re-formed. There was no reserve; the Portuguese had fled the field. The 20th would be overwhelmed, annihilated; all Wellesley's precious cavalry destroyed at a stroke.

"He's gone too far, damn him," Wellesley muttered. MacAllen glanced at the general, and hard blue eyes stared back. "He's gone too far," he said again, hastily scribbling a new note.

"Is there nothing to be done?" MacAllen looked disbelieving.

Wellesley ripped the page from his notebook, thrusting the order towards an aide. "My compliments to General Fane," he said out loud, so all could hear. "The 50th will advance in support of the Light Dragoons." He faced MacAllen again, shaking his head sadly. "That is all I can do. It is in God's hands, now."

Carvilho was at first shocked, then angry, and finally ashamed, but he could not bring himself to call fellow-countrymen cowards. He dismounted to stomp about, hands behind his back, until finally he halted by Lock's side.

"You may not believe, corporal" he said, looking up, "but we are not all like...like them." He stabbed a forefinger in the direction the Portuguese cavalry had run. "My men have honour; they will fight...give them the chance."

Lock grinned. "I'm just sat here waiting for you, colonel," and he drew his curved sword and kissed its bright blade.


A small voice called out urgently, "Sir!" Another of Wellesley's aides, "Sir!"

Sir Arthur did not raise his head from his notebook. "What is it?"

The young man kept his eye glued to his telescope, "Sir! Cavalry, sir! On our right: between General Fane and General Anstruther!"

Wellesley grunted. Probably the damned Portuguese, for God only knew where they had run off to.

"Sir!"

Wellesley sighed. "What is it now?" he asked in an irritated voice.

"They have lances, sir!"

"What?" Wellesley heard shock in the aide's nervous voice. His heart missed a beat: only French cavalry regiments had squadrons of lancers. And moments ago he had ordered a battalion of Fane's infantry to advance onto the field. They would be slaughtered; skewered on sharp-bladed spears that outreached a man armed only with musket and bayonet. He had seen it happen before - in India. "Where, man, where?" He prised the tubes of his telescope open with urgent fingers.

The aide pointed, eye still glued to his own glass, "There, sir! Oh..." the young man's voice became less frantic, "...and a galloper, sir, from General Anstruther's brigade, by the looks of things."

Wellesley relaxed a little. If Anstruther had despatched a messenger, the lancers could hardly be French. It must be the damned Portuguese cavalry after all. He returned his telescope to its saddle-holster before jotting a reminder in his notebook to speak to their commanding officer about his men's indiscipline.

The infantry captain's horse skidded to a stop in a shower of dirt and stones.

"Who the bloody hell are you?" he demanded. Lock simply smiled. Carvilho walked his horse slowly forwards from the corporal's shadow, the old man's braid and bravado taking Anstruther's messenger by surprise. The captain sketched a hurried salute. "Didn't see you there, sir."

"And what can I do for you, captain?" Lock noticed that Carvilho sat ramrod-straight and had managed to look down his nose at the newcomer.

The captain licked his lips nervously. "General Anstruther's compliments, sir; he wishes to know your intention."

"My intention?" Carvilho raised his voice, "my intention? My intention, captain, is to run those..." he pointed toward the French lines, "...those bastards, out of my country. You may tell your general that."

"But, sir..."

"And I further suggest," Carvilho icily interrupted, "that you get out of my way. Unless, that is, captain, you want a lance up your arse. Good day!" he shouted, and the messenger gave Lock a sick look before spinning his horse around.

"Where did you learn words like that?" Lock watched the captain gallop away.

"One day, corporal....."

"I know," Lock said resignedly, "one day, you'll tell me. But we'll most likely all be dead by tomorrow."

Carvilho shook his head. "You have forgotten, Joshua," he said, using the corporal's Christian name for the first time, "that God is on our side."

Lock pushed and chivvied the Portuguese into line. He put every man with a lance in the front rank, sandwiching swordsmen in between to help out if any lancer found himself in trouble. Marco would ride on the far right, doing his best to keep the men out wide in check.

Alonso's partisans formed the second rank. Lock had thought hard about how best to control them; they had had no practice, after all, and if they rushed forward, racing one another, they might cause havoc among the lances. In the end, he put Paulo on their right. The boy could certainly use a sword and seemed arrogant enough to let the peasants' surliness sail over his head. To be fair, they had caused no problems during the journey, but there was…something. Lock could still not bring himself to trust them.

Carvilho, meanwhile, waited patiently. The sun felt warm on his face. If he had to die, he thought, he would want it to be on a day like this. He closed his eyes, remembering his dream of victory; of how God's horsemen had swept away the French, convincing him of the path he must take into this valley of darkness.

"Sir!" Someone was calling him out of his reverie.

"Colonel! Sir!"

Joshua. Joshua was calling him. The old man opened his eyes. He stared at the hill in front of him, a hill running down into a shadowy valley. He saw the French, still in flight. A breeze fanned his face. The cannon smoke seemed to lift, and just for an instant he could see far away, to the hilltop beyond; to dragoons riding forward, and to walls, great walls of stone protecting his enemy.

Joshua - look!" Carvilho's eyes widened, as if he saw but could not really believe, "Walls…." he turned to stare at Lock as if still in his dream, "…of Jericho."

But through the smoke, Lock too had seen the enemy, and understood something more. Galloping out of control, the 20th were almost at the second wall. On tiring horses, with dragoons advancing at them from in front and behind, they had no means of escape. "Come on, sir!" Lock knew they must hurry.

"I do not know the words," Carvilho said, shaking the dream from his head. "I have never fought," he admitted, too late. "I was an administrator; a clerk. Paper was my battleground."

"For God's sake, just shout anything!"

The old man closed his eyes again in prayer. He prayed that God would give them all strength, that God would keep them safe, but most of all he prayed that God would deliver up his enemies. Carvilho opened his eyes, shook his sabre, and what he shouted was a cry for vengeance.

*"Evora!"*

He rode forward, and the Portuguese followed.

*"Evora!"* More men took up the shout. Sixty throats thundered the city's name at the sky.

*E-vor-a! E-vor-a! E-vor-a! E-vor-a! E-vor-a!* Call His name seven times, the Testament said, and the walls will tumble down.

The partisans' horses fought their riders, frustrated at being held.

"Corporal," Carvilho shouted, "the trumpet! Blow the trumpet! Six blasts!" Lock remembered the scripture from long ago, but this was madness! He pulled the instrument from under his arm to put to his lips, and though he was afraid he might have forgotten how, the sweet, rising notes flowed easily. Horses broke into canter. Carvilho smiled a grim smile and to Lock it seemed that creases of age faded from the colonel's face.

But then he was forced to let the trumpet swing free, to draw his own sabre, for the Portuguese had pulled their lances from the stirrup-cups. The wicked blade-points dropped forward as the peasant horsemen galloped hard toward the French.

Toward the walls.


Captain Pedro Martinez, though forever cursed to bear his Spanish father's name, was a proud Portuguese. Or he had been. For now, ashamed of his flight from the field of battle, of his cowardice in leaving the British cavalrymen to fight alone, he skulked behind the town with his comrades.

At first, when the shout went up, he thought he must have misheard. But then it came again.

*"E-vor-a!"*

And again, this time unmistakeable.

*"E-vor-a!"*

Martinez turned to question the nearest man, but he had heard it too.

*"E-vor-a!"* A cry of pain for a dead city: voices demanding retribution. The Portuguese made the sign of the cross.

*"E-vor-a!"* Martinez vaulted onto his horse, yanking its head in the direction of the battlefield. He kicked it into a gallop. *"Come on*!" he screamed at the other troopers as he thundered past them, *"Come on!"* and most followed, for a miracle was happening. The French had stripped him of his pride, but now he would wrench it back; they all would.


Lock heard more horsemen come up behind and risked a backward glance. He did not recognise their uniforms, but Carvilho did, and his smile grew wider. "I told you men would come," he shouted, and he raised his sword again, screaming in delight, for the walls were drawing closer, and God would smash them down.

# Chapter 37

No! It should not have happened!

Killen vaulted from The Tempest to crouch at his colonel's side, dropping the animal's reins so they trailed on the ground. Lock had taught the horse to stand like that, he thought suddenly, *Joshua.*

The colonel's face looked relaxed, peaceful even. Killen tore off a glove, reaching out to touch one cheek. Taylor's still-warm skin moved flaccidly under his fingers, making him snatch his hand away. A fatal wound, the huge bloodstain still spreading across the front of the colonel's jacket could not be made better. He was dead, and that was Killen's fault; he ought to have been at Taylor's side.

A sudden noise made him start nervously, but no-one was there. Smoke closed in around him: sounds of battle seemed muted and distant. Killen straightened up. With growing terror he realised he had no idea what he should do next.


Carvilho's men were in amongst the French. The first line of dragoons, reformed to turn back up the hill in pursuit of the 20th, now found themselves assailed from the rear by a new enemy. They tried to turn about, to face their danger, but many reacted too late. Portuguese lance-blades sought them out, stabbing at unprotected backs. Dragoons yanked desperately at their horses' mouths in their haste to get clear.

Lock slashed with his sabre at a running infantryman and felt the satisfying jolt as the sword bit into flesh. The man screamed as he fell, then the horse was galloping towards another. The corporal watched Carvilho's sabre rise and fall, then rise again as the old man took his revenge on the French, and they ran, terrified, before him.

The remaining Portuguese spread out, seeking their own targets in the smoke. Lock hoped they would take care, but he could do little to help them. He kept his eye on Carvilho as he had promised, until cannon-smoke closed in around the galloping horsemen.

Chaos ruled the hill. Grenadiers reaching the comparative safety of the high stone wall near the top threw themselves over in desperate attempts to escape slashing swordsmen. Some crawled through tight gaps in the stonework, and now the whole milled about in hopeless disorder. Officers and sergeants tried in vain to beat the men back, but many had abandoned their weapons; battered and exhausted, they had seen too much horror. It would take time before they were ready to fight again.

Louis-Henri Loison watched the returning rabble with disgust. They had failed again; failed to break through what seemed like a pathetically thin line of defenders; failed to turn and stand against a few hundred cavalrymen. Bonaparte's finest had been chased away with impunity. Now the enemy must surely pursue them up the hill to complete their victory. He would disappoint them.

Loison trotted up and down behind the wall, screaming and shouting at the returnees. They must make ready for the British counter attack. A few men, old hands at war, listened and stood to reload their muskets. It was a start. Dependable sergeants grabbed others, manhandling them into files. Loison squared his shoulders. Order began to return.

Arriving at a gap in the wall the general stared downhill, into the smoke. Wraiths moved in the murk, but he could not tell whether the shapes were his own men or the enemy. Then unexpectedly, horses cantered up from behind. More green-coated dragoons, held in reserve, moved quickly towards the gap. It was about time. They would attack downhill, quickly clearing out the damned British horsemen.

Loison turned his horse away from the wall, but the dragoons were in a hurry. They caught the general, surrounding him, and it seemed to Loison that his horse was lifted off its feet. He shouted at the horsemen in a panic, dropping his reins to beat at the nearest dragoon with his right hand, but it was no use. Caught in the crush, Loison was carried through the gap in the wall and dropped onto the field of battle. His horse ran downhill, chasing dragoons until the general eventually managed to get the animal under control. But just as he turned its head back towards safety, something cannoned into its side and he was falling, falling.

Loison hit the ground and lay there, winded.


Killen heard the thump of hooves before he saw the Frenchman. Out of the smoke the dragoon galloped at him with sword raised, screaming, and Killen thought later he had never been more frightened in his whole life. He drew his sabre. The weapon scraped out of its scabbard agonisingly slowly, still glistening with French blood. As the dragoon's sword reached towards him he lifted his blade, and a stray beam of sunlight reflected from its polished edge. It flashed in his eyes, blinding him, and in that instant a lance appeared from the smoke; a huge weapon, wielded by a dark knight. Its shaft smashed into the Frenchman's body, hurling the dragoon from his horse with a strangled cry.

Then the lance point turned towards Killen. A shadowy figure materialised from the fog, mounted on a horse that seemed the size of an elephant. Killen raised his sabre to defend himself, but the apparition reined to a halt, dropping his lance-point to the ground. Killen saw a swarthy, stubbled face beneath the man's wide-brimmed hat and breathed a small sigh of relief. The big Portuguese pointed at him, speaking strangely.

"Jericho!" he said clearly, and he beckoned, "come, come!"


Lock cursed. His dragoon had been a wily opponent, but now the man lay twitching and bleeding on the ground Carvilho had disappeared. He thought of his promise to Isabella, to keep her grandfather safe. But the old man was nowhere to be seen.

Lock shoved his sword into its scabbard and kicked the horse to a canter. He must be close to the hilltop by now; close to where the French gathered to re-charge their muskets; re-fit their vicious bayonets. He had to find the colonel.

Suddenly, he was surrounded by horses. A squadron of big men in maned helmets stormed past, riding for their lives. In the smoke and confusion the dragoons missed him completely. His horse jinked sideways to avoid an obstacle on the ground, and then there was a huge impact. The animal staggered, scrabbling to regain its footing, but tripped and fell, throwing Lock sideways. Instinctively, he rolled as his mount went down. Something caught his jacket on the way, ripping off buttons so that the front flapped open. Then his shoulder hit, throwing him flat on his back.

Lock jumped to his feet. Another man must have fallen in the same collision. Seeing him struggle upright, Lock grabbed at his sword hilt, but could not draw the sabre. The fall must have dented its iron scabbard, trapping the blade. Desperate, he felt for the short knife in his boot-top, forgetting he had lost it in the hills.

Then he saw his salvation. Another sword, torn from a belt, lay on the ground to his left. He stooped to it, dragging the blade free of its snakeskin-covered scabbard.


Loison realised the cavalryman would come for him. He felt for his sword, but broken leather slings flapped against his thigh. The Englishman had it. He cursed under his breath, and then he could say nothing. The stink of death was in his nostrils, for the Englishman had his own blade at his throat.

Lock stared. He could not believe it at first, but...it had to be him. The Frenchman's left sleeve was pinned up so the elbow hung loose, like a stubby wing. "Loison?" he asked, incredulous, and the other man took a pace back.

"My fame goes before me," Loison said, in English. His face was calm, but he swallowed, because the blade-tip followed him, pressing again.

Lock's face grew hard. "Murderer!" he spat the accusation out. "Child-killer: rapist!" He put more weight on the sword hilt.

"I have done none of those things," Loison denied hotly. The sword-point forced him back another pace. He kept his eyes on Lock's.

"I should kill you now."

Loison looked into the cavalryman's face and must have seen his anger burn. He shrugged, as if accepting his fate. "Do as you will..." he said bitterly, gaze dropping to the wooden crucifix that had worked its way outside Lock's torn jacket, "...no doubt your God will forgive you."

Lock hesitated. Slowly, he let the sword-point drop. "God abandoned me, Loison," his bitterness matched his enemy, "a long time ago."

The Frenchman stepped forward onto Lock's blade so the point dug into his chest. "You are a fool, Englishman," Loison snarled, waving his arm across the battlefield. "*I* am God, here." He grabbed the sword, though its edge bit into his palm, forcing the tip to his heart. "Kill me; *you* are God, now." Loison's eyes drilled holes in Lock's face.

"*Non!*" The Frenchman raised his hand suddenly, releasing the sword, and Lock saw the scarlet line on his glove where its edge had cut Loison's flesh. Riding up unseen from behind, two dragoons galloped past, one each side. They would have killed him. The first man pulled his horse round, making a barrier between Lock and his general, while the other hauled the Frenchman up behind his saddle.

"Remember, Englishman!" Loison called out, as the dragoons and their passenger wheeled to speed back uphill towards the wall; towards the French.

And Lock had lost Carvilho.


Killen swung himself up onto The Tempest. It would be easiest to go with the big Portuguese; to follow him back down the hill toward the British. But something nagged at him: something felt different. He had been scared witless, riding into battle for the first time; galloping into the unknown. But now he had fought. He had thrust at the enemy with his sabre; he had drawn blood, and probably killed a man.

He gazed into the smoke and dust. There must be others out there like him: frightened men; men alone; men with no Portuguese horseman to save them. With sudden realisation, he knew what his father would have done; what he must do.

"20th!" Killen stood in his stirrups, shouting the rally at the top of his voice, "20th; to me!" His cries would draw the French, too, but now he took the risk gladly. *"20th; to me!"*

With little hope of finding the old man, Lock retrieved the snakeskin scabbard, buckling the Frenchman's sword over the top of his own before he cast about for a loose horse. Eventually, he caught one; a French dragoon's mount judging by its saddlery; a red horse, mane slicked chestnut with its rider's blood. Vaulting aboard he trotted up and down, back and forth on the slope in front of the wall, but saw no sign of Carvilho's sky-blue coat.

Sounds of battle began to fade. A pair of dragoons trotted past on their way back to the French lines, but they seemed in no mood for a fight and Lock was glad they let him go by unmolested. He had started to zig-zag further down the hill when he heard the rallying cry. Christ! It sounded like John Killen's voice! Lock made in that direction, reckoning he would be safer in a group of cavalrymen. He would just have to face Isabella's wrath when he got back.


Men responded to the call. In ones and twos at first, survivors of the $20^{th}$'s charge formed up around The Tempest. Charlie Harris was there, white-faced. A sabre cut to his right arm bled profusely, staining his yellow jacket-cuff dark brown, though he insisted he was fine. A half-dozen troopers arrived with Sergeant Tyloe, wild-eyed but alive and brandishing a bloodied sword. There must be others, Killen prayed, for the group he had gathered so far was pitifully small; easy prey for any marauding squadron of dragoons. He called again, and again, until the cavalrymen began to attract unwelcome attention from wandering French infantry and were forced to move on.

But Killen had done enough. Other troopers took up the rallying cry, drawing more and more of their comrades; even a number of strange Portuguese peasants with lances joined in. Very soon, even large parties of Frenchmen gave the motley troop a wide berth, seemingly unwilling to risk a fight they might lose.

Then a ghost appeared on Killen's left, and he had to rub his eyes to be sure because they were pink and streaming from cannon smoke. But when he saw the grin, the nonchalant wave, he knew. Lock was alive.

"You look like a dead fish," Lock laughed at his friend's open mouth, "sir."

"And *you* are on a charge," Killen managed humourlessly, "of being absent without leave."


At the base of Vimeiro hill, close to where the British had pushed out their front line, Lock found Colonel Carvilho propped against the body of a dead horse. The corporal caught a glimpse of sky-blue through the throng of dowdy Portuguese and leapt to the ground. Isabella reached her grandfather first, glaring at Lock as he pushed through the crowd. The old man had been shot. Lock crouched beside him. Blood stained Carvilho's coat, and his face was screwed up in pain.

Isabella grabbed Lock's shoulder, forcing him to stand and pulling him round to face her. "You promised," she hissed, eyes white hot. "You promised you would look after him!"

Carvilho overheard. "Leave him," he groaned.

Lock scrabbled to the old man's side. By the looks of his wound, the bullet was lodged in his shoulder. Lock was relieved he could see no sign of blood on the colonel's lips.

Carvilho noticed his scrutiny. "I will live, corporal," he managed through gritted teeth. "Did we beat them?"

Lock struggled for an answer. Had they won? He examined the chattering crowd around them. Thankfully, it seemed a great many Portuguese lancers had returned. "I don't know." The old man grimaced. "I saw him," Lock said.

Carvilho's eyes flicked open in shock, "Loison?"

"On the hill."

"Did you kill him?"

"Did your god break down the walls?"

Carvilho shut his eyes and groaned once more.

"He had no sword - I couldn't kill him," Lock admitted. "He called me a fool; said *he* was God." It sounded strange when he spoke it straight out. "That *I* was God."

Carvilho opened one eye, reaching for the crucifix that hung loose around Lock's neck. "You *are* a fool, corporal." The old man tugged the scorched wooden cross towards him, forcing Lock's face just inches from his own. "*You* are not God," he said, his mouth twisted with the effort, "God is *in* you, Joshua." Then suddenly he released the cross, flopping back against the horse's carcase. "Now go away, corporal," he said tiredly. "My people are still lost."

Lock stood up. Unbuckling Loison's sabre, he laid the snakeskin-scabbarded blade across the old man's lap. "This is his sword," he said simply. "Your people will see that you took it from him."

Carvilho grasped his enemy's weapon, hugging it to his chest. "Go," he said.

Lock saw his pain.

"Just go."


A gaggle of horsemen threaded their way through crowds of Portuguese. Now the guns were silent, hundreds of townspeople ventured from their homes to mingle with their countrymen; Portuguese who had bravely fought the French and survived! They pointed excitedly at the long lances, covering their mouths in horror and awe at the men's gabbled stories.

Sir Arthur Wellesley must have caught sight of Carvilho's uniform as he passed. He stopped, unexpectedly dismounting. Lock stepped back. Wellesley stared at him thoughtfully but caught sight of the lieutenant close by.

"Mr. Killen?"

"Sir!"

Wellesley stooped to the old man. Lock moved away, out of earshot. He noticed Isabella had found Paulo and was looking up at him in apparent adoration, hand resting on his thigh, while the boy no doubt bragged to his admirers. She turned towards Lock with a smug look. He sighed.

"He's pointing this way," Killen warned his friend, and Lock saw that Wellesley was staring at him. More trouble! The general straightened up. A mounted infantry officer stood at his side, a colonel, and when Wellesley waved in Lock's direction the colonel looked across too. Wonderful, Lock thought.

"Mr Killen!" Wellesley remounted. Killen went to him, Lock following several paces behind. "Lieutenant; you remember, I take it, my headquarters?" Killen swallowed, nodding an affirmative. "Arrange for Colonel Carvilho to be taken there," the general commanded. "My surgeon will attend to his wound. And assure me, please, lieutenant, that you had absolutely no knowledge of this...this foolishness?"

Killen was dumbfounded, "Of course not, sir."

Wellesley grunted, "I am delighted to hear it. He glanced at MacAllen, who gave a barely perceptible shrug. "Although," the general conceded with a wry smile, watching the noisy celebrations of the Portuguese, "in due course you may find that fact a matter of regret." For some reason he glared at Colonel MacAllen, and in the distance cannon-fire boomed once more. "Come, MacAllen; gentlemen," Wellesley turned his horse to the east, "I fear my talents are required elsewhere."

And he galloped away, trailing gaudily dressed aides like streamers at a fair.

# Epilogue

# Promised land

# Vimeiro Hill, Portugal

"I truly believed," Killen said to his friend, "that I had lost you. We did search…"

Lock interrupted with a lopsided smile, "Francis Kitto told me you pestered the general. I never thought you had it in you, John." He spotted a lieutenant of the 20th walking his horse slowly away from town. "That bastard left me for dead," he said stonily. Melville Rapton's uniform was pristine; his horse polished to a shine. "He wasn't in the charge!" Lock realised with amazement.

"He's been ill."

Lock knew what illness Rapton suffered from. Anger tightened his throat. He drew a deep breath, then it was gone. Turning towards Killen to speak, Lock found the lieutenant's attention elsewhere.

Two horsemen approached. One wore the bright red uniform of an infantry colonel; the other a plain grey cloak with a bicorne hat pushed onto the back of his head. Killen sat bolt upright in the saddle to salute as the officers pulled to a halt.

"Lieutenant," Sir Arthur Wellesley greeted Killen, looking displeased, "do I find you at a loose end?"

"I wished to thank you, sir…" Killen began, but Lock walked his horse forward to interrupt.

"It was I, sir, who wanted to thank you," he said, "for Colonel Carvilho."

Wellesley gave a look of surprise, as if unused to being addressed by a mere trooper, but then offered an almost imperceptible nod. "It would seem," he spoke directly to Killen, "that the intervention of these Portuguese…*irregulars*," he pulled a face at the word, "has given me back my cavalry."

It was gratitude, Lock acknowledged, of a sort.

"What happens now, sir?" Killen heard that another French attack had been repulsed to the east of Vimeiro. Rumour had it their whole army had fled.

Wellesley's face turned to stone. "I suggest, gentlemen," he said, and his voice was like ice, "that you return to your regiment. There is nothing more for us soldiers to do this day."

Dismounted, Lock stood on the battlefield, staring uphill towards the walls. He had galloped there. He had fought there; might have been killed there, and he had proudly watched his Portuguese stabbing their lances at the French.

Now, the enemy gone, the hill was a place of the dead. Bodies lay strewn on its slopes. Men mostly, grey-coated infantrymen slashed by sabres or torn apart by shot. Their blood soaked the dry grass. Soon, vultures and foxes would come to feast on their remains, drawn by the death-smell. Even now, corpses were defiled. Some Portuguese, eager for revenge, moved amongst them, stealing weapons or stripping clothing. They took away anything that could be carried.

"Alonso!" Lock recognised the partisan who had joined Carvilho's band. No wonder he felt uncomfortable in the man's presence. Alonso was a scavenger; a human vulture. That was why he had allied himself with the old man. Lock watched as the Portuguese and his followers picked over French casualties, slicing off fingers or ears for jewellery; silencing weak protests with sharp knives.

Killen saw them too. He shuddered. "How can they? I always believed them a God-fearing people."

But Lock could not answer. He was staring at other casualties littering the hillside between the walls - horses. Tens of fallen animals lay prostrate; the innocent dead, riddled with musket balls or shattered by artillery fire. Yet more were wounded; nearly-dead; stranded on their sides with legs barely moving. Some struggled, desperately trying to rise on bloody stumps; others sat up, calling vainly for their masters.

The carnage reignited Lock's anger. Like a flame fuelled by his grief it grew, burning ever more fiercely until no amount of counting would extinguish the blaze. Loison was right, or half-right, damn him: if God did exist, he had abandoned his creations, just as he abandoned Lock years before.

"Have you a pistol?" The words stuck in Lock's throat. He snatched at the weapon his friend handed down. Its finely chased silver barrel made it far too frivolous a tool for execution, he thought, "Cartridges?"

Killen fished in his ammunition pouch and passed down a handful. "Why do you need them?" He sounded surprised at Lock's harsh tone.

"I have to go," Lock said, "up there."

"Do you want me to...?"

"No!" Lock snapped. Killen saw the muscles tighten in his jaw. "No," he said again, more softly. "I need to do this alone."

"Do what?" Killen was bemused.

Lock glanced up at the lieutenant. For the first time Killen saw, through the dirt on his friend's face, two clean tracks running down his cheeks.

Lock hefted the pistol. "*I* must be god," he said bitterly, "and still the north wind."


# The End

# Author's Tail

The Battle of Vimeiro saw the first of what many historians dub 'disasters' that befell British cavalry during the Peninsular War. With no infantry or artillery support, the single squadron of light dragoons making up the whole of Wellesley's cavalry charged across the hillside south of the village. Brought up by a high stone wall and assailed by French cavalry reinforcements, the 240-strong force should have been wiped out. In fact, given their predicament, the 20th sustained a relatively small proportion of casualties. The reasons behind this apparent stroke of luck have never been satisfactorily explained.

Colonel Charles Taylor, commanding officer of the 20th Light Dragoons, actually led the charge; his first major mounted action. The Portuguese regular cavalry did run away when fired on, the 20th did leap the first wall before being trapped by the second and Taylor was sadly killed in much the same way as the story tells.

Joshua Lock, John Killen and the officers and men of Major Hughes' squadron are, however, entirely fictitious.

Printed in the United Kingdom
by Lightning Source UK Ltd.
135348UK00001B/389/P